ELEVATION

THE CAVE LOGS OF NEW HALE, TIBET

Also by John Teton

Appearing Live at The Final Test

Upsurge

ELEVATION

THE CAVE LOGS OF NEW HALE, TIBET

JOHN TETON

www.elevationtibet.com

Published in the United States by
Earthlight Pictures, Lake Oswego, Oregon.
Cataloging-in-Publication data is available from the Library of Congress

ISBN 978-0-692-40547-5 (cloth)
ISBN 978-0-692-40632-8 (pbk)
ISBN 978-0-692-40550-5 (ebk)

Printed in the United States of America
First Edition

to

H. lucis

ELEVATION

THE CAVE LOGS OF NEW HALE, TIBET

INTRODUCTION

Suspended in a mandala etched in golden-white flames above dark-grumbling clouds, this gently powerful, sensual angel swept her six arms in benediction, pacifying the wrathful demons, stilling their viral replications and guiding them to evanescence in the thunderhead rim glimmering in her light.155

Not quite the sort of text researchers of my ilk normally come across, that. Who knows what would have happened, had a colleague's sheaf of photocopies not opened to that bizarre reference to viral replication? Perhaps I'd never have crept through the wormhole so far from the Division of Life Sciences of the esteemed institution wherein I've built a career in evolutionary biology over these past nineteen years—an eyeblink to a university entering its ninth century of continuous scholarly activity, but far too long for me to put my professional reputation at risk in reckless disregard for the classical academic culture in which the faculty cloaks itself.

The document—photocopied text of three handwritten books—was handed to me one evening in 2008 by a bioengineering professor I'd become friendly with in a weekly discussion group. She had received it from one of her graduate students, a native of India, who had come into possession of the material in Tibet and was seeking my friend's assistance in getting the material published. Knowing of my work in human and animal behavioral patterns in evolutionary biology, my friend brought it to my attention, not to take on as a project—she being well aware that I would be loath to imperil a hard-earned name for academic rigor by associating it with so strange a mystery—but because she knew I couldn't resist such a thought-provoking take on evolution.

The manuscript provoked more than my thoughts. It compelled me to action on behalf of both itself and the world by bringing the one to the other. My actions have been haunted by a Janus-faced danger, in that releasing this material could lead to dire consequences both if it takes root in our fragile global social structure and if it does not. But there was little contest between the two: history shows that hiding from the truth is a poor prescription for guarding against danger. Danger must be faced if it is to be defanged.

So it is that, after years of investigation, travel, and mental gyration as to how to share this striking tale with the general public, I've come up with a solution that—my timid anonymity notwithstanding—shall accomplish the task.

I count on the reader's understanding of my need to hide in the shadow cast by an alias. Publishing the material under my own name is out of the question and leaving it for posthumous publication—a technique heralded in all seriousness by Mark Twain as an ostracism prevention strategy—would waste precious time, probably delaying this vision-seeding for decades.

With those doors closed, a new one was opened by a dim memory I'd been carrying of two book covers I'd noticed in a bookstore a couple of years before. These were wrapped around novels by John Teton, an American writer and filmmaker unknown to me. Being far too burdened with professional reading to spend time on fiction, I nonetheless did find the cover images intriguing so I glanced at them just long enough to get the gist of their blurbers' claims that the fiction within melded realistic treatment of urgent global crises with intense speculative fantasy.

At the time, I construed that meshing to be an odd task the author had set for himself and gave it no further thought. However, for reasons that shall become clear in these pages, reading them blew a recollection of Mr. Teton's purported métier from my lower memory like a geyser. I dug up his two novels and by the first page of the first book, *Appearing Live at The Final Test*, I suspected I might have found a solution for my *Elevation* dilemma. The book opened with a quote from the preface to

Star Maker by Olaf Stapledon, who had been a colleague of my great-uncle's in the Philosophy Department at the University of Liverpool. The reference to the value of seeing real-world crises against a backdrop of evolution on a grand scale chimed in harmonic resonance with themes of the present manuscript. I sought out Mr. Teton and, after a few months' mutual deliberation, sealed the partnership with him that has led to your standing on the precipice of what you'll likely find an extraordinary adventure.

The work is presented in its original three-volume structure. We have inserted just thirteen words—*Terma One, Terma Two, [remainder of paragraph blacked out by author]*, and *Terma Three*—page numbers, and bracketed passage numbers based on the text's seven major sections. Besides that, with the possible exception of a handful of words that might have been misread due to ambiguous penmanship, the typed text seen here follows the handwritten original exactly as it was found from the first line page to the last. Even the title was provided by the authors.

The questions raised by this book press us to confront a plague embedded in civilization so long that we've become blind—or at least inured—to it, even as Yeats's rough beast slouches ever nearer. The story strips scales from our eyes, liberating our vision from its self-inflicted myopia. We busy ourselves like cedar moth larvae burrowing so deeply into the bark of a tree that we're unable even to conceive of a whole tree, much less perceive one, much *much* less recognize a poisonous organism threatening to obliterate the forest. Nonetheless, we're entering a determinative critical phase in a natural selection experiment operating on a one-shot-per-species protocol. May *Elevation* tip us off as to the best stratagem to pursue.

(alias) Charles G. Sloan
Fellow, _____ College
University of Cambridge
September, 2014

Terma One

[1-1]

<u>March 7, '91 - Western Pacific Ocean</u>

Galileo failed to recognize a great new world, even though he stared right at it a couple of times. He sketched its portrait, using a different colored ink for it the second time, as if it had briefly crossed his mind that there might be something really important hiding in the tapestry of stars he was observing in his primitive telescope. But, lacking any reason to suspect anything extraordinary was there, he apparently dismissed it as unworthy of mention. And so Neptune remained undiscovered for another two and a half centuries.

In laying my life on these pages, I've got one huge advantage over the Italian genius. For reasons I can't explain, I'm positive that the mysterious search I'll be recording here will lead me to a discovery of enormous significance. I'm not sure that will be a good thing, for what looks like a beautiful treasure box might turn out to be Pandora's in disguise, but I'm committed to the hunt, come what may.

The haunting storylines I'm trying to untangle include an electrifying beauty emerging from the sea only to shake up my life and vanish into foam, a number of gaspingly colorful, outrageous demons calling me to a fearful reckoning with evil, and barking questions as to what I'm doing near the top of a steamship's radar mast in the middle of the ocean night en route to an undisclosed destiny at the top of the world. I've logged enough years in both research and SAR—search and rescue—to convince myself I've got a shot at finding the answers if I keep accurate notes.

I'm anxious to set down an account of the curve ball I just got thrown off Oahu, but as a trained lab tech, I'm compelled to begin this report of my experimental study with the identity of the chief investigator and a summary of the project's background.

So let the byline read Terma Den "TD" Sherab. Lacking a Ph.D. to append to that name, it's tempting use the title Elder Chief, bestowed upon me by my latest crew of eager beaver SAR volunteers shortly before I up and left the crew three months ago to set this expedition in motion—even though I was only twenty-seven and only a sub-chief at best.

I did earn some of that respect, though, I'll grant myself that. As I head into an exotic unknown replete with risk, it's good to know that some fifty-odd alpine adventurers had their lives handed back to them over a six-year period, thanks to my keeping a clear head and a firm footing on many a Rocky Mountain slope. And for the dozen or so families who got back nothing but the remains of loved ones who'd gambled with wilderness and lost, well, they were grateful too, given the even sadder, sleep-troubling alternatives. I've been trying to keep that in mind since coming out of my one-man huddle before the biggest play of my life, catching a pass on a leap that was thrown so hard it lifted me out of bounds, out of the stadium, and out of my native country, thousands of miles west with a few more to come toward the stars.

I'm writing seated on the uppermost platform of the *S.S. Iyerpadi* at about 4 AM some five hundred miles west of Hawaii, en route to India. Packed onto decks far below me is a motley assortment of made-in-America goodies for customers on the subcontinent hungering for Ford F-150s and Mustangs, wire-making machines, and aluminum siding. Up here, there's no sign of anything man-made other than the radar scanner in front of me and this blank book, hand-made from bleached newspaper and marijuana chaff picked up at a hippie booth in an arts and crafts encampment lining the main road to the harbor in Honolulu. In the wake of a strange experience in the sea a few hours before, I heeded the book's silent advice that I chronicle this expedition in its pages.

Up till last fall, I was minding my own business as Assistant to the Director of Search and Rescue Operations out of the Estes Park Ranger Station in Rocky Mountain National Park in Colorado. But the sweet deal I'd cut—exciting job, beautiful location, foxy girlfriend—had begun to lose its luster. An invisible force tugged at me, gripping the back of my neck and growling that my running rescue ops in storms on icy mountains (and snaking through a guerilla-war-infested jungle) were puny surrogates for the adventures I'm destined for on the other side of the world and that I'd better set my heading where it belongs.

So I up and left, and now I'm sliding on a mighty vessel towards hazards I may be ill-equipped to handle, wondering if I'm any more secure than the rats we used to poke with viruses in the microbiology lab when I was a research assistant at Mountain State College. Since this time I'm the experimentee as well as the experimenter, I'm logging my observations for later review, it being unwise to make judgments on the fly about which ones will prove critically important later on. In an obsessive search for a hidden key, everything looks suspiciously like a key in disguise. So it does to me, at any rate, and if I'm wrong, nothing more than a pen and a modicum of paper will have been wasted; but if I'm right, who knows what breakthrough might result?

At least, writing is grounding (or so my mother used to maintain) and with the hallucinations I've seen looming in the midnight sky, I could use a little grounding. Too much indulgence in staring at wrathful deities can be dangerous to your mental health. My inner stabilizer sputtered the night before we reached Hawaii, when I imagined an army of demons rising out of the sea from beyond the horizon, hell-bent on lighting me up with their flames, turning my skin black and causing my eyes to drip blood and my jaws to sprout fangs. They promised to swell me with second sight enabling me to see for thousands of miles and direct great power at whim toward good or evil, my choice.

The demon dance was abruptly splashed away by a couple of my shipmates who hollered up at me from one deck below, inquiring as to why I was nestled by the ever-watchful scanner with a penlight. I replied "Chilling," a convenient half-truth that got them out of the way.

I've socialized thousands of hours with guys like them in the past, but presently I need some solitude to prepare for whatever's catapulting me all the way to Tibet. I grew up in Colorado, the son of a single white mom who spent much of her life mourning for my Tibetan father, an unrecognized hero in an off-books war to undermine Red China's usurpation of his ancestors' land. That was back before America scuttled her justice-championing instincts at the behest of cheap labor vultures who didn't give a damn that the Chinese government was stealing the most awe-inspiring land in the known universe.

True, I haven't seen the place in person and won't for some weeks yet, but pictures of Tibet have been out there for more than a century, proving that Tibet is Earth's capstone of gorgeous majesty, a planet-topping headwater source of visual and spiritual exaltation and hope that, maybe after all, the world can overcome all the sorrows that its errors have kicked up since the beginning of human time.

I see now that, as a son of Tibet, I've been headed there my whole life, even though I didn't realize it till this past winter, when I was picking through the pieces of my childhood after a disastrous accident struck home. It's as if it took twenty-seven years to wake up (overlooking the possible naïveté in assuming I'm fully awake now) from a lifelong dream seeing nothing of Tibet, knowing no Tibetans, and laying eyes on not even one Tibetan-American anywhere but in the mirror.

I shouldn't lay it on too thick about being a stranger in an unstrange, vanilla land. I didn't get treated like a stranger once football and I found each other. Americans will forgive a whole lot of strangeness if you can catch a football while sprinting past a bunch of meaty rhino-men tearing towards you to pancake you on the turf.

I can pinpoint the moment my identity was changed to the fourth quarter of a game when I was rostered with the Leadville PeeWee Miners at the age of ten. As one of the shorter kids on the team, I'd been tied to the bench for the first two months of the season, like a pug kept out of the dog park supposedly for my own safety, until a classmate twisted his ankle in our second-to-last game and Coach unhooked my leash. We were four points down, so I was surprised when Coach chose me over the other defensive bench warmers. He must have sensed that I could make good use of my anger at him for two months of implicit put-downs by channeling it into laser-sharp focus on the ball. On the first snap our linemen got the enemy's QB into trouble, triggering a double launch of his pass and my body to the spot I knew it was headed. The smack of that whirling leather into my outstretched hands triggered a rifle shot run to the end zone to pull Leadville into the lead with thirteen seconds to go. Riffing on my odd name "T. Den," the coach, the team, and the fans started yelling TD! TD! and it stuck from that day on (except with my mom, who was not about to give up calling me Den.)

I played cornerback on four more teams between the ages of ten and nineteen, including one that came adorned with a handsome, much appreciated scholarship, managing to stay unconcussed and accepted despite a name, background, and look that struck everybody as "different."

That look came courtesy of my father, Dorje, a doctor from Nepal (so I was told) whom I was not blessed with the opportunity of seeing but for a single week of my life, and that when I was only one year old with a memory still too undeveloped for a firm grip on that transcendent moment. I know it was transcendent because of the expression on my face in a photograph showing me with him, along with my mom. It's a black and white snapshot showing my parents from the waist up with me in my dad's arms. My mom kept it framed in a swoopily curved matte resting on the Bible on her dresser.

I always thought my mom looked a little odd in that photo. My dad is gazing at me like he's staring at eternity with hope and joy. My mom and I are staring right back, each radiating our own kind of awe—my innocent wonder in poignant counterpoint to the dissonant chord lacing fear through my mother's lovelit face as she clutches my father in poorly masked desperation. Once I heard the story that he'd been killed—while trying to protect some friends from some criminals is how she put it—I saw her in that picture clinging to the short end of perilously long odds foretelling that there would be no further pictures of my father's face but that half-inch high image on my mother's bedside table. But even that was enough to show how much he loved me and my mother, and going to school in Denver with some kids who knew nothing about their fathers, that made up for a lot.

For a long time, my attempts to glean more information about him from my mom came up dry. That was when I was young enough to accept what I was told and too enchanted by the world's wonders to get fixated on one personal puzzle. The greatest of those wonders was the Rocky Mountain range, which spellbound me even from distant, hazy

Denver. My entreaties to my mother to take me there were met with vague promises of "Some day." I envied the kids whose families went skiing or had second homes up there. Recreation for my mom and me meant bowling or playing catch down at the park, servings of fun that did little to sate my hunger for the mountains.

Then one day the summer before fifth grade, my mom announced that she had some news. She'd gotten a call from her old friend Brenda up in Leadville, the former silver mining town where she had lived before I was born. Leadville used to be where America went to raid Mother Nature's secret silver stash, a trove of precious metal hidden by rock, dirt, creeks, waterfalls, and trees, all camouflage that was no match for metal hounds, the grizzled prospectors and beady-eyed industrialists who could smell precious metal from hundreds of miles away. A lot of them, including one of my own forbears on my mom's side, had surprised the native Utes in those mountains a hundred years before, combing through them for silver. By late this century, the mines had been largely worked out and the silver and miners were gone, leaving behind the residue of a colorful history that draws occasional tour folk.

Brenda had called with the news that the town's original schoolhouse was being turned into a heritage museum and they were looking for someone to run it. Within the hour my mother called the chairman of Leadville's historical commission, whom she knew from her days teaching ESL at the community college ten years before, and the guy hired her over the phone.

So I was going to get my wish and go to the mountains, to live. She might as well have announced we were going to move to Oz or Mars. I was troubled about leaving my buddies, but I was willing to pay that price to get inducted into the hall of mountain magic.

Within weeks we were out of our apartment with everything we decided to keep in a rented trailer hitched to the back of our '69 Mercury Comet, making our way in low gear up miles of twisting roads to our new home in a small town a hundred miles from Denver and another mile higher, the highest town in all North America. We rented a small house that nobody'd lived in for a year and my mother said that before I finished high school, she would own it.

I devoted my first few weeks in Leadville to manual labor, helping my mom set up the house, hauling in used furniture, painting, and weeding the garden, all the while sinking deeper into mountain thrall. Even at ten, I was convinced that the mountains' enormity reflected the scale of the mysteries they hid from all but a blessed few. Who those lucky people were I didn't know but I was pretty sure they weren't kids; I assumed you'd have to dwell in the mountains by yourself for a long time before they'd share their secrets with you. No matter—at night, staring at their dark silhouettes against the stars, I was certain I could hear them whispering that I'd come to the right place, and that some day, when I could ascend to their heights, they would reveal all that they were holding for me in trust.

Then one morning, a couple of weeks in, my mom caught me staring at the distant peaks from the top of a ladder when I was supposed to be cleaning pine cones from the gutter. She sighed and announced that we'd stop by the drive-through and head up into the mountains for a car picnic. I trembled with excitement at the prospect of getting closer to the center of heaven.

An hour later we were in the Comet with a bag of burgers heading towards Tennessee Pass. After a while, we pulled off the road onto a wide shoulder near overlooking a broad valley. Once she got our food scene going, she stared out the window and I got a feeling she was readying herself to tell me something. Summoning my patience, I let her be and got out of the car with my milkshake to check out the brass historic landmark plaque posted at the turnout. It read:

CAMP HALE
RED CLIFF, COLO.

**In the valley below this spot during World War II,
the United States Army trained thousands
of 10th Mountain Division troops to prepare for battle
in Italy's Apennine Mountain range.**

I bounded back into the car, bubbling with excitement over the mountain battle scenarios that had been acted out practically in our home town. She nodded slowly and said, "Come with me." She took me to the edge of the canyon, looking up to the mountains across the valley with her arm around my shoulders. "I met your father in that valley, Den. He was a great man. Not the least bit famous, but as wonderful and brave as any famous-great man I've ever heard of." Noting my puzzlement as to how anyone could run into a doctor from Nepal just up the road from Leadville, she took a deep breath and looked at me. "Den—you know there's a country called Tibet?"

How could I not, with all the books she had on the place on her bookshelves? But, I told her, I'd not been able to find it when I'd looked for it on the globe at school.

"You didn't see it on the globe because China wants the world to believe Tibet is part of China, but Tibet is a country unto itself, a land very different from China and from everyplace else. The Tibetans are a great people. Your father was one of them, which means you're Tibetan too, and so is your name."

"What? You said Dad was from Nepal!"

"No, I told you Daddy came to America from Nepal and that I took you to see him in Nepal when you were a baby, but he was born and raised in Tibet. He came here with hundreds of Tibetan men to be trained by our country's spy agency to reclaim Tibet from China in a guerilla war."

Even though she sounded serious, she had to be kidding, so I enthused about how fun it would be to join a band of fighting gorillas. She managed a smile at that before clueing me in about human warriors who operate in small groups from hiding and conduct raids and ambushes against larger, better equipped armies.

I asked her if there were still some Tibetan warriors down in that valley. "No, Den—you might be the only Tibetan in Colorado now. All the Tibetans at Camp Hale were taken back years ago."

Still trying to get a fix on my father as a warrior, I demanded to know why she'd told me he was a doctor. "He was both," she replied. "The Tibetan resistance leaders and the Americans helping them knew how smart your dad was and they told him how valuable he would be to their tiny fighting force"

"Cool!"

She turned on me, shaken and angry. "No, Den—it was not cool. Those fighters were duped into a suicide mission. A few hundred brave men going up against a well-armed giant never had a chance! Your father learned that the hard way one day nine years ago, and it was the last day of his life." She turned my head from the mountains to her urgent eyes. "Don't you *ever* think of risking your life on a lost cause!"

"That's nuts, Mom," I exclaimed. "And I don't know what you're talking about. Dad was killed in a war? You told me he was killed by criminals!"

"The rulers of China committed countless crimes against Tibetans." She interrupted her quiet tirade for an obligatory acknowledgment of China's virtues. "The Chinese have a magnificent history and culture and have achieved more in the same land with the same language over a longer time than any other people. They have enriched human civilization with awesome accomplishments in science, philosophy, the performing arts, athletics, and on and on. But their recent leaders have behaved insanely, gripping Tibet by the throat. Every time they tortured a monk for information or killed a Tibetan like your father, they were committing a crime. Tibet didn't threaten China. Tibet was an innocent country with good people like your father and his family who just wanted to be left in peace, but China muscled its way in and took command over the whole territory and even tried to stamp out the Tibetans' religion by destroying thousands of their monasteries."

I asked her what Tibetan monasteries had to do with World War II. "Nothing, honey," she replied. "The Tibetans came here in secret long after World War II was over. Even people in Leadville didn't know about the Tibetans up here till just recently. Our government didn't want China to know how we were helping to undermine them."

"It couldn't have been that big a secret—you met Dad here!"

"I was one of the secret-keepers. I worked here, teaching the Tibetans English. I met your father in class."

My parents enlisted in a secret war? My mother marrying her student?! She corrected me on that score. "Your dad was two years older than I and he was my teacher too, in so many ways—more than I was his, given how good his English was to begin with. He taught me about Tibet. It sounded so wonderful. When I was pregnant with you, we dreamed of living there as a family some day. But the same damned war that brought us together made it impossible for us to live together, ever." She looked back up at the mountain across the valley and sighed. "Your father was such a loving, generous, deep-thinking man with a delightful sense of humor. He was incredibly handsome and strong but also very spiritual. His name, Dorje, means lightning bolt, which is how meeting him struck my life"

"—*Lightning bolt!*"

"Yes. It's a Tibetan word, like Terma." I registered my fierce objection to her never having told me my name was Tibetan and demanded to know what "terma" meant. "Terma is a Tibetan word for 'hidden treasure,'" she explained. "Tibetan monks, called lamas, used that word for sacred insights they wrote by hand in books they hid high in the mountains."

"I knew the mountains held secret treasures. I'll bet they have ghosts, too, who study the termas."

She looked up to the tree line a thousand feet above us and murmured, "I don't know about ghosts, Den, but sometimes I wonder if, when a place becomes important to us, we become important to the place too and it ends up keeping some memory of us when we leave." She swallowed, clearly building up to something, so I didn't utter a peep. "There's been no place more important to my life than a tiny glade up on the other side of Eagle Mountain, the peak over there with that high crag at the top. At night your father and I used to hike up there to a special hidden spot we found about a mile off the trail. It looked down over the valley, which the Tibetans thought was so beautiful they called it Dhumra, their word for garden." She faced me with a big smile. "We called our perch with its high-up view of Dhumra Garden "The Den."

"Hah!" I blurted. "So that's it!"

"That's right—you're named for a hidden treasure and a magical mountain glade by a sparkling spring with a view of half the world."

I demanded to be taken up to the Den right then but she turned me down, saying something about it being too painful and pivoting to a claim that we had to go shopping for school supplies as she whisked me back to the car.

I ground my teeth, fixing on the day she would show me around Camp Hale and take me up to the Den, never imagining that that day would never come. But at least I had placed another piece in the puzzle of my childhood. Notwithstanding a few dates she'd had when we were in Denver with the guy who ran a horse ranch down in Colorado Springs, the way she'd looked when she talked about my father tipped me off that my fatherless future would be stepfatherless too, and that this invisible substance, love, could transform your life entirely, long after its catalyst had disappeared.

Damn—night's almost over. Though I've barely started this report, I've got to call for an intermission. I've got a lot of cables to grease today on no shut-eye. I'd best swing by the mess for some coffee and eggs and try to ease through the day till I can hit the sack at sundown.

[1-2]

<u>March 8, '91</u>

Disregarding snarky calls of "Herman Melville!" from my Aussie crewmates who spied me leaving my quarters with this journal as they straggled out of the nightly poker game, I headed straight to this alcove under the scanner and the stars. Gotta focus and get to what happened in Hawaii before we reach Asia, when the Discovery River will overflow its banks.

That first view of Camp Hale was a dramatic curtain opener on fifth grade, the year that began my transformation from city boy to mountain man. I took some razzing about my name in school, but I bought protection from more serious hassles with the universal currency accepted in playgrounds around the world, prowess in sports, namely football and track. Having read a kids' biography of Jim Thorpe the year before, I cast myself in his mold, destined to bask in glory as an anomalously Asian-American athletic superstar. I knew Jim probably hadn't had any Asian progenitors, at least for the most recent three hundred generations, but I was hard up for Tibetan sports star role models in the US since, for all I knew, aside from my mom and the CIA up at Camp Hale, the US had never seen a Tibetan athlete besides me, or a Tibetan anything.

For a while my mother's revelations while overlooking Camp Hale provided sufficient food for thought about my origins, but by the time I got to junior high and girls started occupying more and more of my mental real estate, I began to realize I knew precious little about the romance that brought my parents together. It struck me that, with Camp Hale being a vale of secrets, my parents must have had to run their adventure together under cover. I couldn't see them hanging out at the drive-in or dancing at the Silverlight Inn on Saturday nights. Questions were popping up, and by the summer before ninth grade, I decided I was entitled to some answers.

The trigger to my inquiry was the birth certificate we took up to the high school to register me for football. I'd noticed a curiosity in Box 11, labeled in tiny print "Legitimate" with "Yes" scrawled underneath it. I timed my investigation to begin fifteen minutes after we arrived at Myrtle's diner for lunch, knowing my mother would be less likely to kick up dust dodging my question if she had a plate of Myrtle's chicken fried steak in front of her amidst a crowd of locals.

Like a polite, precocious prosecutor, I opened with, "Legitimate means you and Dad were married when you had me, right?"

"We certainly were," she replied, as if we'd been discussing the issue for half an hour. "Your father and I had a perfect marriage. We loved each other as deeply as humanly possible till death did us part. How many married couples can say that?"

"I don't know; maybe not that many."

"All right then. Remember that."

"I'm just wondering how you managed to get married if everything to do with the Tibetans had to be kept such a big secret."

I caught a wry smile flicker on her face, as if to admit that she should have expected as much from a nosy punk like me. I could hear the jailer reluctantly unlocking the cell door for the story of her great love.

"What a clever young man you are, Den."

"Just the facts, ma'am." I'd heard that on TV once and trotted it out to prove her point. I sat back and waited for the story to unspool.

"All right, Sonny." She took a deep breath. Brought to the shore again after four years, she waded back in, "You remember my telling you about the hideaway your dad and I created high up on Eagle Mountain?"

"Uhhhh, yeah—'the Den' I was named after, which you won't show me."

"We've been through that, Den."

"Go on."

"For over two months, that sweet spot was our real home. Anything we had to do at Camp Hale or which I had to take care of back in Leadville was a minor nuisance to dispatch as quickly as possible before returning to our home in the sky. More than once we stayed up all night talking under the stars and we'd have to pass the next day's work in dreamy fatigue. The sounds of our laughter and observations about our different worlds and nature and the universe mingled with those of the winds blowing through the firs and spruce capping the tree line, the river rumbling far below us, and our heartbeats.

"To take some written snapshots of our time in the Den, I bought a blank journal down in Leadville so we could write down our reflections, jokes, dreams, and conversations. We kept it in a waterproof canoe bag I'd gotten at Beaver Creek and stored it with some camping supplies in a small metal footlocker.

"Weeks passed and the growing sense that we were becoming bound together for good came to the fore on our first full moon night up there. We'd been noticing a pattern in the moon's sky-crossings as it waxed that promised an amazing phenomenon. The Den fronted on a ledge overlooking an enormous drop of two thousand feet to the valley below, right where the river takes a ninety-degree turn to run straight south for a good fifty miles. Absent any party-pooper clouds, around midnight when the moon is full, it's positioned due south so its light ignites a fifty mile-long cool moon fire on the river. It creates a gleaming path straight from the Den through the darkened valley to what looks like a lunar altar, one far more thrilling than in any earthly church.

"It was there, when that shimmering ribbon of moonlight appeared, that your dad offered me this ring that his great-grandfather had carved out of yak bone in the late 19th century." She caressed the ring I'd seen on her left hand all my life. "I kissed him. He asked me if that meant yes and I buried my face in his neck, fighting back tears of joy. Then he showed me a marriage certificate he'd drawn up in our journal. It had a beautiful drawing of Kailash, the holy mountain near his home village. We spoke spontaneous vows to each other and signed the certificate by moonlight.

"I could hardly believe it—so soon after its recent wonderful, unexpected turn, my life had made another quantum leap in happiness. We began to brainstorm ideas for the many things we could do together over the rest of our lives—living in both Tibet and America, the dazzling childhoods our kids would have moving fluidly between these two magnificent lands and cultures, each so amazing on its own and so different from the other. Dorje would practice medicine in a city near his family's village in western Tibet, so our kids could get to know his brother and niece—"

"—Wait—Dad had a brother? Like, my uncle?!"

"Yes. His name was Yeshe." I demanded that she take me to meet him, preferably within the hour, but she shook her head. "I'm sorry, darling. Your father's family lived in a tiny remote village called Gnam Yuljongs." Noting my perplexity at the gobbledygook, she repeated the name and told me it meant "sky view" in Tibetan. "It was high up in the mountains where there was no mail or telephone service, not even a road to get there. We couldn't even find out if Yeshe is alive without going on a major trek in Tibet and that's not going to happen."

My entreaties to reconsider were promptly shot down. She informed me that China's boa constrictor hold on Tibet can get you arrested just for displaying a picture of the Dalai Lama. How warm a welcome did I think they'd give to the family of man who helped lead a militia bent on running China out of Tibet?

Expecting but getting no comeback from me, she calmed down and asked if I wanted her to finish telling me about her marriage. Yes, Mom; please.

"I was saying that we would alternate between Tibet where your father would carry on his medical practice and America, where at first I would pull in most of our income as a teacher while Dorje would scrounge together workshops on integrated medicine for healthcare professionals. All this moving about with children wouldn't be easy or make us rich, but we'd have plenty of the wealth that counts.

"It was the kind of dreaming young married couples do. Yes, our marriage vows were made without the dubious blessings of the state of Colorado. We had no choice. But no other couple's wedding ceremony could be more legitimate or profound than ours. No clergyman or justice of the peace with a rubber stamp could have made our commitment any stronger than it already was. There are half a million divorces a year in this country, every one of which had a government certificate at the start. We made our own certificate, and it was a work of art."

"I hear ya, Mom." As I nudged my mashed potatoes around my plate, I made a note to ask to see that certificate sometime.

"There was just one catch," she continued. "To realize our dream, Dorje and his compatriots would have to prevail in a battle of wills and bullets with China—hopefully all the way to Tibet's national liberation, but at *least* to the point where the killing would stop and people could move freely in and out of the country. We knew it would be tough going. They weren't playing games down there in camp—they were learning to use lethal weapons and to plan dangerous raids against a powerful and well-equipped foe. The risks inherent in the campaigns they would be launching only too soon were painfully obvious and we didn't discuss them.

"At least till our last night there. I'd just discovered I was pregnant with you a few days before and we were so excited that you would be with us the following year. But earlier that day, the commanders in camp had informed the Tibetans that they'd be returning to Asia on the weekend, two weeks earlier than we'd expected.

"That news ratcheted up the intensity of our time together. Plainly Dorje wouldn't be back in the States any time soon, and my visiting him would have to wait well over a year, till you were old enough to handle the long journey. Every minute in the Den that night seemed so lush and poignant at the same time, as if a mammoth pendulum were hanging from the moon, ticking off the seconds remaining to us. Your father was deeply pained that he would not be here for your birth, so just before we left, as the darkness began to lift, he wrote you a message in our journal, a letter to his child, whom he could not be certain he would live to see."

"Mom—Dad wrote me a letter?! Why haven't you shown it to me? I've got to see that!"

"I wish I could show it to you, Den, but I've not seen it myself since that night, because a few minutes after he finished it, we tucked the journal into the footlocker and buried it in its hiding place miles up on that mountain range."

"But you knew Dad was leaving—why didn't you bring everything down?!"

"Burying it there was a way of declaring our faith in our future, of forcing ourselves to be confident that one day your father would come back, that we would hike up there, the three of us together, and dig it up. We needed to believe that in order to handle all the descents we were facing—leaving the Den and Camp Hale, a stilted farewell before the men were stuffed into their transports for the trip to Peterson Air Force Base, and the rearrangement of my life before I began to show by moving to Denver, where nobody would question where I'd met my husband. The next day Dorje left the mountains and, in a few weeks, I did too, to become a single, married mother-to-be in a second-floor apartment in the thick of the largest city on the Rocky Mountain plateau.

"Each day in Denver I prayed that I'd find a letter from your father in our mailbox and each day I wrote him, too, at the mysterious and vague address he'd been given for the camp the CIA had helped the Tibetans set up on the Nepal side of the border.

"I missed him dearly, but I wasn't alone, because someone else very important was with me. And that was you. And on April 4, 1963, as I held you in my arms for the first time, a nurse asked me politely if Mr. Sherab and I were married, and I told her the truth: Yes. We were married and we remained so till death did us part, because we shared a love for each other that lives on every day in my heart and in your every breath."

I wished she'd told me that sooner because it made me feel ten degrees less dadless, a priceless balm for having seen my father for only one week of my life.

In that soft finale to her epic tale, my mother smiled and stroked my cheek, a gesture that she could count on to disintegrate my usual adolescent response mechanisms—jokes, complaints, or bellowed one-upping—had they not already knelt down before the biblical power her tale held over me. But in the silence that followed, the simmering image of that journal with my dad's letter to me burst forth.

"Hah! Now I know why you sounded so secretive when you told me what my name means the first time you showed me Camp Hale—hidden writings! You hid that journal with the letter Dad wrote me right in that mountain. Well, I've got a right to see my mail, Mom. You've got to take me up to the Den to find it!"

"Honey, I only told you about that letter so that you'd know how much your father cared about you. You'll have to be satisfied with that. Going back up to the Den would be way too hard for me."

"I thought you said it was only a few miles' hike!"

"Not in that way—it would make me too sad. Besides, the wilderness can change so much in fifteen years it could be all overgrown and too hard to find. We chose the location so that our campfires couldn't be seen from Camp Hale down below. The CIA wouldn't have fancied one of its workers getting romantically involved with a 'foreign operative,' as they called them."

Noting my steaming lack of sympathy, she took my hand. "I'm sorry, Den. I know how important it is for a boy to connect with his dad, and that's why I took you half-way across the world to Nepal, so the two of you could look in each other's eyes and play together, so he could rock you to sleep. That trip took four days each way under rugged conditions and cost all my savings, but it was easier to take you on that fourteen thousand mile journey than it would be for me to hike three miles to the Den."

I could see I wasn't going to get anywhere badgering her, but I felt cheated. Till then I'd had nothing to go on about my father but that one picture on my mother's dresser and a few stories, and now I was being denied something tangible that my father had created *for me.*

But beneath my anger purled a new warmth, an awareness of how much my parents had loved each other and me, and that was a blessing one couldn't take for granted in Denver, Leadville, or anywhere else.

[1-3]

<u>March 9, '91 — Another Midnight Under the Radar Umbrella</u>

I got the picture. I was to take what little information my mother offered me about my father's background and be grateful for it. Fine— I'd just have to dig up more on my own.

I began by becoming an amateur scholar. Leadville wasn't Oxford, but our high school did have a pretty good library with a few frayed old books that dealt with Tibet, plus magazines and journals I could pore through with the aid of the fat dusty reference catalog. There were even some LPs produced by lonely ethnomusicologists who'd dragged primitive recording equipment into far-flung villages of the Himalayas to capture ethereal haunting rituals that had been carried on up there for centuries and, I suspect, are being performed still, perhaps this very night.

By sophomore year I was spending almost every study hall in the library with my head enveloped in listening station headphones, suffused with whatever I could find out about the history, society, and religion of the society atop the world's roof. I learned that Tibet's culture was rooted in Bon, a religion based on shamanism and animal sacrifice, long before Buddha was born and remained so for more than a millennium afterwards, till a Tibetan king took a fancy to Buddhism and invited an Indian guru to come teach it to him and his people. There, Bon and Buddhism and even some elements of Hinduism and Tantra mixed it up in different ways, resulting in a uniquely Tibetan brew featuring some spectacular unSiddartha-like deities, both good and not so good (as in staggeringly evil).

It puzzled me that, alongside its badass rep for concocting demons, Tibet was adored by the world as Shangri-La, a heavenly utopia where everyone might live for centuries in love and peace and isolation from the rest of the world—and it was *also* a haven for a religion that made room for intense sex acts at the center of its ritual practice. Between super paradise, super demons, and super sex, I wondered why everyone wasn't heading to Tibet to see what was up. Yet, oddly, when the white bread teenagers in the library saw me with clanging ceremonial horn blasts leaking out of my headphones and my eyes popping out at tales of the hideous monsters leaping from my books, they didn't crowd around and beg me for some show and tell.

There was one exception, though—Linda Hawkinson, my first girlfriend. Linda and I took Asian History together. She wanted to know about my background and I let her have it. It was liberating to relate the odd circumstances of my birth and childhood and see someone I was infatuated with become mesmerized by the story. Hm—maybe my strange background wasn't such a bad thing. Linda's was conventional enough—the daughter of a fireman in a longtime Colorado family of three kids—but she was excited to be coupled with the school's human curio, me being the closest the school had ever come to having an Asian foreign exchange student.

Things sailed along pretty smoothly until the day she asked me if I were a Buddhist or a Christian. I told her neither.

"Oh. I was hoping you could explain to me why Buddhists think Christians are too uptight about death, yet *they* meditate on death so they won't be obsessed with it. But I think their meditating on it so much means they're more obsessed with death than we are."

"Okay, maybe they're a little obsessed, but their angle is not to be *afraid* of it. Often, when someone dies, Tibetans burn the body and while it's burning they talk to the dead person to make sure they stay calm while passing to the phase of life between death and rebirth." I'd picked up that in *The Tibetan Book of the Dead* on my mom's bookshelf.

"They're barbecuing the person they're talking to?! That is *so gross!*"

"They're not cooking them; they're cremating them and offering comfort to the soul."

"Instead of praying to God? After seeing their demons in class, the Tibetans are the last people I'd turn to for comfort. Most of those deities looked crazy perverted to me."

Linda had shuddered at the wrathful deities we'd seen in the Tibetan art slide show, but I couldn't get enough of them, even though the more I saw of them, the more puzzled I became about the mindsets that had given rise to them. However, the unspeakable violence perpetrated by bloody monsters etched in detail into cave walls, fabric, or paper was a little too far from the gentle baby Jesus in Mary's arms for the likes of Linda. I could hardly blame her. What was a blue-eyed cutie-pie from a rural county in the bosom of middle America supposed to do with a boyfriend who fantasized about going to what seemed like another planet to truck with grotesque demons?

By the time summer rolled around, our dates had become tinged with awkward silences, till finally, on the Fourth of July weekend, I let her off the hook. That sent my summer rolling downhill and I took refuge in plotting a way to get to Tibet to revel in its mysteries in person. The problem was I was still too young to get there on my own and my mother wouldn't hear of taking me. And the more I read about Tibet, the more I began to get some idea why.

My father had been the love of my mom's life for the last eighteen years and for sixteen of them he'd been dead as a result of his involvement in a fervent Tibetan self-defense movement that had been going on since long before the Communists took power. China notched its first defeat of a Dalai Lama back in 1910, causing him to flee to India, just like the current one had to in 1959 after the Communists had used their newfound power for a decade to make things worse than ever, and when *he* escaped, they got worse still. Tens of thousands of Tibetans were killed or thrown in jail and tortured or forced into slave labor to cut down forests or build dams and railroads.

It was hard not to compare the fate of the Tibetans in this century with what befell Native Americans in the last one. In both cases a land-grabbing government bullied its way onto ancestral lands, but for China that wasn't enough. They set out to crush Tibetan culture as well. They trashed monasteries and religious art, killed lamas, and herded everyone into so-called "study groups" where they hammered their subjects with Communist propaganda and threatened dire consequences for anyone who failed to turn in neighbors they suspected of resistance.

Still, some brave Tibetans did resist, enough that China put another hundred thousand troops into Tibet along with plenty of ammo and hardware. That hampered the rebels' recruitment campaign, which was facing tough going already. Many Tibetans were suffering from the same catastrophic famine as their Chinese counterparts, thanks to Mao's Great Leap Forward that ripped peasants from subsistence farming into heavy industry. The rebels had to flee to India and Nepal to regroup.

When the cross-border guerilla campaign entered the picture, my library resources gave out. I had to press my mother for more details about my father's involvement in it. It wouldn't be easy getting her to address the source of her great sorrow, but I hoped she'd relate the happier story of how my dad came to show up in a secret classroom of hers ten thousand miles away and how she got me and herself across the world to be with him in Nepal.

I picked a Sunday over a brunch of homemade waffles and fresh Elberta peaches to pose my question. It was a late summer morning and we were eating out in the back yard. She had a pair of chaise lounges set up facing the mountains—away from Red Cliff I noticed, although the wide view from our property faced that direction as well. She agreed and her eyes softened as she glanced up at the mountainous skyline, preparing herself for immersion in a bath of mixed memories.

"The reason we have the CIA to thank for bringing your father here," she began, "has to do with their having diddled around in Tibet for years, even while the Dalai Lama was still there, as part of America's ongoing effort to keep the Communists from taking over the world. They'd cultivated a homegrown Tibetan guerilla rebel band led by a trader-turned-militant named Gompo Tashi, enticing him and his followers with some technology and the sci-fi phantasm of airplanes. The Tibetans didn't know much about America, but they welcomed any help they could get, especially from a foreign tribe that hated the Chinese as much as they did, equipped with sky boats and gifting them with weapons and hand-cranked radios.

"Signing on to a CIA operation code-named ST Circus, Gompo and his men flew off in a military plane to the Pacific island of Saipan, where they were drilled in spying, communications, fighting, and parachuting out of airplanes in the dark so they could be infiltrated back into Tibet under cover of night. Then, seeking a training environment more like the Himalayas, the CIA realized it already had just the place, lying dormant in the mountains of Colorado, which the 10th Mountain Division had left behind thirteen years before. So in 1958, the CIA took their first handful of guerillas and brought them half-way around the world to Colorado, and resurrected Camp Hale.

"None of us in Leadville had any idea what was going on up at Camp Hale. We'd known Red Cliff to be an army town when we were kids, during the war, and the word was out that some activity had started up again at the camp, supposedly for development of explosives. There'd been a curious rumor once about a bus carrying a bunch of Asian men breaking down near Colorado Springs, but no one connected that with Red Cliff. We had no clue that the US was interested in Tibet, much less that Tibetans were training for war right in our neighborhood.

"We did notice that a few locals had been hired for jobs up there that they spoke about in unusually vague terms. I was twenty-five then, teaching English as a Second Language as an extension course over at CMC (Colorado Mountain College) oblivious to the whole thing, when one day a man in a suit and tie and high-polished shoes walked into my classroom as I was dismissing a group of Mexican immigrants. He told me he was from the federal government and wanted to give me a chance to serve my country.

"He took me out for coffee, swore me to secrecy, and offered me the opportunity to assist the United States in its battle against the Communist Chinese threat by helping some Asian allies learn English up at Camp Hale. Whether he'd tickled some lust for adventure in a small town girl or I had an unconscious premonition that this move would light the way to my meeting the most important man of my life, I jumped at the opportunity.

"I became a Camp Hale regular, teaching foreign men different from any I'd ever encountered at the college in the most beautiful environment any American teacher could hope to work in. I thought I was the luckiest ESL teacher in the country.

"Meanwhile, your dear father was living in Tibet, an aspiring doctor from a little village in the southwest who'd moved to Lhasa, the country's capital, as one of just a handful of men from the whole country selected to study medicine there. When the Chinese closed down the medical center, he found his way to Nepal and continued his studies in Kathmandu, periodically making trips back across the border to Gnam Yuljongs to visit his family.

"Dorje loved working with patients, but the more he heard about the oppression of Tibet and the burgeoning resistance movement, the more difficult it became for him to concentrate on medicine. One day early in 1962, a few months before getting his degree, he visited a resisters' camp in a remote border area called Mustang. It was mostly surrounded by Tibetan territory with access to several possible paths across the mountainous border. There he met Gompo, who was still feeling his oats from the success of a raid his guerillas had staged on a small Chinese military convoy several months before. The raiders had snared a satchel that they'd turned over to the CIA with more than a thousand pages of internal Chinese documents, which exposed the disastrous famine and internal discontent resulting from the so-called Great Leap Forward. It didn't take Gompo long to recognize that your dad's intelligence, education, fluency in English, and international outlook could be a major asset to Gompo's band of largely unschooled rural tribesmen.

"Gompo beseeched your dad to join their forces. Dorje demurred at first. He'd been thinking of going to Dharamsala, India, where the Dalai Lama had set up the Tibetan Medical and Astrology Institute, but after returning to Kathmandu, he made up his mind that he couldn't pursue his medical career while there was still hope of liberating Tibet. He headed to Mustang, and within a couple of months he found himself riding into Camp Hale in an Army personnel carrier. The next morning he entered my classroom and my life."

I would have been glad to hear more about how young people not much older than I from such different backgrounds fell in love, but I had to make sure she got to the resistance and what happened to my father. I commented that it was mighty ambitious to travel to Nepal with a one-year-old baby.

"It was a challenge from the get-go, having to pull that much money together. Taking care of you in our one-bedroom apartment, my options were limited, but I picked up extra cash taking in essay grading overflow from faculty at the city college nearby.

"Once you earned your toddler stripes, I went into serious trip-planning gear. I was impatient to get going—I told myself I was just eager to see your dad and introduce you to each other, but the truth is I lived in fear that if I waited too long, it could be too late. I'd spent too many days going to the mailbox not knowing if I'd find another letter from Dorje sharing fantasies about our future or some terrifyingly strange Tibetan handwriting delivering catastrophic news.

"By the late summer of 1964 I'd scrimped together three thousand dollars, which was barely enough to cover all the travel expenses I'd calculated for a round trip from Denver to Northern Nepal, with no margin for safety. Taking a long hard look at the diamond and ruby bracelet my great-uncle had given me when his wife passed away, the urgent present trumped tattered sentimentality and off I went to an antique jewelry shop where I picked up nine hundred dollars for it, and we were ready to go. I packed everything we would need into one suitcase, strapped you onto my back and headed to the Denver airport.

"I talked to you about the trip all the time, showing you pictures of the Himalayas and a little drawing I'd made of your dad one sunshiny dawn up at Dhumra Garden. I taught you the name 'Daddy' when I'd show you his picture and told you of our travel plans for airplanes, buses and a jeep. It as all mommy babble to you.

"It took us three days hauling through New York, London, and Bombay to get to Kathmandu. Your dad and I had agreed that you and I would rest up at an inn near the airport for a day or so, partly to recover and also to wait for him in case he was able to get away and drive into the capital to pick us up. If not, on the second day, I was to hire someone with a four-wheel drive vehicle for the journey, which would take almost two hours. He sent me a detailed, handwritten map in case it was needed. After a day I found a taxi driver who was able to borrow a World War II era jeep from a local mechanic and we hit the rough road.

"By the time we rumbled over the final pass in that rattletrap, it had been four days since we'd left Denver. When I saw men scurrying around in the valley below, knowing that one of them was your father, who'd been absent from my life a lot longer than he'd been present in it, my heart started pounding. I fought back tears of joy and told you we were almost home.

"In ten minutes you and I were in your father's arms. My head swooned with the beauty of the sky as the crowd of curious and envious warriors stared and the newly enriched taxi driver turned back to the capital."

"Envious?"

"They were soldiers encamped in a foreign country, Den. Just being a woman was enough to be attractive there, and having young, fair skin, auburn hair, and blue-green eyes didn't hurt." I nodded, a little abashed for not having figured that one out myself. "Gompo took pity on your dad and let him delay his training drills for the first twenty-four hours, most of which we spent sleeping and hugging your father. With a sleeping bag tufted under and around you, you were a real mountain camper at age one.

"When your dad went back to work, we set up a routine. I helped in meal preparation for the men, stashing you in a portable play pen your father rigged up by the makeshift kitchen. It was liberating to be part of a community where your father and I were recognized as a married couple instead of having to skulk around in the shadows as we had at Camp Hale. You and I were together with your dad in the early morning, when he got in his best play time with you, during his lunch break, and at night.

"Once we'd put you down to sleep, your dad and I talked about what was going on with the war, tempering the anxiety that engendered with plans for our future. I would return to Denver to keep you safe from the war. We'd communicate by mail, looking forward to the day China was forced to relent or at least lighten its pressure on Tibet to the uneasy level that had prevailed before Mao, leaving it more or less to its own devices. A year or two at most, we hoped. Then you and I would return to your dad and move to Gnam Yuljongs, while he worked as a doctor several days a week in Kham, a city a few hours away. There he would blend traditional shamanistic medicine with modern Western approaches and help villages like Gnam Yuljongs all over Tibet by setting up transport mechanisms to get patients to regional medical centers for cases local healers couldn't handle. In time, we would bring you to America so you could know this part of your background. You would be our world baby, knowing and loving both sets of your roots."

At that point my mother looked down at her mug, where a half-cup of coffee had gone cold. I guessed that she'd reached rougher territory and needed a moment to think about how to go on. I hopped up with her mug, figuring to make sure her story engine stayed fueled up. I came back bearing some hot Maxwell House, silently beckoning her to cough up the details she'd been shunting aside my whole life. She was quiet for a while, but I had the good sense to know that she respected my right to know how the fairy tale that had catalyzed my life had ended, so I waited her out for five minutes till she spoke up.

"At night, cuddled up with your dad and you bundled next to me, I felt safe and protected by a destiny that had led me to our canvas cubbyhole in the Himalayas. But my security blanket kept getting ripped by the sounds of gunshots fired in target practice and the shouts of the men running war games. When you pointed in the direction of the shots, I made up a song about giant magic popcorn that elephants made over their campfire at snack time.

"When your dad came in for dinner on the evening of the fifth day, he told me they'd moved up the time for the next mission. The CIA had picked up intelligence that another convoy of the so-called People's Liberation Army—"

"—the PLA," I threw in.

"Right. The convoy was expected to make a move through the mountains later that week, offering a good opportunity for a hit. Also, the agency wanted the Tibetans to plant earth movement sensors in certain locations to help them detect signs of atom bomb testing. The mission could last for weeks and was set to start in two days, during which Dorje would be prepping for it day and night, so you and I would have to leave the next day. Daddy had already arranged for a driver to take us back to Kathmandu.

"I steeled myself against crying that night. Your dad gallantly accompanied me on my shaky imaginary excursions to our happy future together, but as dawn drew near, he told me that while he was sure it would all work out, he wanted me to know that if something happened to him, I should feel free to love and marry someone else and that the marriage would have his blessing."

She choked up and dabbed at her eyes with her napkin. I aborted my fruitless search for something comforting to say. Just let it roll. "So that was bad enough. But when we got up and your dad went off to find our driver, I noticed some of the men lined up by the supply shed where one of the team leaders was showing the men how to fasten something that looked like a medicine capsule to their left wrist. I had a horrible feeling about that and went up to one of the men after he left the group and asked him in Tibetan what it was. He replied by making a choking gesture on himself and rolling his eyes, which stood in well enough for "cyanide.""

"Moments later when your dad showed up with the jeep, I was in a near panic state. I tried to hide my emotions by digging around in my purse, and in doing so I came across my little camera, and realized I had yet to get a single picture of the three of us together. I'd thought about that camera every day but it always struck me as a distracting interference with the intense high I was experiencing whenever your dad was with us. Now it became desperately important, so I grabbed the driver, whom I'd not even met, and thrust the camera in his hands, showing him where the shutter button was, and marshaled the three of us into position. I put you into your dad's arms, and with you two looking in each other's eyes and me hugging you both, the driver snapped the picture that's been standing on my dresser for the last fifteen years.

"Unable to let go of what I feared might be my last embrace with your father, I buried my face in his chest so he wouldn't see me crying, though my heaves and the soaking wet spot on his shirt might have tipped him off. I braced myself, tacked on a big smile, looked up at him, and told him I would love him forever and would be waiting for him in

Colorado to help us move. He told me to count on it. A minute later, you were in my arms as we bounced up the dirt road and over the pass, heading towards Kathmandu and its little airport, beginning an eternity of not knowing what was happening with your father."

She swallowed and I damn near choked up myself, but I could not let up. "I'm sorry to ask, Mom, but I need to know what did happen to Dad and how you found out about it."

She flinched but carried on with a performance she'd no doubt rehearsed in many variations as I grew up. "The trip back to Denver took four days, but seemed like four years. I wanted to sleep for weeks so I wouldn't have to endure waiting for the mail all day, every day, for the five weeks I told myself it would take the letter your dad would write me after the mission was over to make its way down the mountains and over the ocean to our apartment. Of course, when you've got a toddler on your hands, there's no time off at all, so sleep was hard to come by, especially with the stress of worrying and trying not to look worried around you.

"But the five-week mark came and went leaving nothing in our mailbox but bills and junk mail. I slipped further into the limbo of chronic anguish that has beset soldiers' wives for thousands of years. I'd look out the window fifty times a day for the mailman, and when he'd come, I'd grab you and hurry down the stairs, my hands shaking as I turned the key to our box, knowing that opening it would channel me into a river of joy, a hell of grief, or a sentence to another twenty-four hours of anxiety, which is what I received every day for three months.

Then one Saturday as I was feeding you lunch, I heard the mailman's keys and it sounded to me like the sharpening of an executioner's axe. I trembled as I held you while opening the box, and when I saw a blue air letter from Nepal addressed in a strange hand, I knew before reading it that I'd become a widow and that you would never see your father again."

I asked her bluntly what it said. "It was written in broken English by a man in your father's brigade. It was a kind but direct account of a report he'd taken from three men in your father's platoon who'd been captured with him across the border during an ambush attempt they'd staged on the convoy. They'd been taken to a crude prison the Chinese had set up somewhere in southern Tibet not far from the site of the ambush.

"Your father understood the implications of the Chinese having immediately stripped them of their cyanide capsules and why their captors were keeping them alive. He hatched an escape plot that placed himself at much greater risk than the others, to increase the likelihood that the others could get away. They objected to his offer of what was likely a suicidal sacrifice, but your dad insisted that a leader cannot abandon his responsibility for the lives of the men under his command. All he asked of them was that, if they made it back to Nepal, they find our address, which he'd left by the lantern in his tent, and get the captain to write and let me know that he would die loving me and you and to remind me that I must be free to start another life.

"Those were the last words I know to have been spoken by your father. When the plan was put into action and the men began their scramble up the ridge, one of them tripped on a loose stone and set off a rock fall. A guard raised the alarm and started firing into the dark. Your father put his desperate Plan B into play and was shot as the other three escaped."

Planning to visit my father's grave some day when I could make it to Tibet on my own, I had to press her for one more piece of information,. "Where was he buried, Mom? Do you know?"

She shook her head. "You deserved to know what I know, Den, and I've told you. Now I need to lie down." She got up and started heading for the house, but then turned back and kissed me on the top of my head.

She slept for two hours. When I heard her making dinner later, I stuck my head in the kitchen and said, "Thanks, Mom. I appreciate your telling me all that." She nodded, adding no further details about my father's death, then or ever again.

But there were reverberations from the darkened energy that coiled and flexed behind her brow, reverberations that still exert a push on the rudder of my life, compelling me to find my way back to the Himalayas, twenty-six years after my first visit there. I cannot forget the clutch of fury my mother felt at my father's killers and the ceaseless, despondent questioning she endured as to what bedevils so many people to so callously destroy the lives of others as beautiful and magnificent as that of her former lover and spouse. Nearly twelve years since that heavy brunch time, I find myself heading to the land of my father's birth and death driven by that same question in the belief that I might discover the answer.

[1-4]

<u>March 10, '91</u>

I'm settled back into my crow's nest on the top deck; the rest of the crew is sunk in night duty, beer torpor, or sleep. Almost all the lights are off and the sky is clear open to the Milky Way, ideal conditions for my internal gyroscope to balance my journeys fore and aft in time.

In recounting my father's death, my mother had shed the protective carapace she'd grown over both of us while mothering a younger child and fulfilled her responsibility as the mother of a man, but at a cost to her equanimity. Within her stirred a turbulent thoughtsream of fear that the aggrieved son of Dorje might someday follow his dusty footsteps into battle against China.

I saw a flash of that fear one evening two years later when I'd returned from work at CMC, where I'd enrolled in an associate degree program to show my mother that I respected her advice about getting a diploma being a good play. I wanted to take up mountain studies and, as the son of a doctor, the science of life processes that made people healthy or ailing or dead.

While hanging out in the bio department, I schmoozed myself into a paid internship in a microbiology professor's lab to learn something interesting while lessening the financial burden my mother was carrying for my education. Our lab was hardly on the field's cutting edge, but we followed what the big boys were doing in the Bay Area and Japan, and every now and then we managed to make a tiny mark for ourselves. We got contracts with the state's department of public health during flu season and pursued our own projects, like our experiment with

Interferon B that earned a spot in the college alumni paper and a citation in an article in *Nature* on emerging trends in microbiological research (footnote #38 of 71, but still, we existed).

The contract I was most hoping we'd land was a genetic analysis project at Colorado Mental Health Institute, over in Pueblo, where they incarcerate the country's ultra-psycho scum—violent haters, mob bosses, serial killers, mass murderers, and, no doubt, someday, the Unabomber, if they ever find him. I imagined ugly viruses oozing out of those creeps that might reveal a lot about evil, but we were too small-time to get that one. Our main niche in the intellectual ecosystem, due to our location in the middle of the Rocky Mountains, centered on tick viruses.

For all their beauty, the Rockies have their share of warts, principally certain viruses that seem to like the mountains as much as we do. They travel widely, courtesy of an endless fleet of vectors transporting them among an endless supply of victims, ranging from porcupines to cattle to humans. Our little team of state college science profs, undergraduates, and staffers did what we could to support the war on nasty arthropods, investigating their m.o.'s so we could throw in our two cents' worth for the development of stronger anti-viral medications.

I was on the team doing microphotography of viruses that ride ticks like minirajahs on tiny elephants, coming up with pictures of them at every stage of infection and replication. Our study chief would wax rhapsodic over the beautiful operational efficiency of the world's tiniest organisms, but I felt like I was watching a creepy horror flick on a half-inch screen in which micromonsters infected healthy cells and hijacked their life systems for their own cell-murdering, reproductive purposes.

On one occasion when I'd pulled an evening shift, I picked up an old copy of *Newsweek* to read over dinner and came upon an article on China and its recovery efforts in the wake of the "Great Leap Forward." Before I knew it, I was tossed about by recollections of the terror China had inflicted upon Tibet during that period. I saw it as a poison entering Tibet's body, attacking the life of the world's most beautiful country to satisfy the invaders' greed and lust for power.

I lost my appetite, left the cafeteria, and hastened back to the lab to try and get my mind onto something else, but as I was poring over a photo of a virus with its injector releasing its genetic material inside a newly captured host cell, I suddenly saw it overlain by a map of Tibet with China injecting it with its foreign culture, propaganda, and oppressive cruelty, leading to the captivity or death of countless Tibetans, including my own father. I sat back to let my breathing return to normal.

That night at dinner, in a blaze of stupidity, I mentioned the incident to my mother and muttered, "I wish I could come up with an antiviral substance to get China out of Tibet. Tibet is a sick captive, abandoned in a prison with no one on the way to save her."

I never should have messed with my mother's embargo on the subject. She froze, holding a forkful of lasagna midway to her mouth and then plunked it back down on her plate. She cleared her throat and glared at me. "Don't start with me, Den, and don't start with yourself. China won its war on Tibet and it's over. Even the Dalai Lama knows it's over, forever."

"That's a little short-sighted, Mom. Forever is a long time."

"China knows forever. It's been around a long time."

"So has Tibet, and Tibet is in the right."

"So? China is run by a band of the most extreme control freaks in the history of civilization and they're controlling a billion people! The poverty-stricken guerillas your father fought with were doomed."

"But the Chinese were sending soldiers around to Tibetan villages and killing the men who refused to join their army. The Tibetans had to fight back. I would want to."

"They had *no chance*, Den. The US should never have encouraged them to fight, not with the piss-ant kind of support they were offering. Life is too precious to waste in a lost cause! You are all that remains of your father's bloodline—and mine, I might add—and you have the responsibility to your ancestors and *me* of *protecting your own life!*"

"So you think the Tibetans should just throw in the towel."

"They already have. They know they've got no better chance of taking back their country than the Sioux and the Apaches do of taking back America. You don't hear the Dalai Lama riling up his followers with that kind of nonsense. The Chinese just have to glance his way and he knows what's on the tips of their tongues. 'You remember Stalin, your phony Holiness?? Or the Cultural Revolution? Try misbehaving and watch us rain death on millions of your people *and* that whole backward culture you cling to.'"

"But the whole world's on the Tibet's side, isn't it?"

"Whoopee. 'On Tibet's side' means a muted chorus of tongue clucking. Ask the Dalai Lama how far that would get him. The PRC honchos would stick out their chests and sneer, 'Do you think for one second we would cave in to a bunch of self-righteous outsiders the way the paltry Afrikaner minority in South Africa did? We have one-fifth of the entire population of the planet, Mr. Lama! Now shut your trap and let us improve the lives of those who inhabit the benighted Tibet Autonomous Region, Chinese all.'"

Having blundered deep into her red zone, I tried to leap my way out, gathering our plates and chirping, "Well, I'll clean up," but her eyes darted to me so fast I put them down.

"Wait until you see what happens with China's one-child family policy."

"What's that got to do with it?"

"I can't guess why, but fewer and fewer baby girls are making it to birth or age one. Watch what having fewer women as partners for Chinese men does to temper Chinese aggression."

"Mom, I get how you feel about it. Can we drop the subject?"

"Do you remember that time in Denver when we went to the funeral for Vinny Nanini's brother, the boy who'd been killed in Vietnam?"

"Uh, yeah, Mom. I was only nine, and it's still the only funeral I've ever been to."

"I'll never forget that moment in the foyer of their house when we got back from the cemetery. Maria was nice to you when you'd play with Vinny, but we weren't at all close. Yet when I came in the front door as she was coming down the stairs, she saw in my eyes how heavily her loss weighed in my heart and she crumpled on my shoulders, sobbing. I hugged her but said nothing because I couldn't, because I knew that what tore her up wasn't just the loss of her son, bad as that was—it was the loss of her son in a stupid war."

"What makes a war stupid?"

"A war that shouldn't be started because it's based on lies or can't be won or both. The Vietnam war had nothing to do with defending our country, despite all the hyped-up patriotic drivel the warmongers sprayed into the fan. Nobody even pretended that Vietnam was a threat to the United States. Maria knew her son had died for nothing. No, it was worse than nothing—he was killed in an evil war along with countless Americans and Vietnamese for the profits of military industrialists and the global dominance delusions of a handful of plutocrats."

Evil. Even though I was only eighteen, that word had begun to sound overtones in my mind whenever I heard it. I asked her if she thought all wars were evil.

"Hell, no. If I'd been an armed soldier in a position to shoot the monster who pointed a rifle at your father the moment before he pulled the trigger, I'd have done it in an instant and thanked God for having given me the chance. But it's wrong to kill for anything less than that, and when it's done for greed, power, hatred, or some sick amusement, it's evil to the core."

The spotlight she trained on evil ignited phosphors in my mind that burned the rest of the night and are burning still, all these years later, casting off fumes of mystery that oppress me with their answerless weight: Where did evil come from? Why does it infect some people and not others? How does it work? What can be done about it?

Recalling that evening, ten years on, in a Western Pacific night with my past left behind, I'm heading all the way to Tibet to get my hands on the answers. It's not a restful quest, but sometimes the straining questions blur into exhausting white noise that covers my consciousness with superficial sleep. I'm going to retreat to my berth and welcome the distracting dawn when it finally shows up.

[1-5]

<u>March 11, '91</u>

I spent the day scraping metal in the galley for a new coat of paint due to be applied this weekend. Fun. What kept me going was the prospect of getting back up here come midnight with my lungs filled with tropical marine night air and my eyes graced with an uncluttered view of the rest of our galaxy.

Thoughts of my time at CMC followed me to sleep last night and kicked up memories of the change that overcame me back then. The more I stared at viruses in our scopes and mainframe monitors, the more unsettling it became. I began to wonder if we grunts were somehow being unwittingly co-opted into producing research for biological warfare agents. The word was out on campus researchers working as hired guns for industrial warmongers who operated from lavish, high-tech warrens deep in the earth, injecting money into the bloodstream of science and tech programs to test new blood-curdling ways to kill people. Maybe some of our virus work was part of a weapons program to literally curdle the blood of soldiers, maybe even civilians, should the government someday green-light a biological attack on the Enemy of the Year, whoever that might be. I imagined the businessmen behind these schemes as bespectacled dark lords, emitting guttural commands to the nominal powers that be, infecting them with compulsions to make and use weapons only they, the demonic manufacturers, could provide.

One spring day, while noting some viral replication details in a computer log, I flashed on the people who worked for IG Farben in Germany during World War II coming up with the business model of setting up labor camps near their plant in Auschwitz. How efficient: put able-bodied slaves to work making pesticides which could be used to gas the women and children to death in chambers elsewhere on the grounds, conveniently placed near cremation ovens. That image swept over me like a tidal wave, dragging in its wake my latent dissatisfaction with having screwed myself into an indoor job that left me pining for the mountains every day. I made some excuse to leave work and hiked into the woods, emerging only at nightfall. I tried to eat dinner, couldn't do it, and went to bed, where I tossed and turned most of the night.

Back at work the next morning, I knew my days at college and the lab were numbered. I liked biology—I respected the intelligence and determination with which its cadres track down mysteries of nature to save people from disease—but I yearned to do some saving on a grander scale, something that reckoned with the hazards of wilderness and the elements. Rooting myself in the plains, flats, or any turf near sea level chokes my spirit the way imprisonment in a landlocked compound would punish a born sailor. The mountains visible out the window chastised me for wimping out in a stuffy flat-floored lab while high winds swept through the trees between craggy peaks at the timberline. They reminded me of the promise they'd held out for me when I was a kid that they were holding vital secrets I could discover only with the breathtaking clarity of view at remote alpine elevations.

I had to plot my escape. What form that would take became clear about a week later when my mountain lust drove me to do something thrilling and incredibly foolish. I'd gone on a high country day hike with a buddy of mine up on Long's Peak. The weather and visibility were perfect, and about 3 PM, when we were starting to head down, I saw a delicious outcrop a couple hundred feet above us and proposed that we check out the view from there. My pal was disinclined but I couldn't resist. I told him he could go back and I'd meet him at the bottom, no more than half an hour behind.

That was risk factor number one, given that I'd be clambering up rocks alone. However, I'd be careful, and I fancied myself a skilled mountaineer. After all, I was nineteen.

But that hubris paled alongside risk factors two through ten, which I threw into the mix forty-five minutes later. I'd treated myself to the exhilarating view of a thousand square miles and was starting down the trail when a revelation swept over me: my visit to the sky perch had birthed me into my true identity as a great mountain man, gifted with instinctive savvy, astute judgment, and an abundance of raw agility. The combined beauty of that state of mind and the mountain forest itself ignited an impulse to attempt a land-flight through the forest. I took off down the trail—not jogging, but running as I had on scores of football fields at a full sprint, even though the trail was scarily narrow and skirted above a rocky slope. I raced that way for more than a mile, leaping over springs and obstructing rocks and across a fallen tree bridge above a creek tributary. I tore through the air, barely touching the ground, invincible, destined to complete the flight without so much as a wobble and to relish my triumphant anointing by Nature as a mountain superman, when I suddenly noticed I was falling down the side of an eighty degree ravine wall.

Lucky for Superman, he survived his idiocy by a last-instant grab of a tree root hovering over a two-hundred-foot pitch down to a torrential waterfall, though not without dislocating his shoulder and screaming *Shit! Shit!! Shit!!* at the top of his lungs as he envisioned the pain and risk it would require to scale the terrifying slope overhead. But there was nothing for it. Too nervous to manage the replacement of my humerus in my shoulder socket, I inched my way back up to the trail over what seemed like one hellish hour, even though it was less than half that long.

Throughout the rest of my hike back, I was overwhelmed with the certainty that, had my hand not secured a tight enough grip on that tree root in the one-tenth of a second available, it would have taken one helluva dog-assisted rescue squad to even locate me, much less get me out of there alive. I was agog at my prior belief that my broken-field running skills could hack starkly non-flat surfaces and how I'd squandered what seemed like a lifetime quota of good luck. I resolved that I would *never* take that kind of idiotic risk again. More, an epiphany—I would prove myself worthy of my mountain ancestors who had survived centuries in hazardous heights by respecting the mountains and I would pay back the universe for my life-saving good fortune by helping others in the mountains who might not be so lucky. I would learn mountain rescue.

That week I saw a notice stuck on the cork board in the break room seeking Search And Rescue volunteers for the Lake County SAR team and I signed up immediately. At dawn on the first Saturday in April I set out on my first mock rescue operation.

Our crew was led by a guy called Cap, a Vietnam vet in his early forties with an attitude that dared Trouble to swagger into his mountains and put one of his residents or visitors in peril. He wasn't noisy about it. He just focused on his work whipping us volunteers into shape while casting his gaze about for the next crisis to come along, which he knew to a certainty it would, passing wartime at the forward base of operations till the next battle exploded.

Working with Cap enlivened me like no other teaching ever had. In training the part of my brain to get a bead on where someone in trouble might be located, he told us that sometimes you had to stand stock still for a moment and quiet your mind to allow clues you'd assembled and clues you hadn't yet recognized to settle into a pattern. Sounds mystical, maybe, but it marked the origin of a real skill I began developing extensively as time went on.

Over the next six months, I grabbed every opportunity I could to train and go out on rescue calls, a series of adventures that reminded me of the time I hitchhiked to Mexico, never knowing after leaving one driver's little world what totally different scene I'd find myself in next.

I saw strange animal dramas—an eagle grounded by a shotgun blast that had ravaged one of her wings, a lost chow frozen along with her entire newborn litter, and the fresh remains of six cattle that had spilled down the side of a mountain from an overturned tractor trailer that took a turn too fast on a state highway three hundred feet above—and lots more intense ones starring my fellow humans. We found one woman trying to fend off hypothermia while breast-feeding her bluing infant in a snow-stranded minivan while her husband was out on a fatal hike to find help. We arrived in the nick of time at an unventilated emergency snow shelter that almost killed the young couple who'd built it and gotten soaked from the near-freezing snowmelt coming off their ceiling. We got a couple of lost college-age snowshoers into an ambulance, leaving it to the doctors at the other end to tell them they were headed for some amputations of frostbitten toes and feet. There were a couple of downed aircraft too—one, the skeletal remains of both pilots and their P-39 Airacobra that had not quite made it to Peterson Air Force Base during an unexpected blizzard in the early days of World War II, and the other, a busted helicopter with a party of badly injured skiers whose exit from Vail had been interrupted by a stand of tall trees shrouded in a cloudbank. And there were many dazed, hollow-eyed hikers nearly speechless with relief and evaporating terror as they saw me coming.

That summer I shed the arrogance that had almost killed me in my hybrid cheetah-mountain goat trance and locked into my groove, treasuring the satisfaction of successful rescues and the quiet thrill of mastering mountaineering. I began to garner respect from other members of the crew, not just for being able to hang in there under treacherous weather and terrain conditions, but for being the first to find a lost or injured party at a rate that was more sharply above average than I realized at first. I remember pausing on a ridge crest midway through a search during my first year on the crew. I'd asked the other volunteers to hush for a moment, as if filtering out the local static would enable me to hear the breathing of the missing hikers we were looking for, and as the volunteers quieted down, I heard someone tell a greenhorn, "Watch that Tibetan dude—he's gets some potent medicine workin' in these situations."

When things were slow, I put my name out to the ranger stations in neighboring counties, reaching out as far as Larimer, where the Rocky Mountain National Park station was based in Estes Park. That's where I landed my first real job, a part-time SAR coordinator's assistant post at one of America's plum ranger operations. The boss had heard about me from my crew chief in Lake County and gave me a shot. I'd just finished finals and was still a week from graduation, but once I got that ranger's call, I was there the next day. He'd made a tricky choice, since some of my fellow volunteers possessed a redneck streak, but no one seemed to question the chief's decision, and we all got along fine.

And so, I turned pro. Over the next six years I worked hard at every aspect of the job, put in lots of overtime, and developed a name for myself throughout the state. I traveled a lot, filling out crew shortages in neighboring states and helping my chief with presentations at conferences as far away as Canada and Switzerland on rescue techniques we were experimenting with. I treated countless injuries and prevented quickly deteriorating conditions from taking a worse toll. I saw death, too, in the faces of people we found too late, victims of cliff falls, avalanches, heart and bear attacks, and the slow-chilling vise of hypothermia, when our job became Search And Body Retrieval, but far more often we found people who could have met the same fate and gave them back their lives, making good on the Larimer County SAR motto "That others may live."

For a while, being hooked on SAR played havoc with my love life. Romancing had to take a back seat to being on call for rescues, most days, nights, and weekends. That was rough. I was a love hunter, as driven to lure, love, enliven, and be enlivened by the prey I feasted with as the game hunter who chases down, kills, and feasts on his. I still am, as an event a few days ago has made only too clear, but the mountain lust that began blossoming in me at nineteen forced upon me the discipline of a drill sergeant grooming an unwashed private in the split-personality army of a one-man state.

I did manage a few loverships along the way—one especially, with Bridget Petrov, that seemed well-suited to my new life. Bridget was a hot ranger who worked out of the same station as me in Estes Park. She was smart, strong, and tasty proof of my theory that full-blooded outdoorswomanliness is a likely sign of other full-blooded womanly talents. Our matching skills and schedules made our ride easy and adventuresome. Bridget was solid, reliable, and physically impressive, but the groundedness I found so attractive in her contained the seeds of our eventual breakup.

I'm known for groundedness myself, but I'd developed one trait that any woman like Bridget would find unsettling, namely a yearning to hunt down the source of evil and bring it to account. While I admired the clean strength of mind that made Bridget uncomfortable discussing evil, we were too close to avoid it.

One night last fall we were relaxing in a tent we'd set up at top speed in a sudden downpour after crossing a swollen creek where the footbridge had collapsed, and we were joking about the pranks the mountain trolls were playing on us. I shifted the conversation to the viruses I used to spy on in the CMC lab, the connection being hazards lurking in the mountains. Next thing, for better or worse, I brought up the story I'd heard the previous week from Roberto Cruz.

Roberto played third base on the city softball team I'd joined the year before, having not quite gotten team sports out of my system in the wake of finally bidding football adios. He worked on the grounds at the junior high and sometimes we'd get together for a beer and a few rounds of pool after work. One evening I'd brought up our team's prospects for the following season and Roberto told me he wasn't sure he'd still be living in Colorado, because of a crisis involving his family in El Salvador. He confided that he was beginning to feel bad about enjoying life in El Norte while the risks to his family were growing more and more grave.

Grave what? I asked. I didn't know anything about El Salvador, other than it was in that part of the hemisphere that seemed riddled with messy, brutal conflicts. I'd picked up some background noise on the news about Nicaragua and the contras and Guatemala, El Salvador—it was all a blurry, unpleasant, remote muddle to me. But Roberto was right there in sharp focus, a warm and vibrant soul, and soon El Salvador was no longer remote to me.

Roberto described the suffering of El Salvadorans in a civil war that's been going on for a decade, with the government battling a bunch of leftist groups including the Communist FMLN in another iteration of the Cold War dynamics that had been driving history since before I was born, including the mess in Tibet that led to my father's demise. Roberto's family had reason to expect a visit from one of the government's killer militias on a search and destroy mission and needed to get the hell out of their mountain village and out of the country.

I'll leave the specifics of that saga to tomorrow. The point here is that when I segued from Roberto's problem to the notion that I might join him on his rescue mission, given that my mountain savvy might be of some value to his family, Bridget sighed and asked, "Can't you just enjoy the blessing of living in a magnificent environment, free of the kind of horror that plagues people in war zones?"

"I'm not sure."

"Are you trying to save the world? And if so, do you think running down to El Salvador can accomplish that?"

"No and no, though I'd salute anyone who thinks so with the balls to act on it. I need to be more aware of what's going on in the world."

She paused for a long sigh. "I respect that need, but I don't have it to the degree you do."

Next, in a boneheaded attempt to explain that "need," I brought up my comparison of the destructive viruses in our mountains that I'd studied in my lab gig to destructive forces in Roberto's mountains: the vicious government-backed militias roaming the jungle hills to scare up forced "recruits" and root out rebels, infecting happy, smooth-running villages with their deadly violence like giant microbes.

Two minutes into that riff, I realized Bridget was becoming a very unhappy camper. I could see it in her hardy Earth woman's eyes. Problem-solving was second nature to us both—we were pros who could look up a 250' slope with a bad outcrop half-way up and know to a certainty that *somehow* we were going to get our injured fall victim out of the creek bed and up to the road—but continuing our love was one slope that couldn't be scaled. Bridget had neither the desire to follow me as I drifted toward the evil infesting a Central American jungle nor the capacity to fathom why I might do so.

Soon the distance between our outlooks on life became too obvious to ignore and, one night, camping, we faced up to it and made ourselves zip up our sleeping bags separately, to force the win for our better judgment over burning desire. In the middle of a long, lonely night, I heard her sniffling for the one and only time in our three years together, and I suppose she heard me swallow pretty hard too. In the morning we packed up our gear, making a little small talk, and came down the mountain.

In the ensuing four months of changes and adventures, sadness about Bridget has diminished to a blinking pinpoint of light in my rear-view mirror. I head to sleep knowing that the weak and short-lived loose-anchor drag of nostalgia will succumb to a cacophony of dreams about what lies ahead.

[1-6]

<u>March 12, '91</u>

The captain has updated our westward progress. We're some two thousand miles from Bombay, on course to reach port the morning of the 16th. I'm determined to complete the recording of this personal history before then. Once I hit Asia, I'll need all the mental room I can spare to receive huge shipments of new stimuli.

As alluded to last night, the breakup with Bridget was hastened by the temptation I saw in plucking myself out of one range of mountains, replete with familiar challenges in the cold uppermost heights of Colorado, and into another, lower in elevation, latitude, and security, in the jungles of Central America.

No doubt there's wisdom in refraining from making major decisions in the first flush of suffering, but some won't get made at all if they're not made then. So it was for my plan to penetrate a snake-infested jungle to help liberate a family from the ravages of the brutal civil war. Had it not been for the breakup with Bridget, I'd have likely just toyed with the idea before allowing reasonable caution to hand down its ruling. Needing to distract myself from the romantic injury I'd incurred obsessing over evil that was only imagined, I began sniffing an opportunity to test myself against the real thing.

Roberto had acquainted me with numerous grotesqueries perpetrated by the Salvadoran military upon thousands of its fellow countrymen. Take my word for it—they were sickening enough for me to grasp the terror his family was living in and why he had to risk losing his precious, steady American job—and maybe a lot more—by going back home to get his loved ones beyond the reach of the death squads. This kind of shit had been going on down there for a decade, but it was getting even worse. Late last year Roberto's sister's best friend and her mother, a cook at a Jesuit university in the capital, were slaughtered along with six priests and dozens of others including the core of an Indian farming co-op.

Meanwhile, the death squads' "recruiting" campaign continued unabated. They had a business to run—capturing, torturing, and executing guerillas, suspected guerillas, families of suspected guerillas, and families who might or might not be friendly to suspected guerillas, what the hell—and they were out to swell their ranks with kids as young as Roberto's fourteen-year-old brother. Their offer the kids couldn't refuse was straightforward: sign on and we'll spare your mothers and sisters from being raped and murdered, a deal routinely welched upon.

The last straw for Roberto happened a couple of weeks before our final tavern talk. Word had circulated among Salvadorans in the US of a story told by a death squad deserter who'd made it to Texas seeking asylum. The noble battalion he'd been part of—one that, rumor had it, had been tutored originally by a US Special Forces detail—had visited a stunt upon a little village south of his family's that was so viciously twisted it made your basic horror flick villains look as sweet and nurturing as Mrs. Piggle-Wiggle. Skipping the revolting details, the point is that creeping massacritis had gotten way too close for Cruz family comfort.

So Roberto was going to do whatever it took to help his family escape to Honduras—no peace paradise either, but a country which had so far kept its national nose cleaner than El Salvador's, where the militias' death toll had already hit high five figures. The family had cousins in a Honduran village ten miles beyond the border. Since the Cruz family's village was thirty miles from the border on the El Salvador side, Roberto figured he could sneak the whole lot of them—eight in all, including a grandmother, two kids and an infant—through the jungle on foot to their destination in nine or ten days.

Roberto had related this much of the story a week or so before, setting off the downhill slide of my relationship with Bridget. Watching the Broncos blow a first quarter lead over the Chargers on the big screen at O'Herlihy's, Roberto observed a similarity between the glum ass-trudging of the Broncos and my own recent demeanor, and hit on a scheme to fire me up. We'd been served refills of our steins when I looked out the window at the mountains and wondered aloud if he were going to miss our snow-capped peaks while back in his home country in a few weeks. "I'll be in mountains all the way, bro—nothing like these, but mountains sure enough, loaded with fruit trees and tropical birds. Real change of pace. I'm looking forward to it, despite the danger. Maybe partly because of it, too."

He let that addendum sit there in pregnant silence, watching his hint register in my ale-sprinkled brain. When it did, my first comment was an expressive, "Hunh," as new notion wheels picked up speed within. Scanning through the implications at much faster speed than I'd expected to have to think when I entered the bar, an odd mix of appealing forces rose through the noise, and before I could consciously deliberate, the words, "Could you use some help?" skipped out of my mouth.

"Oh, yeah. If you're applying for the job, you're hired. We gotta leave at Thanksgiving."

That simply, I'd reset the course of my life in ways I couldn't imagine. Preparations for the trip south and a visit home for Thanksgiving whisked by in a six-day blur. I hadn't seen my mom in two months, and even though I was certain to be home a month later for Christmas, I didn't want to leave her alone at Thanksgiving, so we tooled over the mountain pass to Leadville for a quickie how-are-ya feast. Mom and Roberto had never met and I figured a short break at the table of a very cool American mom would fortify him as well as myself for the challenges ahead.

The grin on my mother's face when I stomped in the house on Thanksgiving eve with my backpack slung over my shoulder was worth the three-hour drive. Roberto and I spent the next morning and early afternoon alternating between helping out in the kitchen and going through camping gear I'd stashed out in the shed.

I confined discussion of plans to haul a party of ten across some rugged mountain jungle terrain to that shed. Knowing how uptight my mother was about anything that even rhymed with "war," there was no way I was going to tell her what we were up to.

Back in the kitchen, cutting up potatoes, I advised her that she shouldn't be alarmed if she called in the next couple of weeks and I didn't get right back to her, because Roberto and I were setting up a hiking trip. I tried to congratulate myself for some clever misdirection, though I knew it was never smart to bet against my mother's intuition.

Come three o'clock, Mom's best friend and bowling buddy Brenda Ryweck showed up with apple pie and champagne, and we were off to the chow-down races. We ran through a chunk of Mom's record collection and heard a few choice tidbits of the ladies' racier adventures in high school, back in the post-war era when the last people Mom ever expected to meet in our remote mountains were a cagey operator from the CIA or a handsome young med student from a turbulent Shangri-La.

The women were interested in our doings as well, and Roberto was properly circumspect in describing his native land. Yes, he visited from time to time, and once his brother had made it up to Estes Park for a summertime discovery of the United States, but not a word about the civil war passed his lips, till my mother brought it up. News of the nightmare going on in El Salvador had made its way even to rural Colorado on and off for years, so it couldn't be avoided entirely. "It's a sad, scary, and nasty business going on down there," she said. I nodded dutifully, trying to think how I could wrench in a segue to the rumors that major league baseball had short-listed Denver for a shot at an expansion team, but not fast enough to head off her follow-up. "As a lot of Chinese young people found out last year in Tiananmen Square, there's no end to what a vicious government will do to crush people it thinks might be rebels. Any sign of brave idealism is target numero uno for their gunfire." Her grim tone blew a hole in my segue plans; I waited helplessly for whatever I had coming. Casting her next pseudo-casual comment to Roberto, she passed the salad bowl our way saying, "Gee, I imagine sometimes you must want to wave a magic wand and whisk your whole family to a safer place, huh?"

Damn. While I was wondering if mind-reading powers come in a New Parent Kit when a baby is born, Roberto blinked and turned his eyes to his water glass before nodding, "Oh, yeah, everybody's had some mixed feelings about home since this war started up. Some folks dream of coming to America but our village has been home for generations and it's so beautiful—no one could be happy ripping up their roots."

There's the transcript, and a wholly inadequate account it is of what that exchange was really about; for as my mother finished her question, I noticed her cast a glance at Brenda before returning her eyes to Roberto. It was a distress call under cover of the friendly smile with which she'd coated her question. I tried to tell myself it was an illusion, but I feared that somehow she suspected me of being up to exactly what I was up to.

I swallowed that thought and grabbed the steering wheel of the conversation. "Roberto's family once saw Rosie Casals, Ma—Billie Jean King's tennis partner? A big-time champ for equality for women."

"I remember her," she nodded, "a tough, smart gal." But I could see that her admiration for Rosie was, however genuine, of secondary importance at the moment. She could see that I was shoving the conversation away from the dangers of El-Salvador in the fall of 1990 and she didn't like imagining why. Nonetheless, she played it out the way I wanted, asking who'd like coffee and letting more delicate questions be.

At least till we left the next morning. When we'd stuffed our backpacks in the car and arrived at good-bye, she fired those famous laser eyes of hers right into mine and said, "You be safe, Buster. Remember—family. Flesh and blood. Longevity. *Common sense.*"

"C'mon, Ma. Does a mother goose have to say that every time her offspring enter the water? I'm a mountain man, remember? That's in my flesh and blood too."

"I know what's in your flesh and blood."

"And there is no such thing as a good mountain man without common sense—"

"—No?"

"No, so relax. You raised me good, Ma, right in the mountains so you could enjoy the satisfaction of knowing I could handle them—"

"—Is that why?"

"Whatever—you know I'm mountain-certified, so reap the dividends. You should be the most relaxed woman in the Rockies."

Neither granting my point nor pursuing hers further, she gave me a hug and a sweet forced smile. "Godspeed, Mountain Man. Call me when you get back. I love you." I ducked my eyes for just a second and then smiled back that I loved her too, and made a quick turn to the car, where Roberto was waving good-bye. As we headed down the road, I allowed myself one quick look at my side view mirror and gulped when I saw her standing on the stoop, watching me drive away.

I knew that, for people like my mother, who've lost someone near and dear, good-byes with loved ones leaving on a great journey can be tinged with a fear that they may never meet again. I learned then that journeyers, too, can feel a sliver of that fear about the ones they leave behind.

But onward. I need to barrel through what happened next in tropical latitudes if I'm to get all this behind me by the time we reach India.

Roberto and I souped up our hiking gear at a mountain outfitters in Denver that day and pulled together a list of supplies like food and tarps that we would get the following day in San Salvador so we wouldn't have to drag them on the planes. Roberto offered to cover my plane fare, but I told him there was no way I was going to let him pay for my vacation. We got up at half past three the next morning for our flight from Denver to Houston where we connected for the flight to San Salvador.

I expected Roberto to be mighty animated flying home, but he went straight to sleep. The ensuing solitude opened up a lot of space in my mind for questions like, "Why the hell am I doing this?" Being a supportive pal, learning more about a different breed of mountainous terrain, etcetera—I knew there was more to it than that.

For one thing, the pox of evil that had metamorphosed some Salvadorans into death squad vermin was more of a draw than a repellent. It bugged me that I couldn't fathom what could impel people to torture their brother and sister human beings to death. I felt that was something I'm supposed to know, so maybe by getting closer to it, I could pick up some clues. It couldn't be chalked up to the passions of personal hatred—these killers usually didn't know their victims. Greed didn't make sense either—yeah, somebody was getting rich wielding the corrupt state apparatus to shovel truckfuls of cash towards their own stashes, but the peons committing the atrocities were not likely to become millionaires off it. I guess I was—and am—still a virologist trying to get a fix on the mechanism by which a killing force penetrates an organism and turns it to its own terrible purposes.

Then I came upon the deeper reason behind my actions. Ever since I heard of my father's murder by Chinese military thugs, I'd felt compelled to expose myself to a similar kind of evil as a way of getting closer to him. Helping to liberate some people from an oppressive government fit that bill, even if it weren't in my dad's role as warrior. The US was building up for the Gulf War, but I could hardly extend the compassion I had for the Salvadorans to the Kuwaitis. Saddam Hussein's would-be conquerors were about to get their asses handed to them by 120,000 of our troops to secure their precious oil fields for the oil habit of our millions and the profits of a few. The Salvadorans had the opposite, far more serious problem of the US lending some of its superpower strength to the oppressors themselves. We'd gone so far as to send a contingent of Green Berets down to El Salvador to train its army in handling troublemakers, such as peasants who wanted a fair shake and workers who wanted to organize to protect their interests dealing with heavy-handed corporations, which, unfortunately, were often owned by Americans able to influence policy and seed undercover wars. In fact, when the rebels made it right into the capital last year and turned the Sheraton into a battleground, they captured a dozen Green Berets and held them hostage till the Catholic Church stepped in to broker their release.

The El Salvador resistance wasn't much like the Tibetan guerilla movement in 1963, which had dried up in the sands of time before I got to junior high, but it was a few steps closer than 1990 Estes Park, so I was drawn to it. Yet the closer our plane drew us to our destination, I knew I was heading in the wrong direction. El Salvador had evil, all right, but for me it would be a colorful side trip at best. I was glad to help and it would be fascinating if I didn't get my head cut off, but it was not the way for me to connect with my father.

I soldiered on in my unsoldierly role. I was uneasy dealing with immigration officials and passing police in the streets of the capital as we gathered up additional supplies, so I made it my business to act like a naïve tourist and met cops' stares with a polite nod. Expressly absent from our shopping list was a firearm. I've had sufficient experience with high-powered rifles from ranger training to use one to good effect—we didn't cotton to stray dogs tearing our deer apart—but there was no good outcome on the menu if our family outing had the misfortune to get into a firefight with a Salvadoran death squad. Our objective was clear: get this party over the pass without getting into trouble.

Early in the afternoon we made it out of the city on a bus for the bumpy two-hour ride to the dirt road that led to his family's home in the tiny hamlet of Nueva Lapitas. Our packs at that point weighed about forty pounds each, and we knew we'd be adding more once we had his family in tow.

Between copious logistical concerns and all the talk of bloodsporting militias, I'd begun to lose sight of the personal strand in the DNA of this trip, but that changed fast when I finally met Roberto's family. They were warm, beautiful people with a humble radiance that exposed unintentional irony in the term "beautiful people" as it's used by American mass culturati. I loved talking with them—they were unduly patient with my broken Spanish—and observing the complex social dynamics attendant to their impending departure. The neighbors' sadness about losing what seemed like a branch of their own families was compounded with heightened fear, as if the Cruzes had had a terrible premonition they all should heed.

They took comfort in the knowledge that they were at less risk than Roberto's father, an activist in the region's farming community who was known to have spent time with the guerillas—he had an obvious target on his back. Roberto's fourteen-year-old brother—ripe militia material—and his doe-eyed sixteen year-old sister and his twenty-one year-old sister, whose husband was with the rebels and who was the mother of their two-year-old toddler, were vulnerable as well for different reasons. Roberto's mother and her parents, who rounded out the troupe of eight we were to escort, were the most deeply rooted in the life of the village and would be missed the most.

The family toughened up for a melancholy farewell dinner before going to sleep. We would be getting everyone up well before daybreak to make the best of the cool part of the day and to minimize the hardships of good-byes. Except for Raquel, who carried her little papoose on her back, everyone had a pack of some kind, even Abuelita who was proud of her fifteen-pound rucksack. Roberto's sibs carried thirty pounds each and Roberto's and mine were in the high sixties. As the visiting mountaineering prof, I provided my share of useful navigation and camping tricks and took care to act as if our expedition were just another interesting wilderness hike. Roberto and his father and I kept our conversations about signs of danger to ourselves.

Step by step, our little family band lumbered our way through the forest, making three to six miles a day, depending on elevation gains. We pitched in boosting each other's morale around evening campfires sharing observations, anecdotes about wildlife, and colorful Mayan fables. There was only one night of rain. We saw it coming early enough to get everyone settled—Abuela, Abuelita, Raquel, and the baby got the tent and the rest of us were comfortable enough underneath suspended tarps. Down on the forest floor there was no wind and throughout the first week we drifted quietly to sleep in misty scents of orchids and izote flowers.

The eighth evening, our last in El Salvador, began with barely audible but blood-curdling sounds of screams and gunfire echoing across the jungle canyon. Although the victims and the perpetrators of the atrocities were a two-hour hike away from us, none of us spoke above a whisper; indeed hardly any of us spoke, other than the baby, whose occasional quiet burbles of discomfort were quickly calmed by Raquel. The incident left everyone praying for an extra layer of good fortune for one more day so we could get out of that natural but god-forsaken paradise.

Late the next morning we crossed over the ridgeline that demarcated the El Salvador-Honduras border, and you could feel the joint sigh spreading relief through neuromuscular systems that had felt tension building up for days, weeks, years. On the afternoon of day nine, we reached the hamlet where Roberto's Honduran uncle and cousins lived.

This place had all the lush, primitive, and soulful hallmarks of generations of tropical isolation. Roberto's cousins treated us as if we'd lived with them for decades. Even I—the first Asian any of them had ever seen—was greeted warmly like a returning prodigal son. They set up places to rest up before dinner, which would be in a couple of hours. I was installed in the back room of a sweet little stucco community center *cum* part-time post office with its exterior covered with murals of jungle animals painted by the local kids. It was charming, but I really couldn't have cared less about anything other than twelve square feet of flat space for me to lie down. Once I did, I was gone in twenty seconds.

But that sleep brought no refreshment. Rather, I awoke with a start from a nightmare I couldn't recall. At first I thought to lay it to the previous night's death squad soundtrack, but it didn't feel like it emanated from evil. It was as if imps had sneaked into my bloodstream and laid down a trail of dry ice pellets that chilled my heart and throat to the brink of paralysis.

I got up and wandered around to shake it off. Roberto's family were up and talking to their new neighbors. I offered to help with the ongoing preparation for a supper of papusas, but I wasn't allowed to do much. My sadness eased up a bit during dinner, what with all the family reunion chatter, which was more loving than lively given the condition of the expeditioners. It wasn't long before we returned to our nooks and crannies to sleep.

Up the next morning at dawn, I was all business about getting out of there, really antsy to get home, without knowing why. I had a bite with the family, got packed, embraced Roberto and his family, and hit the trail. Once back in El Salvador, I'd make it out to the road and hitchhike. The last plane out of San Salvador would leave at 5 PM and I wasn't going to take any chances on having to hang around that sweltering wretched war-torn town another day.

With the cargo on my back reduced to twenty pounds, I felt like I was wearing a rocket pack, and made it over the pass by 9. I took a short-cut to the state road, stuck out my thumb, and was soon relaxing in the cab of a rusty pickup with a flatbed full of recycled plumbing supplies, tooling down the highway. I reached the airport by 4, in time for an early dinner of non-airplane food.

I should have felt good, mission accomplished and all, but I felt rattled all the way back to Denver, where we landed a half-hour before midnight. I found my car and made it back to my cabin in Estes Park by 1 AM.

When I walked in and saw the blinking red light on the answering machine, that ice feeling shot through my vessels again. I had a terrible feeling something was very, very wrong, and I made myself hit the playback button. The litany of trivia started up, messages from a pal who didn't know I was out of town offering a poker game, a call from the library about some books I'd forgotten to return, etcetera. I kept tapping the fast forward button till I heard Brenda's voice on the last two messages. The first, left around 7:30 the night before, asked me to call as soon as I got the message, and the second, left at 9:30 repeated the request, adding that it was important and not to worry about how late it might be.

I felt a wave of dizziness. I walked around on jittery legs, setting my jaw in determination not to panic, that whatever was wrong—and, oh, I knew generally what it had to be—I would deal with it. I wrote down Brenda's number with a shaky hand, sat down, stood up, sat down again and dialed. In a few seconds, Brenda answered in a sleep-sodden and saddened voice and delivered the news: "Your mom passed away, Den. I'm so sorry."

"What!?!?" I hollered back, in shock. "What happened?!?"

"It was a hiking accident. She went up on the mountain for a walk yesterday and apparently broke her leg falling into a ravine. Then a snow came in and she was overcome. I called the sheriff around 5:30 when I noticed she'd not returned and a search was launched right away. Fortunately she'd told me what trail she was planning on hiking. Seemed like half the town was already on the search and the other half on their way when they found her a mile up the trail a around 6:45. The paramedics estimated she must have passed about three hours before. "

Even in the first minute of dealing with the death of the entirety of the immediate family I'd grown up with, my SAR instincts compelled me to ask, "I don't get it—if she'd broken her leg at the bottom of a ravine, how is it they found her on the trail?"

"She'd somehow clambered back up the slope." Brenda paused a moment before adding what I was already thinking. "The rescue guys thought she was trying to make the search easy for them." As I absorbed that news fitting into my mom's ways like a key in a lock, Brenda went on, "They took her body to County Hospital, hoping you'd return some time in the next few days to decide what to do."

I thanked Brenda, told her I'd leave at dawn, and got off the phone to face my first moments knowing I was truly on my own. I put on my parka and sat out on my back deck looking at the stars. I tried to beam a message to my mother through the winds whistling through the tree line a few thousand feet above—a message of love and gratitude and immense regret that I hadn't been there when she needed rescue. Unexpectedly, in a moment saturated with grief, the pain I imagined her experiencing while dragging herself up the side of a snowy ravine faded away and I flashed on her face in the sky smiling at me, her eyes aglitter with love and happiness, as if there'd been no great loss because the best of the life we'd shared together was unhurt by the fate that had just befallen us.

Shock loosened its grip and I drifted off. It wasn't till I stirred some time later and made my way back to my bed for the first time in weeks that the arithmetic of the paramedics' estimate clicked on in my mind and matched the estimated time of her accident to my afternoon nightmare in the Honduran village the day before, causing gooseflesh to lift the top of my scalp surface a couple of millimeters further from my skull.

Even after three and a half months, the sting of that memory remains a clear and present danger to my sleep, some of which had better come my way before sunrise, only a few hours away. I've got to function in the engine room all day tomorrow, and I'll need a full ration of night hours up here over the next few days to make my way through the rest of this story before the next chapter in my life opens up on the Asian sub-continent.

[1-7]

<u>March 13, '91</u>

Amazing how well the night skies from this perch just 125 feet above the sea can compete with what we enjoyed at 11,000 feet back home. It shows up the light pollution civilization pours into Rocky Mountain air. Out here we're seven hundred miles in all directions beyond the reach of any grid or any distraction from the memory of those first days back in Leadville.

I'll skip the next morning's trip to the morgue (thank you), but I will record what else I learned about my mother's final day.

While we sat at Brenda's kitchen table over coffee, she noticed me staring at the blue Rocky Mountain sky. "This is how it's been ever since Thanksgiving, except for late the day before yesterday. The ski resorts have been in a serious sweat. When your mom came by two mornings ago, conditions seemed reasonable for a late fall hike. I offered to go with her—I've always been kind of a ninny about going into the mountains alone, but Julie said, no, she knew I'd promised to help with the church auction, she'd be fine, and besides it was something she wanted to face alone."

"Something she needed to *face?*"

"I tried like heck to draw her out about that. Finally she told me it was like a rite of passage to get over an old phase of her life and provide you with a gift for your future. Her destination was a place she referred to as a kind of Garden of Eden she used to hike to with your dad."

I *knew* it. And I had a feeling it was no coincidence that Mom was willing to return to the site she'd avoided for more than a quarter-century the very week I'd ventured into the middle of a bloody civil war.

"She told me she and Dorje had left a journal they'd written buried in a metal case up there and she wanted to retrieve it." I nodded, more pieces falling into place. "She said she'd always refused your pleas to take you up there to get it, but that now she'd had more time to get used to the loss and a new reason to retrieve that journal."

"A letter my dad had written to me."

"That's right! She told me how badly you wanted to hold it in your hands and read it for yourself and she'd realized that you should."

"She didn't tell you what was in the letter?"

"No—but there's no need to guess, because she did make it all the way to her Eden and did dig up the journal. She was on the way back when the accident happened." Brenda got up and went to the laundry room off the kitchen. "When they found her, she was curled up around this." She removed my mom's red rucksack from a shelf and handed it to me, with her telescopic shovel and Nalgene water bottle still strapped to it. The sack was open at the top; visible inside was an old green canoeing dry bag with a strong-sealing roll-top closure.

I felt like I'd been given a relic unearthed from a cave outside Jerusalem. I could feel a hardbound volume the size of a notebook inside the dry bag. "The rangers gave it to me to hold for you." I looked it over, imagining my mother unearthing it less than forty-eight hours before. "I opened the sack 'cause there were some smelly orange rinds in there, which I found wrapped in plastic and threw away. I didn't look at the book."

With a surgeon's care, I opened the dry bag and saw the journal lying there, the reality of it displacing the version that had stood in for it in my imagination for seventeen years. I didn't remove it; for the moment, I just wanted confirmation that that it hadn't turned to mush. I gave Brenda a hug and took my leave with my most important inheritance under my arm.

The first thing I did when I walked in the house was place the journal with the long-awaited letter on the mantel. I didn't want to open it till the memorial was over and things had quieted down. It sat there, catching my eye thirty times a day, waiting for me to come around.

We held the memorial Friday afternoon at Leadville Airport in a circle of chairs set up a hundred feet from the county's helicopter—provided as a kindness by the sheriff—awaiting its mission, a flyover of the mountain nestling the Den. Leadvillians are proud of that airport, higher than any other in North America, or Asia, for that matter. It seemed a fitting location for a good-bye to the beloved Leadville widow of a Tibetan. When I let the ashes go, a lot of my past accompanied them, a swarm of sunlight glints floating down to the forest, bearing some of my mother back to her favorite place in the world one last time.

The reception at Brenda's gave me a chance to thank a lot of the searchers in person. Even though I'd not spent much time in Leadville the past several years, people who'd meant a lot to me there showed up. I sure could feel the love but it felt awkward in ways I couldn't understand at the moment, like when a few of my old high school and college chums invited me to a reunion poker game. I grinned non-committally, counting on figuring out later what was holding me back.

Returning to my mother's house and its imposing demands, I entered with a hardheaded determination to take care of business and move on, whatever that might turn out to mean. I turned to yard work for a while and then checked my answering machine in Estes Park. There was a message from Roberto from a couple of days before, who'd called from the village post office in Honduras to ask if I could pick him up at Denver International in a few days. He would be crushed to hear what had happened and to have missed being with me in support.

When the descending sun reached the mountaintops, the journal's time had come. I unplugged the phone and took the journal out back. It was strange to realize that the last time the book had been opened, it was probably a few inches over me while I was still an embryo in the high mountainside glade for which I was named. I imagined the echoes of the winds whooshing across the canyon, stirring up the vanilla-tinged Ponderosa pine air that buoyed my parents' romance in the sky.

It was a hardbound blank book of maybe a hundred and twenty pages with writing that stopped about a sixth of the way in. Its entries spanned a period of more than a month in the summer of 1962. A quick glance confirmed that the last page had the letter to me in my dad's handwriting, but I kept my curiosity at bay to read the rest of the book first, which, except for the letter itself now lies in the box I stored at Brenda's last month. I'll have to rely on my memory for the highlights that need mentioning here but since I read the whole thing at least three times, my recollections will be pretty close to the mark.

Most of the passages were written by my mom, especially in the beginning, when she laid out how important it was that they capture this marvelous chapter in their lives by logging their most vivid memories as a hedge against the coming time when they'd be far apart for many months. Then my dad's squarish printing began to appear for short spurts, no doubt encouraged by his English teacher. Almost thirty years later, I could feel the reverberations of their budding romance in her account of how she blushed as their eyes locked in class while she was trying to explain present participles, as if they'd been caught making love in a crowd of strangers, how her knees weakened when he told her a little about Gnam Yuljongs after class, and how two hundred finches swirled up into the air when they met in the courtyard the next morning. "Had I seen that in a movie," she wrote, "I'd have thought it too contrived while wondering how the filmmakers made it happen. I heard in the sound of their wing whistles the clear voices of God and Nature telling me they had conspired to make sure you and I got the message, that all had been arranged for us to be together forever."

And so it went with entries from both of them capturing the excitement of crystallizing plans for their future, the jolt of Dorje's departure being moved up, their beautiful homemade marriage certificate, emblazoned around the edges with small mandalas crafted by my father, and my mother's last entry about leaving the journal under a tree as their own terma, which they would recover together at some point in the next couple of years.

Then there was the final page, written by my father in some haste near dawn before leaving Dhumra Garden for the last time. I excised it from the book before leaving Colorado almost two months ago, and, with the help of a few inches of gaffer's tape I cadged from our shipboard maintenance supply room after dinner, I shall now place it permanently in this, my own journal, for it has already had a greater impact on my life than any other piece of writing ever to come my way (and may end up greater still). It was his long-awaited, one and only letter to me:

July 16, 1962

Dear Terma Den or Sonam,

Son or daughter, whichever name you will carry, I hope you'll feel my love through the long months until I can hold you and tell you of it in person.

Both names fit you. You are "sonam," fortunate, like me, to have your mother Julie in your life. And you are the mountain treasure of your parent's love for each other that has grown strong in our Den in the land of your birth. I hope to take you and your mother to your other homeland, Tibet, when freedom and peace come.

But if they don't, and if I'm no longer in this lifetime, and if you are Terma Den, my son, I plead with you not to follow the warrior path, as I have done. If Tibet is still not free when you become a man, war with our foe could lead you to an early death. That would deeply hurt my soul, even in another life.

Sonam or Terma Den, some day you will learn why our ancestors gave our village a name that means Sky View. As eagles do not prowl through grass, Tibetans cannot thrive long without a view of our world from above.

I shall dream of your learning our language when you come to Gnam Yuljongs, breathing our air and hiking our mountainsides.

You can begin with this:

བདག་གི་བརྩེ་བའི་སྲུ་གུ་ལགས།

ཁྱེད་ནི་ཆེས་ཕུལ་དུ་བྱུང་བའི་མཐུན་ལམ་སྟོན་པའི་རྣམས་ཆེན་གྱི་མི་ཚུ་ཞིག་ཏུ་འགྱུར་རེས་ཏེ། རྒྱ་མཚན་དེ།

གནས་ཚན་བོད་ཆེན་པོའི་ཕུན་མིན་གྱི་རིག་གནས་དང་། ས་ཆེན་ཨ་རེ་བའི་ཧ་གསལ་རྟོན་པོའི་རང་གཤིས་ཀྱི་

སྐྱོང་ནས་འབྱུངས་ཚོག་ ལྡད་མེད་ཀྱི་དུང་བ་རབ་མོ་ཕན་ཚུན་ལ་འབྱུད་ཅིང་གཉིག་གི་ཞན་ཚ་གཅིག་གིས

བསྐྱངས་བའི་རང་རྒྱགས་བཏུན་བའི་མི་གཤིས་ཀྱི་ཁྲག་རྟོན་པོའི་འབར་སྐྱིད་གིས་ཁྱེད་ཀྱི་ལུས་ཁམས་ཡོངས་ལ

ཁྱབ་ཡོད་པས་སོ།།

བདག་གི་རེ་སྨོན་ལ།

ཏུ་ཚོའི་ཁྱིམ་ཆང་ལ་གནས་དགར་ཏེ་སེ་བཞིན་རྩ་ཆེ་བའི་ཧུ་ལི་དང་དེད་གཉིས་ལ་འཁྱངས་བའི་ཁྱེད་ཉིད་གནས

ཚན་བོད་དུ་སེབས་ནས། བོད་ཀྱི་ཕུན་སོང་མ་ཡིན་པའི་རིག་གནས་རང་རྒྱུད་དང་སྐྱ་རེ་ཉེ་དུ་འགྲོ་ཞིད།

ཁྱེད་ཀྱི་རྣམ་རིག་དེ་ཡང་ཏུ་གཉིས་ཀྱི་ཕ་མ་ཁ་བ་ཅན་སྲི་ལུ་སྐྱ་མེད་དུ་འགྱུར་བའི་སྨོན་འདུན་དང་བཅས།

རྐྱ་ཆེས་བཟག་པོ་ར།

With great love,
Your Father

With those words and a fetching little drawing of Mt. Kailash, my parents' terma came to an end.

I had to get my father's mysterious message in Tibetan translated on the double. Most of us in Colorado knew there was a Tibetan Buddhist institute over in Boulder. I had the impression that the place was populated by 2% Tibetans and 98% Anglos, and, as a non-religious none-of-the-above, I'd never had any great urge to go over there and hobnob. Still, I recognized a good resource and I knew I'd be on the phone to that institute first thing the next morning.

After throwing together some dinner, I took a trundle light up into the attic. It was time to wrap up my past and ship it off somewhere. Wending my way through some small furniture and various boxes, I found my first skateboard and various football medals, a bunch of old toys, an antique typewriter and camera, some mildewed drapes, and a lot of other junk I'd have to dump, give away, or sell. It was a wearying affair until I came upon an old wooden box, the size of a large cigar box, with an inlaid pearl design on the cover. My mom wouldn't have relegated a box like that to storing trivia. I sat back against an old trunk and opened it up.

It held a stack of letters, most with Tibetan stamps and return addresses. All but three of the envelopes held letters written by my father to my mother during the nearly two years they were apart—all proof of the depth of the romance that she'd described to me on numerous occasions.

The first of the exceptions was an oversized envelope with a return address reading "Leadville Photography," with "Nepal, '64" written on the front. Inside I found a slightly cracked black-and-white snapshot. It was a picture my mother had of my father, her, and me, identical to the framed one on her dresser, except that it showed my parents' full bodies. It had to be the original, which she'd evidently had enlarged but cropped. The full view revealed a gun holstered on my father's hip and armed guerillas in the background. Apparently my mother had been protecting me from the association of my father and his warrior métier long before I even knew the word "war." Well, no surprise—that was her lifelong obsession.

The second exception was certainly the most painful message my mother ever received—the broken English communiqué from July, 1964, penned by a Captain Pasang, the commander at my father's Mustang base camp informing her of my father's death. It sketched out the fatal incident essentially as my mother had recounted to me that summer in high school when I made her tell me about our trip to Nepal. Captain Pasang informed my mother with regret that her husband's remains could not be recovered. He closed expressing his sympathies, adding that the sadness the Tibetans felt for the loss of such a hero must be almost as great as her own. I imagined my mother thinking about jumping off the Tennessee Pass Bridge when that showed up sifted into the junk mail till I remembered that she had a toddler to raise.

The last letter was written by my mother to my father on my seventh birthday, about six years after he was killed, a poignant love letter to a departed spirit. It slid from a report on the party and her delight at my "round-faced innocent surprise" when she had to bargain with me about climbing up a rock face at the party to ruminations on whether somehow he were helping her raise me from wherever he was and how I would turn out. She ended declaring that posting the letter was as unnecessary as it would be crazy because she was certain he was receiving her every word even as she wrote them.

Near the end, she asked him if I would follow in his footsteps, fighting for liberty as a noble necessity for which I would risk my life in battle, or if I would extract from her stories about him the knowledge that sacrificing my life as he did would undermine the meaning of his sacrifice. Then she added a thought that bears repeating here, one I read enough times that I quote it verbatim:

Den's a gutsy little guy. The way he's going, I don't think he's going to be any more afraid to fight evil than you were, and that will spark fear in me, as well as, I admit, some admiration.

My surprise that she picked up on that possibility before I'd ever thought about evil mingled with an inchoate depression. I fought off recognizing what was behind it but it didn't take long: standing in front of me, long-faced and hollow-eyed, was my guilt about having inadvertently triggered my mom's final, fatal hike. Blue skies or not, my mother knew the kind of risk a December hike to 11,000' entailed and I knew what had set off her urgent need to go up there.

I reminded myself I'd said not one word to my mom about venturing into the El Salvador hellhole, but I had carelessly scattered about some clues. Indeed, I'd placed them on her dining room table. But how could that have been avoided? Shrinking in cowardice from helping my friend? Deserting my mother at Thanksgiving? I'd tried to be discreet that night, but my mother's number one cause in life was to convince me to never venture anywhere near a war zone, and her number one skill was intuiting my thoughts, so undertaking the venture to the high-mountain earth where she'd buried her trump card, crafted by my father long ago, followed naturally as night follows day.

That hurt. My mother deserved another fifty years. I craved the chance to turn back the clock a couple of weeks so I could assure her that, okay, we were going to El Salvador but we'd be doing everything we could to *avoid* conflict. But I suppose that just bringing it up would only fan the flames of her fear. I guess that's what can happen to someone who loses one of the two people she's loved most in her life the way she lost my father, when she sees the other heading any direction other than a hundred and eighty degrees away.

With those morose reflections tossing me around, I traipsed off to bed in my old room, looking forward to daylight, when I hoped an unveiling of my dad's final, Tibetan message might deflect my thoughts from the past to the wide-open future.

[1-8]

<u>March 14, 1991</u>

Dinner was a particularly humble affair this evening. Exhaustion due to last night's late-night scribing felled me after my shift and I napped too late to show up at the mess hall till it was closing. If it weren't for a can of creamed corn I scored courtesy of the ship steward, my stomach would be rumbling louder than our three-story-high engine.

But to my purpose, explaining how and why I got from my mother's hollow house to this perch under the tropical winter stars in the Pacific...

The morning after my foray into the attic, I hit the phones to find a competent Tibetan translator. I soon reached a kindly Kansan scholar by the name of Polly Tenzin Whitney, who offered to get to my dad's final paragraph that afternoon, declining my offer of payment. I copied the bottom of my father's letter at a copy store and had it faxed to her office. Back home, I kept busy transforming my mother's house into a cross between a minimally furnished apartment and a rummage sale. Not very homey, but it was no longer anybody's home.

I picked up the return fax at 6 but postponed opening it till I'd cleaned up from dinner, put a fire in the fireplace, and settled into the armchair. As a cultural warm-up, I started leafing through my mother's Tantric art book. Holy shit, there've been some wild heads bobbing around in the Tibetan atmosphere over the last millennium or two. The book teemed with deliriously crazed demons, sex fetishists (I hadn't noticed a sculpture of a cobra emerging from a woman's vagina when we toured the European Masters gallery in the Denver Art Museum in third grade), passionate lovers, and mandalas as stunningly designed as the Taj Mahal with tiny gods and goddesses you need a magnifying glass to appreciate.

After an hour, I closed my eyes and drifted off, imagining what it must have been like to be one of those artists back in the day. Not much noise in old Tibet to drown out the whispered wailings of demons to those select few who could hear them in the high mountain winds. At one point in my reverie I was crawling for hours through a cave that angled downward in the interior of a mountain till I was a hundred miles below the earth's surface, when I heard rhythmic, reverberating thuds punctuated by high-pitched screams. I crept along the rocky sides of a dark corridor toward a red glow emanating from beyond a corner. I forced myself to edge one eye beyond the wall and beheld an insane dance performed by black demons with snakes for hair trampling on screaming babies. A fiery arm from a pit reached out to grab me and I awoke, believing myself for a moment to be cloaked in fire with no idea where I was. Discovering that damn book in my lap, I tossed it onto the couch, angry at it for showing me what I'd sought. I checked the clock on the mantel: past midnight. My translation was still sitting inside the copy shop folder at my side.

I didn't want to read it till I recovered from the nightmare, so I turned on the college jazz station, washed my face in cold water, and checked the stars out in the backyard. Reassured that no demons had taken possession of Orion, I returned to the armchair and opened up the folder. Underneath a nice cover letter from the translator and a copy of my father's Tibetan message was the translation, which read:

> *You will be extraordinary, my child, as the first to grow up with the wisdom of Tibetan sages, the wild colt spirit of America, and a heart pumping the blood of two strong peoples, each with great instincts lacking in the other. May you have the good fortune to deepen that wisdom in Tibet, where our land can be enriched by Julie's and my child, as dear to my family as Mt. Kailash.*

While attempting to extract every drop of meaning from that message, powerful night winds streaking through the high peaks dared me to go out and face them. I grabbed the keys to my Wrangler and drove a few miles past the edge of town, parked on the shoulder of the road, and maneuvered my way down the slope to a narrow trail that had been etched into the mountainside by decades of wildflower pickers and view seekers. I used a flashlight, but the stars were so bright I hardly needed to.

Crunching the thin snow crust underfoot, I felt tectonic shifts cracking apart my former conception of what my life would be like. My thoughts were barreling ahead at a good clip toward an unexpected future and the sooner I embraced it, the better. I've never had much tolerance for shilly-shallying; rescue work cleans that out of your system but quick. I stopped at a natural boulder bench I used to retreat to with my friends during high school, a spot that looks out over the creek rippling through the valley eight hundred feet below, and imagined I heard my father speaking the words he'd written to me.

He hoped I might discover in our homeland some fundamental Tibetan wisdom. Maybe I'm biased, but given what I've learned of the ancient Tibetans, I suspect it involved unlocking the mysteries of good and evil. I wouldn't be able to find that in my mom's books with the heavy-handed Buddhist spin their authors put on my ancestors' Bon religion. Those tomes seemed crafted by a religious p.r. team to gain Buddhist market share among a population whose indigenous religion differed from Buddhism in countless ways. But I was developing a real hankering to know what those wrathful deities really meant to their earliest biographers in the centuries before Padmasambhava showed up and "bound them over" to Buddhism, the new faith in town. Y'see, guys, all those angry, lusty, hate-filled greedy baby-trampling demons were just trying to convince us to overcome our anger, lust, hate, greed, and cruelty. *Obviously*.

Nah, something dicey had to have been going on in Tibet for the Buddhists to have to feed the locals all that "bound over" sugar candy mumbo-jumbo for the last thirteen centuries, and my dad's message made me see that I had to discover it for myself. So in that sub-freezing starlit stillness, I discovered that my soul was already hurtling towards

Tibet. My body still had chores to do stateside but would catch up soon, for the time had come for me to reckon with the Tibetan half of my past and future.

Trying to fit an extended vacation for overseas travel into the ranger station calendar would not cut it. I would not be returning to my job, not now, probably never. Short of some minimal training assistance the chief might need for my replacement, the Park Service chapter of my life was ending. No wage slavery, no returning to school to dicker over B.A. credits, no American standard operating procedure was going to keep me from finding out why I'd been born. I'd sell my mother's house—it was mostly paid off, so I could likely clear at least twenty or thirty grand off it, enough to cover me for *years*. I imagined hearing wind chimes of ice ringing a call to me from Himalayan caves to see the skies and land my father and our ancestors saw and breathe the air they'd breathed, maybe even find my Uncle Yeshe, if he's still alive, or at least his survivors. I was committing to this journey as fully as I'd ever torn for the goal line with an intercepted pass through a hopping minefield of panicky offensive linebackers.

There would remain one problem, however, a little detail about as inconsequential as a missing left ventricle—what was this expedition going to do to my love life? I harbored doubts as to how well my commitment to adventure would hold up in a fast of long-term solitude and celibacy. Maybe the mission required finding a gorgeous lover whose own evolutionary state would interlock with mine like two helically-bonding strands of DNA, a woman who'd lived throughout the world and was out there somewhere to the west at that very moment, destined to join me in discovering new constellations in the stars we'd see glittering over Southern Tibet, above meteors streaking beneath us the way I spotted falcons soaring far below me from Long's Peak. I could miss the love of my life entirely if I don't venture that way to find her.

But while the rewards of finding a woman like that in the thinly-peopled mountains of Tibet would be fantastically high, so would be the odds against it happening, especially given my game plan of holing myself up as a hermit in a land where I couldn't speak the language.

Well, too bad. A hidden world beckoned, no matter how dark and dangerous, and I could not withstand the disgrace of hiding from it in the shelter of my comfy US Interior Department employee's cabin in the heart of the known and knowable USA. Upper atmosphere currents were sweeping me towards high peaks on the other side of the world. I was being dared by demons and seduced by angels, and I'd not be able to live with myself if I were too cowardly to confront either of them. With my course set and the temperature dropping, it was time to get off that boulder and on with the rest of my life.

Extricating myself from my Colorado life proved disconcertingly easy. My boss in the Park Service accepted the news of my resignation with regret and understanding. I made one trip to Estes Park to help my former assistant with the transition and clear out my cabin. I was invited to a Christmas party, which turned out to be a farewell party for me. They converted the visitors center into an after-hours party venue with a band and big sign reading "Happy Himalayan New Year TD!" Must have been more than a hundred people there that night, some from neighboring counties whom I hadn't seen in years. I loved that crew and it was great seeing them all, sad as it was knowing that another reunion lay somewhere between a long time away and never.

A realtor my mother had known came up with the nifty idea of advertising the house in newspapers on the West Coast. In the first week we got six offers, sight unseen, one of which was from a buyer in Tokyo, where the value of the real estate was rumored to equal that of the entire United States. When the deal closed in a month, I cleared $33,000. Between that, a few grand I'd managed to save from my SAR work, and my plan to travel cheap, I was ready for anything.

I flung almost every molecule from that house to the four winds, keeping with me only my mom's wedding ring, the letter I've stuck in this book, the original of our family picture, and the trusty waterproof sack in which my parents had buried their terma. I placed the terma itself in the wooden letter box and prevailed upon Brenda to hold it for me till the unknown time I would return for it.

The one large possession meriting special care was my mother's library, two hundred books in excellent condition on subjects ranging from Tibet and Asia to art, nature, and literature, and quite a few fine kids' books, acquired for me decades before. I decided to make a gift of them to my dad's village in Tibet, where I was sure I'd be relying a lot on family as I acclimatized myself to their world. Even if few (any?) of them could read English, the books would hold the curiosity of the kids and the grownups there for many years. And if Gnam Yuljongs had been buried under a landslide or sublimated into the cold mountain air, *some* damn library or school in Tibet was bound to take them. I found a hotel—The Cloud Peak Friendship Hotel in Zhangmu, a border town the Chinese call Zham that my mother had once told me was supposed to lie less than a hundred miles from Gnam Yuljongs—and asked the proprietor if they'd hold the books till my arrival for a fee. No problem! Price very low! I didn't have a clue how I'd get half a dozen heavy book boxes from a Nepali-Tibetan border town up into the mountains, but I shipped them off anyway. It was a wacky way to blow a few hundred bucks, but the appeal of such an unusual gift was too much resist. It was a charge having money to blow on such a worthy lark.

I got my passport and squared away a Nepalese visa "to visit family." I didn't say the family members were in Tibet, nor did I put in an application for a similar visit to "China," since the last member of my family to cross into Tibet was executed for his trouble. I read that the Chinese are planning a big whoop-de-doo next month to celebrate the 40th anniversary of their annexing Tibet, and, expecting them to be even more paranoid than usual, I'd rather avoid any conversations with them that might lead to my opinions of the annexation, my paternity, or linkages between the two.

Besides, I don't need their stinkin' visas. My dad and hundreds of others managed to cross that border over mountain passes, and I've got the chops to pull it off myself. I got a hold of topo and satellite maps and I just might choose a route that heads out from one of the long-deserted camps in Mustang Province.

Rather than book airplanes to get to Nepal the way my mother had, I would enter explorer's mode from the get-go by hitchhiking to the coast and making my way to Asia by sea. It bugged me that I was so ignorant about something so fundamental to Nature as her oceans. Taking my time and saving some serious cash doing shipboard work would be much better suited to my mission, vague as it is. I closed my bank account and kept my real estate windfall in bank check form till I got to California. There I'd translate it into a portable universal investment commodity like diamonds while setting about scoring a job on a cargo ship.

I left home after a fresh snowfall on the morning of January 23rd with all my physical assets on my back. I walked through town to the highway and stuck out my thumb. My first lift was from an egg farmer with a full truck bed and careful driving habits. Two trip legs later, I crossed into Utah in a graying hippie's VW van, having logged just under twenty-eight years in the state of Colorado.

I reached California the next day, thanks to a trucker who bent company rules for me and let me snooze through the shank of the night in his big rig. It didn't take much intel beyond one look at the port of Oakland's waterfront colony of giant cranes to know where the container ships hung out and where I'd need to set up my base camp. I found a cheap hotel over a tattoo parlor down near the docks, one notch spiffier than a flophouse, and settled in.

For the next month, I majored in shipboard job hunting daytimes and minored in Tibetan history and culture at night, absorbing what book learning I could while rumbled by the heavy metal favored by the tattoo artist and his clientele below. With a copy of Kerouac's *Dharma Bums* and a book on Tibetan shamanism, I slipped further into the East and the distant past, right in view of one of the world's highest-tech freighter facilities.

The job search entailed learning how to circle around union requirements that have so long caused trouble for low-level job hunters. Picking up on advice I gleaned from a guy in a bar near the docks, I targeted those carriers most likely to accept temporary workers and had itineraries that matched mine. Indian freighters were high on the list.

Not having subjected myself to entry-level job hunting since I chased down a job as a manual laborer on a construction site at age nineteen, I got acquainted real quick with its draining and demoralizing effects. I just wanted to get *moving*, and all this delay and disguised pleading did not sit well with me, so I decided to balance the deleterious effects of the process by building up a new strength in my spare time. I would build upon my past success as a mountaineer and conquer a new environment—the sea.

In retrospect, given the daunting emotional roller-coaster plunge that later fell out from that decision, I've wondered if that arose from a prank by the gods or precognitive masochism, but at the time I told myself it was intolerable for me to be helpless in a biome far larger than all the world's mountains and that I ought to be able to rescue anyone anywhere. I would become a competent scuba diver with a view toward scoring a visit to the kingdom of tropical fish on my way to Asia, maybe while in port in some place like Hawaii or Singapore or on the Indian coast before heading upland.

I signed up with a scuba instruction outfit in San Francisco that ran through fundamentals in the pool at the medical center up on Mount Parnassus. The course wrapped with a dive off Monterey, which was surreally beautiful, despite the frigid temperatures, and which made my mouth water for what I might see in equatorial climes. I became confident I could handle depths of thirty meters or more, which lifted my spirits as I spent most daylight hours scouring the docks back in Oakland for freighter work.

When the *Iyerpadi* hove into port, I finagled my way on board where I won over the first mate by showing off my facility with ropes and larding on my familiarity with hard work. He hired me on the spot as an ordinary seaman, due to depart for Hawaii and India the next day.

From the docks I headed downtown to a jeweler, whose alchemy metamorphosed $31,000 of my savings into nine diamonds. I sewed six of them into the outer linings of my hiking boots and diversified my portfolio by keeping the other three in my wallet, the inside of my left backpack frame pole, and my shaving kit.

With one night left in North America, I walked into the tattoo parlor at ten o'clock stone cold sober, planted the drawing of Mt. Kailash from my parents' terma in front of the tat man and told him to hit me with it, just as Dorje had drawn it, complete with the name of his home village

གནས་   ཡུལ་སྦྱངས་

and one grace note I had the artist add: a thunderbolt vajra above the mountain. A fortnight on, the tattoo has settled into the life of a work of art likely to outlast that of its bearer.

[1-9]

<u>March 15, '91</u>

My last night at sea; no room at my inner inn for procrastination. Before my heady whirlwind makes landfall on the Arabian Sea coast of India tomorrow I must set down the incident off Hawaii that made a sweat lodge of my cranium and obliged me to lay in all this history.

We set sail late in the afternoon of February 27th, gliding under the Golden Gate bridge toward the setting sun. I looked back at San Francisco as she donned her glittering evening wear and got caught in an emotional crossfire. Spectacular romance, traceable from the beauty of the receding port to the mountainous adventure lying in wait in Tibet, ripped at my instincts, which hungered for the perfect woman to share it all with. This trip was a discovery vehicle with an empty seat labeled Lover and a poor six-month forecast for recruitment.

Lame, I chastised myself—no guy should have to have a woman with him to seize an adventure. But that charge was unfair: I'd been doing all right without a woman for a few months, and I've raked in many an adventure on my own. The abstinence I'm bringing upon myself is just a temporary necessity, similar to that endured by soldiers like my father throughout history in times of war. It's the price of discovery that must be paid. And so on, while the irrational sense that against all odds I'd meet The One on this journey kept up its muffled, helter-skelter drumbeat.

Such was my state of mind as we slowed our vessel on approach to Honolulu, a sister to San Francisco in the family of tantalizingly romantic landscapes graced by the Pacific. We had chores to attend to in the first few hours upon arrival in port, but as the local longshoremen got up to full speed, the first mate freed some of us for the rest of the night. A number of the guys with adrenaline levels exceeding those of kids entering Disneyland headed for the city's red light district in a leering lather. I repaired to my bunk, intent on making it to a coral reef for a dive early the next day, as I'd been planning ever since my first dive lesson in San Francisco.

Come morning on March 4th, I hit the island, glommed onto the first dive trip I could find, and was back out on the ocean ninety minutes after leaving it in a boat one four-millionth the weight of the one I'd been working the previous five days, blithely unaware of the double whammy that was about to descend upon me.

With a derelict at the helm of the skiff and a couple of Italian tourists, we motored out three miles offshore of Oahu, my eyes getting stoned on the beautiful tropical waters. When we halted at our destination, our "guide" announced that I could commune with the wildlife by myself for half an hour while he went spear-fishing. We dropped over the side, and off he went. I thought his lack of concern for the hazards of solo diving was pretty cavalier—it doesn't take an SAR pro to recognize that being sixty feet below sea level could be more dangerous than being fourteen thousand feet above it—but I am a certified diver so I went with the luxurious flow of the Hawaiian current.

Before long, the show began: a visually luscious cast of marine characters arrived, carrying on their eons-long ballet, showcasing the stunning craftsmanship of Nature's lead wildlife designers. At least that's how I thought of the mystical sea turtles and the exotic puffers and parrot, damsel, surgeon, and trumpet fish that swam by me as I melded with the bath-warm sea, unaware that I was about to come upon a creature in the ocean far more bewitching than any outfitted with gills.

I was following a pod of butterfly fish towards a kelp glade when some activity in a cluster of divers fifty yards off sounded an internal alarm. Perhaps SAR work sensitizes you to trouble, regardless of environment; I just felt something was off. Then I noticed agitated movement by an overweight middle-aged man. He was fidgeting with his mask and tank straps. A reflex kicked in and I started swimming towards him. I've told myself that my instinct to do so had nothing to do with the sight of another diver—a woman with a camera casing and a gorgeous body about 5'9" long—swimming towards him at the same time, but I've had to abandon that theory.

By the time I reached the troubled diver a half-minute after the sensuous videographer, his classification was slipping into the red zone labeled Diving Accident Victim. His mask was off his face, tangled with his tank and tank straps which were hanging off one shoulder, and he had his hands clamped on the outreached arm of the woman, who was planting her own mask over his face in a heroic act of buddy breathing. Crisis or no, I could not help savoring his savior's heavenly form, but my rescue discipline kept my focus on the need at hand. The troubled diver let go of the woman's wrist so she could take some air herself but losing contact with the mask inflamed his panic causing him to grapple toward the surface. Whether through drowning or the bends, the man's actions placed him on the brink of death. I shot myself his way and arrested his hasty ascent while giving him my mask to breathe. As the woman caught up to us, giving me a thumbs up, I made eye contact with the man and signaled to him that he was all right and would be well cared for as we helped him out of harm's way.

I confess that I had to fight off a flash of excitement at having tripped into a dramatic partnership with a beautiful-legged mermaid who, mask notwithstanding, was a thrill to behold. Fortunately, my SAR calm remained in control and within moments we slipped into a groove with our troubled diver, alternating buddy-breathing duties in a careful ascent punctuated by measured pauses for pressure accommodation. As a fourth diver, a man who had been part of the same troupe, hastened our way, we could feel our big fella's breathing and tense musculature calm, recognizing that he was in four good hands, soon to be six.

The four of us broke through to the sunlight together, triggering two separate dramas that cleaved my consciousness. One dealt with monitoring the recovery of the victim, an obvious diving newbie, as his crisis subsided. As his gasps for air normalized to more relaxed breathing, the fourth diver—a wiry, tanned, take-charge guy with a wet shock of gray hair plastered on his forehead—took over care of the sputtering tourist and signaled for the crew at the stern of a formidable nearby yacht (bannered "*The Farewell Queen* – Road Harbour, B.V.I.") to send over a dinghy. The recovering fat man thanked the woman and me and accepted his handler's guidance in boarding. The guide called back to us, "Fast thinking and perfect execution, Calieze! You too, bud."

I managed a pro forma acknowledgment but he and the other men were swiftly becoming phantoms as my mind tried to keep its balance amidst the earthshaking attractiveness of my rescue partner. Lifting her mask up to rest atop her head, she unveiled a breathtaking face surrounded by dark, shoulder-length hair sparkling with russet highlights. It wasn't just the sculpture of her features that jolted me— talk about Nature's design masterpieces!—it was like standing in front of a woman-shaped wind tunnel blasting glowing health and joy of living from her pores.

"No big deal, Jake," she called out in a clear, melodious voice to her colleague, who had helped the boatman heft their charge into the dinghy.

"I'm going to get Paul re-situated," Jake added. "Please carry on with the rest of the family and bring them up in about fifteen." The crew turned the dinghy with its puffy cargo toward the yacht.

My description of the two minutes that followed will bear about as much resemblance to what I experienced as the schematic of an inert Tesla coil does to the sparks billowing out of one that's all-out electrified.

"Will do," Calieze called back, exchanging waves with the rescued man. Then she turned and looked at me for a moment with a growing smile on her face. "As for you, mister...."

"Sherab. Terma Den Sherab," I answered, surprised that I'd given her my full name instead of TD and unaware of why I'd done so. I did know that my heart nearly stripped its gears upratcheting and that I was diving around in her eyes, shining green, bespeckled with gold and brown, flagship features set off by scandalously well-rounded cheekbones and lips. Her skin tone, darker than that of most people I've known with such a generally Caucasian look, hinted at roots in the Mediterranean rim or perhaps much further east and radiated an exotic erotic force field that utterly overcame me.

Awash, I heard her reply, "Sherab, eh? You, Mister Sherab—"

"—Den will do—"

"Den, you appeared in the nick of time. My client's guest was going wobbly and I was afraid we weren't going to make it back up without real trouble, until you showed up." I mustered a sheepish shrug. "An underwater Lone Ranger, you are," she went on. "You strike me as a pro at this sort of thing."

She had a slight accent I couldn't pin down. I bounced it off England, India, and Eastern Europe trying to place it as I put together my response. Like her face, it struck overtones of a polyglot background, hinting at having learned English abroad, perhaps from British instruction in a non-English land, only to be tinged American over time.

"Tangentially," I replied, determined to keep up the conversation despite the welter of fireworks she was unwittingly setting off in me. (But just how unwitting can such a beautiful woman be of her effect on men? Really.) "I've worked in mountain search and rescue for six years, but I'm a newcomer to the ocean. This is only my second dive." It felt like boasting, but I couldn't stop myself, as if this encounter seemed like nothing less than the cosmogenesis of the rest of my life that must be handled just so. Yet part of me felt warmly relaxed at the same time, even though I knew I had only a few precious seconds remaining with her, seconds in which I had to impress her of my qualifications to see her again, all the while feeling like an idiot for falling for her so hard and fast.

"Ah, search and rescue—there's the source of that calm-and-strength cocktail that relaxed big Paul."

"Wasn't much strength required. It's not like I had to carry him on my back."

She surveyed my arms and shoulders. "True, but I'm guessing you could have carried him to the mainland, if you'd had to."

I sought a deft follow-up to that heart-palpitating flirtation, a smooth reflex that I'd fancied as natural to my former self as Ted Williams's swing, but with mental guy strings popping in all directions, that self had fled the scene. In the thousand-millisecond gap, I seized on her camera as a target for my wavering spotlight. "Looks like you're the pro working this dive."

"True." She saluted her camera with her eyes. "I got this gem for marine life documentary work, but I moonlight for private clients who can afford their own personal documentaries." Her eyes roved back to my upper body and stopped on my tattooed left shoulder. "Hey—Mount Kailash! You're Tibetan!"

In all my years showing my half-Asian mug around, nobody'd ever picked up on my Tibetanness without help. I told her, "You got that faster than a shooting star."

That seemed to catch her up short for a moment before she glanced back at my shoulder, raised one eyebrow and added, "Nice vajra."

"Thanks." This woman was getting more interesting by the second.

She lifted her video camera, encased in a pricey-looking underwater housing, to her shoulder. "May I?"

"Be my guest." She held the camera on my face. As I went on, I noticed her panning smoothly down to my left shoulder and adjusting the lens. "So how did you know my shoulder mountain hails from Tibet?"

"I kinda guessed it wasn't in Colorado, with a caption in Tibetan.'"

Whoa—who was this Sherlock? How long had she been following me? "How'd you know I'm from Colorado?"

She pulled the camera aside, looking pleased and surprised. "You are? Far out—I just pulled that out of thin air." She looked back through her viewfinder with the camera trained on my shoulder.

"That's the view of Kailash from the village where my father was raised. I'm on my way there for the first time."

"Shoot—I envy you," she sighed. "I visited Tibet when I was twelve and it's rocked my dreams ever since. I'm going back some day."

I fended off a wave of dizziness, brought on by the brilliant sun reflections surrounding this sea goddess and a stirring welter of arousal and romance. "You're Calieze?'"

"Short for Cali Zigana," she volunteered, extending her hand.

"Cali Zigana—there's a two-word poem," I replied, unconsciously echoing what my mother had said about my name long ago. I shook her hand, holding it one embarrassing second longer than necessary, in the grip of a high-intensity pleasure charge. Her hand stayed with mine without resistance. I've always believed I can tell a lot about a woman's personality in general and her talents as a lover from her handshake, and hers roasted my vision of my future in the fear that our circumstances and her imminent departure likely meant I'd have to spend the rest of my life yearning for a soul mate I'd never see again.

"Why, thank you. Cali Zigana Moss, actually,"

"Three, then. From?"

"All over. Not yet Colorado, though, much as I'd like to. I crave wilderness."

"This ought to count," I declared, gesturing to the surrounding ocean.

"It surely does, but I was thinking of places higher and drier with mountain vistas."

"Either way, wilderness is good for you. It sustains you for when you have to deal with the opposite."

"The opposite being?"

"I don't know—the supernatural wilderness, I guess. Or jungle gunfire."

"Jungle gunfire?"

"I meant a forested jungle, as in El Salvador. Not New York."

A second whoa. Color fled her face as her expression changed from simple curiosity to a thrown-off pallor, shot through with traces of pain and incredulity—and, if I'm not mistaken, longing. Why the hell did I have to bring up gunfire while floating in bliss? Whatever emotional solution she'd had been injected with, it only intensified the beauty and depth I saw in her soul.

"I'd tell you more, Den, but I have to get back to my clients down under."

"Understood, Calieze. It was a pleasure working with you." She reached over for a second handshake that I hope I didn't respond to too quickly. Having done thousands of timed sprints ranging from five to forty yards, I'm pretty conversant with tenths of a second and this one lasted nine more than necessary to say good-bye. I relished all nine till the spell was broken by the call of her name from the yacht.

She looked back for a moment at the *Farewell Queen* where crew members were checking out exhausted Paul and his gear, and signaled Jake that she'd heard him. Turning back to me, she smiled as she put her goggles and mask back in place. "Till next time, on land or sea. Say hi to Kailash for me."

I nodded with a dumbstruck smile and watched her arch into a porpoise dive, slipping the full length of her masterpiece of a body past my gaze en route beneath a sun-dappled wave. I was angry at whoever had sadistically added that coup de grace, unsatisfied with the degree of anguish losing her would inflict on me.

After a half-minute of staring at her receding form, I threw on my goggles and mask and plunged into the water to catch up with her, but it was too late. She was nearing the other divers, some of whom had begun moving on in the opposite direction. I looked at my pressure gauge and my watch—my air was getting low and my boat was due to leave in four minutes—and came to my senses. I let her get on with her work. That is, I let her go.

In the eleven days since, I've been trying to get on with my work and my life, with only limited success. My post-Calieze stumbling began as I clambered to the surface and made my way back to our boat, silent as the guide showed off his speared king mackerel to the Italians. I was weathering two simultaneous storms hitting me from different directions: a high-pressure, brains-to-loins romantic erotic system buffeted by a tropical depression for having lost the woman of my life forever.

I'm well aware of how unmacho it is to become so jellied by a woman—at all, let alone in two minutes. Machismo flows freely in the veins of SAR culture, but my circulatory system had to contend with some heavy-duty endocrine charges altering my blood pressure. I asked myself, how it could be legal for a woman to be so sexually attractive? America's a free country, but come on: If Cali Zigana Moss isn't required to wear an ankle-length parka, even in the ocean, how is the world supposed go on functioning? A strong man can crave a strong lover the way a great ice dancer cannot be fulfilled without a matching-caliber partner. The chakra-jamming feminine strength in Calieze's handshake hijacked my imagination with fantasies of what it would be like to grip and be gripped by her entire body and soul as we breathe into each other's mouths and eyes.

It wasn't just lust that threw me off—for me, attraction is always more than that. It was a sense that my life to date had been a setup to enable me to meet Calieze and begin a series of adventures as life mates ever after. I'd misread the signals drawing me west all those months. The real target had been a few cubic yards of seawater off Hawaii where I would meet *her*. Even the most majestic mountains couldn't hold a candle to a woman who churns the air and waters around her with waves of such intelligence, strength, sensitivity, competence, grace, wit, and incredible sexiness. With all that, her beauty was a divine lagniappe certifying her as Nature's crowning achievement in the art of womanhood. To have allowed that historic launch to fail was intolerable. As our motorboat wended its way back to the harbor, I determined to find her again.

After gathering myself together on shore, I found myself a traditional, well-appointed steak house in downtown Honolulu with a couple of old-fashioned phone booths equipped with a door, light, seat, and a few large, ragged phone books. This was going to take time and patience. I brought over a lager from the bar and settled in to begin plowing through the Diving, Photography, and Yachting sections of the yellow pages, digging and dialing till my index finger got sore, asking every voice I heard if they knew of a marine videographer named Calieze Moss.

As I plowed through the list, I fought off questions from within as to whether I was just imagining that she had seemed at least somewhat attracted to me and why I was so enthralled by a woman I'd known for only two minutes.

After an hour and a half of fruitless scratching around, I got a referral from a secretary at the yacht club to a guy named Scooter who ran an upstairs camera store in Waikiki. This chap, it turned out, had rented Calieze an underwater camera housing a week before. When I asked him for her contact information, he replied, "You trying to hustle this girl?"

Great—a volunteer big brother. I could understand his reticence, though. I'd be disinclined to set a strange guy on a woman with the kind of superstar body that could be tracked by radar from Stalkerville. He grudgingly agreed to take a message, warning me that he didn't know when he'd hear from her. I left my name and a request that she leave word at the US National Park Ranger Station in Estes Park, Colorado as to how I could reach her.

A sizeable remainder of my beer sat flat in my glass, testimony to my preoccupation with my detective work. I hate not succeeding on a mission, but my feelings about this one had become so tangled, I thought I'd trip on them if I tried to walk, so I sat in the booth and brooded for a while. Questions flowed in under the door: What made me think Calieze might even be available to me? She must have innumerable options when it came to men. She might well be hooked up with some lucky sonofabitch right now. (Nothing to see here, move along.)

That line of questioning overstayed its welcome and catapulted me out of the restaurant back onto the sunny Honolulu streets. I don't take well to ruminating about myself, especially to poking around my feelings with analytic probes. I headed back to the *Iyerpadi*, where I had plenty of reading awaiting me. I had no need for sightseeing, having had more than enough visual stimulation for one day.

It was on the mile-long walk to the harbor that I came upon the street market with the blank book booth where I picked up this volume. Logging notes about my research endeavor would be a lot better use of my time than suffering over some hot chick who bowled me over for a few minutes, or so I told myself while noting that my pep talk sounded like that of the Leadville Miners coach in the locker room when we were down twenty-eight at the half.

Nonetheless, by the time I got back on board and down to the mess for supper, my inner coach had gotten the upper hand. No way would I allow myself to languish the rest of my life with a schoolboy crush yearning for the one that got away. I directed that Calieze must become no more conspicuous in the firmament of my soul than a supernova that has completed its explosive stage and is dimming to invisibility by the hour. A discipline was called for that would brook no introspection. Any journal writing would have to await such time as I'd put a little distance between myself and that afternoon's emotional gear-grinding. I sucked it up and reported to the first mate, asking for a chore to ease our departure, which was scheduled for 2300. I pulled deck swabbing duty and threw myself into it.

But grunt work, mindless by nature, could only do so much to ward off further fantasies of Calieze. I imagined an angel imp, sneaking a regulation-busting concentration of beauty into one unit in the female human product line as a prank. I could see the amusement on the face of that closet artist, relishing the effect of his handiwork on virtually every man who would get a look at Calieze once she grew up, how every one of us would feel reduced to the state of a wriggling sperm weighed down by the knowledge that he was just one of hundreds of millions of males seeking the same divine egg. Some would struggle mightily upstream fearing we had no chance, some would cockily surge forward assuming we would best all other contenders, and the rest of us would sally forth on a fuel mix of nine parts desire to one part confidence, on the hope and prayer that somehow we might prevail against all odds to make it to her, and with her, for good.

The thought of losing got my hackles up, but I had to accept that, for a moment there, I'd had two loves, Calieze and the Himalayas, and I'd lost one. That made it all the more crucial that I appreciate and focus on the other. With that mindset, buttressed by hard work over the following two days, I regained my balance and was able to keep visions of Calieze in check.

By the third night after leaving Hawaii, I'd resumed my post as a spiritual researcher and I began setting down my back story in this book as a cleansing exercise that would leave me ready for the deluge of new sensations that will greet me upon arrival in India, now less than sixteen hours away. Crossing the finish line of this nine-night review, I'm satisfied that I've set that table with the well-tempered clarity that befits a good investigator. I've acknowledged the sharp sense of loss arising from the Calieze incident and even the danger of some warping it might wreak upon my love life over the long haul, but I've not allowed it to sink the larger mission. Indeed, these notes have put Calieze in perspective. No magnitude of personal love, gained or lost, can diminish the drama of the mysterious struggle that's been working itself out in Tibet for thousands of years.

I'm going to do my damnedest to penetrate that mystery and examine its innards. If last night's dream is any indication of what I'm in for, it will be a non-stop flight from normalcy that could last a half-year or more. Since I'd not gotten to bed after writing till almost 3 AM, I thought I'd sleep like a log, but an hour later I found myself looking out my porthole at the moon, shaking. Despite my best efforts at keeping Calieze at bay during the day, she had reappeared in my dream, at my side, as the two of us sought to fend off a terrifying demon that was threatening a village in India, with the fates of the village, India, and the world depending on the speed and intensity of our countermeasures. And, bizarrely, the sexual attraction that had jolted us in the waters off Oahu not only persisted in the height of battle but burst forth in an erotic craze, interleaving all our cells and supercharging our skills and endurance in the fight.

So, getting over Calieze won't be so easy after all, but as I've got some serious exploring to do soon, traversing figurative and literal glaciers at elevations even I have never experienced, I'd damn well better be paying attention. In the darkness of the Western Pacific, I can feel the ocean floor's rising beneath our ship as we approach the Asian continent, this time heading not to my father as an infant, but to the land of my fathers as a man. We'll dock in Bombay in the morning and I shall be ready to leave the womb of this immense ship and my past life behind.

[2-1]

<u>April 4, 1991   On A Boulder, Miles Beyond Gnam Yuljongs, Tibet</u>

Atop a boulder perched two and a half miles into the sky and several hundred miles inland from the location of my last entry, I'm celebrating my birthday gazing at a royal array of mountains caught in a magnificent freeze-frame of Earth's tectonic plate action. I'm in the middle of the scene where India rams into Central East Asia, punching the Himalayas skyward to twice the height of the Rockies. The Himalayas reign supreme; all of Earth's highest one hundred peaks are here.

I'll have to skim through what I've seen since the ship I was working on long ago (twenty days?) nestled into port in Bombay. I could have spent years exploring India's pungent riot of noise, color, and dusty, baked spirituality that has resisted modern homogenization with preposterous success, but I plowed through India and Nepal in a few days, heaven-bent on Tibet. This experimenter's log can afford little room for travel gabble—the focus must be on the mission, which requires detailed logs. In basic research, you often don't know what you're searching for until you find it. And you might not even recognize it when you do find it, and even if you do, others might not till much later, so I count it wise to protect what I might discover by setting it down in print, as a hedge against death in case the odds against immortality prove predictive.

My last moments in civilization before heading for Tibet were in Kathmandu, where I paused to place a couple of long-distance calls, one to the ranger station in Estes Park to see if Calieze had tried to reach me (the new CU grad who answered had heard nothing from or of her) and the other to the Cloud Peak Friendship Hotel in Zhangmu, where a cheerful chap named Lin-Chee confirmed that my mother's book collection was in storage awaiting retrieval—news that made the Gnam Yuljongs of my imagination feel closer and more vivid. I made a quick stop for food supplies and set off in search of the real thing by trekking from Nepal into Tibet.

My heart beat louder as my Nepalese driver lifted us out of the Kathmandu Valley into the haunting, mountain-shadowed landscape at the border I'd glimpsed for the first time as a toddler. I sent the driver on his way at a spot I guessed might have been the location of the long-gone Mustang encampment of 1964. I caught a whiff of spookery as I began my first mountain hike in five months, scaling the same mountains through which battle-toughened guerillas had once re-entered our homeland.

Taking into account early spring conditions and time to acclimatize myself so I could safely cross a couple of seventeen thousand feet passes—no minor matter after months at sea level and zero experience over fourteen three—I figured I'd make it in five to seven days. At the ridge crest marking the Nepal-Tibet border, I paused before setting my left foot down for the first time on the descent, grateful to God in my irrational certainty that I was entering a sacred world, the offspring of a splendorous marriage of earth and sky air pleasuring my eyes and lungs. One giant leap for Tibetan-Americankind.

My first sighting of a Tibetan in Tibet came at around sixteen thousand feet. Near a crude stone hut erected in an upland meadow a few hundred yards off the trail, a solitary herdsman tended a dozen yak lumbering through a meadow in their ungainly grandeur, loading up on tasty grass they'd not had access to during the previous six months. Unable to afford glacier glasses like mine, the herdsman had wrapped his braids over his eyes to ward off snow blindness. I envied his wealth of wilderness solitude and looked forward to accumulating some of my own.

Still, I was delighted to have solitude boisterously blasted away late the following afternoon when I wandered into a village the locals call Tisgra in the midst of an annual spring festival. What a sweet spot of paradise, nestled in a valley by a lake at the foot of a mountain with a monastery planted high up its side. A thousand celebrants from all around bobbed on frothy waves of life love, cheering and clapping in syncopation with buffalo horns, copper bells, finger cymbals, and the clatter of the celebrants' drums and nether-world horns. The cacophony and color riot added synesthetic spice to aromas of tasty goodies and mugs of barley beer wafting past wind-horse flags flapping in the gusty breezes. Pony men with pigtails coiled atop their heads galloped down corridors dividing the crowds, grabbing targets from the ground on the fly. Small children twittered uncertainly before a fanged black monster Walmo dressed in bones with a giant head adorned with bug-eyed laughing skulls wagging its blood-red tongue ferociously at them in a spasmodic wrath dance. Their parents had told them that Walmo and her fellow demons are our protectors, but they'd be entitled to their doubts. I've still got mine.

The only note of real-world demonry I detected in the festival's harmonics emanated from some solemn Chinese soldiers hovering gratuitously around the proceedings, ever vigilant in scanning for signs of treasonous love for the Dalai Lama. The Tisgrans paid those grim sentries little heed, dancing and singing right in front of them. Perhaps it was a gesture of defiance. A grandmother informed me that clapping hands is a Tibetan defense against wicked deities and monsters, a cultural detail the Chinese were unaware of when they were pleased to be greeted by waves of "applause" from the natives when they invaded in the 1950s. A fishmonger who supports his family of six with the blessings of the lake told me he views Communist Chinese control of Tibet as a passing illness of short duration in the grand scheme of things. His ancestors had hauled tons of marble, granite, paint, wood, and metal high up that formidable mountainside to build the monastery to protect an image of the Buddha discovered in the rocks up there. Five hundred years later, his family continues to feel honored to serve its monks whose temple had thus far escaped Chinese destruction.

I spent that night in a meadow a quarter-mile upstream under a canopy of stars. On my hike the next morning I found myself drawn to another striking sight by a siren call of chirruping laughter coming from a nearby creek. Four young women were bathing in a water hole. To avoid jolting my nerves any further or theirs, I slipped back out of sight, in no need of another reminder of how exciting it would have been to be exploring this magnificent country with Calieze, or to be exploring magnificent Calieze in any country.

Over the next couple of days I trekked another forty miles into the gorgeous tenth of Tibet graced with lush forest by humid air wafting up from the Indian Ocean. Excepting a few shortcuts across oxbow curves, I followed a river that would lead me to the head of a trail to Gnam Yuljongs (or so I'd been assured by a goatherd over a lunch shared exchanging goat and cattle jerky). As the sun set on the fourth evening I rounded a bend and got my first sight of Mount Kailash, the nearly twenty-two thousand feet high peak of white-capped black rock depicted on my shoulder. I wasn't one of the countless religious pilgrims who'd journeyed to set their eyes on that peak over the centuries, but I'm guessing that the sight of it packed as powerful a wallop for me as it did for them.

Late the next afternoon, I reached the trailhead below the final pass to Gnam Yuljongs. Wisdom urged settling in for one more night before beginning the haul over another seventeen thousand foot pass under a hot sun, but wisdom had been shoved into the back seat by the force driving me to my family's ancestral village after a lifetime of exile, so I pushed on and up.

I made it over the top all right, but not without a temblor of trouble. The thrill of spotting Gnam Yuljongs resting a couple of miles below was dampened by touches of dizziness and nausea, signs of borderline altitude sickness that I'd helped hundreds of others deal with without ever experiencing myself. Carefully mixing rest and descent to lower elevation, I managed a clean recovery and began to breathe normally somewhere below thirteen thousand feet. Excited as I was to have reached the final thousand yards, I set down my pack and my body right on the path, hoping to appear rested when I met my family for the first time. It was stony but I was too tired to care. A shiver passed through me as I thought about my mother coming to her final rest on a mountain path, but I reminded myself that I was fundamentally in great shape, warm, dry, and uninjured, and sleep took charge of my brain in thirty seconds.

I awoke an hour later to the sight of a Tibetan woman a little older than I and a girl about eight, hovering over me and whispering. My professional pride kicked in and I pretended it was perfectly normal to have settled in for a snooze in the middle of a high, rocky trail. The moment I stated my name the woman said, in Tibetan and eye-popped surprise, "Dorje's child!" I nodded, starstruck, and she enfolded me in a delicate embrace, identifying herself as my cousin Sonam, the daughter of my uncle Yeshe. She introduced me to her daughter, Lasya and led the way down the path, sailing me into the valley of my dreams, still sleepy, but awash in gratitude for having made it home at last, after a journey of twelve thousand miles.

Recognizing my fatigue, Sonam took me straight to her squat two-story house along the tiny town's main drag, a stone walkway. She urged me to rest up before facing the waves of attention my arrival would stir up in the village and meeting my uncle, who was tutoring her eleven-year-old son, Renzin. She showed me to a ladder leading to the upper floor living area where I found a pallet of blankets to collapse on. By the time she turned up again five minutes later with a cup of tea, it was all I could do to thank her in Tibetan and gulp it down before falling asleep.

Sonam woke me an hour later, offering me a bowl of water to splash my face. She was looking forward to my meeting my uncle as much as I was. I pulled myself together and set out on the twelve-yard journey I regarded as the approach to a tiny stone Oz.

We reached Yeshe's doorway as he was helping Renzin clean up from a post-lesson project, sculpting a Buddha out of yak butter dough. I stood outside the doorway as Sonam greeted Yeshe and told him in a giddy voice that she had a wonderful surprise. When she introduced me as Terma Den Sherab, he exclaimed, "My nephew!" with a joyous smile crinkling his Sherab features, so similar to mine and my father's.

Yeshe opened his arms to embrace me without getting up, telegraphing the agility tax that age had imposed on him. He told Renzin to place his Buddha on the shrine by the fireplace and shake hands with his cousin Terma Den. When he invited me to sit across from him, I called Yeshe "Uncle"—a new experience for me since my mother had been an only child—and he smiled. Sipping tea furnished by Sonam, we got acquainted alternating between Tibetan and English sprinkled with off-beat synonyms and occasionally resorting to sign language. Like several others in the village, Uncle Yeshe had acquired some English from travels as far as Lhasa and Nepal.

Uncle Yeshe is a widower in his sixties, the village scholar who spent some of his youth in a monastery and who devotes much of his time to teaching the youth of Gnam Yuljongs. (The lure of monastic life is strong hereabouts—Sonam's husband left home a few years after Lasya's birth to join a monastery two hundred kilometers from here and Sonam and their children have visited him only once since.) I was eager to hear stories about my father but that had to wait as a crowd of curiosity seekers had gathered in Yeshe's doorway, inspiring Yeshe to lead me on a guided tour to introduce me around the village.

Measuring only a couple hundred yards, the tour needn't have taken much time, except that everyone wanted to meet me, even Kyoru, a tail-wagging mastiff-shakhi cross, who was hobbling around on leave from her human yak herding teammates on account of a foot injury. Most entranced were the older villagers who had known my father and looked at me as if I were both Dorje resurrected and, as the only Euro-Tibetan they'd ever seen, an alien from another world. I'd passed through a cultural looking glass only to find myself still an exotic oddball, this time for having a Caucasian nose, green and gold flecks in my eyes, and, at 5'11", a towering height by local standards. The villagers greeted me with warm smiles (or giggles from the half-dozen girls in their teens) outside their weathered, brightly colored houses with prayer flag turrets and sloping walls of mud and stone.

After so many years of trying to imagine Gnam Yuljongs, every house struck me as an Asian landmark. That's a lot of landmarks for a town that makes Leadville look like Denver. There are no cars or street lights because there are no streets or electricity. Just a few score lovely people going about their business in the fresh spring respite from the Himalayan winter, tending their gardens, potato plants, and barley crops, making dinner, and cheering each other on in a chunk of heaven.

An unusual chunk it is, too. One boy shook hands with me while holding a pail of cow dung, which he proceeded to carry inside his house. That being the reverse direction I'd have expected with respect to animal feces and houses, I peeked inside and saw him daubing cow pies on the walls of the ground floor room, which tripled as a fuel-drying area as well as a hay-laden stable and a foyer to the living space upstairs. In some houses a stash of dried fuel is also stored on their rooftops, sandwiching the living space between layers of dung. *Architectural Digest* won't feature that home layout, but in a land as cold, unelectrified, and sparsely forested as rural Tibet, a free fuel supply trumps arty interior decor.

After reaching the ice house at the north end of the village, we turned back and I noticed how closely the view of Mt. Kailash in the distance resembled the drawing in my dad's "terma" letter, now reincarnated in ink on my left shoulder. I thought of Kailash as a massive, proud watchdog, resting but alert, ever watchful from a respectful distance to protect the denizens of Gnam Yuljongs and the surrounding territory from demons only it could see.

Uncle Yeshe stopped to pet his yak—a dri, actually, being the female of her kind—currently on home leave in the ground floor stable of a neighbor's home. She was awaiting the herders' summer tour of the alpine meadows higher up the mountains, for which the herders would receive a share of her milk. Yeshe calls her Dawa (Tibetan for moon) to recall the calfy lowing he heard emanating from her throat during her first moonlit night in the pasture beyond the village. He claimed the sweet, scruffy bovine was relaxed with him because she knew he would let her live out her natural life, a destiny denied the males in this country, where butchery and carnivorism have been around a lot longer than Buddhism.

Our last stop on the tour was a micro-construction project at the south end of town near a large fenced-off community garden. The beginnings of a wall were rising at the edge of a slate foundation laid near a charcoal stove. The villagers are joining forces to build a shower house with a pulley-and-bucket hot water system and a dressing room, warmed, like the water, by a fireplace—no little luxury in villages like ours, where the only plumbing is what you're born with. It sparked an image of a resident relaxing with a book after the cozy luxury of a hot shower. That reminded me of my mother's book collection, still waiting in storage for me in Zhangmu, the nearest city to our village, which I'd bypassed wending my way into Tibet over mountain passes on foot.

That evening, a lavish Welcome Terma Den Sherab pot luck supper was put together by family members and neighbors crowded into Uncle Yeshe's living room, featuring mutton, chicken, a vegetarian roast of savory barley, and tea. I sat on a stack of quilts between Uncle Yeshe and a Buddha statue decked out in silk, lapping up the friendly hubbub in the orangey glow from yak butter lamps.

Much of our stumbling bilingual conversation was given over to developing my chops in Tibetan and Life in Gnam Yuljongs 101, during which I picked up some details about my father's life there. Yeshe and my dad were raised in Gnam by my grandfather, a trader in yak skins, and my grandmother, the daughter of a shaman from a village about five days east of here. Their father was also a builder and had constructed several of the houses in Gnam including Yeshe's. Neither trade nor building tempted my father. Uncle Yeshe said his little brother wanted to be a healer ever since he'd seen their grandfather perform a healing rite when they were little. That changed when the Tibetan resistance caught fire in the wake of the Chinese takeover in the late '50s. Having been born six years before my father, Yeshe had already started a family by then and the course of his life did not allow for guerilla warfare. My father sought his family's blessing as he changed course (temporarily, it was assumed) from medicine to an undertaking with immeasurable risks. The family was distraught about what they saw as a desperate campaign unlikely to end well, but they respected my father's idealism and, knowing that the land they and their ancestors had cherished for so many centuries was in peril, they hugged Dorje farewell and pleaded with him to be ever watchful. Once my father left for Nepal, all they learned of him—and his American family—came through his letters and one fellow fighter from his Mustang cadre who showed up a couple of years later. They never saw my father again.

In the two days since my arrival, I've spent mornings lending a hand at chores like grooming the charcoal pit, a process that requires much wood and effort but pays off with a fuel that burns longer and yields far more heat per pound than raw wood. (Note to self: offering to help the women dragging buckets of water up from the creek is a no-no. Men need not apply. After my one smiling attempt to relieve a lovely neighbor of that burden earned me a weird look from her husband, I felt like a rodeo bull in an ancient social china shop.) I also took on a brief apprenticeship to the stonecutter trimming slate for the shower house. His masterful fitting together of the natural edges of the slate without refined cutting produced a more pleasing, natural look than a primly-filed mosaic, even if it wouldn't have cut the tony Dijon mustard in Vail.

I've spent my afternoons up in the mountains to the west, far from grazing land, scouting for a site to put down roots. On yesterday's foray I carried nothing but water and a piece of Sonam's barley cake for lunch. Today I hiked up empty-handed, feasting on wild berries and stream water. (Anti-giardia tablets? With the pristine glacier runoff I'm following upstream, those are about as necessary as a low-jack and a car alarm.)

Both the village and the wilderness nourish and strengthen me for a mission which will be anything but sweet, one commenced by my ancestors here long ago. They were bold enough to grapple with the horrors reflected in Tibet's bizarre, out-of-control imagery of wrathful gods who, no matter how much the Buddhists try to spin it, look like unvarnished, big bang engines of evil. I'm ready to follow suit, miles of hard hiking away from the beloved metropolis of Gnam Yuljongs, by setting up my own wilderness observatory, a base camp with a view of Mt. Kailash and breathtaking clouds where I can conceive and execute a plan to hunt down evil.

[2-2]

<u>April 13, 1991   Higher Up Still</u>

I've hiked up to about fourteen thousand feet, whopping high even if less than half the elevation of the throne of Qomolangma and his immense court (Qomolangma being the ancient Tibetan name of the mountain a British bureaucrat felt entitled to rename "Everest"). I'm a tiny geo-surfer pausing on the side of a great cresting wave created by India crashing into Asia over the last ten million years, causing these mountains to rise at ten times the speed of the Alps.

That big picture view has functioned pretty well as an antidote for my romantic fantasy overdosing in Hawaii. I confess there've been a few flickering thoughts of Calieze being here, illuminating facets of an imaginary joint Tibetan expedition like a cut diamond turned in moonlight, but my better self has promptly administered a well-deserved butt kicking: So you saw a hot chick for a couple of minutes out in the ocean. No guy gets to take to town (and bed down) every good-looking woman who crosses his field of vision. Sober up and embrace the power of solitude.

Work serves as a constructive distraction. A salubrious project occurred to me on my way back from the forest on an early morning wood-hauling run the other day, when I saw a flock of some exotic geese flying north. As I was wishing I could get my hands on the Himalayan wildlife book my mother had dreamily acquired for her library, I came upon the slowly rising stone shower house. That re-fired my image of fresh-scrubbed Gnam Yuljongsians, huddled in towels and blankets with wet hair, scrambling down the path to their homes with the sweet prospect of curling up with a book. I went straight to Uncle Yeshe's house and pitched him a proposal to build him a library, nearly two hundred books arrayed on shelves I'd build into his ground floor room.

Over a bowl of warm milk—that's yak buttermilk, not the thin liquid I poured on Grape Nuts back home (former home)—I described my plan to hire a yak herder to bring Dawa down the trail to the road with me in time for me to catch the rickety bus en route to Zhangmu. At seven miles, that trek will take a good chunk of the day. Dawa and her keeper will have to spend the night down in the valley while I take the bus to town, reclaim the books at the hotel, and taxi them over to the station the following morning in time to catch the northbound bus. Once Dawa, the herder, and I make it back to the village, I could have the Yeshe Sherab Library up and running in a flash.

The scholar-teacher in him lapped it up, but he was concerned that I'm impoverishing myself by such exorbitant spending. I replied that I had to repay at least a bit of the debt I owe the family for housing and feeding me and for teaching me the techniques of high-country vegetable gardening. I told him that I had to symbolically bring to life my mother's dream of coming to Gnam Yuljongs as part of the family. For my finale, I insisted that if he wouldn't accept the gift, I'd have to throw the money into the river to protect myself from the curse of not having used it as I've been called to. Sold, he picked a site for the library where a couple of hypnotic deity masks were hanging.

So it's on and the neighbors are stoked. They see hauling a heavy load of books up here for a library as a peculiarly American scheme, fitting their image of me as more American than Tibetan. They're right—at times, pioneering corpuscles race through my blood vessels filling me with dismay at people yoking themselves to an ancient mill wheel living the same lives as their ancestors, content to weather their skin at the same old tasks and walking in circles with prayer flags, and I catch a voice within hailing from the ambition-bristling land of my birth, asking where are the new ideas, the production schedules, the moon shots, the big projects at dawn?

Yet when I'm immersed in an after-dinner lesson with Uncle Yeshe, all that gumption dissolves in the dim candle light as a soft rain drips from the roof onto Gnam's sole cobblestone thoroughfare and a murmur rumbles up from the throat of one of the yaks dwelling in the ground-floor stable of the neighbor's house, and I float on the spiritual waves of Tibetans who've lived on this very mountain over the centuries. I gaze at my uncle's face as he pours us some chang, a warm fermented barley brew, through a bamboo pipe, and count my blessings that, despite being raised American, I've been offered the chance to steep myself in the soul-satisfying hot spring that has warmed my people for a thousand years.

As we eased into a conversation about our ancestors' religion the other night, after Sonam and the kids had retired to their place next door, it hit me that other people had created their own rich and ancient culture in the land recently renamed Colorado about as long as they had in Tibet, but that history had been mostly stomped on, squashed, and kicked out of sight in the shiny glim-glam of Americazation. Where I grew up, we were imbued with a sense that The World That Counted began not with the births of the universe or even Jesus, but with those of the USA and Colorado in 1776 and 1876, all of it building up to the glory that is America in the 1990s on the brink of The American Millennium. But sipping chang by lamplight in a village miles from the nearest road and a world away from the nearest country and western bar, that whole construct looked as ridiculous as a naked, bloviating clown, body-painted in flag stripes, strutting and tootling around the square as the villagers go about their business, patiently waiting for him to run out of gas. I'm proud of the land I grew up in, but sitting in my uncle's little house in an ocean of quiet illuminated only by yak butter candles, light hearts, and deep souls, I had to ask myself where America's melee of interstates, computers, quiz shows, malls, stadiums, and unnecessary wars had gotten her.

As my thoughts slipped into Yeshe's groove, he began a humming chant. It soothed me for a while, then beckoned me to join him in it. I hoped that some macromolecular sequencing in my cells qualified me, a green western novice, to take a bold step closer toward the light of a Tibetan village elder and spiritual master. Like a tenderfoot violinist attuning himself to a chamber music virtuoso, I was nervous till Yeshe nodded almost imperceptibly in my direction, mid-chant. I swallowed in grateful relief.

Without prodding, Uncle Yeshe picked up the thread of Buddhism's story in Tibet, from Buddha Shakyamuni's revelation in India through the Theraveda and Mahayana schools in different parts of East Asia to the organic flowering of Vajrayana in Tibet, where it eventually achieved equilibrium with its family relations, Hinduism and Bon. The denouement is Tibet's lama-based religion replete with magic incantations, colorful deistic imagery, oracles, and rites of sacrifice and demon destruction. Yeshe freely admitted the whole mélange would be unrecognizable to the Buddha (were he to be so fortunate to be granted safe passage in Tibet by the PRC).

The religion table here in East Asia has been set with a vast spiritual smorgasbord of dishes sharing one ingredient, a call to lift oneself above the trappings of the illusory state mistaken for reality. Fine—they want to rise above it all. That's a luxury unavailable to most victims of evil. So, much as I respect all the canonized history, intellectual jujitsu, and calm om-ing, I gingerly pressed Yeshe to explain the evil violence depicted in so many of Tibet's thangka paintings. I was hoping to get beyond the flattening p.r. bromide about the wrathful deities' having been "bound over" to Buddhism as protectors and guides, yadidahyadidah. Uncle Yeshe dodged the issue, describing Bon and Buddhism as former rivals who have arrived over centuries at quiescent coexistence, having exchanged so much between them that distinctions are negligible. Either he doesn't know what gave rise to the world's most grotesque religious depictions of violence in the Zhangzhung Valley centuries before the arrival of Buddhism or he's sticking to the company line.

I love Uncle Yeshe. I'm convinced he is an enlightened saint-like man whom I'm incredibly fortunate to have in my life and family. I understand the tensile strength of the cords tethering him to his cultural roots and I treasure my genetic resonance with those roots. But neither my upbringing nor my soul is cut out to tie myself to the past as he has. I'm not going to drink any batch of conclusions brewed by people who have been dead for millennia. My red-blooded American roots are in the Rockies as much as the Himalayas and I believe people should be free to make discoveries for themselves. Every once in a while someone ought to be able to come up with an insight that's just as much an improvement on the revelations of the ancient elders as those elders improved upon the insights of *their* elders. As for the billions who do seek comfort ensconcing themselves in hoary traditions, may the blessings of God (whoever or whatever that might be) be upon you. As spake The Right-On Reverend Isaac Hayes, do your thing. We may meet at random crossroads, but we shall not journey as one. There is no pre-existing "path" for me, other than the lead left behind by those ancestors of mine who had the guts to confront evil and to convey hints of what they learned before Buddhism papered it over. I intend to pick up the search and find out what evil is, how it arose, and how to cut it down. The quest churns around me more every day, like a plasmic bronco materializing out of the cold mists that some day I'll day have to wrestle and ride. I've got to make a commitment of at least half a year to this mission and I'm looking forward to it. Bring it on, Himalaya, with all your ghosts and brilliant majesty.

[2-3]

<u>May 19, 1991   Home On Earth As It Is In Heaven, Tibet</u>

Ballsy and brilliant or deadly and dumb, I've made a new home out of a very old one in a location unknown to all other living human beings—a fantastic hidden cave at some fourteen thousand feet in the Himalayas.

Sipping chang (using starter brew Uncle Yeshe bestowed on me as a housewarming gift "to share with Yeti"), I begin this report at the end of my first night in my new-ancient homestead, gazing at five thousand square miles of Himalayan magnificence spread out under a saffron and rose pre-dawn sky, the sky's coda to its opening night performance featuring the Milky Way so thick I could imagine it dripping all over the Earth. Shooting stars; Jupiter and Mars introduced by a crimson crescent moonset; for this aspiring spiritual detective, a fitting climax to a good first day. Whatever hits I've taken in life thus far pale alongside my past and present blessings and the future that awaits me up here over the next several months.

Was I called to the extraordinary coordinates of this long-abandoned cave? I don't know how else to account for it, because the cave is all but invisible from the natural route down below. I was hiking nearly a hundred feet lower down the mountainside a few weeks ago when I noticed an odd grass pattern in a flat spot higher up. Checking it out I found a micromeadow the size of a box garden near a jumble of basketball-sized rocks with a large, dark space above them reaching into the side of the mountain. I rolled a couple of the boulders out of the way and found a treasure greater than a chest of gold doubloons—a perfect Himalayan cave home, probably uninhabited for at least a century by someone who left only a couple of faded paintings on the ceiling and back wall and an iron pot and a ceramic mug lying by the traces of a fire circle where hot ashes last cooled a long time ago. My scalp prickled as if I'd found Angkor Wat buried in the jungle.

I know my cave's wall painter won't be returning except in ghost mode because a juniper tree has been obstructing the view for many a decade and *nobody* would live up here and let the view from God's box seat get blocked off. My landscaping has been minimal, but re-assigning that tree to future firewood duty with my axe topped the list.

I made ten day-trips getting all the tools and materials up here, including seeds and bird netting and barley, jerky, and other foodstuffs to tide me over till the gardens start producing. It took two trips just to haul up the hides, blankets, and tarps—I'll never spend a night shivering cloaked in covers that have kept yaks warm through hundreds of thousands of Himalayan winters. I've graded the gardens that will keep me alive, built a charcoal pit, cleared a convenient path down to the creek, and cleaned out the soil and debris that have stopped up a smoke vent in the roof over the fire circle.

In short, I've constructed a Tibetan palace of solitude, invisible to all the world except for some dragonflies, birds, and an occasional marmot. The tiny meadow patches around here are too insubstantial to support even one yak for a summer, so no herders will come this way. This home is mine alone, rent-free, till the day I abandon it for the next user a century on, like the shell left by a sea snail later put to good use by a hermit crab.

Freeing my mind and time for this long-term expedition required wrapping up a couple of compelling loose ends. The more cheerful of the two was fulfilling my promise to re-settle my mother's books in her brother-in-law's humble home, that they might at long last begin their new lives in the land my mother dreamt of when she bought them.

After weeks of living in Gnam Yuljongs and its adjoining wilderness, the trip to Zhangmu to retrieve the books felt like parachuting into Times Square, even though Zhangmu is really just a small border town with a resident population only fifteen times that of Gnam Yuljongs.

Still, with all the Chinese and Nepalese going back and forth along its jammed road clogged with traders and diesel fumes, it packs in a lot of bustle. Lin-Chee, the manager at the Cloud Peak Friendship Hotel, took me to a back room where my book boxes were sitting under some shelves storing paper towels and napkins. He was apologetic that they'd been opened by Chinese inspectors. Four of the boxes, with the art, literature, reference, and children's books, had had their seals broken but appeared essentially as I'd packed them in Leadville. The fifth had been ransacked. It had contained my mom's history books, of which six or seven were missing, naturally the ones that had to do with the horrors of Mao's regime, the life of the Dalai Lama, and God forbid, the Tibetan resistance movement. Good thing I'd not put my name on those boxes (not that they know I'm here.)

I booked a room for the night. Having ascertained that I'm part Tibetan, Lin-Chee showed me to my room, furtively volunteering that his government's treatment of Tibet embarrassed him. "China is a great country, we don't need yours too," he said, along with a plea that I not quote him to any of his fellow Chinese.

I went down to the hotel's little lounge and planted myself on a bar stool for my first beer in two months. Seated next to me were a couple of Nepalese traders who'd crossed the border to import wool. Finding out that I'm Tibetan, they asked if I'd been questioned by the police during the round-up. Sure enough, to celebrate the 40th anniversary of the annexation of Tibet, the PRC had conducted an arrest sweep of more than a hundred Tibetans they described as criminals.

Little to no blowback from the rest of the world for that arrest orgy, apparently. Nobody wants to rankle an emerging superpower willing to bare its military fangs against its own people, especially after the pin-the-tank-on-the-dissident game they played in Tiananmen Square the year before last. Party hearty, China! Israel annexes three square miles of Jerusalem, respecting the Arabs' right to worship at their mosques, and endures worldwide condemnation. Iraq annexes a place not much larger than Los Angeles County and the world kicks its ass in a shock-and-awe shooting war. China annexes a country of half a million square miles, destroys monasteries by the thousands, kills natives by the tens of thousands, and the world, even America—*especially* America—bellows, "China—*babe*—let's do business!"

Criminal activity around here includes stashing a cassette of a Dalai Lama speech under your bed. The wool traders told me some Tibetans are expecting trouble when the Dalai Lama dares to identify the new Panchen Lama—the old one having died shortly before Tiananmen Square, curiously just days after delivering a speech condemning the Chinese for wrecking Tibetan culture. There's a suspicion that the Communist overlords will take it upon themselves to pick the new Panchen Lama, which would sound like a Saturday Night Live sketch if it weren't too believable to be funny. Goebbels was so delusional he thought the Third Reich would last a thousand years, but even he wasn't crazy enough to think he could appoint a Chief Rabbi of Europe and make it stick.

The next day, Wangdak the yak herdsman, Dawa, the books, and I made it back over the pass to Gnam Yuljongs in time for dinner. Once the bookshelves were installed and filled, Uncle Yeshe smiled like a wizened kid glimpsing a tree fruiting presents on Christmas morning. He now presides over one of the more formidable gaggles of books to be found in off-off-road Tibet.

The books have been a boon to me too. One slim volume on high-country gardening has supplemented what I've learned from Sonam and the other villagers. Another on Tibetan medicine prompted a lesson on the subject from Uncle Yeshe, who pulled from his spice shelf a witchy-looking bundle of leaves called "mugwort moxa." The traveling healer he calls Amchi burns his acupuncture needle with those before placing it in a patient's body to aid the flow of qi (a/k/a life force). Then there's caterpillar fungus for certain infections. One of the villagers here scrounges through pastures in the spring to harvest those fungus blossoms and sells them for a handsome price in Xigaze to merchants who tout their supposed aphrodisiac properties. It takes a colorful potpourri of actual medicines to back up a healthcare system based on curing the poisons of desire, anger and ignorance through meditation on appropriate deities.

The library is a certified hit in the village. Sonam cooked up a library inauguration celebration dinner, at which I was offered the honorific sheep's tail, something I'd not had the dubious privilege of sampling before. Uncle Yeshe has been lending out the books and another half dozen kids who previously had passed up the chance to study with him are suddenly showing interest.

The last step to be taken before I could emigrate from Gnam Yuljongs was to ask Yeshe to fill out the sketchy knowledge I'd acquired about my father's death. I could hardly embark on a journey to discover the roots of evil without facing up to the catastrophic hit it had delivered to our own family. So after the library dinner, when Uncle Yeshe and I had returned to his place for a cup of chang, I asked him what had happened to his brother. Reluctantly, he began his story.

Yeshe confirmed the reports I'd gotten from my mother and Captain Pasang's letter, adding that after Dorje had joined the rebels, word had gotten back to Gnam that he was leading operations back inside Tibet, finding locations for parachute drops and keeping tabs on some of the military bases the Chinese had set up. But information was infrequent, uncertain, and contradictory. One rumor that scared the bejeezus out of Yeshe and my grandparents was that Chinese soldiers were trained to shoot to cripple, not to kill, to capture the ultimate prize, a Tibetan resistance fighter. Information from citizens they cowed into telling on their neighbors they prized as pearls, but the agonized sputterings they tried to torture out of captured resistance fighters were gold. Their alchemical techniques included electric cattle prod shocks, scalding with boiling water, and suspension from the ceiling by the wrists.

After a while, word of Dorje's whereabouts dried up. The family later figured out that that must have been while he was in America, the far-off land where he'd met his wife and fathered a son.

In Gnam Yuljongs, the family lived in fear for Dorje every day for almost two years, until one day late in the summer of 1964, a man named Cering from the brigade operating out of the Mustang province in Nepal showed up in Gnam Yuljongs and informed the family that Dorje had died a hero's death fighting for our country's independence. After embracing his parents for a while as the visitor sat before them with his head bowed, Yeshe took him out in the pasture to press him for details and the location of his brother's body. Cering had been instructed not to discuss that with Dorje's family unless asked, but now was obliged to continue.

Cering was one of the three men who had been captured with my father on his final foray back into Tibet. In the next few days, while enduring their captors' regular torture binges, my father plotted the escape with his comrades by whispering in Tibetan at night in their prison blockhouse. Before dawn on the fourth day, they put their cell guard out of commission with a blow to the head from a chair, freed themselves, and lit out for a wooded hillside a few hundred yards away. My father had instructed the men that if anything happened to alert the guards that an escape was underway, they should keep going for the other side of the hill to the east while he raised a distraction heading west. He insisted that he should exploit the guards' fixation on him as their commanding officer and save the lives of the other three, who could make it back to Mustang and provide the intelligence gathered during their mission.

Once the rock fall my mother had told me about alerted the guards, my father pulled a killdeer, scrambling conspicuously down a ravine and across the adjacent hill into a different draw, as far from his companions as possible, issuing commands as though they were all together. The ruse worked, luring the pursuing soldiers in his direction while the other three Tibetans slipped over the ridge and on to safety. Just before crossing over the ridge, the escaping fighters saw my father fall from a rifle shot and five soldiers race towards him. While the soldiers dragged Dorje back down the mountain and two of the guerillas fled, Cering remained hidden at the ridge top, watching through binoculars to see what happened to Dorje.

Yeshe paused and I returned his look without flinching. He said that Cering saw the soldiers make Dorje kneel on his tied, bloody legs at the edge of a dry watercourse as they threatened what they would do to him if he didn't tell them what he knew about their plans and those of the rebels. Cering could hear Dorje shout back, 'Tibet shall be free!' They offered him a document to sign, probably a confession to justify what was about to happen to him, which he also disregarded. Then he went silent, even as they smacked him in both ears with rifle butts and burned him with lit cigarettes all over his face and body. When Dorje collapsed in pain, spitting blood, they threw him in the creek bed and buried him alive. Cering watched the soldiers stand over Dorje's grave till their victim's jerking movements beneath the dirt came to a stop, piling more dirt upon him all the while. Crying silently, Cering left to catch up with his fellow fighters. They made it back to Nepal by nightfall the next day.

I closed my eyes and swallowed, aswim with hate-filled yearning to ferret out the names and locations of any surviving members of the vile gang that had murdered my father so I could pay their long-overdue wages of sin with heavy interest and let them know why they're about to die a painful death in front of their families.

With that thought setting my gizzard to boiling, Yeshe chimed in, "The Dalai Lama tells us that a true hero is one who overcomes his anger and hatred." That was embarrassing. Had my train of thought been rumbling that loudly?

However Yeshe had detected my revenge fantasy, his comment made me recoil at it. Jesus, I thought, what's the matter with me? I'm here to prevent killing, not plan it! I thought back to the night Roberto's family and I crouched silently in the jungle before we crossed into Honduras. Then, too, I felt punishing revenge lust in the fruit-sweet darkness weighed down by the humidity and agonized screams and gunfire echoing across the canyon. I had to keep batting away my own fantasies about making those bastards' comeuppance come up, even though I knew that revenge killing does not qualify as "helping." It pretty much guarantees war in perpetuity. Vengeance is so toxic it led to Ghandi, the champion of non-violence, being killed by a fellow Hindu just because the Mahatma tried to stop revenge killings against Muslims. Once the killing of kin by an Other raises a man's warrior hackles, you can bet he'll reach for the sword.

But, I told myself, tracking down the location of the outpost where my father had been imprisoned and buried didn't have to be vengeful. Maybe I could find his remains and bring them back to Gnam Yuljongs for a proper funeral. (If that sounds a mite ambitious, blame my genes: my father thought he and his friends could overpower the People's Republic of China in Tibet.) I ran that idea by Uncle Yeshe and he gave me the kind of sympathetic look one would when breaking sad news to a child. "Your idea is well-intentioned, Terma Den, but not necessary."

He laid it on about my father's soul having long ago vacated that body to be used by other life, as is the way of nature. Furthermore, my asking around about where that prison was could expose me to great risk, so that even if I were to succeed in discovering my father's grave, I could end up buried in the same ditch and my father's line would perish for nothing.

I shivered at the thought of gasping for air, wounded, twitching around underground and cracking my father's barren bones beneath me. I had the spooky feeling that my mother's ghost was sitting next to Uncle Yeshe, praying that Yeshe could get through to me. I blinked and looked away.

Yeshe underscored the futility of binding myself to the worst days of our past by telling me how the resistance had ended when the Chinese got the Nepalese King Birendra to send his soldiers after the last of the guerillas. The Dalai Lama had pleaded with the rebels to surrender in the interest of peace and to devote their lives to preserving our culture. Some took his advice; a few refused and killed themselves. Yeshe concluded, echoing my mother, "It is over."

"Over!" I cried. "It's not over. The Communists are no different from the Romans who thought they'd permanently absorbed Judea by kicking out the Jews and destroying their temple. The Jews kept their culture alive long after the emperors were gone and made their way back."

"Yes, in nineteen hundred years. And they didn't make their way back by hunting down Roman imperial soldiers. They counted on justice taking its course in the fullness of time."

Reading between the lines, I guessed Uncle Yeshe wouldn't think much of my scheme to track down the meat robots who buried my father alive and mete out a little homemade justice, Mossad-style, some counterprogramming for brainwashed dogs leashed to the idée fixe of a tyrannical power that taught them the command, "Crush!" But while it's all well and good to be anti-evil and pro-peace, if those ideals have anything to do with justice, they don't eschew punishment, they require it. And if the world is still too primitive or intimidated to dish it out, I had a mind to step up in the tradition of justice that doesn't cotton to snarls of "Get over it."

In time, I cooled off and recognized that that blood-heated train of thought was not going to help me acquire the wisdom I've sought in coming half-way across the world. My performance in class at the feet of Uncle Yeshe was less than stellar, but I did eventually admit to myself that evil had survived the revenge play being called from the sidelines and on the field for thousands of years. I had come here to think up a new one—not that noble one of J.C.'s either, about loving your enemies and praying for them, recently translated into Tibetan by the XIVth Dalai Lama, he of the heroism-of-conquering-one's-own-anger philosophy. Well, love, forgiveness, compassion, and control over negative emotions are all fine and dandy, but when it comes to *ridding the world of evil,* millennia of bloody empirical evidence has piled up proving that, on their own, loving quiescence and pacific self-centering have failed as miserably as justice by vicious execution.

As I mulled over that conundrum, Uncle Yeshe sat on the other side of the candlelight, murmuring "Om mani padme hum," the Dalai Lama's favored chant to invoke devotion to developing one's compassion and wisdom in striving for the purified body and mind of a Buddha. When he stopped, I stood and bowed, thanked him, and went outside for a walk to the pasture overhung with stars at the edge of the village.

I stopped where I imagined Cering might have concluded his frightful report to Uncle Yeshe long ago and looked up, hoping to get a glimpse of my father at peace in the galactic tapestry to comfort me. And in a moment, he did appear, in a demeanor that stunned me. Rather then peaceful or resigned, his face at the zenith looked me in the eyes, brimming with what seemed like joy and pride. When I saw my mother's face alongside his, a couple of tears began a slow, silent flow down my cheeks. Perhaps that vision was a reconstruction or a long-buried recollection of how my parents looked at me when I was with them in Nepal at the moment our picture was taken. Whatever, my anger at the killer-thieves who stole my father's life washed away in the love our family was blessed with that could never be taken away.

It was the next day that I discovered this hole in the Himalayan wall I now call home. A few weeks later, I'm settling into the life of a pioneer, protected from the distractions of interacting with noisy minds, a necessity since my own mind is noisy enough, as evidenced by its reaction to an eerie painting I discovered tonight by lantern light flickering on the cave's ceiling. Partly obscured by old soot and moss, star-like eyes arcing within a mandala seem to be peering down at me. If the hits I get off it are a sign of what this place can do to my mind, I could be in for more than I bargained for.

No, scratch that. I know some battles lie ahead, much stranger than the ones my mother enlisted Leadville Photography to hide from my sight. But she and my American forbears helped prepare me for this as surely as my ancestors here and I'm scanning for opportunities to engage. A potent candidate site for them lies atop a stark, imposing promontory off to the west at around nineteen thousand feet, with a steep, craggy final ascent. I'll make it up there before long, on the hunch that there's a connection between Tibet's high elevations and the Bon artists' inspirations to paint the most wrathful deities ever seen by a mind's eye.

I'd hoped my elderly uncle might shed some light on it all, but he's been pretty stingy with that light, if indeed he has any to shed. Maybe he's so bought into Buddhist Boundoverism that he really can't think past the official take on what those baby-stomping demons were up to. Or maybe he knows the secret but fears I can't handle it (my revenge fantasies having left room for doubt on that score) or that the world can't, and he's made a pact with God knows whom to ensure that the secret doesn't get out till the time is ripe. Many would scoff at the notion that clues to the mysteries of evil lie hidden in these mountains, but only time will tell whether it's the Tibetan seers or the scoffers who've been out of touch, unwittingly propitiating conditions for the cancer of evil to metastasize. In the meantime, I must forge ahead in search of that secret or I'll never be able to forgive myself. It'll take time, but I'm prepared to commit myself to these upper reaches of the planet at least till fall.

I'm going to call this home New Hale, in honor of the birthplace of the love that led to my birth. Long and winding though it seemed, the trajectory of my path from there to here has been as straight as that of a well-shot arrow on a windless day. I shall embrace Himalaya and hope to win her over.

[2-4]

<u>June 11, '91   New Hale, Tibet</u>

I now consider my new home named as much for the observatory with one of the world's greatest telescopes as for the place my parents met, because it feels like I can see the whole universe from here, employing only the optics I was born with, aided by elevation and isolation.

The first time I scaled Long's Peak with two buddies, we spent twenty-five minutes at its 14,259' top. No more treacherous, seven-hour, ass-dragging rock climbs needed to reach such alpine heights—all I had to do this morning to catch this spectacular view was open my eyes. Ensconced in my yak hide-covered, meadow grass-stuffed throne bed, I behold a kingdom of thousands of square miles of land and eighty thousand cubic miles of atmosphere, a gallery for breathtaking cloud sculptures evolving as they float silently through the sky, doubling as way stations for cloud hopping over Asia.

I got my first taste of that kind of traveling when I scaled the Spire, the promontory that anchors my western vista, and found a view even more intoxicating than New Hale's, spellbinding swirls of energy, currents of dazzling light, fresh air, and winds sweeping the forest and valley far below. I spent two hours in cloudscape-inspired meditations like riding the cusp of night shadow from a thousand miles up as it retreats endlessly westward, immersing myself in the earth and ocean by subtending a chord through the planet to emerge in places like Aruba or the Antarctic ice shelf, and beholding the solar system from one astronomical unit above its plane, listening for whispers of the rumored Atman. As I imagined flying over a cloud bank with a flock of geese, I became aware of an odd sensation that I'd chanced upon a mode of travel that was as real as railroads and as liberating as aviation, a form of non-Newtonian sensory propulsion that can be employed by anyone with the patience to project his imagination up to the stratosphere and stay a while.

Once a hint of dark cloud materialized on the northwest horizon, it was time to descend. You don't play games with steep slopes in the Himalayas on a cloud-heavy June afternoon, just in case the monsoon drops in for an early visit. I made it back here about twenty minutes into the rain—not yet the monsoon, but a wet enough foreshadowing of it to issue an alert.

Doesn't matter—I don't need the Spire for cloud-hopping, since here at New Hale I see clouds topping out far higher than the Spire from my front door. A few evenings ago, a luminous cumulus cloud five miles high beckoned over the southern horizon. I decided to climb it mentally as I would an earthly mountain physically. The initial ascent was a dreamy, sumptuous feast for the eyes, scaling soft, brilliant white fluffs to the crow's nest of an airborne vessel sailing through the atmosphere. It was hard to believe that such a lovely-looking world could contain anything sad, much less evil. The whole tableau seemed designed to beckon souls to explore a great mystery, to spark a latent instinct worked into nature's design like the DNA embedded in the cells of snapdragons to entice dragonflies to take part in their reproduction rites.

I've launched myself on many such sky voyages over the days and nights since then. Inspired by a technique Superman once used of dividing his own body of hard-packed cells into two, each body only half as dense but able to act independently of the other, my mind parts ways with my corporeal self, leaping between clouds as I survey the land below me.

I flew that way for hours last night, touching down on cloud tops as rest areas, the way I used to ski up to the side of a trail in the middle of a steep run and pause to soak up the pristine air and views of the mountains burstingly fresh.

When the rush of surveying Himalayan peaks frozen mid-soar beneath me made me dizzy, I returned to the sky above New Hale and floated down to my throne bed, where I began fermenting ideas as to what I might do with this new power. Perhaps it could enable me to travel above any spot on the planet. Better yet, maybe it could catalyze enhanced sight like a scanning radio telescope that detects invisible signals from far away, maybe from *people* far beneath my stratospheric altitudes. I decided I would attempt to engineer visitations of a kind that would never occur to the earthbound. Perhaps I've been granted an opportunity that's a command in disguise, one I'm lucky to have been given and must obey.

My stomach swooped up against my diaphragm as I projected that fantasy onto the towering moonlit cloudscape where a mystical vision appeared: a horse and hooded rider were cantering down towards me, no doubt bearing a personal invitation from the spirit of the clouds to return immediately, so urgent was the revelation that awaited me there. I was ready to go till the rider arrived and lifted off her hood, revealing the sparkling, riveting eyes of Calieze.

Whoa—I stomped on that fantasy as if it were a burning ember that had sprung my campfire and landed in dry pine needles. *None of that business.* I tried to focus on the moon and the path it had traveled while I was gone, but that put me in mind of the solar eclipse coming up next month in Hawaii, where *she* had appeared to me out of the sea.

Agitation oncoming, I kicked that image away, only to see its place taken by a memory of the total solar eclipse I saw when I was fifteen. My mother and I had driven us all the way from Leadville to Eastern Oregon, barreling through a blizzard in the mountains on the slim, fervent hope that by the time we made it down to the valley near Bend, the clouds would part and nature would reveal her holy of holies—and our prayers were answered. The skies cleared just as the new moon's nibbling mouth reached the solar disk and proceeded to trace a perfect alignment of the diameters of the two lights that rule our planet. We'd been appointed to a temporary triumvirate of celestial mechanics—just the sun, the moon, and ourselves—as the sun graciously allowed his beloved granddaughter to sweep before his face, the better to reveal his brilliant corona mane blazing outward in the eastern sky into the mid-morning starscape.

Though only a high school sophomore, I thought then, as I have countless times since, how extraordinary it is that our planet has been positioned so that the disks of these two celestial bodies should appear exactly the same size to us, the only configuration out of an infinite number of possibilities that could allow the inhabitants of a planet to see its sun's corona. As the only world in the universe that we know of to be so privileged, perhaps we've been granted placement in this astronomical sweet spot as a sign, a tripwire set in place millions of millennia ago to clue in a species intelligent enough to appreciate it that it had qualified for a unique challenge: to prove that we deserve such a beautiful world by treating our own kind and the planet itself with great care and by rising so far above our basest instincts that they wither away.

Further, even at fifteen, I saw in a total eclipse signs of romance and eroticism, the perfect fit of male and female, a celestial mechanics rendering of the yin and yang principle I'd read about in one of my mother's Asian art books that made me yearn for a girlfriend whose celestial body and spirit would fit together so perfectly with mine.

Regrettably, that recollection crumpled my resistance to ruminations on Calieze. I was convinced that Calieze and I had fumbled our destiny, as inexplicably as if the moon en route to the center of the solar disk had suddenly ducked down and wandered off, ridiculing God's sign of our special place in the universe. I'd blown my one chance at the life I was supposed to be leading out of some ridiculous mix of timidity and false cool. Her blood was coursing its way through her exquisite body and brain at that very moment, her eyes either closed in dreams or perhaps gazing at something breathtaking—breaching humpback whales? Moonbows in the mist? Some other ecstasy, perhaps one unbearable to contemplate—

—That was the last straw whine. At last my archetypal coach materialized to administer an overdue ass-kicking. Look at you—whimpering like Little Miss Petticoat bewailing the cad who knocked her up and left town. You're an SAR pro, you pussy! You can't afford to succumb to tough conditions of any kind! You sound so deranged, it's conceivable you made this whole thing up in a dream! Maybe there was no Calieze other than some concoction of your horny, romantic ocean-tossed sleep. Think about the havoc that fixation would wreak on any future prospects for love the world offers you. You'd deserve the fate of a self-crippled cowboy, riding out your days on your own to spare every new might-have-been lover the pain of getting involved with a nostalgia addict who looks at her wishing she were someone else. Man up and get your work done here before you turn loser for good. Let your blockers run interference; your job is to receive The Secret and run for the end zone.

Nothing like a well-deserved, coach-grade ass-whupping. I awoke this morning, shook off the embarrassment of the whole solipsistic episode, and headed for the Spire. I got to the top in two hours, filled my lungs for a while with the purest natural oxygen in the solar system, and made it back here shortly after noon, a new man. I'm free at last to tackle what lies ahead in the next three months.

[2-5]

<u>June 12 – late</u>

The wrinkles of this page tell of my hands having been drenched in cold sweat from gripping my head and neck. Something spooky shot through with traces of thrill has just happened.

I awoke an hour ago and couldn't get back to sleep. My mind was pacing back and forth like a distressed wolf. I gnawed on a thought bone: what if the capacity for mental flight I'd discovered has a purpose far beyond sightseeing that I've overlooked?

I sat up on the throne bed and vaulted to the top of the nearest cloud bank, surveyed the circular horizon, and observed in silence, as a birder might when convinced he's near an ivory-billed woodpecker, a species not seen for half a century. I subsisted in that state for a long time. Eventually, I began to hear a quiet cacophony of thoughts which were not my own. Like hands possessed by Ouija, my mind was pulled somewhere unknown. I flew over darkened East Asia in an acutely alert state, scanning for souls that might be rattled by the spirits of evil that had exerted such a hold on the imaginations of my Tibetan ancestors.

As I listened to white noise of unspoken thoughts, I began feeling my way through the upper atmosphere as I would through a trailless forest. In time, one thoughtstream rose above the others, gripping the needle of my inner compass. Like the first time we used Corpas-Sarsat signal tracking to locate a downed single-engine aircraft in the mountains near East Desolation Peak, I felt like a trained hound picking up a radio scent.

I flew to the southeast, the dance between scent and sensor intensified moment by moment till my physical surroundings dissolved to a non-descript fog. I had arrived at an access path into the subconscious mind of a total stranger surrounded by an ethereal membrane in a translucent gray-walled chamber the size of a cabin. I declined to press forward, fearing discovery by my subject. This diminished the detail I could make out, but I was close enough to determine this much: I was peering into the soul of a man in torment as he considered bringing far worse torment upon someone else. There was no way for me to be sure how closely his appearance in the chamber resembled the way he looked outside of his "soulspace," but from what I could tell, he was East Asian, fairly young—mid-thirties at most—and in throes of anxiety, mentally jerking around like a PCP-saturated warthog.

The quarter-sphere in the direction he was facing was the window through which he saw the real world in front of him. Shadowy images hovered in the walls, ceiling, and floor of the surrounding chamber. At the rear, a weak brownish light blinked on and off. The man stared through his window like the solo operator of a haunted tank in a storm, shifting the focus of his gaze between the figures in front of him and a dark, floating cluster the size of a volleyball approaching him from left of center.

Like a hound, stink-disturbed while on the lookout to protect us both from danger, my nose recoiled at a putrid smell. A piercing uneasiness churned about, perhaps originating in the subject I was observing and refracted within me. Tension arcing between him and another person outside engorged him with a sense of power to enact something dreadful and he was teetering on the brink of carrying it out. He was tempted to do something with the cluster which hung before him, passive and uncoercive.

My conscience pricked me for prying into someone else's mind, but I couldn't afford to nettle myself about privacy invasion. I was a field scientist gathering invaluable data on a vital dynamic of human behavior, perhaps being called upon for an act of crime prevention as well. Both roles required that I observe my subject from a blind within his own mind and get a fix on what he was preparing to do before he did it.

For a while too strange to measure, I spied upon the man who was spying on his prey. My mind jumped about among sundry schemes of prevention of the crime and rescue of his presumed target, all fettered by my inability to see what he was up to. The scene continued in anxious stasis so long I realized it could have been going on—and might continue—for hours, days, perhaps intermittently for years.

Strained by the endless uncertainty and my impotence to help, I retreated and reset my internal compass to the northwest. I was soon relieved to find the Sapta Gandaki river system where I'd last seen it down below and headed on to the valley overlooked by New Hale, where I eased back to my throne bed to absorb what I'd just been through.

Whatever happened out there covered my head and body in gooseflesh. Maybe I've been equipped all along with an on-board radar device to navigate through stratospheric air currents to the mental abodes of individuals who have no idea they're being observed. If this recurs, I could be standing on the brink of a monumental discovery.

[2-6]

<u>June 20, `91   New Hale; Daybreak</u>

Maybe Mt. Pinatubo finally blew its top—there are weird colors in the sky. Odd weather too. Last night's summer solstice frost obliged me to fuss with the tarps I dragged up here from Zhangmu to give my fruits and vegetables a fighting chance against the cold. But I'm not complaining; pampering my high garden is a small price to pay for having this magnificent turf all to myself.

Though still in its earliest stages, my research here at New Hale Lab has become as disciplined as anything we undertook back at CMC, and I'm beginning to reap rewards. After writing that last entry, I remained awake much of the night reviewing my findings. They confirmed the wisdom of having invested seven months escaping the distractions of Colorado and Gnam Yuljongs to pursue the secret wisdom of my ancestors. By separating myself from a few pools of humanity, I may have gained indirect access to a whole ocean of it.

This kind of talk is uncharacteristic for me. I'm a science-trained antiflakist with no tolerance for hare-brained, wispy-waffle wannabe mysticism. Yet I also have little tolerance for those egos too brittle to brook the present inability of science to grasp the entirety of how the world works. Often enough during the embryological stage of a new field of science—the genesis of general relativity being a perfect example—conceptual breakthroughs precede the development of circumstances and tools of measurement requisite for scientific proof. There can be times when thought experiments and other kinds of non-quantifiable investigation can and must be nurtured, and that's what's going on here at New Hale. I'm not going to back off from reporting what I experienced just because I couldn't photograph it or subject it to mass spectrometry. I saw what I saw, not just that first night but in six more such flights I've taken since then. These are legitimate field observations of a phenomenon previously unknown (to me, at least), as real as the strange sea life that floated in the windows of Beebe's and Barton's first bathysphere trips a thousand meters beneath the Bermuda sea in the 1930s.

But new knowledge is often wrapped around discoveries of new ignorance. My visitations to another half dozen souls since that first night have been as mysterious as visits to other planets, where I still can't fully comprehend what's going on. It's as if I've traveled hundreds of miles to one specific house where an intense crisis is unfolding, only to find the door locked and windows shuttered while signals emanate from within in codes I can't decipher.

However, codes can be cracked, as Sherlock Holmes, Watson (J.D.) and the Turing machines the Brits turned on the nazis all demonstrated, and I'm determined to crack this one. It may be my destiny to glean an understanding of what goes on inside people's souls as they wrestle with the clashing temptations of good and evil competing for spiritual turf in their soulspaces.

The solitary brooding of the subjects in these early experiments has bolstered my sense that devil myths are preposterous fictions generated in most cases by and/or for primitive, superstition-hobbled minds. The freakish hemorrhaging of mores that lead to evil behavior are private and wholly internal. Whatever role those dark clumps might be playing in these intense inner dramas, external demons have nothing to do with it. I bet the ancient Tibetans demon painters knew that, which makes all the more intriguing their creation of the world's most lurid demonic imagery.

By training my brain to refine this newly discovered skill the way I trained my body to master rappelling or skiing steep mogul fields, I may be on the verge of answering that question, and it's incredibly exciting. The rain has started in earnest now, but that's fine by me. I'm going to accomplish things in this cave nobody has imagined. Bring it on, Monsoon.

[2-7]

<u>July 11, 1991   N.H.</u>

After three more weeks of this massive rain dump, I admit I jumped the gun with the "bring it on" bullshit. Turns out there's a good reason we use the word *rain* in the States and not *monsoon*. The monsoon is a different beast, one you can get to know intimately when you decide to hole up on the delivery dock where the fresh water supply for all of India and China is unloaded. When I took this place I must have missed the fine print where it mentions that taking a five minute round-trip to the eco-friendly organic latrine up the hill means risking your life. The wrathful deity on my back wall must be a storm demon who wants me off his territory, and his wall o'water, slippery slopes combo tactic looks scarily effective.

Calm down: no one's going to succumb to a mountain storm. I'm not going up against this unprepared, like my mother. I'm TD Sherab and I can handle mountain challenges, including the aerated tsunami that belts me in the face the moment I poke my head out of my cave. It can't continue like this for eternity—it has to stop eventually and the sun god shall again come in for his shift. I just have to stick it out, continue my work inspecting dangerous souls, keeping in mind SAR Cardinal Rule #1 for victim and rescuer alike: *Keep a clear head.* And when a victim can't, the rescuer's got to do it for both of them. And when the victim and the rescuer are the same person, the auto-on brain circuitry we wire up in training has got to kick in. A clear-headed, guiding inner voice, divine or otherwise, trumps babbling fear and panic any day.

The ones needing rescue are the prospective victims of the sickos I've been encountering in nightly visitations. I've increased the degree to which I press forward in the subjects' soulspace membranes without being discovered. The attempts I've made to impact what was happening by shouting and threatening the subject went unnoticed but the closer vantage point has provided a much clearer view of what's going on.

Last week I visited (and, unfortunately, smelled) the soul of a pimple-faced teenager with his buddies hunting down a gay man. As before, the cluster appeared near the kid's head, but this time I saw him suck it into his lungs. The moment he did so, pustules appeared on his inner face in a nauseating surge of violent energy that led him to beat the gay man to death with a nail-studded two-by-four as he and his pals whooped it up in a Texas twang.

So it has gone in each incident since in which the subject went ahead and committed an evil act. He—they've all been male so far—sucked in the ugly clod of dark filamented gas right before taking violent action. Perhaps I was drawn to the microbio lab job a decade ago because a suspicion was lurking in the back of my mind that evil functions like a virus. Now, I've detected what appears to be a spirit-rotting virus that infects people who welcome it into their souls.

I'm calling this virus *eviola,* a soulpox vector that has laid waste to a far greater segment of the human race than smallpox ever did, one so widespread that eradicating it isn't even on the world's to-do list, much less being actively pursued. *Eviola minor* is associated with non-fatal evil like rape and torture, that, however brutal, scarring, and deserving of unremitting punishment, allows victims to live out the rest of their lives. In souls who infect themselves with its deadly variant, *eviola major,* fundamental human respect for life is so atrophied that murder can be committed with dispassion, satisfaction, or glee.

The gang that murdered the gay man differed from those Roberto feared might come looking for his family. Those kids were intoxicated brats, probably pulling a one-off motivated purely by bigoted hatred, unlike the Salvadoran thugs trying to put down a broad resistance movement. But both engines ran on hate in the complete absence of respect for life.

Witnessing that beating brought my blood to a hard boil, but I'd asked for it. There's no clean and easy way to get a handle on what underlies evil. I've had to admit that joining Roberto in El Salvador wasn't all about altruism or burnishing my rescue credentials: I was *attracted* to the chance of confronting evil, which stank in countless murder sites throughout that steaming jungle. Evil is an unrecognized feature of nature that draws in my intellect the way evolution hooked Darwin. Hence my hazardous laboratory, in which emotions must be carefully titrated. If you can't bring yourself to imagine the grief and horror of families like those Salvadorans who discovered or saw the mutilation of their loved ones, you'll not sign on for the mission or you'll abort it if you do; but if your imagination dangles you too far into the abyss, your grip, sanity, and life could be lost.

I can hack it. This is the perfect place to develop investigational techniques to study human interactions with these organisms and strategies for preventing infection. Conditions may become critical but I've been trained in crisis control and I'll not be rolled.

[2-8]

<u>Aug. 3 - New Hell, Tibet</u>

Location name changed to reflect mental status. Been cooped up in here a month and a half, prisoner of a siege that's filled the atmosphere with a falling body of water the size of the Caspian Sea. I wasn't expecting Monaco, but my notion of "summer in the mountains" was no match for the Himalayas. "Monsoon" must have its roots in "monster" and "swoon," the latter to suggest a loosening of mental mooring that will befall anyone trapped by it too long with nothing else to do.

Or nothing healthy, cheerful, or stabilizing to do. Diddling around with evil with no guide but my novitiate self qualifies on none of those counts. Admirable pluck you evinced last month, mate. Badass General Sherab, Supreme Commander of Tibetan-American Forces in the Himalayas—he don't take no shit from demons, *do* he! Stuff him in a dank 14' by 35' isolation cell 24/7 throughout a raging storm for a couple of months and he'll just get stronger confronting evil the whole while.

Whoops.

They don't train you for this in SAR, the military, or anywhere else I know of, unless maybe that's what those original Bon demonmeisters were up to. I know I wasn't ready for hovering near so many souls on the verge of committing evil and being unable to do a damn thing about it. As an SAR vet, being utterly powerless to rescue the victims nearly kills me.

Easy to be a virus examiner when you're enjoying a quadrillion times size advantage in a clean lab with colleagues, smooth jazz, and a vending machine down the hall—but stare long enough at the working innards of sick souls committing unspeakable evil and you can fall into a vortex with the sucking power of the bloody one swallowing El Salvador. Your own blood will beg to be spared having to circulate through a brain taking in such god-awful sights.

Night after night I've witnessed souls scarfing down eviola and perpetrating acts of repellent, degrading, deadly violence on victims they see through the windshields at the front of their soulspaces. A head-sized eviola virus hovers in front of them, offering to penetrate. "Bite me," eviola seems to hiss, "you know you want to." And the twisted soul does, a host welcoming its positor visitor, embracing the injector with its mouth, opening its innards to receive eviola's gushing, poisonous RNA. The host invites the virus to remake itself hundreds of times over, a process reflected in ugly pustules breaking out all over his inner face and body as he springs into mayhem action, his eyes bulging with sick pleasure as he carries out atrocities upon the gagged, screaming mercy-pleading victims of rape, limb-chopping, and gunshots to the head.

I can see why the world's arranged so that, even though everyone knows such mayhem goes on, no one witnesses such a varied array of it night after night. It's too much to take. A couple of nights ago I saw a guy in a dark alley fill himself up with eviola and stab the prostrate body of some bloke trundling home from a pub. Twenty times. The night before last I saw a European in uniform joining his comrades on a firing line killing unarmed civilians lined up against a village silo and dumping the carcasses, not all quite dead, into a mass grave. Must be some war going on over there I don't know of. His face was so scarred by eviola pustules it took a moment to locate his eyes—a hideous appearance so unlike anything I've ever seen in photographs of criminals that it's obvious these eviola pustules are visible only within the perpetrator's soulspace.

In one incredibly bizarre scene eleven nights ago, I saw a white man about thirty struggling with another man in a dingy apartment with photos of mangled bodies on the wall. He'd managed to get some handcuffs on one of his victim's wrists and was trying to stab him with a butcher knife, but the captive knocked him down and escaped the apartment. I watched as the solopsycho ran around his apartment in a panic. He lifted the lid on a barrel to check on a decomposing corpse. He opened his refrigerator where he was storing a human head. He scurried around uncovering other body parts, skulls, penises, hands. I had to steel myself against vomiting and I retreated. That one was the worst.

On second thought, there can't be any true worst in the league of pseudo-human eviola suckers. The nazis (I won't dignify "nazi" with capitalization) earned the mass murder championship but they cared too much about clipped German efficiency to take personal time to draw the baths of evilsick horror relished by the Salvador death squads. I didn't want to mention this before, but, to illustrate the point, the pride and joy of one team of Salvadoran death-squadders was a work of horror art mounted in a jungle hut in which they propped up the bleeding headless corpses of a family they'd just decapitated around a dining table and placed the victims' heads on plates in front of their bodies (with the baby's little off-balance hands nailed onto its own head) and a bowl of blood as the table's centerpiece.

That was their kicker, a vicious, permanent, life-shortening, visual assault on the relatives and neighbors who would discover the slayings. For those death squads, perpetrating evil is motive as much as means. Quashing the rebel movement in El Salvador was a convenient excuse for the gang to take a long, satisfying swig of eviola. Doubtless it was a similar thirst slaked by the automata who buried my father alive. They must have dug it, because, I can't see anybody doing something so ghastly to another human being as a mere counterinsurgency tactic. As far as they knew, there weren't any other Tibetans around to frighten, so it couldn't have been to intimidate the enemy. No, they *got off* on it. They were brutaliphiliacs.

Special thanks to the cave's former tenant for bequeathing to me the painted mandala that adorns my back wall. It never fails, but when I get up the gumption to take a candle to it, I find yet another sooty bon-bon. Like last night's find down in the lower right corner: a tiny colored image of a demon pouring something awful into the crotch of a prostrate, naked woman, while other demons busy themselves nearby sawing off body parts of other anguished victims and cook up a cauldron full of heads. Ah, but there's an uplifting Buddhist Bound-Over message in it after all, by golly—good ol' Shakyamuni is redeeming some of the karmically challenged with golden threads, transporting them up from their hells on an ascending cloud. Go, Shak! Undunk those sinners from the Lake of Fire.

Well, forgive me, bound-over believers, if I'm not sold on your assurances of the benevolent intentions of the wrathful deities. Now that I'm living in a home equipped with satellite evilvision, I don't believe that any abiding managed by the original Tibetan monster painters was all that calm. These images smack more of desperate self-therapy, calls for help, visual screams of alarm—anything but a bodhisattva's reminiscences of sweet samadhi. Witness the power of faith: here's an entire culture so self-bamboozled it overlooks the emperor's lack of clothes *and* his bug-eyed, buggering, ox-headed perpetual perpetration of rape.

Hell, sometimes I wonder if that thing on my back wall *is* a painting. More than once I've been convinced that the eyes of that fat, six-armed, skull-draped, blood-licking Heruka in the center are following me around the cave as it crooks its finger at me. "Come," it beckons. "You're ready for your initiation. Enter charnel grounds at night and dig up skulls to lace around your neck. Encrust your body with a carapace and surround yourself with flames. Grow your toenails and fingernails ten inches long and file your canine teeth into sharp spikes." When I caught him looking at me last night in a crack of lightning, I leapt out of bed and roared right back in his face, mimicking his hideous dance moves and screaming curses at the top of my lungs. I can play your wrathful deity game, you vile bastard! But Heruka just cackled in derision at my pitiful chest-puffing. I scurried to the cave entrance and scooped up handfuls of mud to slap on the wall and cover him up, only to watch it drip to the ground as if Heruka himself had pushed it away to make sure I'd be lanced by his laughter.

Okay, mud was dumb. I should get some paint and cover up the damn thing for good.

Oh, that's smart. Stop by the nearest the paint store, cart a gallon all the way up this mountain, and destroy a painting that has eluded destruction from all elements including humans for at least a century because you can't handle living with an image of a Tibetan demon while on a mission to understand the meaning of Tibetan demons.

When I was a kid, my intellect pleaded with my fears that the wood grain ghost I saw on my closet door couldn't really have been moving toward me when I'd stare at it. Now I'm wondering if it really *was* moving, presaging the haunting lying in wait in my future. Before dawn this morning, when the downfall had the nerve to turn to snow for an hour—in August!—I became convinced that if I had the guts and tools to examine enough of those snowflakes I'd find some microdemons in white crystal disguise entering the world from another dimension, pre-coded with instructions that only the eviola-infected can decipher.

Maybe there's a good reason after all for not trucking with Tibetan mysticism without the guidance of a guru. I really don't know shit about the fire I'm playing with up here, and I can't turn for help to the guy next to me on the bus because this bus is a driverless Hell Express and I'm the only passenger on board.

Gotta face it: I'm a raw, foreign, self-drafted rookie. I've put myself in play in the Terror Bowl only to find I don't have either the chops to stay in or a clue how to get out.

Well, I've got to bail, that's all. Wimpy chump-shame be damned, I'd evacuate to the village right now if trekking through this downpour weren't tantamount to suicide. My dying in a mountain storm fall would cheer my mother's ghost about as much as my running into a hail of Red Army bullets screaming "Free Tibet!" But the moment it clears enough so I can count on at least two good hours, that would give me enough time to descend past the steepest terrain and from there I could make it the rest of the way even in hard rain if I have to.

Of course, if and when I do make it down to the village, there's the problem of explaining my showing up there like a mad, drenched wraith. I could pretend I was on a supply run, even though the only supplies I need are the sights and sounds of real people in the flesh. Normal people, healthy and loving people.

I can cart down some squash to trade and tell everybody I liked the exercise. Wouldn't have to tell anyone what I've been going through.

Are you kidding? Uncle Yeshe probably knows *right now*, and everyone else could see it in my face the moment I show up.

Enough. If you're gonna sail solo across the ocean, you can't complain in the middle of it that you want to find a nearby Club Med to chill out at for a few days till the weather mellows out. Break off this spiritual mission and you're a failure, just another hapless sperm that never makes it to an egg. No can do.

By the way, that enchanting mergoddess I'm not supposed to be thinking about? Thank God she isn't here to witness my disintegration. What a dream-crashing would be there, my romantic fantasy cracking open like a tasty-looking farm-fresh egg with nothing inside but a cockroach.

I gotta get some mercy here.

Take heart—there's more than mercy about. I sense a small blinking light in the darkness, trying to remind me that sometimes "That Others May Live" has to be applied to ourselves, that somewhere in the back room of my mind I can scrape up enough residue of the right stuff to make it through. Cardinal Rule #1 cannot be followed by anyone who too easily abandons hope. If I just take each hour as it comes, I shall prevail.

[2-9]

<u>Aug. 16 - Grand Central Nervous System, Tibet</u>

All right, I had a rough spell. I was under monsoon fire. That was a couple of weeks ago; no need to dwell on it.

Gotta thank God for scientific analysis and physical endurance for enabling me to avoid collapse. And while I'm at it, thank God for the beauty of the night skies when the clouds have deigned to clear away for a few minutes and allow my eyes and soul to take a Perseids meteor shower. Visual bliss.

As I was saying before I rudely interrupted myself, I've been pursuing post-midnight basic research with a view towards developing eviola infection prevention strategies. This is not a new wing of the peace movement. There are good fights, and the people who've stepped up to fight them, like the Tibetan resisters and the Allies in World War II, have been heroes vital to the restoration of justice. But noble warriors are like a pack of smart wolf puppies who've managed to haul a few pots of creek water to douse little spots of a forest fire that's burning a thousand square miles. Both efforts are short-term, temporizing measures when viewed against the backdrop of what's really needed, which is taking down evil itself, a big picture challenge requiring vision, intelligence-gathering, logistics, and execution no one has yet imagined. The very concept of ending evil is so alien, I've never heard it mentioned. Ever. We've got to get our act together as a species if we're ever going to see a headline about the virus of evil like the one I saw in high school—*Smallpox Eradication Completed.*

For that, we'll have to avoid confusing eviola with biological viruses, microbial rapists that take their victims by surprise. Eviola is a mindless spiritual virus with no more good or evil properties than a stone. Eviola merely presents itself and awaits an invitation from its host, who can choose whether or not to inhale the virus and commit a vile act.

My research is all about that choice. Freed of the mimicry and hoary paradigms shackling institutional labs, I don't have to pay obeisance to conventional wisdom, like those who regard genetics as a one-stop explanation store for everything under the sun. When I worked at the CMC lab, I heard about the 1960s fad theory that XYY chromosomal abnormalities led to violence in males. The theory had already gone bust by then, but even had it proven true, all it suggested was that the XYY anomaly correlated with a "tendency" toward violence. It certainly wouldn't help explain violence in women, one of whom I witnessed a few nights ago stuffing coins in a baby's throat to make it stop crying, which it proceeded to do once it stopped breathing. Permanently. Even in men, what could an increased statistical likelihood have told us? A tendency is neither a guarantor of an effect nor a causal mechanism. A genetic tendency might have reflected a statistical frequency with which *some* commit an act of evil violence, but there's all the difference in the world between doing it and not doing it. Those geneticists, like all fundamentalists, got tripped up trying to explain everything through the lens of a single belief system. Blaming bad genes for evil reflects a witlessness on the level of those who don't get it that "The debbil made me do it!" is a joke.

The devil is a fabricated scapegoat, a primitive construct like the god of the hunt. There is no god of the hunt, any more than there's a god of the touchdown. I never thanked God when I made it into the end zone; I thought it would be insulting to God to think that he had nothing more important to attend to in the whole universe than whether I helped put another six up on the board against Rangeley High. Devil tales are comfort food cooked up by cynical, manipulative opportunists for consumption by the simple-minded and weak-kneed who can't accept that regular people *choose* to commit evil acts of their own will. Blaming it on Beelzebub cradles them in the assurance that evil is a force external to humanity that can be escaped or defeated through brainwashing, exorcism, or holy war. Too scary the truth, that it all comes from the souls you might encounter on the street, in your home, or in yourself.

Well, grow up, Virginia—there is no Satan. But the good news is that the worst evildoers are different from you and me. The worst are not simply defective members of our species: they constitute a distinct species that co-exists with *homo sapiens sapiens*, similar in appearance but lacking the functional immune system capable of resisting eviola, the respect for life instinct that characterizes a true human. They're freaks of nature with severe congenital spiritual deformities.

Maybe that's what the Tibetan demon painters, the world's most lurid religious depicters of evil, were getting at from the beginning. Maybe they buried the truth in plain sight, placing a terrifying demon in the center of their thangkas as code for the locus of evil germination lying in the center of the evildoer's soul, a visual clarion call to future generations seeking to eradicate spiritual plague to look within.

Well, I've heard the call and I'm bringing to the table a scientific outlook. Regardless of what the National Academy of Sciences might think, I'm positive that the research I'm engaging in here is as central to the understanding of life as Darwin's. Darwin focused mainly on biological evolution and speciation leading from the amoeba to *homo sapiens*; I'm focusing on the continuing evolution and speciation within the genus *homo* that, over thousands of years, has led to the rise of a species alongside *homo sapiens* that ingests eviola and manifests soulpox. It takes centuries of brainwashing or dull-witted sheep-thinking to believe that the vermin who nailed the Salvadoran baby's hands to its severed head are organisms of the same species as Florence Nightingale or Uncle Yeshe.

I've named this other species *homo anipoxis*. Even the vast nazi plague inflicted only a small fraction of the harm done to the human species by anipoxi throughout history. Their strain must be brought to an end.

To pull it off, we need to get a handle on some basic questions, like what are the different forms of soulpox? In what ways are they fundamentally the same? How and why did the disease arise in the first place? And why has Nature—okay, God, The Creator, whatever—

forced these two species to contend with each other? Nature's intricacies are so elaborate and well worked out, I can't help wondering if there's a *reason* for forcing a sentient species endowed with a fundamental respect for life to live under an omnipresent threat of the most atavistic predatory behavior of animals.

Like what? The Creator's own personal amusement?

Okay, let's call that Opposing Tropism Theory #1: The Creator gets off on the drama of it all, maybe like an opera fan.

Grand, soap, or space?

All three in one, must-see cosmovision special.

Maybe it's all a careless comic toss-off. The Creator splits its sides laughing at us every day.

Enh…keep brainstorming.

All right, OTT #3: Meltdown. The grand experiment of intelligent life has spun out of control. The Creator is not amused to find out that Its invention ain't worth nothin' but a God damn.

So God made a rock too big for God to move?

Lame. #4 please.

Unfinished and Abandoned Project. The world we're all so wound up about is just one minor forgotten mess-up, like some faulty substrate I might have made in the microbiology lab that didn't look right and got dumped in the biowaste bin. Just because it went down the drain didn't stop the chemistry between the reagents carrying on on their own.

Dumped and forgotten? That's big league nihilism, worse than being laughed at for eternity, or for whatever time we've been allotted.

Okay, here my best shot: OTT #5—The Preoccupied Gardener. The Creator set this hybrid experiment in motion like a gardener crafting a wide variety of new candidate species to feed Its insatiable curiosity. Basic research on the grandest scale. We're one of thousands or trillions of intelligent animal species planted in Its cosmic garden. Our outcome is of real interest to The Creator, as part of a larger data set It's compiling. Whether It cares about or even notices every sparrow's fall, or even notes the fall of so fine a sparrow as Ghandi, or just checks up on us every month or millennium or so in the rotation will have to remain unknown for the foreseeable future, but the results do matter to Its Holiness.

I dunno, pal. I think there might be something else going on here. If that last scenario is right, it doesn't tell us whether evil is just an accident or a phenomenon with a real purpose in the grand scheme of things.

Let me get back to you on that.

I do think my chances of success in finding the answer would be enhanced if I had a partner, one whose strength, like mine, must be potentiated through the fitting together—

Drop it.

A momentary slip. I'll keep compiling data on my experimental work with an open mind, as behooves a good researcher. If I can't manage a breakthrough by summer's end, I may have to accept that the challenge is beyond me at this time in my life and move on to something else.

[2-10]

<u>Sept. 3? (losing track) NH (Still)</u>

Here's a handy hint, Himalayan campers: if you want to see no evil, seek no evil. Because seek and ye shall find works real well up here, and what you find might deliver a hard kick to your viscera.

Case in point from last night—I had the displeasure of spying on a guy pacing back and forth in his soulspace, snarling at his TV that provided the only light in his street-level apartment. On screen was a newscast showing a gang killing someone, cheering each other on in some Latin language I could barely make out—Spanish or Portuguese, I couldn't tell which. Then the sound was drowned out by the throaty roars of a mob thundering down the street. A thrill shot through my subject's body. He grabbed a lead pipe he had stashed by the door and ran out in the street, where he saw twenty or thirty men chasing down three teenaged boys dressed in rags, running for their lives. He joined the mob, smacked one of the kids in the neck with the pipe, ripped off the kid's pants, and yanked three wallets out of his pockets. A couple of the men had brought ropes and a momentary tussle ensued as to which one they would use, while the kid, who couldn't have been more than thirteen, blubbered something like *"Por favor me perdoe!"* My subject stepped forward, yanked one of the ropes out of the hands of one of the combatants, and looped it around the kid's neck. He was so excited fashioning a crude noose that his hands trembled. Another lyncher shinnied up a lamp post and called for the rope; in seconds, the boy's jerking body was casting a swinging shadow on the street.

At various points before getting myself from the Rockies to the Himalayas I envisioned myself in a bunch of different roles with respect to evil—amateur scientist, pastor, cop, coach, detective, rescuer. But now that I've spent two and half months up here encountering evil almost every night as it unfolds, I realize I've become none of those. I'm just a helpless, useless voyeur, and I don't like it.

In the absence of anything constructive to do for my subjects' victims, I've channeled my frustration into a taxonomy of evil. Out of habit and predisposition, I take some comfort in organizing troubling, inchoate thoughts through the familiar process of classification. Classification makes us science vets—no matter how low a rank we might have held upon discharge from the service—feel like we're gaining mastery over whatever phenomenon of the natural world has preoccupied us. But that faux mastery can be redeemed only by the real thing. How long can we cower away from taking on the phenomenon that's caused more suffering than all others throughout history? And how long can we shield ourselves from the humiliation of cowering behind the cover story that evil is an inextricable part of the human condition?

I'd rather face evil head on and see what might be done to clean its clock, maybe disassemble it altogether. I'm analyzing it to formulate a strategy of attack, like a field marshal in a battlefield tent plotting maneuvers by lantern light.

This will take more time to lay out—maybe more time than I can stand immersing myself in this misery—but I've started by noting the various motivational triggers of evil acts: Power. Greed. Hatred. Brutaliphilia. Revenge. And various mixtures thereof.

For example, the guys in last night's lynch mob were brutaliphiles, all right, the way they practically creamed as they beat up the dumb street kid who thought he might secure himself his next week's food by picking a few pockets—but they weren't haters like the goons in the KKK. The Klansmen that reveled in the agony they inflicted on the victims of their game of unpin-the-balls-from-the black-man at their lynching parties—those guys threw off a stink of hate that lingered throughout much of the American South long after the perpetrators had gone underground, literally or figuratively.

And let's not forget the KKK's hater kin in Arabia. Last year, when the FBI investigated the Arab who assassinated the extremist rabbi Meir Kahane—himself not a killer but such a hater the Israeli parliament banned him from running for election on account of his anti-Arab racism—they raided the assassin's apartment and found papers linking him with a multimillionaire jihadist named Osama bin Laden with plans to blow up New York skyscrapers. *Skyscrapers.* You gotta have a mighty high concentration of eviola circulating in your blood vessels to murder thousands of innocent Joe Blows and Jane Does just trying to get through their day shuffling papers in a cubicle or washing dishes or bathroom floors in an office tower. And for what? The FBI couldn't find any clear demand behind it, like the Algerians trying to get the French to leave town. Seems the bin Laden gang just want to blow up skyscrapers full of Americans thousands of miles away. Think how many kids you could orphan in a few minutes blowing up a skyscraper. They must have.

Those who kill thousands of office workers in a few minutes and those who kill thousands of monks and peasants in a few years have differing proximate motives, just like the Medea who kills her own children, the uniformed meat robot torturer, the murdering rapist, and the weapons merchants fomenting war by corrupting politicians far from the front lines where their products slaughter civilians. But deep down they're doing the same, ultimately damned thing: welcoming eviola into their spiritual bodies and inflicting atrocities upon others, pouring poison into the veins of intelligent life. The challenge of global eradication of such a ubiquitous, pernicious phenomenon as evil will be colossal, but so would be victory. It would dwarf the defeat of the Axis powers and let the sun radiate a healthier, brighter future for all.

That said, I'm not sure how much more isolated intimacy with evil and fruitless attempts to push it back I can handle. I'd sure hate to bail—I'd feel like I'd failed to find what I came here to find, like I'd be retreating from the calling I heard in my father's letter empty handed. I can make it through the monsoon outside—it's showing signs of relenting already. I just hope I can weather the inside one too.

[2-11]

<u>Sept. Something (a few days after equinox?)   Au Revoir, Tibet</u>

The sun is setting further south every evening as the planet swings from advantage North to advantage South in solar favors bestowed on its hemispheres. It's time for most animals to get on the move and there's no sense in my being a hold-out. This adventure is ending.

Watching the smoke from what could be my last cook fire up here for a long time wend its way skyward, I'm knotted in ambivalence about abandoning the upper mast of this granite celestial schooner. There were some rough times, and I'm still far short of the embarrassingly ambitious goal I set for myself, but there were heavenly times aplenty. One occurred just ten minutes ago, when an eagle owl called out from overhead and I answered back in her language as best I could and saw her turn and fly back in my direction for a good two hundred yards before figuring she must have been imagining things.

More important, I've derived two findings from my study that will give me a jump start on this project when I return some day: Evil arises solely from a choice within a soul to allow itself to become infected and it is possible to observe the internal and external experiences of a soul from a distance. I don't claim to be the first to have made these observations; I suspect that quite a few seers came up with them long before me, perhaps a preponderance of them in these very mountains. Nor do I claim that my results have attained the status of scientific facts. But they do resonate sufficiently with common sense to merit preliminary respect in advance of proof. Science ultimately depends on solid facts, but there's a continuum stretching between ethereal fantasy and hard proof. Reason, judgment, instinct, and faith all come into play between those poles. In exploring uncharted territories like the soul and evil, I keep in mind the well-tempered wisdom of physicists who suspended judgment about Einstein's once outrageous declaration that mass can bend light until a solar eclipse provided proof of it.

The next chapter of my life should lead to greater momentum for the hunt for proof when I return. Life among people will help me figure out what makes them sometimes go wrong. Whether those people are in Tibet, Asia, or who knows where and how long it will all take, I'll find out when I get there, however many theres and years that might entail.

There are risks leaving before the job is done. I'll have to wrestle with suspicions of a failure of conviction. Exposure to too much standard issue reason could cool my ardor and persuade me that I'd been imagining things or that even if what I've discovered is real, that the answers I'm seeking are beyond human ken, like the beginning and end of the universe. Such doubts could leave me in limbo wondering forever if I've seen the light or forgotten it.

And I may take a detour into family life. If that happens, I may never return, except perhaps as a wistful tourist with my family in tow— oh look, children, there's the cave where Daddy lived for a while when he was young and foolish and idealistic. Hell, that might even be the way it should be. Maybe I'm not cut out to take this all the way. Maybe I won't even want to. Solitary spiritual investigation taketh away as much as it giveth, no? There must be a lot to learn from your kids you can't get otherwise.

You can't have it both ways. I don't care what Siddhartha Gautama or Swami Whatchamathingamajig did. I credit the Buddha with scoring some of the greatest spiritual insights of all time, but here's one ball he fumbled: forty-nine days of enlightenment under a bodhi tree ought to clue you in that it's not cool to walk out on your wife and newborn son. I don't know whether I'm going to take on fatherhood or not, but whichever hand I bet on, I'm going all in.

Now hold on a minute—it needn't be so cut and dried. The Hindus figured out that a man can have a full life raising a family and participating in a community before joining the pro sage league. Maybe I'll come back here when I'm sixty. With my wife, even.

Well, trying to plan it all out is an exercise in futility. Life's unpredictable even if you stay put in your home town working at the community college for forty years; it doesn't get any less so combatting evil across the world by soul projection from the Himalayan wilderness.

Whatever the risks, I've reached Impasse Pass and it's time to turn back. I'm trained to recognize exhaustion, and here it is. Not physically—nothing like the exertions of no-frills homesteading in the wild and countless miles hiked in thin air on steep trails to put you in great shape—but spiritually. And, frankly, emotionally. For a guy under thirty with a history of ample socializing, I'm not bad at handling solitude, but I've got my limits. Bully for the high-altitude elder sage who can sit in a cave for months at a time without fluttering an eyelid as insects treat his flesh like a smorgasbord delicacy—that's not me. I'm hungry for the sight and sounds of other humans—and yes, the touch, smell, taste, and mind of a woman with entrancing eyes.

As for the vexation that befell me on account of one such woman I met under the surface of the Pacific seven months ago, I've gotten that under control. It doesn't help to deny the attraction I felt—it was the real deal—but I've still got seventy years in my wallet and I'm not going to spend them on sighs. You lose something, even something very valuable, let it recede into the past. You still have to keep your eyes forward so you don't trip over a snag or a sleeping leopard.

I realize it won't be easy to find someone to fill the vacuum left by the disappearance of Calieze, but I've got to do it. This isn't about getting my rocks off (okay, not only about that). My plan up here has been flawed from the beginning by being designed as a male-only mission. The same goes for the ancients' teaching that a man should seek his enlightenment after he's done with his family. First off, that ignores the woman's enlightenment. But the main thing is, those ancients must have had third-eye cataracts: how else could they fail to see that the quest for spiritual revelation might work *even better* when pursued *with* your love instead of without her?

Hominids have produced some striking improvements mixing and matching male and female genes over the last few hundred millennia, so it makes sense that spiritual evolution might enjoy the same kind of acceleration by mating the spiritual genes of the two genders. Seems to me that must have been the Creator's plan from the beginning. It's bizarre how few have caught on to it. (I don't count among the recognizers any conniving Sri Svengali hawking yabyum yoga as he works his lingam into a gullible "consort" who ends up more enlightened than he, at least as to what constitutes an exploitative jerk.) I admit it's just a theory, but I intend to put it to the experimental test of a lifetime as soon as I can find the right collaborator.

I'll look everywhere for such a partner, if I must. (Almost everywhere—Hawaii and Colorado have been scratched. No *Vertigo* obsessions, please, or moping in saloons surrounded by rheumy guys draining mugs of Coors bellowing at the Broncos.) Maybe I'll go down to Australia. Or Africa. Any place where I can check out more of the world and give my brain a break after a tempestuous summer's work.

I'll start moving this strategy into play tomorrow. Except for the gardens and a few supplies I'll stash neatly here in the cave as a courtesy for its next denizen, I'll cover all traces of myself.

This book? Might as well leave it here—it's about full and it's done its job. My folks had the right idea about the power of a keepsake: leaving it somewhere important can serve to remind you to come back for it another day.

There's the first glimmer of Scorpio's cat's eyes, heading toward the spot where the sun just slid over the horizon. Sometimes I can't escape the feeling that they're watching me, awaiting my next move, and have been all along, as if—

—Hm. Thought I heard something.

Well—I did. Like steps. Somewhere down the "trail." A most unfamiliar sound, and not like the marmot's scurrying I heard uphill from me last week.

Hey, let your imagination live it up. Soon enough you could be places in Delhi or Bombay where you won't be able to hear yourself think.

Yeah…but…I thought I heard steps. Never thought about what I'd do if another person showed up.

A shepherd, maybe? Nobody who cared about his animals would drag them up a treacherous mountainside to some place as pastureless as this. The only eats around here are insects, tree bark, leaves, and my garden to which they would not gain admittance. Besides, no shepherd could get within half a mile of this place without my hearing his flock bleating.

Equally unlikely would be anyone out to make trouble. That never even occurred to me in a place so opposite of Delhi and Denver.

Maybe it's Yeti, at last!

…Okay…Someone is walking down to the left and he's getting closer. I'd just as soon not have to make Tibetan small talk with anyone. Would he have to know I'm here?

How could he know that? And if he knows I'm up here, why would he approach?

Hunger?

Who would come out this far without food? Makes no sense.

Whoever the hell he is, he's coming this way. I'm going down there to face him. Gently. If he doesn't know I'm here, I'd hate to trigger a mortal shock.

[2-12]

9/27/91
New Hale, Tibet

The esteemed author of the preceding work of autobiographical research has asked me, a newcomer and humble servant of Lord and Lady Nature—

—Cut the false modesty, love goddess—

—Pipe down, bub. Act like an esteemed author.

As I was saying, I have been asked to provide an afterword for the author's account of his fascinating travails in pursuit of a fundamental secret of the universe from the highlands of Tibet, and it is my great pleasure to do so (as, I must say, there has been a great deal of pleasuring in the last thirty-six hours).

Is that documentarian lingo for a sexual marathon?

Ahem. This peer-reviewed journal has taken a personal turn. Granted, our brains, once exercised out, have repeatedly raced back in for yet another go with the insistence of ball-fixated retrievers, but they have proven multi-faceted—

—I didn't mean to suggest that's all we've done.

Nor I. I have much enjoyed getting acquainted with Mr. Sherab's anterior lobes every bit as much as I fancied after being obliged to abandon him at the sun-dappled surface of the Pacific seven months ago. And he appears to be sufficiently taken with our conversations to invite me on a still-to-be-revealed mission he has begun here in New Hale. We shall therefore need to find another volume to record the progress (and setbacks) in our research partnership, one that is bound to take us places we can scarcely imagine.

I love you and I thank you for every step you took to get here.

My pioneer patient is pleased with my house call, and I am equally grateful to him for having provided me last March with a crucial hint as to his future whereabouts.

I tried for months to convince myself this trip was all about groundwork for a nature documentary on bar-headed geese, but that illusion has concluded its service and gracefully retired. In hindsight, my life, that had seemed so scattered over so many parts of the world now appears to have been heading straight here from the beginning.

My life up to the day before yesterday feels like a disguised prologue to a God-knows-what of staggering proportions.

Even God might not know. Perhaps it will be our job to help him find out. For now, however, this being the bottom of the last page, my initial report is concluded.

Cali Zigana Moss, out.

Terma Two

[3-1]

Chk out Canadian B. Lishman plan to lead young geese in their 1ˢᵗ migration w/ ultralight aircraft

9/28/91
Evening, New Hale Cave
CZM

I've left the sentence fragment at the top of this page as a salute to the thirty pages of ideas and data I'd compiled over the last month, while this notebook was still serving its original purpose: notes pertaining to my documentary film from conversations with Asian ornithologists, regional video production outfits, and Chinese travel and communications bureaucrats. Now, with the radical change in circumstances that's exploded before my bedazzled eyes in the last three days, those pages had to be removed so that the book can be redeployed to another mission *entirely*. Bar-headed geese, I still love you, but we're taking the project in very different direction, setting it in spectral cumulonimbus clouds and the mouth of a Himalayan cave.

Rain, in what may be its last hurrah for the year, has forced us indoors—doors? there's no door for miles around—inside, and led me to take up Den on his suggestion that I record some impressions from the recent and distant past. I've not read any of his journal other than that one page we shared way back 1½ days ago, so I'm not sure what he's after, but since it was more of a request than a suggestion, I'll give it my best shot. He's set me up with a yak fat candle at the back of his limestone domicile and I've settled in for the flow, here in the middle of nowhere above everywhere.

I once shot video of pond salamanders for a film on forest creatures of the American Northwest. There were bundles of them engaged in a silent rite, at least a dozen of them tangled in a ball. I felt like we'd stumbled upon a secret society's most sacred and profane annual ceremony. Weird, but the forces that combined to land me on this mountainside seem just as tangled and mysterious as the creatures in that ball, going about their respective business without regard for what others deem normal.

Among the few who might not have been surprised by my story I must count my late parents. Surely a pair of holocaust refugees who found soul mates in each other, despite having emerged from such drastically different backgrounds as theirs, could expect that their only child would create an exotic life for herself. They understood that what gets beaten out of beaten paths is life's luster.

A few weeks ago Rajasthan offered me a dollop of the exotic that tasted oddly familiar even though I'd never been there before. My arrival there felt like the natural completion of a millennium-long circumnavigation, beginning with the departure of my mother's Roma ancestors from North India, migrating westward at millipede speed through their subsequent diasporas in Western Asia, Europe, the Near East, and "the New World," en route to East Asia to dig for my roots. A strange story made all the stranger since every other gene in my cell nuclei came from my father's bloodline of Hungarian Jews, a very non-Indian people who, distinct as they were from the Roma, nonetheless faced similar, parallel struggles with violent bigotry that eventually converged in the genocidal labor camps at Birkenau.

Fortunately that shared history of sorrow produced a shining silver thread—my parents' meeting in the newborn state of Israel, where their eventual marriage led to my birth in the Caribbean and my upbringing in some of the world's most colorful habitats, including India, where I spent some of my childhood with a Tibetan nanny while my father did soil science research for the UN. Recollections of that enchanting time stirred a longing in me to get back to Asia ever since. For the last half-year that quest has been bound up in a scheme to produce a television special on bar-headed geese, Nature's ace aviators of the Himalayas. Someday I just might make that movie, but for the time being, that project has been shunted aside by enticing mysteries crooking their fingers at me from the cave shadows of Tibet, beckoning me to step up my explorer game in the company of a startlingly exciting man named Terma Den Sherab.

I owe a debt of thanks for this felicitous turn of events to the rotund member of a Hawaii client's diving party who got himself into a tussle with his oxygen gear in a rather scary underwater emergency last March. I had the situation minimally under control, buddy-breathing for real for the first time as I tried to guide the man to the surface, but it was touch and go—until, out of nowhere, a hard-bodied human dolphin appeared and, with a commanding mix of reassurance and skill, lent patient assistance to our ascent. His evident strength—from the looks of him, he could have lifted my two hundred and fifty pound charge as if he were no heavier than a dog toy—reassured me that our rescue would succeed. I've proven myself sturdy in crises in the past, but not without suffering youthful memory tremors of one that convulsed my life in a hail of bullets fired on a New York street. This time though, it was smooth sailing, confidence and elation. My masked man and I took turns sharing our air supplies with our panicked pal for a short time and we were home free.

My father had admonished me long before that drinking holes are undesirable places to make the acquaintance of a man. Better to keep your eyes open at work, he said, where a guy had to have passed some kind of professional muster and would share some fundamental interest with me. How prescient, Dad. I was on a job composing a backlit shot of a Yankee yachtsman's fiancé communing eye to eye with a sea turtle when circumstances led me to a grinning, fascinating, dashing Amerasian hunk with a consuming passion for Tibet. I was strained, wanting to swim with him and knowing I had to return to my diving party, a tension I resourcefully resolved by grabbing a shot of his shoulder, where he'd conveniently emblazoned his destination, the name of his father's village—a helpful clue I figured could come in handy some day in case I couldn't get him out of my mind.

A couple of weeks after that sparkling encounter, I dropped off a rented camera housing with a ballast release system at the Waikiki Marine Photo Shop and the clerk relayed a message from some guy named TD Sherab who had called for me, asking if I would be so kind as to leave my contact information for him at his old work number in Colorado. I'd been wondering whether Mountain Man was with someone. Clearly he'd been attracted to me—men can't disguise that very well, much as they might fumble about pulling a hat down to shade their googly-eyes—but that didn't mean he was single. However, he was diving alone and seemed to be going to Tibet on his own, so it was unlikely that he was up to his eyeballs in a relationship. And now he'd asked for my number. Ooookay…

So, flitting unknowns notwithstanding, I dialed the number and reached a national park ranger who'd heard that TD had checked in by phone a few days before, inquiring as to whether I had left a message for him. Hoping to ingratiate myself with the ranger to glean clues to TD's whereabouts, I engaged him in some small talk, during which he told me, "TD Sherab is something of a legend around here. It's not unknown for locals to check in with mountain rescue to know if TD is going to be on duty before setting out on a risky climb. He's been offered some hefty rewards by grateful rescuees."

"Offered?"

"Offered, not accepted. He asks them to contribute instead to the non-profit outfit that trains our rescue dogs and cares for them in retirement."

That missed connection tinged my imaginary reunion as both more desirable and less likely. Nothing to be done about it, though—internal regulations forbid obsessing over a romantic phantom and inflating simple coincidences into auspicious omens, much less embarking on a globe-trotting manhunt. I accepted that I'd probably have to chalk it up to an intriguing near miss.

At the same time, I didn't have to extinguish the fantasy altogether. There was a perfectly sensible rationale to advance my film career with a project that just happened to take me to Tibet. I'd been wanting to produce a TV nature special, running my own show for the first time. The subject: the world's highest-flying migrators, the geese who gaze down upon Mount Everest from the jet stream on high. Everybody loves geese—they're the dogs of the bird world. A natural nature flick, thought I. So I crafted a two-front strategy: Between shooting nature docs and scuba tourists in Hawaii, I'd keep fattening my savings account, while at the same time putting together a proposal for my own show that one of the new cable stations focusing on nature might fund to the tune of $275K. Plus, I'd make it into the film record books as one of the first female executive producers in a genre overrun by guys. Come on, sisters—we shouldn't cede all those rich natural resources to men-folk, no matter how fair-minded and eco-friendly (or hot) they might be.

Heck, I didn't need a career excuse to go back to Tibet. Tibet is the sky-land of Bon deities I'd dreamt of returning to ever since my four-day glimpse of it in the company of my nanny fifteen years ago. Now, as an adult, I wanted to re-confront the demons that had so rattled the brains of my ancestors and me alike, demons I'd been riffing on in canvas, fabric, paper, and stone ever since I'd first seen their thrilling and frightening faces in their native land.

Further, the journey would afford me the opportunity to reconnect with my mother's ancestral people, who still inhabit Northern India. I've had an intense hunger for anything that could connect me with my mother ever since she was torn from my life by a drug-addled psychomaniac drive-by shooter on the Lower East Side.

We'd kissed my dad good-bye before she took me to school that morning, intending to continue on to the Ukrainian Community Center near my school, where she was doing social work for boatloads of recent immigrants, but neither of us got to our destinations. As we were laughing, recalling a goofy impersonation of our landlord Dad had done at dinner the previous night, rapid-fire explosions and screams ripped the air. My mother covered me with her body and dropped us to the ground. I could feel her lurch on the way down and when we hit the ground, I felt a warm liquid soak my hair. A moment later the explosions were over but the screaming intensified. I asked my mother if we could get up and run away but she didn't answer. Then a babushka mama pulled me out from under my mother with a look of tragic terror on her face and I looked down and saw blood on my sweater and skirt and a gaping hole in my mother's neck. As her blood drained into the gutter on Avenue B I took the lead in the hysterical screaming.

That recollection has raked me over its coals a million times and it still shakes me to the core. I believe that that soulless humanoid with the sawed-off shotgun was somehow connected to the evil killers of the ancient demonology of the East. He didn't know or care about collateral damage caused by his slugs as long as one of them nailed his sales turf rival. But I cared, especially since the one that passed through my mother went on to kill my father years later, when his heart finally gave out in exhaustion from the struggle to survive his grief over the loss of his beloved. Had he not been determined to live long enough to see me off to college, I doubt he'd have made it even twelve months.

Mother…I can feel your warm hand leading me from the island surf on St. Kitts through the forest of tall legs to our cottage. I hear your soft-accented Romani lullabies comforting me during the hurricane as you tucked me under my poinsettia print blanket, and your stories about the monkey god while we ate popsicles on summer nights up on the roof of our East Village apartment building. I remember the costume of Kali, "the goddess of positive destruction," that you made me for Halloween in New York, so crazy none of the other kids would go near me. You were just ahead of your time, Mom. Eight years later, while studying at the San Francisco Art Institute, I resurrected that costume for Halloween in the Castro, and I was the talk of the crowd, or at least of those crushed around me among the ten thousand other partiers jammed into two blocks.

I had to come back here. I sought new images to subdue the memory of the street crime atrocity that took her away from me at age eleven. At first those images hung me dangling into nightmares so wicked my dad had to take me all the way to India to escape the environment where they'd caught fire. But the demon killers came along for the ride. I'd imagine them popping up in cows' ears, toasters, seashells, candy wrappers, even hovering over the unwitting face of a baby in a pram being strolled on the boardwalk. Staring into the glowing charcoals of a bonfire on Juhu Beach, I pictured their eyes dilating and constricting as they pounded on the drums with all their huge ears, noses, and genitals, and poking out from behind the heads of people stealing glances at me on the bus. And later, in a club in San Francisco, when a mosh pit screamer went berserk, I felt sorry for him, because the wrathful deities assailing his soul brooked no mercy. I went up to him as security was taking him away, and shouted over the band's sonic hammer blows, "The demons are real, but you can overpower them!" And for just a moment, as they took him away, the screamer fell silent and looked me in the eye, thankful for one understanding touch.

It's no wonder I went to art school. I was a natural candidate for art self-therapy. Painting those deities made them mine. By forcing them to my will on canvas, I slowly but surely took command, until one day I realized I'd gone a full six months without a single nightmare of Yama the death god firing a shotgun at my mother. I'd been graced with a spell of inner peace.

Having then sustained that peace for more than six years called for a voyage to Asia to crown my achievement in psychological strength, to show that I can practice what I'd preached to the mosh pit screamer.

And there were the stratogeese, plying the heavenly winds, awaiting my tribute.

And, oh yes, there was that man who struck me as pretty damn heavenly as well, but I was awash in worthy goals, so I could pretend to ignore any ulterior motives darting around like archer fish just beneath the surface. What was wrong with printing out a frame from the video and showing the words on the guy's shoulder to my friend at the Tibetan art store in Mill Valley? Gnam Yuljongs, she said, Sky View. If my thoroughly legit, professional wild goose chase in the Himalayas *happened* to bring me through the town of Gnam Yuljongs, and if a Colorado search-and-rescue vet happened to be there at the same time, there'd be no harm in saying howdy. I had logic, expense, and ego covered regardless.

So I pounded out a preliminary proposal for a film to feature my star geese, pulled strings to get it to acquisitions people at a few cable networks to gauge their interest ("maaaybe" doesn't sound like much but it's enough to fuel the hopes of filmmakers), and threaded the needles at the Chinese and Indian consulates for my visas. The idea was to use this trip for pre-production research, checking out the local conditions and trolling for leads on local crew, equipment, and logistics (a sailplane pilot?) that I'd need for the full proposal when I got back. Now, who knows when that will be?

Not I. At the pace the adventure ride of the last three days has been pulling me, I can't spare a moment to lift my gaze much above the zinging now.

Indeed, my life had been speeding ever faster for weeks before I found myself in New Hale. I wasn't lolling about in a hammock in India. Like a hockey forward hip-checking an opponent, I deflected jet lag at the arrival gate in Delhi and forged ahead through the city's chaos to the train station, determined to touch down on four sites sacred at least to me, before heading into the Himalayas. But India hip-checked me right back before I could even board the first train, searing me with sights of destitution that should not be part of Earth's story.

I tried not to get overwhelmed by the skinny girl relieving herself of diarrhea in a busy street, the baby boy lying naked on a busy train platform with no one watching over him, and, alongside the tracks on the outskirts of the city, the gagging stink of a massive squat of homeless people permanently encamped in destroyed, roofless concrete hovels along a creek that multifunctioned as water source, sewer, and cemetery. It was heart-wrenching to realize that some of the parents trying to tend to their children in that bottom-level slum may well have spent their own childhoods in places like that. India must reckon every day with a population so huge I could match up an Indian for every American man, woman, and child, and still have a billion Indians left over. And hundreds of millions of those are buried neck deep in a swamp of poverty far beyond the imagination of most non-Indians, baking under skies that even when cloudless can be gray with pollution so thick as to make the green eco-projects of Western environmentalists look ludicrously futile. I had to shield myself against discouragement about the weight of the world's problems. It's a blessing to be able to help solve even one of them, which is impossible if you take in all of them.

So I took a guarded deep breath and kept a tight grip on my itinerary, the first stage of which took me to Rajasthan, the land of my mother's ancestors, where I came upon many a person with green eyes who I figured could be my tenth cousins. A Kabeliya woman I found dancing one afternoon for a crowd of tourists on the edge of Puskar enthralled me with the hypnotic swoops and swishes of her people-charming ceremony, as mysterious as the snake-charming exploits for which her people are celebrated. When we accidently locked eyes, I perceived a flash of germinal recognition in her face. Her all-male troupe of musicians, connected to her by long invisible neurons, caught on and gave me a look suggesting that my cross-bred features had given them something to wonder about.

At a melodic interlude in her dance, the performer startled me by sweeping over to me and pulling me into the center clearing, volunteering me to pick up some switchy dance moves. The crowd's cheers left me no room to escape, so I gamely spent a couple of minutes with her, acquitting myself without much embarrassment before bowing to my mentor in gratitude and making my exit.

At the fringe of the watching crowd, a little Indian girl about ten years old caught my eye. A bright-eyed sweetheart, her face lit up with a shy smile she tried to bury in her mother's sari. As the performers dissolved into the crowd, she persuaded her parents to bring her to talk to me.

Her name was Jyoti. She was on a family vacation from Bombay, where her father worked as a bank branch manager. We hung out for a while at a nearby tea stall, where Jyoti peppered me with questions about my life in far-off America, all in fluent, softly-accented English. "Where are you from?" she asked first, to learn the origin of such an unusual looking being (I being the only non-Indian around).

"Many places," I replied, " including India. I lived here when I was about your age." That finding excited her further, as if her native land, which she already loved, had suddenly become even more interesting.

Jyoti was especially intrigued to hear that I'd helped make movies about science and nature. Her parents observed their daughter's excitement with a mix of pride and unspoken reservations. Perhaps they were alarmed at the prospect of their unusually intelligent child getting too drawn to the wilds of America, where girls freely chose their own spouses and built careers far from the family kitchen. Nonetheless, they remained friendly and gladly facilitated an exchange of addresses when we parted.

My remaining three mini-pilgrimages connected me with an all-star triumvirate of architectural sculpture masterpieces. First was the Taj Mahal, an exquisite tomb built by a Mughal emperor for his beloved wife. Sadly, its magnificence has been marred by an Indian horror story centering on the emperor's evil son Aurangzeb, one of India's most vicious and loathed leaders, who called himself "Conqueror of the World" and went on a long killing rampage in an effort to impose his ultra-Orthodox version of Islam on the whole country. I wondered why humanity hasn't mustered the creativity and determination to prevent that kind of hideous mania from breaking out, over and over, down history's infinite hallways.

I found respite from that historic nightmare in the unsullied joy radiating from the beautiful, earthy sculptures created at Khajuraho half a millennium before the Taj was built, depicting myriad scenes of life lived fully, including some of the most explicit sexual imagery ever committed to a permanent record, all radiating Botticelli-grade classiness.

Last, I found my way to Ellora and its "caves"—literally a sculpted basalt mountain crafted by such artistic geniuses that calling them caves is like referring to the Sistine Chapel ceiling as colored lime mortar. At "Cave 10," I sat for an hour in the darkness at noon at the feet of the fifteen-foot high 8th century Buddha, letting him fill me with a cosmic grace I'll never forget. Unfortunately, I was also unable to forget Aurangzeb, and once again my joy in the exalting potential of humankind was pierced by sorrow for the cancer in its underbelly. Evilsickness keeps breaking out at so many times and places, how can one maintain the Ellora Buddha's bliss even by oneself, much less expect to see it spread through the world?

I bid the Ellora Buddha farewell and left for Tibet to get on with my date with bar-headed geese. With my papers accepted by Chinese authorities at the airport in Lhasa, I boarded a train to Xigaze, a hundred and sixty miles southwest. This being the end of summer, I still had weeks to locate flocks of the geese in their feeding areas on the Tibetan plateau. The south offered good sighting opportunities, and when a bus dispatcher told me he understood Gnam Yuljongs to be located there (thanks to a nephew of his at Tibet Vocational College who had a classmate from that village), I bought a ticket for the border town of Zham. There, a leather merchant I met in a Nepalese cubby-hole restaurant told me that his tanner periodically picked up yak hides from a Gnam Yuljongs trader. There was no road up there, he said, so he'd meet his connection by pre-arrangement at a trailhead some fifty miles back up the road I'd just come in on.

Outfitted with basic camping gear, food and water, and binoculars, I set out the next morning hiking north, as comfortable as if I were roaming a road in the Sierra foothills. I asked the occasional shepherd or truck driver I'd come across if, when, and where they recalled having seen bar-headed geese, and did they know happen to know where I might find a village called Gnam Yuljongs?

By mid-morning, I learned the location of the hidden pocket in which Tibet kept the Sherab family's ancestral home. A porter who'd been to Gnam Yuljongs himself a dozen times, offered to take me to the trailhead, so I hopped on the back of his sputtering motorcycle and held on for an hour-long wild ride in confidence spun from fantasy and high mountain air.

I disembarked at the trailhead, compensating my escort with a couple of apples. Before he'd disappeared into the vanishing point on the horizon, I was on my way up the trail. (The operational word there is up—that pass tops out around seventeen thousand feet, but I was energized by the vistas and heart-thumping anticipation.)

When I first sighted that jewel of a village inset in a pristine creek valley, I could hardly believe my eyes. I guess I'd subconsciously assumed that Gnam Yuljongs was an imaginary place, like Hobbiton— but, no, there were real homes and animals and people down there. It was charming, in the magical sense of the word. I told myself I didn't care a whit whether or not TD Sherab had ever set foot in the place. (Untrue, but it made me feel better to tell myself so.)

As I descended to the village, I could see the effect of my bow wave on some of the villagers who became aware, even at five hundred yards, that someone out of the ordinary was headed their way. I was greeted first by a woman named Kurukulla who was carrying a berry basket from the edge of a community garden at the end of the narrow strip of a path that stood in for Main Street. Her sweet, wrinkled, lighthearted Tibetan smile melted me.

Kurukulla introduced me to some of her neighbors, who deferred their curious questions until I was settled in the home she shared with her son and his family of four. They invited me to luxuriate in the village's clever shower house, a hot dinner of barley stew with a sampling of the yak cheese dangling from a line overhead, and a bed for the night, all of which I gratefully accepted.

Over dinner, I told them (with help from the English-speakers) about having come to Tibet as a girl and some of the stories my nanny had put me to sleep with featuring characters with names like Drashup and Nyema. I told them about my geese, which they see typically a couple of times a year, and the nature movie I had in mind. In a community consisting mostly of people who had never seen a television, that must have struck them like a mission to Mars.

Naturally I was asked how I'd heard about their village in far away Hawaii (which one of the kids thought was near Africa). The mention of Terma Den Sherab set off a whoop. One of the kids ran out of the house and returned a minute later with a boy and a girl and their mother, Sonam, who were Den's cousins and who had seen him a few months ago, before he moved higher up in the mountains, some unknown distance to the west. I asked what village he'd relocated to and got a laugh for an answer. No, no village, no people there, Terma Den all alone.

Really? I'd thought Den had come all this way from the States to get to know his father's family, but there must be more to it than that.

Sonam took me to meet her father, Yeshe. As it was late for him, I stayed only a couple of minutes for a little small talk but that was more than enough to be smitten with his gentle wisdom.

I returned to Kurukulla's to find conversation bubbling about the adventuress who'd made it all the way from America to Gnam Yuljongs after receiving a message from Terma Den. They were too polite to ask nosy questions but they exchanged twittering looks when I expressed an interest in hiking around the mountains to the west in the interest of avian filmmaking.

At one point that evening, I noticed Kurukulla staring at me across the lantern with yearning in her eyes. In smiling back, I slipped into her mind and found a yearning for what she perceived as the glamorous adventure of my life. I silently replied that I do enjoy my life but that I also envy her beautiful, settled family life and hope that some day I can create a scene so lovely myself. I swear I could see her eyes soften and relax in a breath of pride.

Ever since I was a girl there've been random incidents in which I seemed to have tripped into a telepathic connection with someone. I don't know why and I'm careful not to question it too much, as if I might scare away the hidden angel responsible for that ability. I just observe it once in a while and get on with the show.

Once the gathering's conversational surf had settled down to a few contented murmurs, everyone retreated to their various houses and beds. On a straw mattress with a yak fur blanket, I fell asleep in Gnam Yuljongs, Tibet, knowing that in the next few days I'd set eyes on wildlands called home by bar-headed geese and, along the way, either meet Den or get that handsome bug out of my system and move on. I'd found Den sufficiently alluring to check him out as long as it didn't pull me too far out of my way, but I was not head-over-heels infatuated with him. If he didn't turn up on this trek, sobeit. I was truly thrilled just to be in the Himalayas.

At least that was the tenor of my internal talk show during my ascending hike the next day. During a lunch break by a boulder-strewn creek crossing, I pondered what might happen if I did find Mr. Sherab. I was certain he wouldn't be dangerous to come across alone in the wilderness, but there could be other unfun possibilities. Maybe he'd turn out to be weird—you can't predict what happens to a guy who ties himself off from civilization for too long—but his family in Gnam Yuljongs were so enamored of him, that seemed unlikely. He could turn out to be a bit nutty or obsessive or sweet-dumb or just plain boring, but the recollection of our one, ocean-bobbing conversation marked those possibilities unlikely. And even if any of those scenarios did prove true, I'd still pat myself on the back for having gotten a brisk workout in a gorgeous wilderness and sharpen my mental and photographic focus on *anser indicus,* sightings of which were likely if I stuck around long enough. The thought that the man might materialize and turn out to be every bit as fetching as I'd imagined did tap on the windows of my mind periodically, but I was not going to let it in and start taking over the house. One step at a time. If that.

I allotted six days to this expedition; if I found neither goose nor guy after three full days, I'd turn back on the fourth morning. I felt rich with time and hiked along without hurry or even a glance at my watch, which I'd stashed in my pack. I set down the pack a couple of times for light-footed side trips up a creek and up to an outcropping that offered yet another spectacular view of the mountains sloping down toward the south. I scanned the skies with my binoculars, on the watch for geese like an aviation fan awaiting the arrival of the Blue Angels. I did spot a number of other fine birds through those lenses—a greater flameback, an eagle owl, and a few barbets—but no geese yet.

The sun touching the serrated western horizon signaled the start of camping hour. I found a serviceable flat spot for my tent by the rushing creek I'd been following all afternoon. I was brushing away little stones when an eagle owl called from a few hundred yards up ahead. There was an eagle owl out for an early constitutional to the south, but the call had come from the northwest, and when I looked in that direction, I saw a wisp of smoke curling up to the sky, rising from a spot about a hundred feet higher than the level strip I'd been using as a trail.

Smoke? Haven't seen any lightning—the sky's crystal clear. "Campfire" flashed on my dashboard.

Well, now: whose campfire might that be? Perhaps a shepherd had established a little outpost up there? But I'd seen no tracks or scat, nor heard any animal sounds for hours, save for that eagle owl, and eagle owls don't build campfires.

There was another possibility and it had to be investigated. I took a deep breath and began my walk uphill, leaving my gear to itself by the creek. I walked at a quiet, measured pace, careful not to alarm a campfire-capable eagle owl. After all, I really didn't know jack about who was up there. It might be (beware: former New Yorker thought) someone with a gun and a nervous trigger finger. But even if it were an unarmed shepherd or some entirely decent mensch, he might not be decent, if you catch my drift. Whoever he was sure valued his privacy and might be disinclined to entertain or even see visitors, even if he were TD and the visitor me.

When I came within a few hundred feet of the smoke, I heard a clink and rustling, as if someone had put down a pot and was moving about. Instinctively, I imitated the eagle owl call in a whistle, telegraphing the arrival of someone of good will.

A moment later a man appeared through the trees. Though more clothed and weather-roughened than the strong-armed angel who'd aided my ocean rescue efforts half a year before, there was no mistaking him: I'd found my man.

"Well, hello, Terma Den Sherab!" I called out airily, as if coming across him at the farmer's market in Sonoma He was gaping at me from between a pair of pine trees, his tongue apparently paralyzed. Helpfully inclined, I chirped "Calieze Moss."

His face projected a blend of elation and dread. Watching him shakily close his mouth for the first time since I'd appeared, I concluded he could use some added lift from his wilderness hermit confusion. "Hawaii—remember?" The dread drained out of his face, leaving behind a bright-eyed, wondering smile. He reached out a hand, as much to see if I were real as for a handshake. I removed my glove to take his hand and said "I'll take that as a yes."

Our touch jump-started his mountain man demeanor. He pulled himself together, managing an attempt at Gary Cooper cool betrayed by a touch of breathiness. "Calieze—what a welcome sight! But—forgive my curiosity—what in blazes are you doing up here? "

We let the handshake linger an extra instant while I answered, "What do you think, silly? Saying hi. I got your message from the photo shop in Waikiki and since I was in Tibet on a job, I thought, what a kick to stop by and see if you were in."

In the brief silence that followed, I smiled, listening to the spinning in Den's brain. When his clutch re-engaged, he came up with, "A job."

"I'm doing research for a nature film on bar-headed geese."

He processed that for a few seconds and the gears shifted again. "Hm. I'd like to hear about that, but I'm guessing you didn't hike all the way up here with nothing but the clothes on your back."

"My pack's about ten minutes downstream."

"Did you make camp already?"

"I was about to when an eagle owl with a campfire drew my attention."

He grinned. "Quite the naturalist. Well, look—you can spare yourself setting up in the cold dark and be my guest up here. There's room, and dinner's not far off."

Now I was spinning, figure skating in delicate balance. "You sure? I'm guessing that a guy who chooses to hang out up here likes his space."

"Yeah, it's tough being crammed into a space with only few thousand square miles to myself, but in the interest of hospitality, I'll squeeze aside." Glancing at sky, he added, "I was going to sleep outdoors anyway, so the indoors accommodations are all yours."

Indulging my curiosity, I inquired, "What passes for 'indoors' around here?"

"I moved into an abandoned cave last May. A fixer-upper with mucho charm."

"Your offer's very kind, mister. I'll take you up on it."

"Shall we get your pack then?"

"Let's do."

It was crazy, hiking down the path watching him negotiate a patch of rock faces with snow leopard grace while I blathered through the chapter titles of my voyage through India and Gnam Yuljongs, all the while feeling that this guy I barely knew and I might soon know each other barely, after a few hours more of tingling, thin-oxygen mind massage.

Twenty minutes later I entered the gates of New Hale, Tibet— what an insane view for somebody's front porch—and the mayor offered to brew up some butter tea. "I'd offer you wine but my cellar's dry."

"Oh, who needs wine?" I replied. Gesturing to the blue and orange-streaked billowing clouds mounted above the spot where the sun had just set, I added "This scene is stuck in high for good."

In the next second, I noted the reckless ambiguity in my choice of the word "scene," accompanied by the inner defense that my remark would be construed as an innocent observation about the physical environment, followed by a smirking *Rrrrright—and what is that bell-*

clanging stirring in your brain, heart, and loins? What crossed your mind when you saw that ample mattress/throne tucked up against the outside wall of the cave? And isn't it plenty clear this man had not forgotten you in the last half-year?—all silenced by a trumpeted *Quiet! I'm in the middle of a performance here. He's saying something!*

"Tea it is, then," he nodded and set to work, and soon the tangy aroma of butter tea soon wafted through the air.

I watched him go through his well-practiced campfire routine. He was more grizzled than the glistening figure I'd floated with in the warm waters off Oahu, and even more attractive on account of it. I gave myself a two-minute warning that if I weren't prepared for the possibility of getting involved with this man, I needed to pick up my things and get on my way; but this vessel seemed designed to go in one direction only.

Den looked up from his fire circle with a carefully carved glance. "Sorry if I came off a bit jangled by your showing up. The whole time I've been up here, the last thing I've expected to see was another human being. Especially you."

"No offense taken. I'd have been jangled too," I volunteered, neglecting to mention that I had been plenty jangled by the sight of him, and still was. Until that moment, I'd had myself convinced that Den Sherab was just one interesting guy among a fair number who've come my way and that I was perfectly capable of checking him out at a careful, measured pace before deciding if I wanted to invest any more time in him. But it wasn't working out like that—at all—for we'd begun what became the longest, farthest-ranging conversation I've ever had with a man. Our families, our past connections to Tibet, the parallels (we were born the same year, seven months apart) and contrasts of our childhoods, our experiences in India, our colorful panoplies of religious curiosities, nature, the blessings of solitude and mountains, and on and on, all the while pretending to ignore that we were falling in love at ten g's. We fought to maintain our balance, gaining giddy altitude from the rush as the helium from the distant twinkling suns elevated our mood ever higher.

As we got to know each other better by the minute, I sensed that he was holding back something about his motives for planting himself in such high elevation isolation for so long. At one point around midnight, he referred to his domain as New Hale Laboratory, so I asked him what was being investigated in the lab. He paused before replying, "This place is ideal for studying many aspects of nature." Tacking away, he tacked on, "You can appreciate a nature haven, having had a one in a million job filming wonders of the sea."

Noting his awkward evasion, I accepted his segue. "True. I've seen many an awesome sea creature and some tropical fish so beautiful I thought the sea had been stocked with them by angels as secret proof of God's existence. "

"I was thinking something like that in Hawaii just before I spotted you underwater. I could just picture the design conference where they came up with those reef fish. God comes into the conference room and announces, 'Wait'll the humans get a load of these!' And he lays his drawings down on the table and angel jaws drop all around."

"But, Lord!" I chimed in. "We're not adding humans to the mix for millions of years. And even then, think how long it will be until they come up with underwater exploration!"

"'Right!' goes God. 'Don't you get it? Once the humans do experience this underwater revelation, they'll understand it's their reward for having advanced enough to deserve a look at The Plan. Think *drama, my fine seraphim—drama!*'

"Brilliant, m'Lord!" I exclaimed on behalf of the cheering angels. "Your reef fish will stun them with the epiphany that they have been appointed caretakers of Life, which they'll revere ever after!"

"Whoops," replied Den with a rueful sigh. "Flag on the play."

"Now, now," I nudged. "Stay with the big picture. Life is a miracle and in time the human race will show it sufficient respect. Inhale this beauty-abounding sky. Even though few people have ever seen as many stars with the naked eye as we're seeing right now, everyone has glimpsed enough of them to warrant some optimism."

"I like your attitude. It puts me in mind to pose you an astronomical question."

"By all means."

He motioned for me to sit next to him on the cozy grass mattress he's got set up against the outside wall of his cave. "You need to sit right next to me so you can get this view of the stars."

"Grandma, what a bed-like observatory you have."

He tried to suppressed a laugh. "All the better to stimulate your vision with. We need to be comfortable, sitting up, with a clear view of the sky."

"Forgive me—sometimes my mind trips right into the gutter."

"No harm, no foul. None whatsoever. But no shoes on the furniture, please." He was removing his hiking shoes. Some fake, coy caution was in order.

"Have you posted all the workplace regs in this lab? I'd kinda like to see those."

"This is a throne bed, from which we shall survey our domain. If you'd be so kind as to remove those dusty hiking boots..." In acknowledgment of his clean return shot, I did as requested. "Now here's something this lab is perfectly equipped for." He lifted his bare right foot out in front of us, blocking a patch of the skyful of stars. "Stick a big toe up against those stars." I complied. "How would you gauge the odds that there's another galaxy somewhere directly beyond the spot where that lovely toe is?"

"Pretty decent," I ventured.

"It's a virtual mathematical certainty that there are hundreds of galaxies lined up behind that toe, and if you hit a galaxy cluster jackpot, perhaps millions. Of *galaxies*. And the same goes for every other random toe-sized sky sample you could pick."

"You can't expect me to take your word for a claim that wild. I'm going to go check it out. And I'm leaving now."

"Be my guest."

"Are you coming?"

"What do you think I meant by 'be my guest?' Stop lagging."

"*Me* lag? I'm past Mars already! Asteroid coming up at one o'clock."

"Copy that. Floor it."

"Bye, Sol," I called out. We soared on, our feet at the prow.

"Wave to the starry neighbors."

"They're asking where we're headed."

"Let their sparkly tongues wag."

"I don't know the answer anyway," I commented, aware of how true that was for the long term and how false at the moment. As I called out, "Supernova ahead, show some respect."

I wondered if it had ever been more obvious that a man and woman whose only physical contacts had been two handshakes (one of which was half a year in the past) were roiling in mental foreplay on the precipice of becoming lovers, even though not one gesture or look in that direction had appeared on stage. I heard Den call out "And on our left, ladies and gentlemen, a sombrero-class stunner!" and I whispered, "They're all stunners, pardner!"

We were cruising above uproarious pre-sensual surf in a non-contact dance, tantalizing and tantric, gradually yielding to gravity with ever-shortening breaths, until finally, he turned his head toward me.

The vibrations in the neural rails of my reptilian railroad signaled something whopping big was barreling my way at streamliner speed. My inner captain stammered a command to slow down for a few moments more.

We looked each other in the eyes without speaking for two heart-pounding minutes before I caved. "Ma—he's making eyes at me. An older man."

"Hardly! " he scoffed in a grinning whisper. "I remember you from Wombland College, Class of '63."

"But I was only one inch tall when you graduated."

"Yeah, but what a little sweetheart. And look atcha now, all grown up—and rill pretty too."

"I'll bet you say that to all the girls in New Hale."

He looked at me another few seconds, swallowed, shook his head the tiniest bit and said, "I'm a goner."

"Good—I'd hate to be stuck all alone on Goner Island."

"Believe it or not, I've imagined this."

"Yeah?"

"Yeah."

"Did you imagine this?" With a touch of gentle erotic sado-masochism, I moved my face ever so slowly towards his and brushed my lower lip against his upper lip. I could feel him shiver with musical electricity.

"How could I?" he replied, trying to mask his shortness of breath. "That's unimaginable."

"Nevertheless, it's coming down the tracks." His wide eyes locked onto mine, vibrant, and rock-still. I murmured "Who'd have thought it possible to make love wearing jeans and a down vest?"

"We've been doing it for six hours."

"Time to change into something more comfortable."

Den reached an arm behind my back and in one move of balletic gymnastics, revolved his body around and up onto mine as he settled me back onto the throne bed. There was no denying the evidence of his arousal, yet for a moment he stayed poised, looking down on me, his head surrounded by the Milky Way.

For an immeasurable spell, I followed him millimeter by millimeter in a time-lapse tango of ecstatic, agonizing slowness, relishing every frame of our improvisatory epic movie. Stroking my face with the delicate touch of his rough right hand, he lifted off my shirt with his left. His mouth dropped open for a moment, but we maintained our equilibrium, showing off our virtuosity in controlling our surging animals, aware that what we were about to ignite would go on long beyond that one birthnight. Then we let go and a massive starquake was under way.

When it was over—Over? What, after three hours? The first three days? Will it ever be over? When the fairy dust settled from that first passion explosion, the first thing I heard from Den was a whisper of thanks. I don't know if he was addressing God, or nature, or whom or what, but it wasn't me.

Maybe it was his parents for making his life possible. I know I've thought of mine for so many blessings that enabled me to reach this beautiful and exciting place in life, among them a generous capacity for desire. I'm not going to deny that the gene gift package my folks bestowed on me included a complement deemed desirable by members of the opposite sex, but, really, what good is that in the absence of someone to take full advantage of it? Well, I'm in the presence of such a man now: Den advantages me to the hilt, and he appears to feel he's getting as good as he gives.

It's hopeless to try and account for everything that's happened in the last three days. The speed with which we'd become intimate that first exquisite night was hardly the norm for me, having long ago become wary of how swiftly my lovers' fantasies could race in alongside their passions. Yet it struck me as perfectly paced, as if our relationship had leapfrogged an interplanetary distance, propelled by a sense that we'd been together for a longer than Earthly time. Everything that had come before appeared recast as milestones along the way here.

The momentum of it swept into the day and night that followed before we penned those few lines that ended Den's journal. We spent a lot of time hiking and taking in some of the endless sweep of vistas the southern side of the Himalayas holds out free for the taking to anyone with the gumption to settle into them at this elevation. I spent a bit of our talk catching my recluse host up on the outside world—Den didn't know that the USSR was beginning to crumble or even that apartheid had met its sorry-ass end in South Africa months ago—but most of it was devoted to discovering some experiences we had in common and others one of us had had that the other could never have imagined. Den introduced me to various denizens of the creek beds and the hardy wildflowers that had hung on to the mountain slopes since spring, and we treated ourselves to lots of jollies on various impromptu beds. No need for curtains or furniture in a skylit bedroom that's a million acres wide—wherever you look, the wilderness offers you prime accommodations.

We've done plenty of joking around too. Thank God, this boyfriend has a sense of humor, one that leans toward earthiness or the counter-romantic when the occasion calls for it. If hanging with him meant constant immersion in cosmic romantic beatitude, I couldn't take it.

Nor, I'm sure, could he. Den's got a romantic streak, but he's still a macho mountain man, so his protocol for love includes a healthy dose of making fun of it. Like last night, as we were settling into each other's arms on the throne bed under the stars, reminiscing about the gorgeous underwater site of our first meeting, he intoned, "It calls to mind that passage of Keats's:

Had the surgeon fish swum colorless, I'd still have loved the sea
Had thy foxy face shone bodiless, I'd still have dreamed of thee

"Oh, yes," I enthused," and I love it when he has her reply:
I thought as you made up those lines to nip you in the bud
But I forgave your lying eyes, you're such a luscious stud

I'm pleased that Den shares my predilection for cloudgazing, and these skies offer some spectacular atmospheric organisms for our examination, day or night, your choice. I've watched clouds for the joy of it all my life, especially when I lived in the Caribbean and Northern India, but I soon realized that Den's fervor for clouds mixes a trace of darkness into his awe. I found out why last night.

It began simply enough. We were sitting on the throne bed around midnight, recovering from a lovefest with mugs of chang, playing with the constellations. Den pointed to Aquarius in the southern sky and said, "Here's a brain teaser: can you use the zodiac as a star clock?"

I was game. I thought about it a few minutes and then it came to me that if Aquarius was near due south at midnight in the late September sky, you could probably find each of the twelve signs of the zodiac in that same due-south spot in some month of the year as the earth goes around the sun. So maybe it's going to be Pisces there next month and Leo in March and so on, with each month having its own south-at-midnight zodiac constellation. It wouldn't be exactly that, since two weeks earlier or two weeks later that same constellation won't be due south right at midnight, but that's gotta work as an approximation. And since a person at any given longitude rotates with the Earth to face all twelve zodiac constellations every twenty-four hours, a new one must move into that position every two hours. With each of the constellations taking about twelve hours to cross the night sky from east to west, it's not so hard to superimpose a kind of sundial over the sky where each twelfth of that arc represents one hour. So, I explained to my attentive quizzer, you locate the south-at-midnight constellation for whatever month it is and see how many visible "sky-twelfths" it is from due south, and that's how many hours it is before or after midnight. Something like that?

I earned a search and rescue guy's version of a gold star. Den said that's essentially it, and he was impressed that I'd figured it out in half the time it took him. I was mainly delighted that we were in a place so conducive to re-learning the familiarity with the stars that industrialized civilization abandoned long ago.

Right about then some beautiful clouds were materializing and the nearly-last quarter moon was up and offering some great visual effects lighting up the clouds' rims and translucent spots, ideal for Rorschach skygazing. I told Den about a dream I had a few nights ago in which I'd come upon a mountain that reached half-way to the moon. People were ski-jumping off the moon, landing high on the mountain and skiing down. I went up to the moon in a convenient elevator and when I got out I saw dog-sized transparent frogs with neon green and blue stripes bounding about.

He shook his head. "That's what comes of plunking a wildlife cinematographer and San Francisco Art Institute alumna in the middle of the Himalayas. Who needs movies?"

Sensing a receptive audience, I went off on a spree pointing out moonlit cloud sightings of an weedy sea dragon orchestra conductor and a white-crowned twelve-headed blazing-eyed she-god until Den put his hand on the conversational steering wheel and asked me to join him in an experiment with mental projection.

Mental projection? That got my attention, given the number of times people have said things out of the blue that seemed to have arced out of my brain into theirs a moment before without their having the faintest idea what had just happened. The first time I remember noticing it, I was in kindergarten on St. Kitts. Our class was upstairs in a community center and the teacher had been reading us a story for what seemed to me the longest time. I could hear the waves lapping up on the beach and an image popped into my mind of my body reforming as a Slinky so I could tumble head over heels down a rubbery stairway and keep rolling all the way to the surf, when suddenly the teacher interrupted her reading and said, "Well, look at little Calieze over there, fidgeting like a Slinky itching to go bounding downstairs. I think it's time for recess."

That kind of thing has happened to me so often over the years that it gave me only a moment's pause when Den and I met in the ocean and he made reference to my catching onto his being from Tibet with the speed of a shooting star—about one second after a memory of a shooting star had flashed in my mind. It had risen up from a fifteen-year-old memory of my first night in Tibet when my nanny took me to her home town for a visit. While we were on an evening walk in a nearby pasture, I beheld the most brilliant shooting star I've ever seen streak across the sky. I viewed it as an omen that someday I would return to the land that lived under such a magical sky. Entirely understandable that that image might pop into my mind when Tibet was mentioned in a warm sea; much less understandable Den's coming up with that left-field reference one moment later.

And then there was his mention of New York gunfire.

I yanked myself away from last March's ocean scene and expressed my interest in whatever he meant by mental projection. He suggested that we use the clouds as stepping stones, as a kind of launch pad "to cruise the skies scanning for signals." He noticed my puzzlement. "Something like radio waves."

The day before Den had referred to his domain as a lab again, glossing over the explanation I'd requested. Lab or not, using our brains as tuners, experimenting with "something like radio waves" was a little unusual for a couple cozying up in a double sleeping bag in the middle of the night. He attempted to sell it as a taste of Einsteinesque mind play, thought experiments having been the wellspring of Einstein's genius. He suggested that the high elevation of New Hale may be conducive to honing a mental skill that may lie out of sight and inaccessible to people immersed in the hubbub of society down below. "If you really release your mind to a problem, the knowledge sensor of the mind can sometimes lead you right to its target."

"The target being…?"

"There's no guidebook."

I was on holiday, what the hell. "Sure, let's give it a go," I said, disregarding for the moment the sense that his idea wasn't quite as spontaneous as he was making it out to be. We'd done a sky trip that first night, of course, high-spirited galactic gallivanting, but this time he seemed not so casual. He said it was important to stay close to Earth, and listening "though not with our ears." When I asked him if this was about communicating with the dead, he said, absolutely not, and that I shouldn't go into it with pre-conceived notions of what would happen. We just had to start climbing the clouds that were drifting by a few thousand feet away under the moon and feel where to go from there without speaking to each other.

All righty, mate, let's set sail. We sat up and began by staring at the moonlit cloud tops, and in short order I was back in the sky with Den, this time floating in the silent, mountain-high surf of glowing water vapor. I felt like I could have stayed right there for days, years, until I felt myself yielding to a gentle pull off to the east. Over the next minute, my awareness of Den diminished until I could no longer be sure he was still with me.

This journey reminded me of a time when I was twenty and on vacation back in St. Kitts, heady with confidence, and decided to hitchhike across the island to visit some friends who lived on the other side. I'd been picked up by a scraggly-bearded islander in a camper with a young couple ensconced in the back. They invited me to climb into the loft over the cab where, exhausted, I drifted off for half an hour. I was awakened when the ride turned bumpy and when I lifted my head enough to peer out the little window, I noticed that we were well off the main road. Wherever we were had not been on the announced itinerary. In fact, calling the terrain we were driving on a "road" was a stretch. But I wasn't worried and I didn't care. It was like going along with a dream that had taken an interesting turn. There was no need for me to help whatever it was that was unfolding to unfold. I just relaxed in the river of time, prepared to glance over my shoulder at what was transpiring on shore, certain that I'd end up at my destination.

The objective of our detour became clear when our geezer pilot pulled up at a rustic hillside cabin, greeted its inhabitants, and scored some weed. Rather than get up and socialize, I lazed right where I was. The vibes were smooth and that was good enough for me and for them. I closed my eyes, and after about ten minutes, I felt the engine chug back to life and the bumpy rolling started up again. When I felt a turn and a smoother surface beneath us, I opened one eye, noticed the

Caribbean's familiar blue-green off to the right, and happily closed it to carry on drifting. After another hour, we stopped, the back door screeched open, and our mellowed driver announced, "All out for Banana Bay."

That drifting feeling had seeped into my body again as I found myself flying over East Asia, but this time the chugging engine was replaced by a sense that a non-material tether had latched onto my head, pulling me in a direction I couldn't identify. I yielded to its magnetism and forgot about where I'd left my body and whom I'd left it with. I was being pulled by cosmic forces that knew a lot more than I.

After a while, I lost sight of the moon. The ground, with its rare flickers of lantern light or cook fires far below, was gone too. I could see nothing but a fuzzy dim light emerging in the darkness. It seemed a few hundred yards ahead, coming closer by the moment. No St. Kitts mellow, this trip. Interesting, no doubt, but not so pleasant. There was something unsettling, or dangerous, or just plain wrong in that spot. I hung on to the tether until it released me at the boundary of a gray blur obscuring the light. I took a deep breath and pushed on through.

I was staring down at a large man dressed in worn military fatigues pacing around an outdoor space the size of my family's cabin on St. Kitts. I'm using the term "outdoor" loosely—it looked like a chunk of woods with brush, grass, and weeds underfoot and parts of trees around the perimeter, blurred at the edges. Positioned at the back near the top was a light like a dim lamp. Its light fluttered, gasping in the gloom. There were blurry, confounding images in the surrounding walls.

The pacing man was below where I was observing him. Though I was within his range of sight, he was unaware of my presence. I felt as if I were spying on him from outside an upper window. He was about forty, light-skinned, stubble-faced and pinch-eyed, and had a dirty baseball cap on his head and a hunting knife affixed to his belt. Agitated, he kept glancing through a large, open space in front of him, like a glassless window. Through it I could see a couple of girls about fourteen or fifteen years old in the distance, wearing school uniforms, apparently walking home at the edge of the woods. As the pacing man's eyes darted back and forth, his view maintained a constant distance from the girls even though they were walking away from him, so he had to be following them. They were as unaware of him as he was of me.

I got anxious—scratch that—*increasingly freaked*. I didn't like the smell of this place. I didn't know where it was, how I'd gotten there, or what had happened to the guy who'd started me down this peculiar path. I wanted to turn away, but I couldn't because I suspected that this weirdo was up to no good. I felt compelled to stay, as if somehow spying on him might enable me to protect the girls who were continuing their innocent jaunt at the edge of a field without a care in the world.

A bizarre black mass, like a head-sized cluster of disturbed scorpions, slowly approached the window from the outside. The man stared at it, fixated, his nostrils flaring, his lips parted. He looked over to the girls and suddenly, a hideous montage appeared in his chamber walls, terrifying images of one of the girls being raped, as seen from the rapist's point of view, alongside the stabbed body of the other girl. The window in which the girls were still visible drew closer to them in swift darting movements. The man sucked the black mass closer and closer to his face and the dim light behind him sputtered feebly. I screamed at him, *"Don't do it, you stupid bastard! The scorpions will devour your head from the inside, slowly but surely, for the rest of your miserable life!"*

Though I was shouting as loud as I could, he didn't turn one degree towards me—but he paused and ceased the sucking inhalations that had brought the festering ball almost to his face. His view became stationary, allowing the distance between his position and the girls to grow.

The man turned his head in the direction of the light that had been sputtering high in the back of the chamber. It had begun to steady, like a fluorescent bulb starting up in slow motion. He looked back to the hovering black mass at the opening. He flinched, backed away, and crumpled to the ground, sitting slumped over. Through the window the girls could be seen turning a corner in the distance and disappearing out of sight. I called out to the pathetic figure below, "Don't ever go that close to the brink again, and you might save yourself."

My skin, chilled from head to toe, began to return to normal, and as it did, my inner ears seemed to pick up a faint sound—a voice. It was Den, calling me from someplace in front of me. I looked up and there at the top of the other side of the depleted man's strange space I saw Den's face, urgent and caring, looking right at me.

I called, "Den!" and the next moment I was hurtling backwards through space, the whole course of my strange journey reversing itself at high speed. Eventually I caromed off the clouds and plummeted back to earth, smoothly slipping back onto our bed outside the cave entrance. Den was there, his right arm around me, his cheek pressed against mine, quietly saying my name.

I wanted to respond but couldn't. I was shivering and woozy, so out of it that when I looked at the sky overhead, I thought I saw a pair of stars tracing a circular path at the zenith. For three days I'd been gamboling with a wonderful new lover in a beautiful paradise of fun and excitement, and now—well, there'd been excitement aplenty, but beauty and fun gamboling had been blasted to smithereens. I hoped Den wouldn't be repelled if I were to tell him what had happened to me. Maybe it had been a dream and when he'd called my name, I put him in the dream before waking up.

My discomfort at the clawing recollection of what I'd just lived through was tempered by the faint sense that somehow I'd had something to do with the creep's backing away from his planned attack. Another thought caught mind-jumping.

Nightmare or nightmarish reality, either way I was spinning in a quandary. Much as I'd fallen for Den Sherab, I realized I didn't know him well enough to be sure how he'd take my story. He'd said he was attracted to me as a woman of strength, both mental and physical— what if this gave him cold feet? I imagined appealing to him by insisting that I'm not afflicted by hallucinations of vicious criminals and that I really am strong and level-headed, yet that imagined spiel itself struck me as a sign of nervous weakness. So I kept my mouth shut and sought succor in the warmth of his embrace and the cool light of the moon that had wandered a couple of diameters west.

I squeezed Den back in silence. He told me it was all right, he loved me, he had been watching me, he was thankful to me for having trusted him. I wanted to place his hand on my pounding heart but was reluctant to disclose how shaken I was. "We can talk about it another time," he soothed. "Let's just enjoy the stars."

So we did, and in time, conversing about the constellations graced us with some welcome normalcy. We spent the next hour playing mind games and recounting stories from our youth. It helped tamp down the occasional shakes I'd get when the hunter's image of rape and murder would butt back into my consciousness. I bathed again in the sweet, funny good-times warmth we'd been enjoying for the previous three days, laughing about strange concepts we'd had as little kids. (He liked my habit of building shelters for sidewalk anthills out of little twigs. I admired his feeding streetlamps by putting sticks down storm drains.)

Such superficially pleasant comfort got us past the shank of the night to the point where I'd relaxed enough to consider telling Den what had happened to me and to ask what had been going on with him all that time. I did not want to look flaky, even to myself, and certainly not to my new lover. I didn't know how much of a scientific hard-ass he might be. This guy used to work in a microbiology lab and superimposes a mental protractor on the night sky to gauge stellar right ascensions as a surrogate for a clock. He might not take so well to finding he's involved with a female who claims to see into people's minds. Oooooh—cue the theme from *Twilight Zone*! But I thought, screw that—I've got my feet on solid ground and I know what I experienced. If I'd seen into someone's mind, it wasn't that different from Den's and my having unwittingly read each other's minds in the ocean, and that didn't bother him. If my story made him conclude he'd been sleeping with a fruitcake, too bad. I'd cross that shaky bridge if and when it appeared.

"Terma Den, you must realize that something strange happened to me during that little cloud-climbing, wave-tuning experiment of yours."

"I figured that much. Please continue."

I up and told him the whole thing, trying not to reveal my anxiety about it. His initial reaction was unclear. He nodded, "Hunh," and got real silent, looking back and forth between me and the sky. I felt entitled to ask him, "What?!" but I thought better of it. Something was cooking in there and I'd let him inform me of it in his own good time.

After a few minutes, he kissed me and spoke up. "You're not the only one with strange news, kiddo. The reason you saw me looking at you at the top of that sicko's place is that I was there. I saw everything and I heard you shout. You're not alone in this."

I shivered. A hundred questions cascaded down the furrows of my brain, too many to even begin examining, tired as we were. I guess he felt the same way, because he scooted down in the sleeping bag, prodding me to join him. He looked up at the sky for a while until his eyelids floated down and he fell asleep. Another few anxious minutes later, so did I.

It was a couple of hours past dawn when we woke up this morning. We went about our morning routine as if nothing unusual had transpired the night before. The subject didn't come up until we were sipping green tea after breakfast. Den said that he had not attempted to intervene with the sicko because he was certain it would have no effect and that he was shocked how my screamed imprecations had seemed to affect the hunter. I wanted to ask him why he was so certain he could have no effect on our "subject," but I thought we'd more than filled our quota of strangeness for a couple falling in love and I let it rest.

Life spun slowly on throughout the day as we tended to home chores like gathering wood for the charcoal pit (a task that didn't make much sense for people who have yet to discuss how long they're going to be here.) We took life an hour at a time and I was happy to let it flow along, nice and copasetic.

But no; another shoe had been hanging suspended over our heads out of sight, awaiting the moment to drop, shortly after nightfall, some six or seven hours ago.

We'd been chatting after chowing down the last of our dinner— warm barley cakes with spinach and mushrooms sautéed in sesame oil, yum. "Quite the feast, TD!"

"Any food is a feast."

"And any sight up here is a visual feast. Look at the galloping seahorse." I was referring to the latest magic mime performance being enacted in the sunset clouds off to the southwest. We tickled each other's imaginations for a while picking out colorful chimeras relishing their minutes on the sky stage. It was fun, but led inevitably to recalling the cloud launch of our disturbing mental journey the previous night. At some point Den made a passing reference to having spent some time up here thinking how evil seemed to infect criminal minds like a virus.

Though a part of me cautioned that talking about evil was a sure downer on an evening like this and would taint our beautiful falling-in-love dance, I was kind of glad he brought it up. Evil had pierced my family and it was comforting to know that Terma Den, with whom I was becoming more and more deeply involved, wasn't burdened by too little—or too much—sensitivity to handle a matter of such significance to me. When he told me the story of how his father lost his life, I knew we had more in common than I could ever have guessed while floating above a school of angelfish off Hawaii.

Talking over what had happened to our parents, I expressed my dismay at the levels of degradation to which a sick human brain can sink. I ignored my ambivalence about getting into such a repugnant subject in this setting and decided to tell him about a story that the press in America had had a field day with this summer, while I was fashioning my plans to come to Asia. I don't have the stomach to go into the details, but it concerned an extreme psycho in Milwaukee by the name of Jeffrey Dahmer, who'd taken up a hobby of subjecting young men and boys he picked up to gruesome forms of torture and murder. This had gone on for years, until one resourceful victim managed to escape the creep's apartment—with a set of handcuffs still dangling from one wrist—and find the police, who returned to the site to arrest one of the creepiest criminals in modern American history.

I immediately regretted my indiscretion. Den reacted with much greater alarm than I'd expected. His eyes widened and he asked in a hoarse voice just when the news of that arrest had broken. I was able to pinpoint it pretty close to July 23rd since I remembered seeing it on the waiting room television while starting my visa application at the Chinese consulate in San Francisco and thinking, whoa, good time to take a break from the States.

Den swallowed and got up, muttering that he'd be back in a minute. He picked up his journal from the stone shelf in the cave and searched through it. He paused at one page, put it down, and walked shakily out of the cave. He paced around for a while out there, looking at the sky, leaving me dying of curiosity. After a few minutes, I couldn't take it any more, so I went outside and approached him gingerly, starting to apologize for having wounded our conversation, but he silenced me and told me I'd done nothing wrong, that he'd explain himself later on.

I returned to our porch and settled onto the throne bed to wait. A few minutes later, he joined me and started talking about the Denver Broncos and how odd it was for him to have no idea where they were in the new season's standings. He wondered what would become of their quarterback, John Elway, a supreme athlete who had threatened to dump his #1 NFL draft pick opportunity to play center field for the Yankees, yet, having thrown in with football, now found himself having lost three of the last four Super Bowls, this year's being the most humiliating Super Bowl loss of all time.

Hunh? Then came the kicker: "I think a lot about recovery from a series of failures. I really hope Elway can crawl out of the near-miss abyss someday and emerge victorious, despite all. I think a sign of transcendence anywhere can boost people's confidence in transcendence everywhere."

Not a word about evil. Throughout the evening, nothing heavier than sports talk crossed Den's lips. If he wants to explain anything about his reaction to the serial killer story, that'll be his call, not mine. All through dinner tonight, I've been happy to brainstorm with him about ways to trick marmots into venturing forth from their dens (for amusement purposes only), supremely silly speculations as to why dogs' lips are serrated, and making Belgian waffles in the wilderness.

And so we healed the spooky mental bruises of the previous twenty-four hours with soothing, burbling froth. We were living entirely in the moment, the only reference to the past being Den's request that I write down a summary of what has happened to me since he and I met almost seven months ago, a task to which I've faithfully applied myself ever since we cleaned up after dinner, some four hours ago.

So there it is, dear Den—I've done my job. I present these notes to you *con brio e amore,* and hope you'll find that they've accomplished what you wished. Bar-headed geese having been put on leave, you're welcome to add impressions of your own to the following vacant pages. Or not, as you please—we're on this adventure together, and that's what counts. I look forward to relocking ourselves in each other's arms as the rain plays itself out on our ancient stone roof.

[3-2]

(a few hours later—9/29/91, maybe 3 AM?)

I've been tossing about for a while, unable to get back to sleep. I've got to set down a coda for the piece I wrote earlier.

I woke up about an hour ago and knew Den was awake. He was lying still so as not to disturb me, but when you're with someone you love, vibes can be as palpable as a paroxysm of fidgeting. I put my arm over his chest to let him know I was ready to listen if he wanted to talk. This guy's no dope; he knew I was right there, disquieted along with him, and that beating around the bush wouldn't suffice. He slipped an arm around my shoulders, sighed, and said, "All right—I'm gonna go all in and pray that this doesn't send you running back to Sonoma County."

"I'm not going anywhere."

"Okay, then—here it is: That Dahmer monster you were talking about—I was inside his mind for the fifteen minutes that preceded his victim's escape in July. I saw it happen through his eyes, just as we observed that hunter of young girls in the woods last night. I've slogged through shit like that at least a hundred times since the beginning of summer, complete with those ugly virusy clusters near their heads, all kinds of people on the verge of committing evil in visions like the one we had last night, many of them acting out the vile fantasies they envisioned in their soulspaces. It's all in the log I wrote during the months we were apart."

My skin was prickling. He went on. "Early on, I tried to intervene, only to have to resign myself to my status as an impotent observer, because I failed to affect the outcome every single time. Still, I felt compelled to continue the experiment, in the hope that I'd learn more about what causes these people to commit such evil. For someone trained in rescue, to just watch, utterly unable to help, was brutal. But the night before last, when I took you with me, you—*you got it done.* We'll never know for sure, but I think that maybe, last night, somewhere on Earth, a heinous crime was aborted, prevented by you, Calieze, here in the heights of Tibet…Hence the mountain of *Now, what?!* in my face."

Now thousands of hair follicles were freezing on my scalp. That wormhole journey to the mind of a prospective perp reappeared on stage as vivid as an open wound, obliging us to ponder what that smattering of the recent past portends for our future. A dimension of reality I had no idea existed had just opened up.

"Now what," I answered, lifting my head from his chest to look at him, "is we're going to find out why we met."

Our tensions tightened our bonds to each other. Den squeezed me for a few seconds and then drifted away, leaving me alone in wakefulness.

I edged away to pick up this book and my pen. By the light of the lantern I lit to scribble these lines, I can see Den's brow furrowed, as he tries to rest in the land of dreams. I'm about to join him there. We're both going to need some rest because, ready or not, something much bigger than A Relationship, or even The Relationship, is rumbling just under the horizon and it's coming up quick.

[3-3]

<u>Oct . 2, 1991</u>

So much for "This adventure is ending." Nothing has ended, except the belief that Calieze and I had failed to meet our destiny together. My 6½ months of anguish over the missed chance of a lifetime was as natural as the pain from a chest full of broken bones. I have been vindicated.

Further, the experiment I was packing in ice a week ago has been relaunched, making contrails in the sky, proving that our two heads are infinitely better than one. Calieze and I are exploring spookily thrilling terra incognita in scientific research, notwithstanding our forsaking the usual nose-stinging, formaldehyde-saturated institutional lab for one of the most majestic study sites in the known universe.

Less than a minute after I set my journal down to investigate the source of footfalls among the trees of New Hale, my life burst out of its entropic resignation like the birth of a star. My heart, famous in Colorado SAR circles for its rock-steady adherence to a pulse of sixty flat, almost leapt out of my chest, already jolted a minute before by the sound of another human on the mountain, now followed within three seconds by three new shocks, each a full Richter grade greater than the one before:

It's a woman! –

—she's stunning!!—

—it's ***Calieze!!!!!!!***

Instantly blitzed by a biochemically mixed burst of joy and fear for the loss of my mind, I thought dreaming or madness were far more reasonable explanations for the vision before me—Calieze standing ten yards away on a remote mountain in the Himalayas. But when she said her name, I realized that my life was changing more in that moment than I'd thought it ever could if I lived to one hundred. My spirit, which had sunk like a fallen tree into a sodden forest floor, catapulted skyward and the sun's rays burst free from physics and bounced deliriously off everything they touched.

But, with the motto of Oscar Brown, Jr. echoing in my brain, I was cool. I moseyed on over, shook the lady's hand, and offered her a little Himalayan hospitality, imposing what restraint I could on my visible elation, even though I felt my head piercing the sky.

I've not read what Calieze has logged since then, but I assume it gets across the gist of that first evening's prolonged, fully-clothed, non-contact tantric build-up of desire. If I didn't have a renewed mission to complete and the prospect of more Calieze-love flowing in from the highland future, I could have died that first night, ecstatic to my bones.

In the interest of observing New Hale Laboratory record-keeping standards, I must acknowledge that the aforementioned ecstasy arose in part from some purely physical causes. In the clinch, Calieze is a world-class performing artist with the responding and rhythm instincts of a jazz master. I told her how much I appreciated her artistry and she generously credited me with inspiring her to exalting heights. I told her I'd never been exalted quite like that even once, much less half a dozen times in thirty-six hours.

I understand that Buddha had other things in his enlightened mind when teaching compassion, but since last week, I've experienced compassion for the myriad men who will never know what it's like to make love to a woman in Calieze's league. Like desert tribesmen who know nothing of alpine lakes, their ignorance protects them. As for the Buddhists, Hindus, and Christians who would dismiss that compassion as the sign of an immature consciousness chained to frivolous bodily existence, I feel even sorrier for them. It's become epiphany-clear to me that setting loose in the world all-encompassing soulful, romantic, erotic, yin-yang love was God's greatest stroke of genius.

Last night in a lapse of cool, I confessed to Calieze an irrational fear that she might somehow disappear from my life a second time and she replied, "Hey, bud, I'm the one who launched a search operation across half the world to rescue us both from destiny deprivation."

"It sure took you long enough," I chided.

"You sure hid yourself well enough. Don't complain to your first responder."

"So you'll stay."

"Stay here?! You mean you're not going to walk me home tonight?"

"I'd like to think you are home."

"Then, honey, I'm home."

Fortunately for the lab's mission, Calieze's telepathic capacity complements my own. I've gotten pretty nimble at ferreting mental distress signals out of the atmosphere—which might explain or derive from my SAR work—but hunting in the soulspace range on my own, I remain stuck in observer-only status. Calieze hasn't yet developed the inner radar to pick up such signals, but she's hooked into me enough to accompany me, and once she's there, she's able to project thoughts into others' soulspaces without their realizing it.

Her mother told her that telepaths have shown up in her family at a rate of one or two people per generation, usually manifesting in an adolescent girl. Roma have a reputation for magic and fortune-telling that stretches back a thousand years. There's an eleventh century record of Emperor Constantine IX calling upon them to use sorcery to protect his livestock from predators. They were known as the "Atsingani," a name sprinkled in Roma families ever since in various forms, including a Hungarian version that became my lover's middle name.

Being different has hurt the Roma more than it's helped, bringing upon them woeful persecution. Like the Jews in Egypt, they were kept in Romania as slaves for hundreds of years, and once liberated, found themselves generations later imprisoned and murdered in huge numbers by the nazis.

Jewish and Gypsy—Calieze has survival power coming at her from both sides. Never better proof that beauty and talent cannot be stomped out of a determined, life-loving people by an evil oppressor.

Indeed, it was that fierce survival instinct that led to Calieze's birth. After World War II, each of her parents joined other young refugees in Palestine, where Jewish and Roma communities had been living for a long time. The holocaust they had survived had taken the lives of all four of Calieze's grandparents. Her mother had been protected as a girl by a Hungarian Christian family that had fled the approaching Russians as the war wound down. Eventually she landed in a displaced persons camp in Italy. When Zionists came offering Jews a new life in the nascent state of Israel, she saw her way out and brazenly claimed she was Jewish, a ruse that made her an Israeli pioneer at the age of thirteen, living in a Roma community in Jaffa. Six years later, as an undergraduate at Hebrew University, she met Calieze's father, a Hungarian Jew a few years older than she, who was doing graduate work in soil science. Three years on, they married and continued their itinerant life stories together, moving first to London, then to St. Kitts, where Calieze was born in 1963, and a few years later to New York, where she went to school and where the whole family eventually obtained citizenship.

It was in the land of the free that Calieze's family was victimized by an evil as deadly as the pox that infected the camps at Birkenau. The bullet that tore through her mother's neck broke her father's heart. He maintained pretty well, taking her to India, where he had been offered a position working on the Green Revolution, supplementing his daddy-daughter time with the aid of a Tibetan nanny, and then to San Francisco where he worked with an environmental consulting firm. (No way was he going to subject them to New York, shot through with painful memories.) But Calieze's reaching adulthood allowed his life ligaments to weaken and he died of heart failure a few years ago at the age of fifty-four.

By then Calieze had graduated from the San Francisco Art Institute, where the tech-friendly genes she inherited from her father kicked in, leading her to change up her major from painting to video and filmmaking. Employing electronic brushes to create paintings that moved, she made one art film and one documentary short, both of which dealt with Tibetan iconography and which did well in film festivals. She made a living in freelance videography and a home in a caboose she'd bought off the Union Pacific Railroad for one dollar after finding it abandoned on a side-rail next to a Nowheresville diner in Nevada. On a dare to herself during a cross-country drive, she'd stopped to lunch on the house specialty, trumpeted on a sign outside as *Gizzard-Burning, Eardrum-Boiling, Guaranteed To Injure, Gasp From The Gut, Hi-Octane Ethel's Ethyl Chili.* Staring at the 1940s era caboose through pepper-stinging tears, it suddenly dawned on her, *that's my new house!* A couple thousand dollars worth of hired truck hauling later, the rail car was reborn as the home of Calieze Moss on a woodsy plot she rented from a kindly pair of elderly former beatniks on the Sonoma coast north of Marin County.

While video gigs, marine and otherwise, would take her far and wide over the next three years, having that coastal caboose to repair to fostered lots of dreaming, much of which led her back to the Tibet of her dreams. In time, she started scheming to make it back here to justify its hold on her or release herself from it. While the geese project germinated, she took cinematography jobs ranging from underwater bridge inspections to nature documentaries on such subjects as coral reef deterioration, spotted owls, sharks, speciation among sea slugs, and an Arctic whale rescue. Somehow the two years she'd allotted for all this had turned into three by the time she set up a pied-à-terre in Hawaii—I think that delay had something to do with a guy designing a bathyscaphe for Scripps—but by then even the glories of surgeon fish and sea turtles had only the most tenuous hold on her. When she found me headed this way, she took it as a sign that the time for her return to Tibet was drawing nigh.

And so we find ourselves together in Tibet, breathing air of crystalline clarity, free of the pollutions of light, noise, smog, dirt, and distractions, in which the acuity of our onboard vision sensors surpasses those of eagles and satellites. It is the perfect place for our parallel thrilling explorations, the one, blissful and intimate, the other, hair-raising and disturbing but, we're hoping, ripe with potential to save lives.

We had another round of both explorations last night, separated by a sobering intermission. We began with an experiment in tantric lovemaking. Our version, which helped fuel the spiritual booster rocket we rode afterward, was improvised sans guru and without regard to the many and conflicting traditional textbook instructions on official tantric technique. Hoary guru warnings about the dangers of engaging in tantra without the guidance of an official master strike me like a dictum from the Certified Guitar Teachers Guild that guitar must be learned by signing up for years of lessons with a member of the guild. Of course there are great guitar teachers, but some of them were self-taught, just like Buddha. I'll bet that, if pushed, the gurus will acknowledge that others can teach themselves too, if they have more time, patience, talent, and drive than those with the inclination to depend on an authority and the money to pay for one.

Our version sure isn't about prohibiting orgasm, the ultimate anticlimax. We create an interlude midway through for a cosmic consciousness mind-body meld to prime the spiritual discovery potential of our male-female team by straddling interpersonal and cosmic bliss, before coming back to each other and our bodily riffs. We need our spiritual strength at maximum pitch before embarking on risky voyages. We view going solo without yin-yang complementarity as handicapping, like trying to swim the English Channel using only one side of your body.

For last night's foray, we boarded the throne bed with multiple blankets and our own synergistic heating system and swept each other up in another intimate round of brain-and-bodystorming. Calieze sat in my lap facing me—she achieves great posture in such situations, a pleasing by-product of her having subjected herself to years of yoga, an apparent requirement of living in the Bay Area for more than six months—and we slipped naturally into our meditation, expanding our union far outward. We felt our intertwined minds and souls expand outward, enveloping the solar system while maintaining contact with the collective consciousness of intelligent life marooned on one blue planet within. After a time of inestimable length, we stirred, completed the dance, and recondensed ourselves back to our earthbound nest.

After a while with our heart and respiration rates back in normal range, we dressed and made our way down to the creek to splash cold water in our faces. Then we let our thoughts recover over mugs of tea before gravitating back to the throne bed. We positioned ourselves as we had three nights before, ready, we thought, for whatever adventure we might find.

It didn't take long to find one. We noticed a cloud covering the lower half of Pisces, making the star-studded fish appear as if they were leaping above the surface of the cloud like a pair of lively carp. Looked like a positive place to start a journey that could prove troublesome, so we projected ourselves to that cloud and put our conversation on silent mode.

We lay atop the cloud, soaking up the view, hearing nothing but the wind, till I felt a now-familiar, subtle tug on the brain. I lifted off, leading Calieze on a flight south by southeast. The Himalayas fell away beneath us and we entered the airspace of India's Gangetic Plain. Between the darkness and my haziness about Indian geography, I soon lost track of our whereabouts.

In less than half an hour, the tractor beam's accuracy was verified as it took on a repugnant odor. Locked onto it, we soon arrived at the edges of the soulspace of a bug-eyed Indian man haunting the edge of a village. Taking up positions in the blinds of his upper soulspace, we saw him approach a girl of about seven who was on her way back from an outhouse. In a flash he seized her and threw her into the trunk of a rattletrap car and sped away.

We could hear the girl's muffled cries as he transported her through a nearby town and miles beyond on a dirt road. We observed his drive through the windshield-shaped front of his soulspace, seeing what he saw through the actual windshield of his car. At some point, I noticed another muffled sound mixed in with the girl's kicks, the engine's grumble, and the driver's loud mutterings to himself: a barely audible, rhythmic pumping that I took to be the sound of blood in his cerebral arteries.

All the while, as the kidnapper's headlamps illuminated the ruts of the dirt road, the walls and upper and lower surfaces of his soulspace pulsated with a panoply of horrible images, showing what seemed to be his thoughts with unprecedented clarity. He was envisioning himself standing by a well in the center of a tiny, rural village, conducting a rite before a small crowd of avid believers. Interspersed with the chanting of the villagers were images of various fanged, skull-draped Herukas egging him on and one especially ugly "shot" of the girl tumbling down the well and being held under water by a demon who then lifted her drowned carcass aloft. As in the other soulspaces, a single sputtering light hung suspended at the back of his soulspace, so dim as to be almost invisible. It was a rank place, as ripe for *eviola* as a dank forest for mushrooms.

The driver took no notice of the light as he bellowed obeisance to the demons, stiffening with a dark charge in his sick, throaty, unintelligible chants over the child's moans. All the while, an eviola virus pushed its way through the space right above his field of view, approaching the kidnapper's head ever closer, its black tangles pulsing with primitive aggression beneath its surface. The virus held the driver's gaze more than the road, causing him to drive through potholes that would draw his eyes back to the road for only a moment before returning to focus on the eviola, which grew in size the more he looked at it. Calieze and I tried calling to him, but aside from an occasional twitch in Calieze's direction, he took no notice of anything but the crazy concoctions of his diseased mind.

We stayed with him as he approached a tiny village identical to the one he'd been envisioning. He parked near a well between the huts and began chanting as a troop of devotees who had been awaiting his arrival gathered around. He thrilled both to their attention and to the eviola, which, having begun the size of a golf ball had now grown to the size of a football slowly being drawn to his head.

Calieze tried many things hoping to turn this evolving nightmare around. We saw him react, looking over his shoulder at her calls without seeing her, but her efforts seemed to make no difference. That had nothing to do with her using English, a language he was likely ignorant of, because her meaning would have been clear anywhere in the world.

The pseudoshaman worked his followers into a frenzy in synchrony with the clamoring demons in his mind. The panting of his spiritual corpus drew the maggoty virus ever closer, anticipating a perverse reversal of Rosemary's fetus in which it would burst fully to life once the virus gained entry its host's body. As the light at the rear of the soulspace disappeared, the crazed creep gulped down the eviola and he smiled with grandeur as pustules broke out all over his inner face and limbs. He stormed over to the vehicle, grabbed the girl out of the trunk by her feet and hauled her like a forty-inch long totem over to the well.

He suspended the piteous, wailing child over the opening as he reached a roaring pitch in his chants and dropped her in, head first. His followers prostrated themselves before him as he carried on his rattling chant, exulting in the child's screams, which dwindled over one interminable minute before submerging into silence.

An ecstatic snaggle-toothed smile split his face. He blessed his followers and bid them rise. I looked across his soulspace at Calieze, who was gasping in tears. The surfaces of the criminal's soulspace showed a gray blobby membrane pulsing with the rhythmic pumping sound, and I realized I was seeing a chamber within his brain, fed by a network of tiny reddish vessels pumping eviola-infected blood through his diseased neurons. The bulbous pustules mottling his inner face formed surface crusts from which infected blood seeped and dribbled down his neck.

That blew the cap off the visitation. Calieze fell back and I fled to catch up with her—or rather to catch her, since she was in an emotional freefall. She'd not undergone the hardening of seeing disasters of that order frequently over the last several months, as I had, and even for me, this evilkilling was one of the most despicable.

I glided swiftly back through the skies over the subcontinent, keeping a close hold on my mute partner. I was sure that her pain from the absurd and tragic loss of the child's life was compounded by an irrational fear that her efforts to prevent the crime might somehow have made it more likely.

When we returned home, I led her to our indoor bed, where she snuggled up to me. Knowing better than to pressure her to talk, I told her that raking through the ashes of our ordeal would be easier come morning. She nodded in my shoulder, which had become warm and wet with her tears. I reminded her that I love her and kept my arms around her all night.

We awoke this morning to skylight streaming in through the cave entrance. We attended to our ablutions, stretching, breakfast, and chores, grateful for the bright blue sky's cleaning off the outer residues of the previous night's pain, all without a word about last night. It was understood that we'd get around to it once we got started on our day hike. (Happily, that followed an interlude in which I found her drying off from a creek bath and allowed the whirlwind forces of our mutual attraction to flood to the fore again.)

By mid-day, we set off toward the promontory, as a first step towards conquering it at some later point when she's had more time to acclimate her legs and lungs. It was a relief to get back to a raw embrace of the beauty of the mountains. By the time we reached our first break perch, at an elevation some eighteen hundred feet higher, we were ready to debrief each other about last night's visitation.

Calieze had generously allocated to our hike one of six oranges she'd packed in up here all the way from India. Peeling that food of the gods and gazing out at the vista beneath us, I spoke first. "I'm guessing that last night wasn't your idea of a fun date that might come of your searching for me in Tibet."

"No, Den, it wasn't," she sighed, "but I'm not slitting my wrists about it either. It was traumatic watching that little girl lose her life, but I knew you were up to something gnarly when I accepted your offer of a research partnership. You never promised me a lotus garden. Our visit to the hunter showed it could get harsh."

"Which it did, markedly, for a while."

"Which it did horrifically, for an eternity. But, painful as it was, I admit it confirmed that we're onto something with powerful potential to connect to other souls."

I offered her another hit from my canteen and nodded uphill. "Shall we?"

"Let's do it," she declared, standing and forging ahead. I buried the orange peels, shouldered the rucksack, and caught up to her.

"How about giving me your take on souls?" I called ahead.

"Ooookay…I have been giving it some thought," she said, unconsciously speaking in sync with her footsteps.

"The way I see it, everybody's got a personal spiritual identity that pre-exists and outlasts the mind and body carting it around. It's as real as redwoods and robins and your heart, but it's without mass and mostly invisible to us, like electromagnetic radiation other than light."

"Like Flatlanders seeing a cylinder poked through their world as a heightless circular wall they have to walk around."

"There you go. Maybe someday science'll get a handle on it, but it's been there all along, the way action potentials in nerve cells were there before scientists figured out how to measure those. But some of us—you and I, at least—can see a manifestation of it in a person's soulspace.

"Your soul is you before and after its association with your present body. It moves into a body like the owner of a new ship equipped with a whole bunch of cool gadgets and features, some of which hum along automatically and some of which remain on standby for you to use when you feel like it. Your soul is not the ship: it uses the ship and sets its course, making its calls based on sense data, memory, and instincts."

"I'm with you, Calieze, and so are a whole lot of others, especially here in Tibet and in India. And I think I know where the soul hangs out."

"Yeah? Where?"

"The prefrontal cortex in the brain."

"Not the heart, eh?"

"The myth of heart and soul linkage got going long before some people had to give up their hearts for artificial ones and found their souls were still present and accounted for. The PFC is headquarters for executive function, judgments of right and wrong, where we commit to actions."

"I've actually seen a prefrontal cortex once, when I shot a medical instructional video of a new brain surgical technique. The utter silence of the brain amazed me."

"Amazing, how decisions made in that gray silence that can change forever the life of the person in whose skull it resides."

"And the lives of many others besides, especially when the decision leads to the evil killing of somebody else."

"Tigers, of course, being exempt from indictment of evil."

"Of course. Animals can't be judged evil no matter how awful their behavior. I once worked on a boat covering an orca hunt, where a band of orcas chased down a baby blue whale, stealing it from its mother who'd exhausted herself trying to protect her calf."

"Holy crap. You saw that happen?"

"I didn't just see it. I captured it on tape for others to see on television. Sometimes shooting nature ain't pretty. When we climbed back on board the boat, we were basically speechless for two hours."

"Shima, our rescue dog in the Rockies, had a beautiful soul and it wasn't tarnished just because he'd occasionally gobble a live mouse. Even Kyoru, that poor little mongrel in Gnam Yuljongs has a soul."

"Maybe Kyoru's fleas have souls too—that's why the Jains panic at the thought of stepping on an ant. But dog, dolphin, spider or flea, they're all exempt. Evil didn't exist till humans came along, equipped with an instinctive awareness that the right of another human to live should not be violated."

"Rule change."

"A rule change that some players scorn." Through stressed breathing, Calieze wheezed, "We call them psychotics or sociopaths, medical sounding terms like hemophiliac or epileptic, but whether or not evil people have a disorder of the brain, they sure as shit have one of the soul, where they let any respect for life instinct they might have decay or die."

She halted her riff as she slowed her pace. "You okay?" I asked, beginning to wonder about her ability to handle this climb, which was getting quite steep. I disregarded her nod and waited to see how long it would be till she steadied her breathing.

After a few moments, she picked up her theme. "The spiritual test of whether individuals are human is whether they instinctively hold that right to live inviolate or they do something like splatter semiautomatic gunfire around innocent people to make a point to a rival drug dealer."

"Or bury a man alive because the chairman of a political party wants them to crush everyone who disagrees with him. Once they succumb to that virus, they've begun transmogrification into something subhuman." Once the viral cluster invaded that pseudoshaman child killer, he looked like he had late stage smallpox."

"Eviola doesn't invade anyone," she corrected me. That lunatic chose to suck the virus into his body. Viruses are mindless—they just need a place to stay and reproduce, like every other life form. Blaming the virus is like laying the blame on the so-called devil or on some boss giving orders. That charlatan shaman sought his own soul infection. He craved it. ”

“He craved it but not just because he was crazy. There are lots of people who are crazy or who suffer some other mental inadequacy who cope with it quietly and get on with life. They don't turn to evil as a resentful substitution for healthy life unless their souls lack the respect for life instinct.”

“No RLI.”

“No RLI.” Calieze was walking twenty feet in front of me and I noticed her gait change. I increased my stride to catch up to her as she struggled to continue the conversation. “My bet is that that sputtering light at the back of the pseudoshaman's soulspace was the last, gasping fragment of his RLI.”

Calieze coughed and stumbled. We'd just rounded a turn in the path to a point where we regained sight of the promontory, and she took one look at it and sat down with her back partly against a boulder. I was struck by the suddenness and extent of her lethargy. She went on for a moment about how the human race wouldn't merit the gift of intelligence but for our RLI, babbling as if to combat the recognition in me and herself that she was not doing well. I checked her pulse and could tell right away that it was at least 120. I said, “I tell you what, let's you and me put this hike on pause for a couple of minutes,” though I knew we weren't going any higher on that trip. Her hands and face had begun to swell. I pointed out that she was acting lightheaded, but she denied it, coughing. “Ladies and gentlemen,” I announced, “we'll be starting our descent to New Hale momentarily.”

Looking up at the promontory, another good nine hundred feet higher in elevation, she said, “But we're almost at the Great Spire. I'll be fine in a moment. I don't want to give up.”

“We're not giving up. We're just taking the Great Spire expedition in stages, as nature requires, and we've completed the first phase, which was to climb only to this elevation, which I'm guessing is nearly eighteen thousand feet. Now we're going to turn back, 'cause, Calieze, you're developing altitude mountain sickness.”

“Nonsense, Den.” More stifled panting. “I just need to rest a moment.”

"All due respect, ma'am, but this isn't your area of expertise." I didn't like pulling rank on her but her condition bore no fooling around. "You're at risk of getting into real trouble if we don't head back down. Home is more than three thousand feet lower and you're going to feel better and better the closer we get to it."

She rolled her eyes at me and said, "Yes, doctor."

"I don't have an MD, but I've seen more cases of AMS than ninety-nine percent of those who do. When we stopped for a drink at the little waterfall, you seemed fine, but not now. We're going to take a nice steady stroll downhill, right back the way we came." I yanked a windbreaker out of the rucksack. "Here, put this on. Preserve your body heat." She lacked the energy to dismiss my advice.

We returned home about five hours ago. Knowing Calieze was headed for an early, long sleep, I threw together a quick dinner, warming up some momos (dumplings) and porridge left over from last night.

Once she crawled off to bed and set her beautiful head on the pillow, I breathed a big sigh of relief. A good third of the mental energy I employ in rescue work, even in such a mild case as this, is devoted to putting just the right English on the conversation ball, line after line, to optimize the potential victim's state of mind. The point is not to blur the focus on the job that must be done, but to paint some optimistic perspective around it, producing constructive entertainment to highlight whatever fragments of normalcy might yet be hanging in the atmosphere. Get that nervous, shaken person onto a glide path to recovery and home. Calieze will be fine in the morning. A few more weeks of careful training and she'll handle a trip to the Spire as well as I.

We've got plenty of work cut out for ourselves right here. Traumatic as last night was, what we've experienced together was too convincing to ignore. So we shall embark on visitations again, and again and again. I'm certain that, like mountaineering and musicianship, our new skill can be built upon.

At the same time, I do wish that we had some real-world evidence to back up our impressions of what we're doing with our embryonic power. We don't know for sure if Calieze's apparent impacts really registered at all in the perps' minds or even if those perps or their targets really existed. Speculation doesn't mean jack without evidence.

We should keep an eye out for some way to verify the effects we believe we're having. We can't afford to invest so much of our physical and mental lives on a meaningless, gut-wrenching fantasy.

Meanwhile, we've got another, more mundane matter to address, which is how long we're willing to brave the oncoming dark cold. I'd never considered spending the *winter* in the remote Himalayas. But why not? For centuries there've been some people who manage to live and work at this elevation. It would be a hell of an adventure. If we can pull it off, we could emerge invincible. I'm thinking go for it.

No need to commit one way or the other quite yet. We can handle at least a few more weeks up here and that will give us plenty of time to strategize. For now, I shall sign off and yield the field to my beloved teammate in profound gratitude for her and for whatever led us to this adventure, even though a whiff of terror does sometimes streak through the wind.

[3-4]

Morning, Oct. 8, '91
CZM

If my father were still around, I wonder if I'd have the audacity to tell him, "Hey, Dad—your daughter's turned scientist, too." He was pretty open-minded, but the experiments Den and I are carrying on are a bit too fringy for the kind of agencies he worked for. Our log notes would doubtless raise eyebrows too, but given the criticality of Den's and my relationship to our research, I feel obliged to insert certain personal details that would be ruled out of bounds in more conventional lab records. So, before logging details of our most recent confrontations with evil, I'll relate a much more pleasing encounter between Den and me that took place the morning after our second, extremely trying visitation. It does bear upon how the hell I ever got myself to go back for a third attempt after the miasmal horror of the pseudoshaman.

The sun had risen enough to render the air bearable for stripping down and I was finishing off a quick bath down by the creek with a lukecool mixture of two parts water straight from the creek to one part boiled up at "the house." I was relishing the invigorating sunshine on my bare skin when I heard Den coming down the path to the creek, about to find me in all my glory. I didn't need to turn around to know what effect that would have on his (likely unclothed) mortal coil. I've spent two weeks this guy, whose hearty appetite had been sharpened by both the better part of a year of solitude and two weeks on a rich diet of excitement. While drying off, I took a look at him and repeated my remark off Oahu. "Nice vajra," adding "show-off" for good measure, pretending not to feel my own desire simmering.

He chuckled and came up behind me, looping his arms around my waist. As I felt his whole-body embrace, I rolled my eyes and said, "God, you're predictable."

"Touché—but please remember that I'm interested in your mind. You're not just some deity consort cheesecake to stuff my face with."

"Who cares? You're nothing but some deity consort beefcake to stuff *my* face with."

With a dash of indignation he declared, "Perhaps it would interest you to know that I have a mind too."

"I believe you, Yogi. And it looks like you're using it to meditate on the Eager Husband pose."

He picked me up, muttering, "My resistance is futile."

I wrapped my legs around his waist. "What resistance?"

Abruptly ending verbal communication, he emplaced me, carried me back up the hill, in flagrante delicto and oh, so delicately, in the awkward but most exciting ninety-yard rush of his life and mine, and grounded me in more earthy sensuality than I'd ever dreamed possible before coming to Tibet.

An hour and a half later, thoroughly spent, Den flopped down alongside me as we immersed ourselves in a warm morning sunbath, and I intoned, "Mmmmm—yabyummy!"

"I think the entire Himalaya trembled at the sight of you naked by that creek."

"Funny—I didn't feel it until you showed up."

"Sex with you compares to all past sex the way all past sex compares to kissing."

I replied, "Coming with you compares to all past orgasms the way my past orgasms compare to the hokey-pokey."

"If you don't mind, I'd rather not think about either your past orgasms or the hokey-pokey."

"You're the last man on Earth who needs to worry about a woman's past." Partly for the amusement of watching him squirm, I added, "You penetrate my mind as much as anything else. I can't imagine how you can understand a woman's feelings so well."

"No need to get carried away."

I caught him suppressing a grin as he rolled his eyes. I was tempted to embarrass him a little more, but I let it be, pleased with myself.

I suppose I'm stalling. I hope I can be forgiven in light of the whiplash from our week-long roller coaster ride that followed. But here goes.

The evening after our first assault on the promontory, we took it easy. We slept in the next morning and began the day in the gardens, babying the watercress, carrots, and turnips and their environs. Mid-day we took a climb straight up behind the cave. There was no way either of us was going to allow my brief knockdown by AMS to go unanswered. I'd never backed away from a physical challenge before and I wasn't going to start now. The incident called only for a recalibration of my training, not a retreat.

Come nightfall, it was time to get back to work. We began the first of a nearly week-long series of expeditions into the substratum of humanity's spiritual life where the potential for evil hides. In the first five nights we visited a wide variety of soulspaces, offering me ample opportunity to duplicate the presumed success of my first attempt to steer a prospective perpetrator away from the vile act he was plotting. One "brutaliphile" lashed a man to death in front of his fellow prisoners in a torture chamber, apparently in North Korea. Another took part in an execution-style machine-gunning of six blindfolded men and a teenaged boy in a Latin American jungle, which could have been El Salvador but which, sorry to say, could have taken place in a number of other blighted lands. In a third instance, a white woman killed a couple in bed with a .45. In every case, we could see what the perpetrators were plotting anywhere from two to forty minutes in advance, and I tried everything I could think of with words and images to dissuade them, all to no avail. I emerged from each soulspace beaten down worse than ever.

Daylight offered opportunities to counter the depletion of my spirit with a build-up of physical strength. Likening our daily hikes to football practice, Coach Sherab put me through my paces to build my leg strength and lung capacity in thin air. I was able to take a few scraps of pride in my physical progress, but it was hard to ignore the dark cloud that hung over me from our nocturnal forays to sites of imminent evil.

Den's confidence, on the other hand, never flagged. Den is hard core. He exudes indomitable search and rescue force. A setback, a rough time, a big loss—none of it fazes T. Den Sherab. He sweeps the debris off the launch pad, calls in the next rocket, and straps himself in, ready for ignition at a moment's notice. He'd been through four months of failure to affect perps on his own before I came along and succeeded the first time out, so that one jolt of hope had reinvigorated his quest. He became more determined than ever to reopen the case against evil, even if it meant badgering the one person on this earth he madly loves to do something that was wounding her. Fine—I won't duck out. Child murder notwithstanding, I advance with the team.

So, two nights ago, we set out again and came upon some teenaged skinheads in an American city park hovering near a homeless man wrapped inside a filthy sleeping bag. It was a bitterly cold night and the kid whose soulspace we'd reached was fiddling with a plastic gas can and chortling with his rude boys about setting the sleeper on fire. A bulging *eviola* cluster gravitated ever closer to the kid's head and the RLI light high at the back of his soulspace was barely detectable.

Nauseated, I was bracing myself for another murder when suddenly an inspiration hit me. I caught a glimpse of the kid's own grandfather flitting by in his memory as seen in the walls of his soulspace. The disheveled old man was gazing fondly at him. I conjured an image of the grandfather stumbling about in a burning sleeping bag, screaming and crying as his flesh burned and projected that into the kid's mind, where it appeared above his window to the outside. At that precise moment, the kid stopped talking with his friends as his internal self stared at my motion picture. The others carried on, not noticing his silence. Suddenly his RLI light flared up a bit, brightening his soulspace. The boy looked back at the unwitting homeless man and blurted out, "Ah, what the fuck, let the loser sleep. We can use the gas on the Radio Shack down the street. The asshole that runs the place sneers at me like I'm a criminal just for looking at the shit in his window."

The *eviola* froze a couple of feet from the kid's head as he looked around at his shaved-headed friends. They were taken aback by his turnabout, since just minutes before he'd been the one leading the charge "to barbecue the homeless dude." My hope soared that my trick had worked and that these thugs would abandon their murderous prank. But then one of the kid's buddies spat, "Chicken shit!" and the others joined in, deriding him for having lost his balls. In seconds, a dark splotch covered over the image of the burning grandfather and the viral clump was reactivated, its surface riddled with slimy, maggoty spikes. With deep inhalations, the kid drew it up to his mouth and he sucked it into his body whole. Pustules broke out over his soulspace face and hands as he declared, "I was kidding, fuckfaces—let's burn this bum!"

And they did. The last thing I saw in the perp's vision window was the gang running from the scene, whooping and hollering, as the terrified victim tried in hopeless, drunken clumsiness to grapple his way out of his burning shroud.

I fled back home, paying no attention to Den's ministrations. I remained speechless, as I had after the pseudoshaman, this time for more than an hour, during which Den told me that he recognized we'd done enough, we'd tried hard, but that he wouldn't ask me to try again "at least for a while." I was neither mad at him nor able to soothe his conscience, troubled as it was for having pushed me to go through with the visitation despite my apprehensions. I was too rattled to settle on what to say.

When we did speak again, we avoided the subject in favor of lighthearted things. A serious reconsideration of our whole mysterious enterprise was rolling towards us from the future, but it had telegraphed respectfully that it would meet us the next day, after we'd had a good night's sleep and some hiking therapy.

The next morning Den asked me if the time had come for us to have another go at the Spire. I was flattered by his confidence in me and I declared I was. Taking the Spire would be a head-clearing morale booster. We took our time, paced the journey with well-timed breaks, and found ourselves just shy of the final assault in less than two hours. Den gave me one more chance to turn back, but I was exhilarated by the gorgeous view and my own increased strength and I ordered us full steam ahead.

Forty minutes later we stood atop a precipice that seemed to overlook the whole planet. It's literally breathtaking up there. (Permanently so if you don't watch your step—it's eight thousand feet down to the first nearly level ground.) Looking down on a few blindingly white cloud tops a mile below us struck one more triumphant chord in honor of my decision to come to Asia last spring. When in heaven, the difficult seems simple and the impossible a logical option.

The high made the trip home feel like paragliding. We had dinner preparations underway an hour and a half after leaving the Spire, as the sun kissed the horizon. We dallied over our humble chow as the stars lit up over Tibet, took a walk under the waxing crescent moon, and retired to the throne bed in our jackets with mugs of chang.

Blessed by a day so abundant in God's good graces, I had no excuse for avoiding the troubling question about our mission that was still sequestered in the wings, having swollen through six consecutive wrenching visitation failures: Why are we doing this to ourselves? Den sighed, "I hear you."

"Den, I love your rock-headed endurance, but let's face it: there's been exactly one presumed success in the four and a half months since you began diving in scum ponds of evil. Is it really worth it?"

"It was worth it to those two young girls at the woods' edge."

"It was worth it to them. But what if that were the only success we'll ever have? Could we keep punishing ourselves this way forever, hoping for another?"

"It's not punishment. We're just working our way back to more successes. Uncle Yeshe once told me an old Tibetan saying, '*Srog gi skyabs byed*—for long life, neither hurt others nor fail to protect them.'"

"I have trouble seeing how this grueling ordeal could possibly contribute to my living long."

"I'm wearing asbestos-skinned armor out there. The only thing that gets to me is the pain I see it inflicts on you."

"Now, don't get too excited. There's no arterial bleeding going on. Maybe I just need a pep talk."

"I'm here to give it to you, because you are the key."

"We're the key, if a key there be. Now please explain how you withstood four months of sorties to hell with no key."

Den lay back with one hand under his head and the other around my shoulders as I nestled next to him. He began by acknowledging that the bit about asbestos-skinned armor was partly bullshit. After all, right before I showed up a couple of weeks ago, he'd decided to jump ship. "And," he added, "the worst heart-losing moment was when I saw the injury inflicted upon you while you were locked in empathy with the girl drowned by the pseudoshaman. As we flew back here, I was tempted to guzzle a gallon of amnesia juice with you. But lying here with you afterward, a steely invincibility charged my spine with determination. Microbiologists graced with evidence that they may be onto a cure for a deadly disease have no right to flee. A charge of hope like that is more than a gift—and it is a gift, whether you wanted it or not—it's an order from above that you ignore at your peril. Should you shirk it, the price you'd pay in lost self-respect—and sacrificed adventure—would cripple your spirit forever after."

I stroked his thick chest. "I get it. If I pressured you to let New Hale turn into a ghost lab, I couldn't live with myself."

"A breakthrough in spiritual antiviral research beckons." Den gently slipped away from our embrace. He stood up and started pacing around the throne bed. I watched him going back and forth, turning my head Wimbledon-style, bemused by and feeding off his fired-up élan. "What is experimental science but getting at the origins and mechanisms of natural phenomena? Our study of evil is embryonic, but so were biology and cosmology at one point."

"I'm with you, Den, though I'm glad we don't have to explain soul science to the *Nova* staff or *Science* magazine."

"Somebody may, some day. And that'll be good, because *Science* magazine weeds out the flakes and nutcases. Some people think that having a soul makes them experts."

"Having kidneys doesn't make someone a nephrologist."

"And neither we nor anybody else can claim to be legit soulologists yet. But we have landed some promising clues that we have to respect enough to follow them up. Everyone in microbiology knows the story of the Scottish pharmacologist who left his lab in a mess when he went on a family vacation in the summer of 1928. When he got back to the lab weeks later, he found a little fungus contaminating one of the staph cultures he'd left stacked on a bench. The curious thing was that the bacteria right next to the fungus had been killed off. He diddled around with it and published a paper on it a few months later, but eventually he dropped the whole business. Cultivating the fungus was hard and extracting the bacteria-killing agent in it was even harder, he didn't know its structure, and he figured it probably wouldn't survive in a body anyway. His interest faded and so did he.

"But eleven years later some scientists at Oxford who'd been looking into the Scot's finding announced that they'd figured out the agent's structure and how to extract it, and when they received word that the Scot was coming to visit, one of them famously exclaimed, 'Good God, I thought he was dead!' And within a short time the penicillin Alexander Fleming had abandoned began saving millions of lives around the world."

"Okay, perseverance furthers. Sometimes."

"That lesson wasn't lost on early virologists. In the '50s some of them noticed that viruses inactivated by heat or ultraviolet light checked the growth of live viruses on a rabbit skin and a chicken egg. They'd discovered interferon and launched a crusade against a slew of plagues, including hepatitis, herpes, and cancer. In our lab we were taught that legend like a catechism."

"I'm following you," I told him, "unfortunately for my eye muscles having to track all your pacing. Could you give it a rest?"

"Sorry." He returned to my side. "I guess I made my point."

"Your point is that what we saw in that hunter's soulspace was our staph culture fungus moment."

"I'm speculating, of course, but—yeah."

"I respect speculation," I replied. "It's stock in trade for black hole studies. A potential big deal that's hard to prove."

"Proving that black holes are real would be a big deal. But a thousand murders a day taking place a lot closer than any black hole have already proved that evil is real and putting an end to it would be a bigger deal still. It would make knocking over the fascists look like winning a bar fight."

"My sixth-grade teacher told us she didn't set eyes on her husband for over four years during World War II. At least we've got each other."

"And no bullets to dodge."

"So hold the self-pity if we lose a few, is that it?"

"Rescue teams win some and lose some."

"Okay, Den. The show must go on." I stood up. "I'm gonna wash up and when I get back, we can give it a go."

I made my way down to the creek in the moonless dark, trying not to tense up for whatever lay ahead. I returned to the cave to find Den doing pushups, getting night game-ready for what would be neither fun nor a game. We allowed ourselves one embrace for the sky road and settled into position on the throne bed, our backs up against the rock face.

I willed my apprehensions to melt away and readied myself to feel Den's psychic tug and soon began soaring with him above the clouds resting on the western horizon. After a while—a half-hour?—the lights of a city appeared up ahead, dimmed as if seen through a thin coverlet, blemished by a telltale smudge signifying a soulspace. We separated and entered it, taking up our positions on opposite sides.

Hunched and prostrate, our subject looked out over a busy urban thoroughfare during an evening rush hour in what appeared to be western or central Europe. To his right were two comrades, a woman with a beret and on the other side of her, a man with a ski hat. They were perched on the rooftop of a building some eight stories high, clad in shabby army surplus clothes and bearing assault rifles. Unlike most of the loner killers Den has come upon—he refers to them as "solopsychos"—this lot were conspiratorial terrorists, possibly a left-wing twist on 1930s Nazi brownshirts. Our subject's nervous glance looked forward and down at an elegant, faux-classic building surrounded by a pointed metal fence that attempted to straddle both aesthetic and security concerns. An American flag hung limp from a pole at the front.

Our subject lay prone, both in reality and within his soulspace. Through his window we could see him holding a rifle when we arrived, though it would disappear and reappear in phases as his attention darted about. When he lifted his weapon to his cheek, a crosshair view of the building's guards' kiosk filled the window. When he looked at the woman next to him, the letters "RAF" carved into the gunstock peeked out from under her left arm. I could smell beer on her breath. The man's hand appeared, holding a longneck bottle and brought it to his mouth below the window; its brown glass tinting its reflection of the sodium vapor street lights that pierced the darkness and highlit the narrow eyes of his fellow would-be killers.

His soulspace walls were littered with images of windows shattering in a brightly-lit trolley and fancy SUV's at the building's gate, accompanied by screams, and followed by bloodied survivors including a mother bearing an infant with blood spouting from its chest, stumbling over corpses as sirens and panic rent the air. A barely visible, sickly yellow RLI light flickered at the back of his soulspace. I was astounded to realize that so much bloody, lifelong pain was about to be inflicted on account of the festering pathology in a few cubic centimeters inside one skull on a nearby rooftop.

Then something caught my notice that wrenched me free from my anxious stupor. In the man's soulspace wall, in a framed family portrait that included our subject, a little girl bloomed large in the picture and recoiled in horror. Twitching, without looking back, the man reflexively kicked backwards and the light and the family disappeared.

Faster than I could think, my memory spun out an image from a troubling thangka I'd painted in school, adapted it on the fly for the West, and flung it into his soulspace wall: a demon with a western face like that of our subject but with upper and lower three-inch fangs and bulging, bloodshot eyes stomping on an infant who looked like a younger version of the little girl in the picture, gagging on her internal organs as they were pushed into her throat. I could hardly stand what I was doing, but I forced a close up of the girl's face onto the man's surround screen, and after a moment, the crosshairs dropped from the window and the view retreated a couple of feet and turned to the woman as he lifted his hand, as if waving her off. She scowled, and an agitated conversation ensued in whispered German, with the other shooter joining in.

The subject and I struggled for control of the imagery dominating his soul. His chamber walls re-erupted in scenes of gunfire, breaking glass, and screams, and the baby-stomping demon disappeared.

Feeling a tug from across the soulspace, I looked up and saw Den, whom I'd forgotten about, gesturing to me to stop. His dim voice sounded as if were on a phone from Saturn. I could make out only the word "peaceful."

For the moment I was too focused on what was transpiring in the subject's window to think about Den's message. The subject's female comrade shifted her look from him to the street below, craning her neck to better see the street down to the left. The subject's window followed suit, revealing a trolley making its way toward us. Our subject looked back at the woman and saw her lift her rifle and take aim. A moment later, the crosshairs reappeared in the window, tracking the distant trolley.

The trolley made a stop one block away to take on passengers. As the milliseconds raced by, I considered Den's apparent urging to replace the horrific imagery I'd projected into the man's soulspace with something calming and peaceful. It struck me as risky to drop the elements of fear and horror, since that approach had just netted us a temporary reprieve from the guy's terroristic juggernaut. However, I flung my imagination in the opposite direction and it landed on a melody that evoked the tragic pointlessness of violence. It was a phrase from the second movement of Beethoven's *Emperor* piano concerto, a musical line that had been borrowed for a song of star-crossed lovers in *West Side Story*. I let the orchestral strains leak into the subject's consciousness; and, sure enough, the crosshairs dropped out of the picture.

They quickly reappeared but the extra moment had given me an opening to switch gears. As the trolley started to move again and the three shooters readied their weapons, I placed the little girl into Van Gogh's *Starry Night*, restful and sleepy-eyed, listening to the grand, sweeping, nostalgic finale of Ravel's *Mother Goose Suite* and laid it in the shooter's soulspace surrounding his window—and right before my eyes and ears, it sprung a psychic letting of the man's overheated blood. His RLI light rose and the orgies of explosive violence in his soulspace drained away. Chunks crumbled out of the bloody visions, leaving behind swatches of silver-lined clouds of a clearing storm.

Through the window, the woman, grimacing as she put her eye to the gun sight, was halted by our subject's hand placed on her shoulder. Another argument in whispered German ensued, during which I maintained the movie of the little girl smiling as she drifted off to sleep. I could feel the pieces of a real rescue tumble together like the works of an elegant combination lock, each in their proper place, and in a moment, the subject's pissed-off, would-be killers put down their weapons and skulked off to the stairwell door.

I was astonished. We'd won. We'd apparently saved—who knows?—maybe ten or twelve lives. As we flew back to Tibet, I reveled in Den's radiating waves of triumph and bursting optimism. When we finally reached New Hale and I saw the beaming relief in his face, I fell into his arms, quiet but jubilant.

"See?" he asked with that cockeyed grin I'm so enamored of. "Who says artists are self-absorbed? How many art school grads can say they saved even one person from violent death in their entire lives? You just saved a dozen in a few minutes. You were brilliant!" I smiled and laid my head on his shoulder, part of me wanting to fall instantly asleep from mental exhaustion, the rest buzzing and bargaining for a little spell of normalcy before turning over my consciousness safekeeping to the unpredictable gyrations of Dreamland.

"Kudos to you for persisting this week. I was done." I sighed. "Now can I go to bed, Daddy?"

Den's answer surprised me. "In due time, but before nodding off, I have one more experiment to propose."

"Please—time totally out, SAR Man. It's savor-and-recover time."

"Calieze, this isn't about nerve-wracking drama. I'm thinking of a boon to recovery, something short and sweet."

"And what might this be?"

"I'd rather not say, Calieze. I've not tried it before, so please don't ask. I promise it will be light and easy, maybe even beautiful and definitely nothing to do with evil. Call it self-lullabying, a real life, real-time bedtime story. If even one sign points the wrong way, I'll swing us back home on the spot. Sunshine or bust."

"*Sunshine*, you say."

"Middle of the night sunshine."

"All right, m'love. I'll trust you. But if this trip smells off by one molecule, I'm fleeing for the comfort of this bed and our Milky Way cover, with you or without you."

"Deal."

"Just let me stretch first." I got up, uncreaked my knees, and rummaged round in the cave for my handy-dandy solar-powered flashlight for a five minute stroll around the neighborhood. The stars were so bright I was sure that, if I stayed quiet long enough, I'd hear their photons making the stratosphere sing.

I got back to our tiny front yard and took my place next to Den. He said, "Let's go," and soon we were back in the dark upper atmosphere, flying west again, faster than ever.

And longer than ever. I was tempted to beam him a question, namely what happened to the short part of 'short and sweet' but the ride felt good so I cut him some slack. As always on these trips, Den appeared ethereal to me, as I might see him in a dream. I could hardly feel his warm skin and firm musculature but the electricity between us and the confidence it fueled were as vigorous as ever.

A streak of light appeared on the horizon over a land mass I took to be Scandinavia. We were traveling back into the dusk preceding the night we'd already lived for hours in Tibet. I saw the sun rise in the west as we gave chase to it over the Atlantic. We charged on for a long while, working our way back into the late afternoon over the edge of North America. Back home for a visit, much sooner than expected.

No sooner had I recognized that the patch of coast where we were headed had to be New York than it all whited out and we were surrounded by a fog like those that had preceded our arrival at soulspaces in the past, except this one shone like a sunlit mist after dawn on the Sonoma coast. Our pace ever decreasing, we came upon a cloud chamber the size of the other soulspaces we'd visited, lit up a brilliant white from within. We slowed and approached it like a spaceship docking at a space station.

We'd entered upon a lovely and comical sight, reflected in a bakery window. A slight, but spry, elderly white woman was walking through the courtyard of a big-city housing project holding a quacking white duck wrapped in a towel in her arms. Taxis, buses, trucks, and cars plowed along what looked to me like 125th Street in Harlem. The sign tagging, stumbling homeless, and a smattering of barred and boarded up windows certainly qualified it for ghetto status, though for the first time in all our visitations, the air smelled as clean as the air in New Hale. I know New York too well to believe that was the smell of the city, so it must have been an attribute of the woman's soulspace.

As she soothed her new feathered friend, she paid no attention to her soulspace walls, which were merrily screening a whimsical array of abstract color patterns mixed with faces of people of all ages and races, a lively collage of joy and colorful contentment, splashed here and there with flowers. A good many of her neighbors seen through her window, almost all of them black or Puerto Rican, looked her way, mirroring the good cheer of those in her imagination. Off to the side a couple of teenagers rolled their eyes at "the funny kook" but some adults on benches near the doorway were more charitable, waving and smiling. A rotund man called out "Here come the duck ambulance!" while the woman next to him elbowed him gently and told the lady "It's the Lord's work you're doing, Anne."

Within Anne's soulspace, her RLI shone like a bright lighthouse beam above the rear of her spiritual chamber. She chattered to the duck, joking and comforting it as she entered an apartment tower through its heavy, graffiti-tagged metal door.

We boarded the dingy elevator and Anne stroked the jittery bird in anticipation of the clang of the rusty gate. When the door opened, a window at the end of the corridor looked out on Harlem humming twenty stories below. We watched Anne and her uneasy guest make their way down the corridor to her apartment door, where she negotiated the awkward task of holding the duck and a small bag of groceries while unlocking the door.

Inside, she was greeted by three more fussing ducks and a pigeon, all of them hobbling along with injured feet or wings on wrinkled, messy newspapers strewn on the floors and furniture. Anne dropped the keys and grocery bag on a hall side table beneath some framed photos of stage productions, a black jazz band, and a peace demonstration. She carried her feathered charge down the hall to a bedroom, where a double bass, its rich spruce grain softened by a patina of dust, stood watch in a corner. A black man with a mostly bare scalp adorned by tight grey side curls was lying on his side. A TV tray by the bed held a glass of water and several bottles of pills. The man lifted a sleepy eye and a beautiful smile came over his illness-thinned face. He appeared to be well into his seventies.

"I could see you coming down at the corner," he said, "and I thought, look at the quacks.'"

The woman stroke the duck's head, and cooed to it, "Don't you mind Theodore, Constance, he's as happy to have you here as I am."

Having introduced the duck to Theodore, Anne placed the bird on the hallway floor where it began a waddling survey of its surroundings. Anne returned to the bed, kissed Theodore, and touched his face. She sat at his side as they raked through the details of how he was feeling and her latest bird rescue. I bathed in the warm glow of the deep love that bonded the two oldsters. I looked up across Anne's soulspace at Den and felt our love headed in that same direction, decades away. He smiled at me and I closed my eyes to the gentle pull away from that sweet microcosm and we rejoined each other in the white cloud to begin our long flight back to the other side of the world.

The whole way back, pushing into the night side of Earth, I was grateful for the gift Den had bestowed on us. He'd not previously attempted to train his inner radar to look for a soul of such light and purity, in which a powerful respect for life instinct was but one part of an environment suffused with wisdom and love. While the intelligence and rich life history in Anne's face left no doubt that she must have seen a great spectrum of human experience in her lifetime—and perhaps had to deal with evil that might have been directed towards herself or people she loved—it was obvious that eviola could never get anywhere near her soulspace, for it would not survive the welder's arc phosphorescence of her RLI. She'd achieved eternal immunity.

Den's gamble had paid off ten times over. When we returned to the high cold mountainside of New Hale, we curled up in and around each other in our warm double sleeping bag and relished our love before, and while, falling into a deep, smooth sleep. I had been reminded of the beauty of life, which made me thankful that we had found a way to protect that beauty, even in such an unpredictable and invisible fashion as we'd concocted over the last couple of weeks.

Q.E.D.

[3-5]

Oct. 30, 1991
CZM

The brawny man hoisting stacks of wood over yonder by a charcoal pit has opined that I've labored enough at woodcutting today and suggested that I catch up on recording the proceedings of the New Hale National International Interplanetary Lab. Having taken on the lioness's share of the writing, I'm dutifully logging in.

We had more time for work for a while after my last entry due to the reading on a thermometer I imported up here from California. It obliged me to share a news flash with Den when he snuggled up to me in bed, murmuring, "Paradoxical though it may seem, even though our dance last night left nothing to be desired…," finishing with a pressing thought that shot straight to my lower brain.

"Sorry, Den, we'll have to let the echoes of last night's crescendo suffice for a few days."

"Uh-oh."

"The thin red line on my thermometer foresees an egg release in my immediate future."

"The Oracle of Walgreen's hath spoken."

"Indeed. Its wisdom is great and trumps pills and devices not readily replaceable in the remote Himalayas."

"Nuff said. Adding a nursery onto this cave would be a tricky enterprise."

I was ready for more visitations anyway, after the inspiring ones to Germany and New York. Den and I have slipped into a mission groove that has continued unabated for three weeks. Our strikeouts are still painful, but they're less frequent and the lives saved when we score motivates me to pick myself up after the failures and carry on.

I shall note a couple of examples from both sides that occurred during the last three weeks. One night Den led us to the soulspace of a man in a butcher shop. He looked Tibetan to me, so he must have been a lot closer than Germany. It was further unlikely that a shop in Germany or anywhere else far from southeast Asia would have a poster like the one on the shop wall of a girl who looked perhaps four years old with large, Mongolian almond-shaped eyes imparting a somber caste to a face surrounded by extravagant gold-threaded, red silk finery, evidently regarded by some as a real-life agent of the divine.

Clutching a knife designed to cut yak haunches, the subject was sneaking past the poster of the goddess girl towards a gray-haired man hunched over his bookwork. It looked to me like someone was about to murder his boss. I suffused his soulspace with a chilling vision of himself as an elderly inmate rotting in prison with his grown child crying outside the prison window. It was close—the subject's foot-long blade was poised, just pre-thrust, over his victim's neck, when he froze. The older man suddenly turned around, shocked, and took the knife from him.

We had limited time to ride the high from that success before encountering a form of evil that's in a class unto itself. It occurred about a week and a half ago, when we came upon a man in his twenties exiting a bus in large city and making his way to an apartment building. The look of the city and the use of Arabic in most of the street signs and advertisements—one of which had the name "Damascus" in English— indicated a location in the Mideast, undoubtedly Syria.

We were confused by the mélange of images in the subject's soulspace walls. His visions of fatally stabbing a teenaged girl seemed to parallel images of himself and others close to him with that same girl throughout a shared childhood, unmistakably reflecting family love. This girl was no sexual prey like the targets of the hunter and several other potential perps we'd surveiled: the girl he was envisioning stabbing was his sister. And there were no indications of her having done harm to him or anyone else. Rather, in a battering flux of memory movies, we saw the pictures of affection repeatedly trampled by images of the girl being raped by three thugs in a back alley.

I knew then that we were up against an implacable foe, evil that stemmed from an interplay of forces far more difficult to reckon with even than the spiritual illness of one individual's atrophied respect for life instinct. What inflamed the mind of this man was an age-old belief in some cultures that, in the wake of a rape of a family member, the family's moral flamethrowers must be aimed at the victim, as if compounding her rape with her execution would remove a stain upon their honor. I'd heard how sometimes such hideous non-judicial sentences are carried out by a family member upon a sister or daughter if the girl dares to get married for love in a match not made by the bride's father. A girl can be offed just for holding a boyfriend's hand, or going on a date without permission from a male family member, or even merely turning to look at a boy, often without the perpetrators facing punishment or even token prosecution.

My blood absorbed a painful chill watching our grim subject make his way through some crowded city streets. I glanced across his soulspace at Den and could see the pained resignation in his face. He had little hope that I could trip up the deadly juggernaut approaching the girl, one she must have feared from the moment the rapists had viciously stolen her virginity. I tried concocting an image of Mohammed, surrounded by revering followers sitting at his feet in ancient Arabia, looking straight at our subject, raising his hands and shaking his head to halt him, accompanied by the stirring tones of a tenor muezzin calling the righteous to prayer. Wrong call—the man's imagined stabbings grew more frenzied, perhaps from a false, sociopathic notion that this murder was required by the teachings of The Messenger.

The brother sneaked into the apartment building, and the eviola beckoning to him grew to the size of a medicine ball with spiky maggot appendages on its surface. I tried projecting an image of his sister and himself twenty years into the future, with families of their own at a celebration, smiling at each other in mutual affection. As he disabled the lock and entered the apartment, I became panicked and flung in images of his family including clones of his bleeding sister stabbing him in vengeful rage for his crime. It was an idiotic choice made in desperation, one that could hardly counter his anticipation of his certain imminent ascent to hero status among his people on account of what he was about to do.

Helplessly, I watched the brother suck on the virus, grabbing it in huge clots and thrusting them into his mouth. He sneaked down the cramped, hallway to a room at the back, thrilling to the infection and swelling his chest with pride. As he passed a hallway mirror, I could see his physical face still looking normal even as carbonaceous waste fire pustules broke out all over his internal face. He peered through the bedroom door to locate his prey, burst into the room, raced to her bed, and pinned her down with her blanket. Through his window I saw the girl awaken and the widening of her eyes as she realized that the living nightmare she long feared had begun. She got out two screams of his name, "Fayez!" before the first thrust of the dagger in her face, followed by four more ripping open her head and neck.

And yet, the horror of that sick and bloody scene had yet to reach its peak. It was surpassed a minute later by one tinny sound—the cheers and hallelujahs of his family coming through the telephone at the girl's bedside when Fayez reported the success of his perverted mission, an entire family of accessories before and after the fact to the vicious murder of their own innocent kin.

The fear that I might have inadvertently triggered the man's final plunge by misapplying violent imagery made me nauseous. I grew dizzy and fell back, briefly losing consciousness. When I came to, I found Den holding me as we flew through the night, over a cloud cover lit by crying stars. Den squeezed my shoulders but couldn't bring himself to look at me, fearful of worsening my sense of sorrow and defeat by revealing his own. I collapsed onto our bed, speechless and spent, and again, we couldn't address what happened until the next day.

The next morning, with the sun good and high, we'd gone downhill to gather wood for the charcoal pit when I piped up, "So, Den, you think maybe, just for next time, we can stay away from Honorkillingstan? I'm apparently not up to the job."

"It's not your fault that everything you tried came to naught. You were fighting centuries of cultural pathology." He swiped at the ground picking up dead wood with each phrase. "Yeah, I can try and avoid greater Arabia next time, if you want, but millions of Arabs despise honor killing as much as we do. And it's not just an Arab thing."

"I know," I replied, chagrined at myself. "And it's not just a Muslim thing. I've heard of honor killings in Italy and Haiti and Brazil, all done by Christians."

"In some places, woman-killing isn't even a matter of honor. For a lot of Indian husbands unsatisfied with their dowry, an investment strategy they get away with is soaking their brides in kerosene and setting them on fire."

"Can we limit ourselves to one cultural psychosis at a time?"

"Okay."

"Fayez's sister was my sister."

"Mine too."

"But Fayez is not my brother. He's not even my species, nor is anyone else in his murder-celebrating family. They're perfect examples of what you call anipoxi. Everyone who glorifies Fayez, every last person in his country responsible for letting him off the hook is an evil killer too."

"No need to exaggerate. The lenient judge is not a sister-stabber."

"How many people did Eichmann personally gas?" I could hear my voice rising, but I had to let it out. "Parse it all you want, the ones who enlist or support or enable murderers or let them go free, celebrated or not, are evil too. In fact, it's mighty sick of the rest of the world for granting Fayez's country sovereignty, entitled to all the benefits thereto. If Fayez had stabbed his sister's head five times on the front lawn of a home in Chevy Chase or Boulogne or Osaka, public outrage would have led him straight to a murder conviction with maximum punishment. Yet because he did it on the other side of a fence marked 'National Boundary,' he'll probably go free, lionized as a home-town hero."

Den sighed and stood up with an armful of cut dead wood. "Shall we?" We stuffed our harvest in our backpacks and began trudging back uphill. After a couple of minutes, he spoke up. "Speciation has been going merrily along among us intelligent primates just as it has among other life forms for the last few billion years. I cannot respect the opinion of any agape-spewing bleeding heart who tries to tell me that

Fayez or the Salvadoran scum who nailed a murdered baby's hands to its head is a member of the same species as regular people, let alone Anne or Uncle Yeshe. As members of the genus *homo,* anipoxi are similar to humans morphologically and they inhabit the same biome, but that's it. Their soulspaces lack a functioning organelle integral to human beings. They almost never interbreed with us. The distinction between them and human beings is the most important development in evolutionary biology since the rise of intelligence. Anipox heads are as different from ours as those of anencephalics."

"They're worse. It's not a brainless baby's fault that a light shone at the back of its head comes out its pupils. Anipoxi have a choice whether to suck on that virus, as do humans who possess a weak RLI. Just because they're more susceptible to eviola doesn't mean they're predestined to ingest it."

"I stand corrected, Calieze. It always comes down to a choice of the soul—not genes, not upbringing, not society, not karma."

"Almost anyone can be tempted."

"Not Uncle Yeshe."

"Okay, now I stand corrected. Saintly people like Anne and Uncle Yeshe have such a strong RLI, eviola can't get anywhere near them."

"I'm not sure they're human either."

"They're probably not. Maybe they're *homo lucis,*" I volunteered, "humans of light. Like *anser indicus,* a species unto itself. There are nine other goose species, all named *anser,* and they didn't just show up on Earth's door all at once. There's no reason nature would kill off evolution in primates the moment it came up with opposable thumbs and larger brains."

"Why would evolution ever hit the brakes? Evolutionary biology ought to flat-out declare that there are three homo species, anatomically similar but sharply differentiated in internal spiritual structure and behavior."

We returned home and unloaded our talk about speciation along with our firewood. After cleaning up from a barley and bean soup lunch, we sat on the throne bed, each of us wearing one more layer than usual against the chill malingering around from the night before. Den was sitting next to me pointing with some ox jerky at an imaginary chalkboard in the sky. Occasional bites shortened his pointer. "No surprise, but that is the lowest I've ever seen the noon sun up here."

"And the daily high temperatures are sinking right along with it. If we're going to stay up here much longer, a supply run is in order. "

Den twirled his jerky stick before me like a baton. "We're about out of these."

I had to give my implicit question a bit harder nudge, whether Den felt ready to face it or not. "Household shoppers generally have a plan. It's one thing to get some ox jerky to tide us over for a few weeks before departing the mountains. But if we dare to brave the high Himalayan winter, a couple of carts' worth of goodies won't cut it. A couple of parkas rated to minus forty degrees would have to top the list. I mean, how long are you in for? Four weeks? Four months? Four centuries?"

"Suppose we make a run to Zhangmu based on the four week plan, and see what happens."

"We could make it to Gnam Yuljongs by sundown if we get our butts in gear. I'd love to see your family. Maybe Sonam will have a stew in the works. And by this time tomorrow we could make it back to the village from Zhangmu. "

"Deal," Den nodded. He stood up and pulled a rock at the back of the cave off a motley stash of dollars, Indian and Nepalese rupees, Chinese yuan notes, and the glittering metamorphosis of his mother's house. He told me that I must feel free to access it, should I ever "need it for an emergency." Ever the rescuer's mindset and ever the lover's protective instincts. I assured him that, while I appreciated this most recent sign of his love, I'd not set out from Sonoma to Tibet shorn of financial assets. I reminded him that I had nearly thirty hundred-dollar Travelers Cheques lining the false bottom of my backpack, so I'd have no need to take advantage of his offer.

Slinging on our backpacks—empty except for sleeping bags and a few basics—we hit the trail and headed down the mountain, returning to our familial outpost of Tibetan civilization at dusk. Sonam, who was churning butter in front of her house, was the first human I had seen besides Den in more than a month and the first besides me that Den had seen since late spring. She was thrilled—and very relieved—to see us. Apparently the background worry radiation Den's family had been living with ever since he'd left had spiked and stayed high once I set out on the same trail last month.

She wasn't the only one who'd been concerned. In a minute we had a crowd of two dozen Gnam Yuljongsians surrounding us and more coming. It was a little embarrassing being treated like movie stars, but the affection on display was genuine and reciprocal.

As we made our way to Uncle Yeshe's house, we heard an odd, feverish chant coming from a house up the street. Sonam's smile dimmed. "Pema's auntie has been ill for days. The shaman arrived this morning. He has been with her all day." I felt a shiver imagining the traumatic trance the shaman was putting himself through, as the hopes of Pema and her family awaited the results of his entry into an ancient battle with spirit-killing demons.

I sure cheered up seeing Yeshe's smile greeting us. I told him, "You're looking great, Uncle Yeshe!" and his smile widened at my addressing him that way. We gave him gentle hugs and he smiled at the evidence of the accuracy of his inner predictions as he saw Den and me together for the first time.

It was decided that we would stay in Yeshe's upper room where, Sonam demurely explained, there was room for a blanket mattress on the floor in addition to the palette bed against the wall. While Sonam finished dinner preparations, Den and I took turns luxuriating in the beloved shower house and wandered around trying and failing to find ways to help. That made us all the more determined to discover what might prove useful that we could procure for the family in the expedition to Zhangmu.

A crowd of Gnam Yuljongsians crammed into Uncle Yeshe's main room for an impromptu pot luck in our honor. Some of the folks came bearing books they'd been meaning to return to Yeshe's library, the shelves of which were half-empty. While I'd relished our largely vegetarian existence uphill, I have to say that Sonam's yema pepper and ginger boiled yak and rice hit the spot for a cold mountain eve. The butcher had come late the week before for the annual slaughter. He'd dispatched the souls of four yaks to their maker, leaving behind the makings of a rare fresh roast feast and stone bins of air-drying meat that would keep a lot of families well fed through the winter.

Throughout supper everyone asked us about adventures we'd had far up the mountains. I felt almost dishonest gushing about the beauty of the wilderness up there, painting a picture of a vacation in nature, without mentioning any of the harrowing, traumatic, and sometimes elating adventures at the heart of the real story.

We could tell that Uncle Yeshe had something on his mind throughout dinner, and after a dessert delicacy of carrot brownies made with nuts and raisins (called *barfi*, regrettably, but they were delicious anyway), he gently shooed everyone away. He could stay up only so long and, after his talks about demons with Den in the spring, he wanted to hear what had unfolded in our mountain hideout.

In the candle-lit quiet, a barely audible chant from the shaman made its way through the cold mist resting on the cobblestone street outside Uncle Yeshe's living room. "We heard about Pema's family calling in the shaman," Den said. The solemnity of Yeshe's silent nod told me all I needed to know about Pema's aunt's long-term prognosis. "Uncle Yeshe, do Tibetan shamans ever conduct rituals to protect people who are far away from them?"

His protective instincts at work, Yeshe didn't say anything at first. I remarked, "When I was here before and told Sonam about my work on a whale rescue in the Arctic, she quoted an old saying about how protecting others helps a person live long. I've heard Den say it too."

"*Srog gi skyabs byed,*" he nodded.

"Yes. I've been wondering if that might be related to what Terma Den asked about, shamans protecting people who are far away."

He sighed, resigning himself to the need to speak his piece. "Common sense must rule. One does not ensure long life by going to war against the great army of a repressive state. Nor by seeking out evil for battle in hazardous circumstances." We were taken aback at both the insight and the pointed nature of Uncle Yeshe's remark. "There are many stories about people with unusual powers, dear ones. One can levitate, another can fly, another can appear in two places at once, another heals a disease from far away. And there have been stories about a man who lived in our mountains long ago who became so adept, he was able to stop evil acts before they occurred. It is said he attained the rainbow body of pure light upon death." He took a sip of tea to give himself another moment to frame his conclusion, then looked at each of us in turn. "Such an endeavor carries much risk. I would certainly respect anyone who could do it. However, you must know that I respect you both already. And, having lost my only brother, it would be all the more painful to lose his only son as well. Or his dear friend. That would hasten the day I lose myself."

"I don't want you to lose yourself, Uncle," Den said. "Believe me."

"That day will come one way or another, and when it does, provided my family is well, it will be no tragedy. I am becoming an old man and I believe what the Buddha taught us about the liberation that comes with death. I'm not afraid of it in the least degree." He paused, readying his conclusion. "But you have asked about protecting others from suffering. The Buddha did not teach us to try and remove suffering from the world. He taught us to accept that life is suffering. That is the first of the Four Noble Truths."

"I greatly value all you've taught me, Uncle Yeshe," Den replied, "but I've got to admit I can't accept the idea that life is suffering from which one should aspire to escape."

"Of course not. You are half American, my nephew."

I tapped Den on the knee. "Uncle Yeshe's got your number, Yank."

Den turned to one-up me. "Granted, but you don't accept it either and you're not even half-American."

"I'm half-Jewish."

"Ah, " he acknowledged, "that'll do it."

"And half-Roma."

"That'll do it twice."

Our exchange had deflected our attention from the sight of Yeshe pulling a small lacquered box from a drawer under his bed. With tension gripping his face, he extracted a tiny white pill from the box, pushed it into his mouth, and swallowed. We kept our concern to ourselves, hoping he would explain what was going on. When he said nothing for ten seconds, Den spoke up. "Uncle Yeshe, what's the matter?"

Uncle Yeshe shrugged. "It is nothing."

"What is that medicine, Uncle?"

Recognizing that the question wouldn't disappear, he pointed to his heart and said, "Nitroglycerine."

"Nitroglycerine—how long have you been taking that?"

"Since summer's end. Nothing serious; just some occasional discomfort. Amchi had tried other things. A mix of flower roots and yak bile and zinc." He studied the dark little bottle as he rolled it between his fingers. "When that didn't work, he brought me these from the pharmacy in Zhangmu." He held the bottle up to the candlelight. It was almost empty.

"Listen, Uncle, if those little pills help, we'll get you some more when we're down there tomorrow."

Yeshe tried and failed to raise an objection to what he considered a troublesome favor, but his insecurity about running out wouldn't permit that. "That would be very kind of you. I shall provide you with a kilogram of butter in exchange."

"That's ridiculous, Uncle Yeshe. You don't need to give me anything. I'm the one who needs to get everything I can for you and the family. After all you did for me when I came here last spring, I should bring all Zhangmu up here."

"Please control your gratitude, my nephew."

I spoke up, amused at the thought of inflicting Zhangmu's chaotic traffic jams on the sweet peace of Sky View. "We'll leave Zhangmu where it is, Uncle Yeshe, but we do want you and Sonam to make up a list tomorrow so we can get everything you need from town."

We'd been sitting up with Uncle Yeshe for a good while since everyone else had left and he was struggling to keep his eyelids above half-mast. We bowed, thanked him for his hospitality, and set out on a walk to the barley field to let him retire.

We held hands as we walked along under the stars. When we were out of earshot of the southernmost houses, Den said, "You know what was odd about Uncle Yeshe's warnings about my undertaking battles with evil?"

"It didn't seem odd to me. He loves you."

"True, but I've never told him I was going to try and battle evil. When he said that, it was as if my parents had possessed him and were speaking with his gravely voice."

The next morning, Den and I hiked over the pass down to the road to catch the bus. It was the first time we'd ever set foot on a road together. No ordinary road it is, either. Waterfalls abound, pouring out of Himalayan forests high above, pouring intoxicating drinks for the eyes in a futile attempt to distract passengers' awareness of the one to four thousand foot drops off the edge of the road, a long skinny trickle of pavement ending in Zhangmu.

That tiny southern Tibet border town a few hundred yards long struck us New Haleans as about as local and cozy as Oakland. But clogged as the air is with the diesel fumes and dyspeptic thunder of truck engines, we didn't mind. We were there to get supplies and to prove ourselves still capable of handling civilization in the flesh. We visited the pharmacy for Yeshe's nitro and trolled several little shops to stock up on first aid materiel and spices, noodles, candies, vegetables, and other treats for the denizens of Gnam Yuljongs and New Hale, a good-sized sack of old-fashioned wheat flour, and some drawing paper, paints, and pastels for Lasya, Renzin, and yours truly.

For a break from the unfamiliar business of shopping, we ducked into a tea stall across from the Cloud Peak Friendship Hotel. While our order was being prepared—count on a *long* time for that in this part of the world—Den went over to the hotel to pay a visit to his concierge pal, Lin-Chee. I sat at the table and wrote post cards to a couple of friends and one to my landlords back home. As an afterthought I decided to write one to Jyoti, the little girl I'd so entranced with my "Gypsy" moves in India. You can see in the dazzling brightness of her eyes that that little girl will someday travel a lot farther from Bombay than Rajasthan.

When Den came back bearing a thin local newspaper, I asked him what he'd advise me to use for a return address and he pointed to the hotel. "Lin-Chee is my personal postmaster—anyone who can be trusted with my mother's library for four months can handle a few letters."

Our Nepalese host brought our chai, whitened with water buffalo milk, and a plate of sizzling fried breaded banana chips. As I scribbled away, Den opened his smudgy eight-page newsweekly—no doubt the product of a staff of two and printed in one of the hillside hovels that make up most of the housing in Zhangmu—and set about struggling to extract meaning from the sea of Tibetan characters with his limited knowledge of the language. He hadn't gotten past his third sip of chai when he sat up straight, eyes glued to an article with a photo of a bedraggled Tibetan man in handcuffs, and exclaimed, *"Thi bombo!"* He bolted up, pale, told me he'd be right back, and trotted back across the street to the hotel, clutching the newspaper.

I passed the next few minutes finishing up my card to Jyoti, wondering what could get such a rise out of Mountain Man Sherab. He returned a lot more slowly then he'd left, his eyes failing to conceal tumultuous news bouncing around his head. He sat down next to me, nodding. *"Thi bombo* — butcher knife!" He slapped a finger on the photo of the prisoner. "Lin-Chee says this guy caused a stir in town last week when he threatened to kill his boss at a butcher shop with a foot-long knife. Take a look at that wall." Guessing what he'd found, my eyes had already widened before landing on the background of the photo of the man being hauled away from the butcher shop. Sure enough, on the wall behind him was the poster of the goddess girl we'd seen in the soulspace window of our visitation subject last week. My scalp prickled all over as Den added, "According to Lin-Chee, the would-be killer had his knife raised right over his boss's neck when he froze and let himself be disarmed."

Your reality check, mum—will there be anything else?

Den and I sat silently for several minutes, absorbing this unassailable evidence that the work we were doing at New Hale was indeed a matter of life and death. Finally, he gave me a look that asked if I realized what this meant.

"You ready for parka shopping?" I asked.

"We have no choice. Lives are at stake."

"No reservations about homesteading through a Himalayan winter at our elevation?"

"There are some year-round Sherpa villages at fourteen thousand. We're only a few hundred feet higher at most, with a lot less need for luxuries than a settlement that needs to worry about infants and elderly."

"Hey, if I can operate a camera on a whale rescue in the Arctic Circle, I can run a brain on a human rescue on the tropic of Cancer."

"Except that this gig is almost three miles higher than that one."

"Enh," I shrugged. "Hair-splitting. It will be fun. Sometimes."

I took a couple of minutes to add a note to the postcard for my landlords, letting them know that my last month's rent deposit would indeed have to be my last month's rent. Then, off we went in search of heavy-duty parkas, thick-lined boots, snowshoes, tarps, freeze-dried fruits, vegetables, meats, matches, a lantern and a couple of extra flashlights for the long nights, a stash of batteries, a snow shovel, an ice pick, another yak hide for our bed and yet another for the cave entrance. We hired a Sherpa—a nice, unflappable fellow a bit older than we named Lhakpa—to help us haul this cargo over the pass to Gnam Yuljongs. From there we'd manage the rest of the freight work to New Hale ourselves in two trips over two days.

We were all loaded up when I asked Den to give me five minutes. I darted into an electronics shop to pick up one precious luxury: a short-wave radio with a little solar panel, a hand crank, and a battery compartment. This omnivore is designed to eat whatever electrons you've got on hand. I could see the drain in Den's face when I came out of the shop with it—he'd consider cutting the handle off his toothbrush to save pack weight—but I told him if I had to go four more months without music, I'd crack up. "I'll play it only rarely and whisper quiet, but I have to pull in a little music from somewhere, sometime. You'll be glad, Den. At certain points this winter, I'll conjure just the right piece of music out of the atmosphere as it threads its way around the planet and guide it into your dreams. It will smooth out the rough spots and polish the good ones to a shine."

He chuckled to himself and stroked my temple. "Let's roll," he said, hefting his loaded pack onto his shoulders, and led Lhakpa and me to the bus station.

Those flashlights were put to good use in the last mile of the trek to Gnam. We made a bit of a stir on arrival, partly for arriving in the dark at dinner time with one-tenth of a ton of stuff on our three backs, partly for the art supply gifts for the kids, but most of all for our announcement that we would be staying at the upper elevations throughout the winter. Uncle Yeshe shared Sonam's concern over our plan, but he reminded her that, aside from the sherpas that showed up sometimes, Den had done more mountaineering than anyone they knew.

After dinner, Lasya sidled up to me shyly and asked me to teach her some English words. During our lesson I glanced over at Den and caught a wistful look. It went without saying: in teaching one of his Tibetan relations English, I had stepped upon a path blazed earlier by another woman, without whom he wouldn't be here, or anywhere.

At bedtime, Lhakpa was offered a spot on Kurukulla's lower floor for the night. Uncle Yeshe looked relieved as he set the new bottle of nitro in the lacquered box before settling himself into bed. Den and I went for a walk to strategize the rest of the move to New Hale. When we got back, I found Yeshe had left a candle burning for us. He looked so enchanting in his sleep that I stayed downstairs for a while to break in my sketchbook with a drawing of him as a sleeping Buddha at the center of a simple mandala, surrounded by family and neighbors and Den and me, watching over, learning from, and meditating with him as he sleeps. I left it on his bookshelf.

The next morning we paid and sent off Lhakpa and sorted out our belongings and provisions, leaving half behind for the next day. We fended off Renzin's and Lasya's entreaties to let them join us for the overnight trip, neither of us being too keen on letting anyone in the village know the location of our encampment. "It could get inconvenient if we were to be invaded by tourists when we're in the middle of one of our intense practices," Den remarked to me, to which I added, "Of either kind."

We made our way back up here, with enough time to unload, get some dinner together, and catch some rest for a long round-trip to the village the next day. No anipoxi or talk thereof, no dreamy stargazing, not even any love dancing for us—just swift-sinking sleep.

Yesterday we strapped on our empty packs at first light and made our way back down to Gnam Yuljongs by late morning. I was a little embarrassed when Uncle Yeshe bowed to me in gratitude for my humble drawing of him, but flattered too. At his request, I helped myself to a couple of his library books—the *Ramayana* and *The Bon-Po*

Book of the Dead—as long-term loans. Just before we set out for our fully-loaded ascent, we succumbed to Kurukulla's insistence that we imbibe a little fresh yak blood to maintain our vitality for the journey. I tossed mine back and, out of range of Kurukulla's beaming eyes, fought back a gag reflex while rolling my eyes at my sympathetic lover. Thus fortified, we gave everyone hugs and left Gnam Yuljongs, heading off to become part of the one-millionth of the world's population that live above thirteen thousand feet, not to return until sometime next year.

We arrived at sunset, a few hours ago. Den hoped for both our sakes I'd go to bed when he did, but I needed debuzzing and decided I'd best acquire it by relieving my guilt at not have recorded a word about all that's happened these last three weeks. Now that it's done, I'm free for whatever lies ahead, beginning with my first slumber as a wintering Himalayan.

[3-6]

<u>Thanksgiving, 1991</u>

Putting pen to paper in this log is like walking into a house that used to be mine, where the furniture and pictures have been replaced. I happen to be crazy about the new owner but I do feel a bit out of place.

Calieze strongly suggests that I make an appearance as Visiting Logger to provide our study the extra dimensionality conferred by binocular insight, especially given the unique nature of this research partnership. While girding for full-on winter—building small coal heaters to keep our cave egress clear of snow, working the charcoal pits—it's occurred to me that we may be the first couple ever to attempt to live through the winter isolated in a cave at such high elevation in the history of Tibet—if not anywhere—not to mention doing so while waging the strange battle to which we're pledging our lives, our fortunes, and our sacred mental health.

Can't help but notice that it's Thanksgiving back in the New Country. One year ago I dined with my mother, expecting to be there with her again this year and for many Thanksgivings to come. Her premature death still delivers a deep pang to my throat when I think about it but I'm not a grief addict. On a hike the other day Calieze and I discovered a stream fed by an alpine lake and lay down along it with our faces an inch from the frothing surface, lapping up the purest water in the universe at will like exhausted, happy border collies. Arriving home and extracting fresh bread from the stone oven—well, Thanksgiving works fine up here too.

Our work continues, as do the heavy taxes it occasionally exacts. There are still more wrenching failures than successes, and even the successes are wrenching until the last moments, but our impromptu strategies for dealing with our subjects (mine offered to Calieze from the sidelines) are proving effective more often. If four months of high mountain wintering doesn't bust us, by the time we next visit civilization (such as it is in Gnam Yuljongs), we might well have completed a winning season.

Two incident reports must be filed to illustrate variants of anipoxi who've devolved in such a way as to kill with clean hands. These are power mongers who employ others to do their evil bidding, both within and outside of the law. We chanced upon an example of the latter when we landed in the bizarre soulspace of a gangster don who must have been Pablo Escobar. The last I'd heard, Escobar had allowed himself to be arrested and kept in a self-designed cathedral-like "prison" from which he continued to carry on his murderous business trafficking cocaine with government protection. Cost of business—a couple thousand lives per month plus bribery peanuts from the same multibillion dollar cash bins from which he occasionally drew to sprinkle p.r. largesse upon the grateful poor of Medellin.

His was the first anipox soulspace we'd encountered where no victims were visible in his window. There were just some casual, even friendly, gendarmes patrolling the grounds in a fecund forest overlooking what must have been Medellin. Also visible as our subject roamed his private soccer field was a satellite phone through which Sr. Escobar gave massacre orders to be carried out by his troops in the crippled remnants of civilization down below. We heard plenty of those orders and the resulting sounds he received from his reporters' phones.

The main theme of Escobar's soulspace décor was fire. Blazing guns, rivals immolated in their limousines, explosions erupting at his command. Calieze and I were no match for this kilokiller. Nothing we tried made a dent. He inhaled eviola and barked orders to his thugs to fire on a cohort of police officers he'd not bribed. While getting off on the screams and automatic weapon fire emanating from his phone receiver, he thrilled at the view of himself on the ceiling of his soulspace with flamethrowing body parts projecting high-pressure napalm fire.

An alternate form of remote control evil cloaked in the guise of law enforcement and national security appeared last week in a splendidly appointed office in the heart of a city by a river in southeastern Europe. Calieze believes it was Belgrade. Our subject's environment was adorned with the trappings of political power: flags, leather, brass and gold, mahogany paneling, and framed photos of himself with bigwigs festooning the walls. Like Escobar, this killer had not a gun or weapon of any kind on him. What he did have was a chilling and bloody inner life playing out in his soulspace as he gave orders to the dapper civilian and military henchmen gathered around his desk who relayed them to colonels and paramilitary puppets.

Surrounding the window in his interior were images derived from the reports he was hearing and from the fantasies that gave rise to his instructions to destroy a city populated by a rival ethnic group. While devouring a succession of ever-larger evioli with wild-eyed gluttony, he relished the byplay between the crisp, articulate, orders he issued in his quiet palatial office and the chaos that ensued miles away. Our ears were battered with terrified screams punctuated by barrages of artillery shells, shattering glass and stone, and rumbling tanks as the city—apparently named Vukovar—suffered World War-class destruction. An orgy of shooting picked off children rummaging for food scraps, a few mutinous soldiers singing "Give Peace a Chance," doctors and nurses tending a flood-stage river of mortal injuries, and shawled old women clambering up the steps to their cracked apartments. As the president's men left his physical inner sanctum, his spiritual one gave way to a scene that brought a glazed-eyed smile to his pustule-rotted internal face: hundreds of staff, patients, and other civilians whose hiding places had been blasted away were ushered from a bombed hospital to a nearby pig farm where they were massacred by gunfire, driving the pigs insane with the noise and blood.

Basta. Living through that shit is hard enough and reliving it for the record can only be taken so far, especially by my partner. I addressed her wobbles the morning after Vukovar as the rising sun took a bow over lovely lavender and green wisps in the eastern sky. It was a gorgeous celestial body performance, but half of its audience sat still and glum, brooding over her morning chang. I dragged myself into pep talk mode.

"Chin up, merwoman. This sky can match anything Hawaii puts up for beauty and you don't have to make small talk with clients."

"At least there my clients didn't dump mortar fire victims into mass graves if I failed to get a shot they wanted on video."

"We're not failing. Our success just switches off intermittently."

"I love your concept of success. You ought to coach Nepal's national surf team. For every couple of wins, we lose three."

"Where I was raised, a .400 hitter is a superstar. And we didn't 'lose' anyone. You can't lose someone you never had in the first place."

"I'm not sure how much more murder-watching I can take, Den. I need some time off."

He paused a moment before mustering a reconciled nod. "All right—deal. A burnt-out rescue squad isn't much use. We should take a week off. Tonight we'll luxuriate in having nothing to do."

Calieze perked right up. "Nothing, my ass," she smirked, standing up. "But now, it's time to collect some wood. If we're staying here, we've gotta keep those charcoal pits cooking every day now. Snow's a-comin'."

The downhill half of our trip to the old fire zone takes only ten minutes. We zoomed through it with muscles thankful for a little action after another long night of stationary stress and fitful sleep. As I started working my hand axe, Calieze harvested some breakable branches and began to muse aloud. "I've been thinking about what you said about evolution of the human soul."

"I thought you wanted a break."

"I don't mind shop talk—I just want to lay off the job itself for a while." So much for a Calieze mood slump. Bottle her energy and it could power Asia.

"Humans have evolved a criminal justice system to deal with evil, but it's still a thumb-like digit that's not quite opposable. There's not much to protect people against the anipoxi in power, like that dude ordering the slaughter in Vukovar."

"He who spoke in eviola tongues."

"Right—it'll be a long time before anyone throws his ass in jail. Or the asses of the moneymaggots profiting from supplying his weapons. They're Farbenites, like the vermin who made Zyklon-B for the gas chamber 'showers' at Auschwitz. There's no difference between them and murderous creeps like Pablo Escobar. In fact, power monger killers aren't much different from Jeffrey Dahmer and Charles Manson either, except that they've mastered the system and kill a whole lot more people." She stood up, having arranged our timber harvest into eight neat bundles, and arched her back forward and back. It would take four trips with both of us to get all this newly harvested wood up to our charcoal plant.

"Need a war cooked up? Call Powermonger, Moneymaggot, Hater, Brutaliphile & Associates. Patriotic, religious, and tribal rationalization options available—order yours today!"

"But good evolution's been at work too," she added brightly. "How about the first cave man whose RLI light gave him a twinge of compassion at his woman's cries. Next thing, he's sitting down by her side and brushing her hair instead of dragging her by it. A hundred millennia go by and his descendant builds his wife the Taj Mahal or writes 'I Walk The Line.' And by then the creeps who drag their wives by the hair are regarded as beasts and thrown in jail."

"Now you're talkin'. You ready to head back?"

"Sure." Calieze tightened the straps on a log bundle I'd hoisted to my shoulder. "Onward."

As we plodded uphill, I thought about Calieze's cheery take on evolution. "The respect for life instinct has evolved into a spiritual immune system," I told her. "RLI light rays function like antibodies that ward off eviola. So, yeah, in some people the RLI is dead and they have no immunity. In most people, the RLI is bright enough for them to resist temptations to evil and keep the virus at bay. In some the light's so strong the virus won't come near, and in a few, the light is so brilliant its rays seem to extend beyond their heads and make the environment around them radiant. But in too many, the RLI is so weak it could sputter out at any moment. Those are the ones we've been visiting as a psychic EMT crew that has to figure out on the spot how to tailor a treatment to each patient's disorder. With that enraged butcher down in

Zhangmu, your injection of a vision of himself rotting in prison with his daughter crying outside was like a dose of spiritual interferon that boosted his immune system into action. If you weren't pulling it off successfully now and again, we wouldn't be holing up in an alpine cave for the winter."

We'd arrived at the charcoal mounds. As I unloaded my pack, Calieze slapped me on the butt. "Okay, fight on, New Hale Snow Leopards—after a solid week off."

So began our week-long breather. By yesterday we were ready to tackle the Spire again with renewed vigor. Calieze gave me a wry smile when she saw me put a sleeping bag in my rucksack, but said nothing about it. Three hours later, as we caught our breath at the pinnacle, she began unbuttoning my shirt, and I knew I would once again swim in the healthy exuberance of Calieze's physicality. She is so carefree and fun I feel sorry for the vast swath of humanity still hobbled by primitive schemata of sex that equates sexiness with dark lady vamping. Whatever turns you on, and all, but Calieze makes that shtick look silly and Victorian.

Some time later, as we jettisoned our last booster rocket, Calieze unleashed a joyous scream. I thought it was orgasmic, straight-up, but this time her skyward eyes signaled that there was more to it. Before I could turn my head upward, a heavenly chorus heralded what I would see—the horn blasts of a splendid squadron of bar-headed geese calling down from the indigo zenith, seeming to hail us from above the Himalayas en route to the sheltering warmth of India. As the flock headed toward the southern horizon, Calieze declared, "It was a magnificent movie after all, recorded on neurons instead of tape."

I couldn't help anthropomorphizing the hell out of the geese, wondering if they hadn't conceived this whole set piece, implanting the idea of coming here in Calieze's mind last spring. It's silly, but it will do for a closing thought. Our furlough of cream puffs and whirligigs is coming to an end. It's back to work with life and death stakes, night after night with a hundred more cold nights to come before the sun deigns to grace us again with melting warmth. My focus will remain fixed in the present and I'll not write again here till we've made it through; my written record of 1991 stops here.

[3-7]

April 21, '92
CZM

I can hardly believe that nearly half a year has passed since I last entered these waters. Especially with so much time spent indoors, one might presume that Den and I have had ample time for log-keeping, but not so.

Far from hibernation, our nesting in a sideways, high-elevation hole in the planet throughout a Himalayan winter required enough work to make the most hectic Manhattanites look like rock-sunning lizards by comparison. We've had to dig deep pursuing survival and habitat maintenance. (And what unusual landscaping we've wrought—amidst a thousand square mile untrammeled snow field, bar-headed geese in northern flight could observe bluish tendrils stretching from one spot on the mountain in several directions, our paths to the food storage chamber, charcoal mounds, and the trail, carefully carved with respect for the pristine.) My arms and back have never been this strong, even with Den handling most of the heavy labor. Sometimes I reached bedtime barely able to move, even to yield to the ministrations of my indefatigable teammate.

One night Den snuggled up to me in our sleeping bag and nibbled at my ear, murmuring, "I'm one lucky guy."

Wiped out and aware that our aspirations for the next hour differed, I nonetheless replied, "And I'm one lucky girl,"

"Maybe you're also jest a girl who cain't say no."

"You're not that lucky."

He chuckled, "I could feel your mind grinning as that one sailed in right over the plate."

But there are plenty of times our luck runneth over, like the time on New Year's Eve, when we were soaked with sweat in celebratory action and just as we were on the verge, the moon came out and lit up snowflakes being blown down from the slope above. We took one look at each other, disinterlocked ourselves, scampered outside, and standing up in the cold, re-fused ourselves into a single, orgasmic organism in a shower of tiny, close cold stars light years under the huge, distant hot ones.

I would hardly claim that we are constantly harmonizing with the music of the spheres. Seeing no one but each other so much of the time does provide ample opportunity for pet peeves to arise. The radio static crackling out of my shortwave when I've struggled to pull in a clean signal does bug Den and I can get prickly if he interrupts my concentration too often while I'm working on a tricky painting—but such irritations are few, far between, and muted. We've never forgotten how fortunate we are to have found each other in the warm waters of Hawaii a year ago. New Hale is no prison. Going out warmly dressed with your honey, snowshoeing through beautiful scenery, and coming home to make a hot tasty dinner and watch shooting stars is not a prisoner's lifestyle. You wouldn't choose it if you and your relationship weren't in good shape to begin with, but doing it you can end up in even better shape and undauntable.

Besides, not everything about life at fourteen thousand feet is so tough. All winter we had one major advantage most campers never have—no water hauling trips down to the creek and back. Encamped in the middle of a freshwater field as broad as the Indian Ocean with a shoreline freeze-framed at our doorstep, you make one simple cook pot scoop out your front door and a minute later, bingo—the world's cleanest water.

And we've enjoyed many satisfactory escapes from cave fever. I got myself a little John Audubon action, making sketches of bar-headed geese doppelgangers of ourselves I'm thinking of painting on our ceiling near the old, smudged star field painted long ago. Den's been practicing writing Tibetan. We read books we'd brought up on long-term loan from the Gnam Yuljongs Library. Once in a while, I fire up the shortwave to see how much of the rest of the world is still there—most notably discovering around Christmastime that the USSR wasn't—and more often to lasso whatever musical gifts might have been sent our way by radio devotees holed up in their own, more civilized caves far away.

One such gift arrived when Den took ill some time after New Year's. I had to tend to him for three days before he felt human again. He had a hard time with that, due to inbred macho and SAR acculturation. On the second night, when I had to help him sit up to sip his soup, he muttered, "I hate appearing so weak in front of you."

"Shut up, idiot, before you have to surrender your title as the strongest man I've ever known. The only weakness you should be embarrassed about would be whining about appearing weak. Let that great body of yours heal itself and you'll come through this tougher than ever. Your immune system is as brawny as your muscular and central nervous systems." That shut him up. I resettled him near the cave-entrance with the radio, hoping to capture some musical waves that would envelop him, body and soul. Right on cue, flowing through the atmosphere, low-fi but intoxicating, came the 4th Brandenburg Concerto. Den imbibed it with his eyes closed, letting a bracing spiritual elixir enliven all his cells.

Of course he recovered and was back snow-clearing, fire-tending, glacier-hiking, and love-stoking with me in a matter of days, tending to the daily fourteen hours of groundwork that free us up for our night job, hunting for souls tempted to self-infection by the world's most deadly virus. Since Den's last entry at Thanksgiving, we've embarked on nearly two hundred more forays to sites of potential eviola infection scattered around our beleaguered globe. We've jacked up our pace to two visitations a night, once before sleep and again in the still-dark wee hours of the morning. It's been a steamrolling grind that could have utterly debilitated us if we hadn't toughened our spiritual muscles as well as those surrounding our bones.

It turns out that telepathic skills are as capable of disciplined development as those of reasoning, performance, athletics and other abilities with which Nature has graced human beings. To illustrate the point I shall relate an incident that began almost two weeks ago, on the night of April 8th. With the throne bed set up outside in the early spring chill, we tripped into our ever-swifter meditation and soon found ourselves flying west, towards Europe. Faster than any jet, we crossed over the lands radio newscasters had begun to refer to as "the former Soviet Union" and descended upon a town that could not sleep for being trapped in a nightmare of inconceivable proportions.

The language spoken sounded like that of the military and political mucky-mucks we'd heard directing the massacre at Vukovar last fall, so we figured we were in Bosnia or Serbia. We had landed in the soulspace of a soldier, part of a ragtag group of uniformed men crudely ushering families towards a lit-up three-story house down the street that backed up against a forest. A sickly mix of screams, cries, curses, and roaring laughter issued from the windows. Our subject's inner window showed him to be in charge of a family of four—a woman with a Muslim's head shawl, her husband, and two girls in their early or mid-teens. Surrounding his window, the man's chamber walls consisted of a hyped-up montage of images of violence and mundane tasks like cleaning out stables and manual construction labor. An eviola virus looking like a slow-motion, lantern-sized tornado approached him from eleven o'clock.

By the time we reached the front door, the girls were crying in fear and their mother seemed to be pleading with her husband to tell them what to do. In his tremulous appeals to her to remain calm, he called her "Ajla."

Upon entering the house, we found ourselves in a pack of humanity as crowded as a party south of Market in San Francisco except that there were more people sobbing or screaming in pain than there were laughing. A couple of the laughers greeted our subject as "Branko," welcoming him to the orgy in progress. They led him and his captives to a corner of the main room, where a crowd of soldiers had cordoned off a family of seven including a couple of grandparents and a girl of about six. The child's mother was being brutally raped by a cackling, swooning monster. She looked right at Branko and begged him to kill her on the spot. As he stared at her, some eight other soldiers began to work on the rest of her family by

[remainder of paragraph blacked out by author]

Sorry, Science. Dock me for refusal to record full and complete field observations. I cannot subject any reader (myself included) to an account of the atrocities being committed upon that family and others throughout that house, vile acts that would have startled Nazis.

But hold—nauseated as I was by what I saw through our subject's window, I did not forget why I was there. As Ajla and her daughters were screaming in terror and images of raping them flickered in Branko's soulspace, I heard Den call me. He pointed to a vivid image high on the side of Branko's soulspace wall of a woman about thirty looking up at the viewer with a gleeful smile. I thought it was Branko's memory of seeing his mother outside from a high inside window until a child's squeal emanated from the memory and the point of view lowered so that the woman was seen from below waist height. When a pair of toddler hands reached up towards her I realized it must have been his recollection of his mother having lifted him joyously when he was a child. At first he'd been seeing her from above her head and then, when she'd set him down, he'd reached up to her, begging for more.

Reflexively, I superimposed Branko's mother's face over that of the desperate rape victim who was still begging Branko to kill her. The images of violence in Branko's soulspace walls froze and cracked, his RLI lit up, and the virus shrank away, vanishing in the distance.

Ignoring both the rapists' invitation to join the party and their victim's plea to deprive the depraved of their prey in a mercy killing, Branko shouted over the chaos to his comrades, apparently indicating that he was going to have his way with his captives in the basement. He began kicking Ajla's family towards the back door.

The moment they were all on the back stairway, Branko continued barking orders and cursing loud enough to be heard in the main room, if anyone there were listening, but he stopped his kicking and shoving. He took Ajla by the hand and ordered the others to follow with a gesture that seemed to say, "Don't worry."

He led them to a door that opened on an outside stairwell, hushing them along the way. They were agog, realizing that this member of a gang of vicious predators had decided to help them escape. A minute later they were picking their way through the dark woods as quietly as they could, with Branko in the lead. Branko waited until they were a good two hundred yards from the rape camp to turn on a flashlight, which illuminated the tangled tree roots and brush so as to speed their progress.

Normally, once an eviola crisis has slid down one slope or the other, we leave the scene, but this time, when I looked up at Den across the man's soulspace, I heard him say, "Let's stick with this." We had been so horrified by what we'd seen in the rape camp that we sought the additional security of seeing that Branko's turnaround would endure and leave the refugees free.

In half a mile they reached the back entrance of the family's home, where Branko gave the family three minutes to grab their passports, money, valuables and a few photographs before whisking them back into the woods.

We stayed with this motley clutch of war refugees for another two hours' hiking through the forest. Along the way the children began to shiver and their father wrapped his long coat around them and gestured to indicate that it was too warm and he didn't want it—an obvious but welcome white lie.

Eventually they emerged into a sheep pasture. A small house sat at the far end, its tin roof gleaming in the moonlight. Hearing only hushed voices, bleats from sleepy sheep, and the crunching of boots on frost-crusted snow, they reached the house. Branko knocked on the door and a shaken man clutching his robe answered. Branko, pointing west, mentioned the name "Foca." As the gray-haired farmwife appeared, dismayed, Branko introduced himself and the family of escapees.

Badly shaken but settling down, Ajla and her family were tended to by their hostess who warmed up milk and leftover fried bread. Den and I couldn't predict how long the family would be nursing the deep wounds of psychological trauma, but they were safe, for now. In relief, I fell back and rejoined Den in the night sky, heading east, where the first hint of light was reaching the horizon.

We made it back to our cold home and sank into our sleeping bags on the outdoor throne bed. Ragged from our nerve-banging night, we couldn't fall asleep. Den lay beside me with his arm under my neck, staring at the top of the sky. Then, jogged by a squeeze of my shoulders and Den's pointing, I looked up and saw something mighty weird near the zenith—a pair of stars moving around in a circle. "What the hell is *that?!*" Den exclaimed. I murmured something about having thought I'd seen something like that after our first visitation together the previous fall. "Weather balloons? I have seen some strange things in the skies back in the Rockies," he answered himself, without conviction.

I welcomed that mysterious diversion, which lasted about ten more seconds, but I was soon dragged back down to the miasma we'd witnessed in the hell house earlier. I buried my face in Den's chest and reconsidered our situation.

Yes, we'd seemed to prevail with Branko and perhaps saved four lives, but there was no proof that our rescue was real. I asked myself how I could stand any more wrestling with the evil abominations committed by eviola eaters, and the simple answer presented itself: I was done with this phantom mission. It was something Den had begun to which I'd willingly joined on with the best of intentions but which had, that very night, proven ultimately intolerable. "That's it, Den," I whispered. "I've had it." He petted my head, but said no more, and we finally drifted off to sleep.

A week and a half passed in a monotonous haze of snow chores and basic living, punctuated by an occasional hike. When Foca forced itself back into my consciousness, I felt like I was walking around with a hole in my chest. At night my breathing floundered weakly in the shallows, tossed at awkward angles by intermittent sighs. Sometimes I noticed Den looking at nothing on the ground, his cheeks sunken and the light in his eyes a bit dimmed. I assumed that he was afraid that our mission had crash-landed due to my condition.

Spring kept on coming. The mountain forest lording over the valley had begun her wardrobe change, with warming snow glistening on the pine needles and our snow piles melting into the reviving creek, all offering succor as we went through the motions of wilderness life. Reminiscences of our adventures in sundry soulspaces scattered around the world were off-limits for conversation. We weren't on a mission any longer; we just were. It had been so many months since the butcher incident in Zhangmu that I'd begun to wonder if that might have been a singular fluke in a string of fantasies stretching on and on, in which we tossed precious months of life into a thresher in a mutually reinforcing binge of delusion.

Then, three nights ago, while Den was copying some Tibetan verse to practice writing, I took a yak hide up to the roof of the cave as a pad to lie on while I pulled in some quiet music on the shortwave. For a while I parked myself at a station out of Bangkok playing a mix of Thai and American pop—Whitney Houston and some band the DJ called something like Boys To Men—till, bored with that, I twirled the dial and landed on the BBC broadcasting its World News Hour. A reporter in Milan had begun a story on the Balkan war, my favorite subject. As she referred to an official campaign by the Bosnian Serbs to "ethnically cleanse" the region of Muslims through systematic rape and murder, I was reaching for the radio's off switch when I heard something that popped my eyes wide open: it was the name "Ajla."

I bolted upright, grabbed the radio, and scampered down to our entrance, motioning to Den to join me. Even covered over by a translator, I could recognize the voice of the woman in the background as that of our Ajla. The translator related how Ajla and her family were Bosnian Muslim refugees who had reached Milan a week ago after an arduous journey escaping from a threatened rape and murder in their home town called Foca. She recounted how a Serbian soldier had helped them make their way through a forest in the middle of the night. She felt guilty that she and her daughters had hid their head coverings and denied their religious identities while a sympathetic farmer who'd hidden them the night of their escape drove them, crammed in an old Fiat, to the Montenegrin coast, where they secured passage across the Adriatic to Italy. She told how she and her husband struggled to hold their daughters—and themselves—together through nights of midnight terrors as recollections of the rape camp continued their mental torture long after they'd been liberated from the threat of physical torture. The reporter interjected that when she'd located Ajla's family, ensconced on the small living room floor of a Muslim family they'd found through the local mosque, the fifteen-year-old daughter was curled up in her mother's lap, heaving dry sobs.

About the atrocities being committed in the Foca hell house, Ajla would say nothing. The reporter stated that Ajla had to channel most of her mental energy to keeping recollections of the Serbian soldiers' perverted, murderous mayhem at bay. But she did mention their liberator. Before he left them at the sheep farm the morning after their escape, their captor and savior confided that he was ashamed of having been tempted to join his fellow soldiers in their orgy, but at the moment a woman being raped in the corner of the main room had pleaded with him to kill her, he had seen her face change into that of his own mother, who had died ten years before. That vision instantly caused him to reverse his course and engineer their escape, despite the risk of being shot on the spot by his comrades if he'd been discovered aiding the escape of Muslims. According to her translator, her closing words were "Wherever he is, we pray for his safety."

Whatever suffering I'd endured observing the horror house in Foca that night two weeks ago was too paltry to measure against the torture Ajla's family had been spared on account of our not having quit the night before. That's how I can stand wrestling with the abominations of evil, and that's why I shall carry on.

As for Den, he never wanted to quit. He'd slogged through so much helplessness in visitations before my arrival that he barrels through our failures like a seasoned boxer taking a few punches in the early rounds. Not for him, any Buddhist liberation from his suffering or even helping others to rise above theirs. He wants to terminate suffering itself, at least the kind that results from evil.

I'm with Den all the way, now and into the future. But as I thought about it in the middle of the night, I began to think that maybe the *best* way to be with him all the way is not to be with him all the time. Having been obliged by the weather to be confined to base so much all winter, I was ripe for the insight that it would be good for me to get out on my own more, so I could bring a fresh perspective to things when we got together again.

Finding those thoughts ricocheting around in my mind upon awakening this morning, I told Den I'd decided to go on a long hike on my own. He was a little surprised, since our shared hikes are a cornerstone of our life together, but he accepted the notion readily enough—he probably relished the idea of a few hours to himself in the spring air—and I was on my way by mid-morning, with the compass Den insisted I take stuck on my belt.

After starting off, I crossed our creek at a bridge we'd set up a couple of months ago when the creek was so solid we could use it as a road. (We'd dragged three skinny trees killed off by a lightning fire, each about 15'-20' long, down to a place with flat anchor spots on either side, rolled a few boulders against the ends to keep them in place, and *voila!*— homestyle civil engineering.) From there I felt my way around the downward slope of our mountain, sometimes taking detours before turning back to a direction I sensed was right for reasons unknown.

I loved every minute of it. I had adventures with the birds and scurrying animals I wanted to share with Den, but I was in no hurry to go racing back to him. On the contrary, I became possessed by the need for a lot more solo time to grow into myself, something that could be accomplished only by being on my own for a good long spell.

And just as that thought blossomed into a full-grown vision, sure 'nuff, a golden opportunity to make it happen presented itself in front of me. It was a cave, a bit smaller than New Hale and in dire need of cleaning, but with a nice southeastern exposure to catch the morning sun and brimming with possibilities. I knew then and there that I would pioneer my own high mountain home in the Himalayas.

I cleared a spot in front of the entrance and sat down for my lunch with my percolating fantasies. Yes, Den might not be too thrilled about this. Mountain Safety Man will worry about me, and he'll miss me— God knows I'll miss him—but we'll still spend most of the year together, and it will be even better than now, because I'll have more opportunities to come up with my own insights and adventures to share with him—and vice versa, for that matter. As for the concerns for my safety that will fire through his SAR circuitry, well, he'll adjust.

Noticing that the sun was a couple of hours past the meridian, I packed up my rucksack and headed back home. Uphill it would take close to three hours and downhill less than two, hardly another world away.

I found Den refurbishing the net posts for one of the gardens. His sweaty, relieved smile at the sight of me betrayed his studied nonchalance. I gave him a big kiss and announced that I had lots to tell him after dinner. I didn't want to hit him with the news while we were putting together our chow, a barley roast with jerked yak. I could tell he suspected something pretty big, but he didn't press me for details.

When we'd cleaned up from dinner and were settled onto the throne bed, we talked a bit about evening stars as Den patiently waited for me to get to the point. "Wellsir," I said, taking a deep breath, "the time has come, the mermaid said—"

"—to talk of her own sea cave," he offered.

"How'd you know?"

"I saw it coming all day."

"It won't be bad, Den—in some ways, it'll be great. I've found a place, less than two hours from yours."

"Mine? I somehow had the idea that New Hale is *our* place."

"Well, it is, but now we have two Our Places. With my having one to myself sometimes, our relationship will be even more wonderful when we get together."

"Baloney. My heart can't grow any fonder. It's maxing 24/7. But never mind—I'm not saying your scheme is without merit."

"It's bursting with merit, Den. Wait until you see the new place! It's in a beautiful location and I'm certain this move will make us even more effective in our work."

"Guess what, Calieze: I don't doubt that part for a minute. Before you showed up here last fall, I loved being alone most of the time. The only bad parts were thinking I'd never get to know you and my sense of helplessness during visitations, neither of which apply any more. My only concern is that I know better than most people—including you, my wagtail love—that all kinds of unexpected things can happen in mountain wilderness, especially to people venturing into it alone."

"Venturing alone? Before I got here, you'd been at it alone for more than four months at a lot higher elevation than my new cave! So I've got to do this in order to be your equal."

"Bull."

"You homesteaded this place, you proved you could make a life high in the Himalayas all on your own. That required a kind of resourceful toughness few people have ever even attempted, and I don't want to continue freeloading on your moxie. I've got to do it myself." Den sighed deeply and said nothing for a minute. I added, "It appears that you're being swayed by my unshakeable logic and good judgment."

"Judgment, shmudgment. Shit happens in the mountains that nobody can control, incidents that make people rue the hour they'd been foolish enough to take on the wilderness by themselves. I've had to respond to hundreds of those incidents. I lost my mother in another. I can and do trust your judgment, Calieze, but I also know for an absolute fact that you could find yourself in desperate jeopardy without my being able to do a damn thing about it if I'm miles away with no way for you to communicate with me."

"But that could happen in the thick of civilization too. We can't book a risk-free trip on this planet. Even if we could, it wouldn't be much fun, and it sure wouldn't be your style. Or mine."

He demurred from further comment on that tack. Finally he sighed, "Maybe I could pick up a couple of ham radios down in Zhangmu. Just for security." The sign that the deal was done.

"Ham radios!? Why not a helicopter? Let's not take chances here." He faked a grin out of courtesy. "I'll show you some security, pal," I declared, leaping on top of him in our sleeping bag. "Hard core, bone-jumping security you'll never forget."

As he put his hands to work on my neck, he muttered, "I see we're going to celebrate our first reunion before we've even been apart."

"And there'll be plenty more where this is coming from."

We proceeded to celebrate with great panache. When I recovered enough breath to speak, I said, "Touchdown, cornerback, and a million extra points of colored light, still draping me from the sky."

The stars were bright enough to illuminate his trademark stifled grin as he swept his hands down and up my body, ending with a hug at the shoulders. He didn't say anything for a while. Den doesn't say much in bed. He doesn't need to. But when I saw his grin cloud up, I felt obliged to coax an explanation out of him. After a minute and quiet throat-clearing, he spoke up.

"Your touchdown remark reminded me of an 83-yard stretch I ran late in the fourth quarter of my final game in college. It took me eleven seconds of opponent-dodging to reach the end zone, but I was in another zone dimensionally from the moment I intercepted the ball. It was a pre-established fact that no human being could stop me and that I would score and win the game for us. A photographer from the Durango Herald got a picture of me at the peak of a four-foot leap in the air over a hapless diving tackle. I was running on elation.

"Funny thing was, I'd not made it out of the stadium before the ecstatic glow of that run got tinctured with regret that my time in that zone was past. And it was. For ten years I never felt elation like that again. But it came back in spades when you showed up at sunset last September, and it came for good.

"Look, I know it isn't very John Wayne of me, but it really rattles me to think of your disappearing again for any of a multitude of other reasons much more disturbing than videotaping divers. The first time, I survived, and I'd just about reconciled myself to living with the hole your absence left in my life, but if anything happened to you now…" I heard him swallow, both of us suspended, knowing more or less the scope of the disaster that had shot across his screen. "Whew."

"Terma Den, you're not the only one here to be acquainted with a shiver of fear. But we have to stay in command here. We cannot afford to get rolled. We must instruct those worries to skedaddle out the back door and never come back. We're going to be fine—better than fine, and better than ever. Our play time and our work time will alternate with moments of rest, just like the muscles of the heart. A soul can use a little rest now and then, even from exhilaration."

I could swear I saw John TD Wayne's eyes glisten up for a moment there, but I withstood the gale winds of my own sudden desire to reverse course and stay in our homey hidey-hole in the mountain. Instead, I gave him a kiss and lay my head on his chest.

That was last night, some five hours before I took up this pen in the pre-dawn darkness. Soon we'll be up and pulling together supplies for my new, ten-million year-old house. We'll need to make a run down to Zhangmu too before this move is finished, but finished it will be, and soon.

(Pssst—just between you and me, whoever you are—please send me a retroactive good luck wish.)

[3-8]

May 24, 1992
The Andromeda Range, Tibet
CZM

It's high spring in the Andromeda Range, which overlooks the wildflower-sprinkled slice of Tibet I've relished gazing upon most of the last month, sharing the view only with insects and birds.

Unlike New Hale, this first home of my own since I left my caboose last summer sits on a more easterly slope and thus bathes in the light of the rising sun, moon, and constellations. My favorite light is the one I discovered when I opened my eyes in the middle of my first night here: framed in my entryway gleamed the fuzzy radiance of the Andromeda galaxy, churning out photons with inconceivable power, a small fraction of which end their two million year journey on my retinas every night. Sometimes I wonder what kind of retinas the photons leaving that galaxy right now will land on when they arrive in these mountains and it makes my heart so full with longing for a sweet future for the human race that I forget to breathe.

The day of my last log entry, Den and I returned to Gnam Yuljongs for the first time in half a year. Rejoining 70+ happy (and relieved) humans after seeing only each other in the flesh for six months was both dislocating and joyous. We spent a great day and night catching up with everyone, especially Uncle Yeshe. He was more unnerved by what he saw as our excessive risk-taking than I'd realized, which made us both feel pretty bad. I don't think he quite appreciated the extent of our experience living with the elements going in. I was touched to see how he'd set my drawing of him on the inside of the door of the cabinet where he kept his writing materials. With a shy smile he told me it would have been improper to leave a drawing comparing him to the Buddha out in the open, but he treasured my gift and had placed it where he could still see it every day. I feel like he's my uncle too, with the concern over witnessing him gulp his heart pills that goes with that.

I was delighted to find a letter from little Jyoti waiting for me at Sonam's house. She'd been pestering her parents to take her to visit me in Tibet, clearly unaware of how complicated a journey that would be. When we got to Zhangmu the next day I wrote her back, suggesting that maybe we could meet again when she's a little older. There's no reason we couldn't entertain them in Zhangmu for a day. I closed the letter saying "Make sure you let me know if you move away so I don't lose track of you. I nearly lost my best friend that way and I don't want that to happen with you."

Den took the occasion to write to Roberto, his compadre from his El Salvador mission, and to his mom's friend Brenda, counting on the Leadville postmistress to know where to forward her mail if she'd moved away.

Our supply-gathering in town this time was easier than in the fall, as there was no need to haul yak hides. We picked up more seeds, food stores, and gardening tools, plus a camera for Lasya and Renzin and a wide-brimmed hat for my first summer here to guard against the skin-drying effects of the low-latitude sun. I informed Den that vanity can survive in isolated, high elevation conditions and he replied "You gotta take care of your skin. Here in Shangri-La you might need it for two hundred years."

Staying another day in Gnam Yuljongs on the way back, we helped Sonam and Kurukulla with their gardening and I taught the kids how to use their new camera. By the time they get their film down to the tourist store in Zhangmu and someone makes another trip up to Gnam with the prints, it may be months, but they'll be tickled to be the first kid photographers in village history.

Two days later Den made his first trip here, helping me schlep backloads of stuff for my new settlement. When he set down his cargo and took in the view, he nodded with what I detected as admiration that I'd scored such a great place. Knowing I wanted to set up the garden and charcoal factory by myself, he left after lunch, keenly sharing my anticipation of our inaugural ball there under a nearly full moon about three weeks later. As he shouldered his pack, he made a point of reminding me, "If you're out hiking and lightning starts up, even if it's blue overhead and the thundercloud is ten miles away, stay away from water, ridge tops, and tall trees. Get into a dry gully or under a cluster of even-size trees and crouch down. Got that?"

"Yes, dear."

"And I left something for you—just in case."

I asked what that might be but got no further details. I took one final kiss and tried not to stare at him as he made his way around the bend.

Later, setting up my sleeping bag, I spotted an envelope at the back of the cave. In it were five diamonds. I wasn't surprised by his generosity or the care for my security reflected in his gift—both have long been apparent. Rather, I was disquieted to realize he had envisioned the possibility of circumstances arising requiring resources of that scale in which we would not be together.

The following three weeks were among the best of my life, despite the big hole left by Den's departure. After being with him night and day for seven months, I was awash in a jumbled appreciation of time on my own and of how much he means to me. I set up a sweet crib, kindled a nascent garden to life, did a lot of drawing, learned a bunch of new constellations with the help of my star book, and thought about what I've been doing with my life.

I welcomed the break from eviola hunting and I was in no hurry to get back to it the first night after Den showed up here last week for our reunion. We had other business to transact then and we took our sweet time at it. Afterwards, I made sure Den slept in position to see the Andromeda galaxy when it rolled up into view around four in the morning. I psyched myself up to awaken at just the right moment (using the old mental alarm clock trick I learned from my dad) and tapped Den on the shoulder. When he looked at me, I just pointed out the entryway and watched him smile. There's no need to tour-guide Den around the night sky.

"My mountain's namesake: I've named this place the Andromeda Range."

"Andromeda? Did you run that name by Quality Control?"

"Don't you like it? I think it's beautiful."

"Do you know Andromeda's story? According to the Greeks, her mother Cassiopeia, the queen of Ethiopia, boasted about her daughter's beauty exceeding that of the Nereid sea nymphs, one of whom was married to Poseidon. Poseidon wouldn't accept such trash talk and sent a monster to the Ethiopian coast to wreak havoc on the country and wouldn't let up till the king offered up Andromeda as a sacrifice. Before she knew it, Andromeda was chained naked to a rock in the sea, awaiting death. Not a very reassuring story."

"But she was rescued, wasn't she?"

"Luckily Perseus showed up in time and liberated her. Married her too. But associating yourself with Andromeda won't particularly help my uneasiness regarding your being here alone."

"Don't worry, D. I'm simply honoring the galaxy in her name. I've gotten to where I can find it in two seconds. To look at a tiny fuzzball of light and know it's made of a hundred billion stars is thrilling."

"That it is."

"Think we could see another Den and Calieze up there with really good binocs?"

"If so, they lived two million years ago."

"Maybe Andromeda's Den and Calieze are looking at the Milky Way right now and wondering if you and I might be looking back at them from inside it."

"If so, they'll have to wait another two million years to see us, and then only if they've got a *really* powerful telescope."

"Aha—you're assuming they could see us only with light rays."

He chuckled and let his gaze fall back on the star field. He shook his head in awe and muttered, "That is outrageously beautiful."

"You've never told me how the stars got you in their thrall."

He seemed to be working around a reply, running his fingers through my hair, eventually coming up with, "You do realize you're probably the only woman in the world to be living on your own in a cave at such a high elevation, don't you?"

"And?"

"For all I know, the first ever."

"Your point, sir?"

"My point is you're Superwoman."

"Non*sense!*"

"As beautiful as Andromeda of Ethiopia with the mental and physical strength of an Amazon."

"Hush, you horny doofus. You know you and I are evenly matched, so you're just praising yourself to the skies, and it's unseemly. Now please answer my question." I employed a feathery finger touch to his lips to soften him up.

I could see the ambivalence in his face as his resistance crumbled. "I wouldn't be surprised if it started in some way when my mother showed me these clear Himalayan skies at the age of one," he began. "But there was no follow-up for a long time. Only pretty tough starlight could make its way through the light-polluted haze covering Denver. But the day we moved to Leadville, as it got dark it occurred to me that maybe I could see a shooting star if I went outside, so I stepped out on the porch and what I saw blew me away. The starscape was as powerful as a vision out of Ezekiel. I took a chair out in the back yard and sat there in the darkness, sweeping the skies with my eyes and thanking God for showing me something that made me so happy. Eventually I noticed some wet streaks on my cheeks emanating from my eyes. I wondered if my eyes had something wrong them. I had no idea that there was such a thing as tears of joy."

"And this was while you were a ten-year-old football jock?"

"Yes. And by the way, I haven't told anybody that before and it's classified."

"Damn—I was looking forward to telling that story on the *Today* show. But now I'm thinking better of it. If I did broadcast that my well-muscled former all-star football ace mountain rescue hunk boyfriend gets overwhelmed with the beauty of the stars, a million women would be storming up here to try and take you from me."

"Whatever, babe, just keep it to yourself, okay? No need to do anything obnoxious, just because you know I'll love you no matter what."

"Likewise. And lovewise."

He was silent for a couple of minutes, staring at the galaxy, before breaking into the quiet. "I admit that I missed you fiercely that first night without you at New Hale. I remember shortly before dawn watching the waning crescent moon climb over the horizon just ahead of the sun like an eager pup and thinking how your determination to go off on your own made me love you even more, which I hadn't thought possible."

"I knew it—I could feel your spirit caroming off the moon's edge right to mine. I launched my love right back at you and I always will."

"You're saying I don't have to worry about your leaving me for a bodhi tree to get enlightened under."

"You are my bodhi tree. I get enlightened every time I'm under you."

"That works for me." He tossed a pine cone down the slope, listening to its skittering fade away. "I feel sorry for Buddha finding his enlightenment after leaving his wife. Any enlightenment without you would be mighty hollow to me."

I kissed my fellow astronomer, and thus re-equilibrated, we drifted back to sleep.

A few hours later, we began our first full day together in our second home with a few chores. Then we went on a gorgeous day hike, troubled only by a couple of Tibet's peculiar hot springs snakes haunting an otherwise luscious-looking spring feeding a leaf-shaded creek. We made it back in time to cook up some tasty *de thuk* soup with droma root, cheese, rice, and jerked mutton, simmered over a juniper branch cook fire to fortify ourselves for our return to work.

Den had taken a couple of stabs at eviola hunting on his own during our time apart, and observed a few signs that he was beginning to get through to his subjects, but he was looking forward to much greater success now that we were together again.

We planted ourselves in a watchtower nook above my stone house and wended our way back through the strange spiritual passage we've traversed so many times before, never knowing where we would land. Without etching more harrowing details here, I'll just say that our sharpness at figuring out how to dissuade our subjects had not suffered. Both then and in our later pre-dawn sortie, we found that we were as adept as ever, if not more so, at defusing bombs of evil in people who were heavily into nasty violence intended for their perceived enemies. Den finds subjects faster and we're honing our instincts for coming up with countermeasures that fit our subjects' mental states. We're getting to be like a jazz duo improvising psychic licks. Sometimes they're off, sometimes they're ignored, and sometimes they show a chance of working only to fade pointlessly into a void, but more and more often they flat-out score. The subject backs off, and his or her intended victims escape a fate that had either terrified them or escaped their notice. Over the course of this past week, we prevailed ten times in fourteen attempts. We've been tempted to let others know what we're up to, perhaps some mystic monks, as a kind of anti-evil troop build-up, but that idea gets the kibosh the moment we think how odd we'd sound—just being the couple we are is odd enough around here. So we continue, drawing satisfaction from our successes and suffering our failures on our own.

The pain of those failures is powerful but so are our resources for withstanding them. We condition our minds by thinking more of the potential victims out there who need us to do the best we can. Hard work and play in many forms help too. After the most grueling sessions, I sometimes aid our recovery by removing the shortwave goblet from its hiding place for a draught of music from someplace like Europe or Brazil or Australia.

Last night an underground jazz maven in New York hit the ionosphere with a piece that reached down to our little receiver in the Himalayas with an impact I'll never forget. It was a long journey that started out with a smooth mellow passage featuring a tenor saxophone full of driving, positive conviction with a touch of meditative romance. But about midway through, a crack opened up in the earth and horrors of pain and violence thundered out of this same band, as if to announce that all that had seemed good in the universe was but a deception, shattered with such violence evoked by the saxophone's screams that I saw once again the blood spurting from my mother's neck wound. God knows I didn't want to hear any more of that, and I was sorry my radio surfing had wrecked the peaceful air of the Andromeda Range I'd just invited Den to enjoy. I reached over Den to turn it off, but was surprised to have my hand stopped by him. "Let's see where he's going with this—there's got to be some point to it," he said, and I settled back uncomfortably to listen.

The screeching went on for another three or four punishing minutes that seemed like hours. Whoever was behind it must have seen a blood-spurting neck in his time, or some equivalent to it, because this was the musical embodiment of high-intensity pain. I was holding my breath just to get through it, when unexpectedly I heard a theme coming up from beneath the trauma and, soon enough, soothing it, settling it down and sending it on its way, lifting us to a higher plane that evoked the mellow beauty from the beginning now radiating immeasurably greater power. It careened me into the bliss I've felt when we've projected ourselves to the cloud tops under the full moon, surveying civilization, persuaded for the moment of the universality of tender loving-kindness that graces so much of humanity. It was a prophet's song of praise of the world's bounty of life, an affirmation that despite all the sorrows evil and hardship visit upon the Earth, love has always prevailed and always would. It brought tears of joy to my eyes.

As the piece settled into its close like a boat from across the world easing into port, I hugged Den in appreciation for his insight that it was worth hanging on through the roughness along the way, and waited for the DJ to identify what we'd heard. After a respectful moment of silence, a deep, reverent African-American voice arose and said, "You have been guided back home by master Pharaoh Sanders, longtime brother to Saint John Coltrane, after an unforgettable spiritual journey he calls Elevation."

Den turned off the radio and we lay quietly together, looking at the Milky Way. I knew a little about Pharaoh Sanders, having seen him play once in San Francisco, and I'd owned some Coltrane records, but Den had had less exposure to their likes in the Rockies, so I was unsure how he'd taken it. He reflected a moment and said, "I'm guessing that Sanders doesn't put much stock in transcendence that hasn't endured and survived the abyss. That music established his credentials for telling victims who survive sorrow and evil and the families of those who don't that if they can hang in there, joy of life can be theirs again."

"I can buy that."

"Me too. That's why I like the song's title. In fact, everything about these last eight months—our home, our relationship, our pasts, especially the visitations where we're trying to raise the potential perps and victims to higher ground—it's all been about elevation."

"*Elevation* should be the title for our log," I replied. "Ever since I got here, I've felt like we're being elevated to a place we can't yet see, as if our individual spiritual DNA is coiling together to create a new, composite being."

Den turned in his sleeping bag to face me. "Towards what end?"

"I don't know, darling. Not yet, anyway."

Den looked me in the eyes till I shivered in wonder of what lies ahead. He massaged my neck and closed his eyes. In his power of suggestion I followed suit.

That's all I've got for now. Den will be awake soon and return to New Hale. What I'll do with my second round of solitude I don't know, but I've given this log its due. Den and I have described the project we've been assigned, our methodology, and our early findings. We're nowhere near done with our work, but my bar-headed geese research notebook has served its repurposed duty, so I doubt there will be many more entries. My focus shall return to the mission, wherever it may lead.

[3-9]

Sept. 25, 1992
The Spire, Tibet

Dearest Den,

I've long thought we'd stay together forever, but your giving me the ring your father gave your mother means more to me than I can say. I love you.

Our life quickened the moment we met. When you appeared in the woods a year ago today, I knew my future lay with you. Nevermore Colorado.

Sayonara Sonoma.

[4-1]

May 3, 1994
Andromeda Range
CZM

Welcome back, Old Log. Make yourself at home in my mind in this sweet spot in the Himalayas and allow me to beg your forgiveness for two years of neglect. The times demand that we make up and catch up.

First, an assurance: Den and I remain Gibraltar-solid in our relationship despite (and partly on account of) our lengthy fall and spring separations. Having recently begun my fifth stay at Andromeda Cave, I miss the man like crazy whenever I'm not thrilled to be alone and some of the time that I am. Experience has proven me right: there are some things you can learn only on your own.

I'm glad Den accompanied me down here last week, though I confess that when he proposed doing so, I protested that it would make me feel like a little girl being walked to school. I promised that if I found my home collapsed, I'd come right back, but he pleaded a yearning to help me put my gardens in, so I relented.

I knew his real reason though: Den is jumpy about spring avalanches and he wanted to keep an eye on slope conditions above us. That suits me fine, since I want him to teach me everything he knows about the subject. I can accept being dependent upon him only for his abundant love.

I'll spend about a month and a half here this spring, puttering in the garden and immersing myself in meditation yoga in the morning light that fills my limestone studio. Den will find plenty to do on his own, picking up some bivouac action at higher elevations for a few days at a time. We've planned to take a few stabs at visitations while apart but so far the results of such attempts have been underwhelming.

Our real work will resume after I return to New Hale before the start of the monsoon. To help me stay balanced through that intense season, I'll have more than Den to keep me company. I'll be spending a lot of time with the two bar-headed geese representing Den and me in my ceiling painting near the soot-masked star field. I spent weeks this winter cleaning and sanding my stony canvas, prepping the surface for my humble masterpiece. We're depicted as a male and female pair as seen from above, flying together, neither ahead of the other. The principal elements are in place now, but getting all the fine detail work on the feathers will consume a good chunk of the summer. This imagery is to my grant proposal descriptions last year as living geese are to the eggs they hatch from—the end was invisible at the beginning, yet would have been impossible without it. Like the once-brilliant elephants on a ceiling at Ellora, the painting's vibrant color will someday lurk silently behind a sooty cloak woven by time, their original message dimmed beyond recognition. Until then, it should continue to please my one-man audience, who tells me that my lifetime of art practice was worth it for this one painting. We artists value praise, especially when it comes from someone who loves you until death do you part.

When I come back here in the fall, it will be for a shorter stay, due to the unpredictability of snow season. At the end of that round, Den will show up to aid me in hauling the harvest he helped plant this week up to New Hale to help feed us through winter.

The life we're building together is *way* off the beaten path, but it works for us, both charged and burdened by our strange mission. Den never takes me for granted, and I count my blessings every night to have found him. We have arguments from time to time, but they don't cut. The other day when Den was helping me tie back a leaning paolay sapling near my house to keep weather and its own fruit from bringing it down, we had a dispute over how to tie an alpine butterfly knot. What a guy thing to argue about. Of course, he is a guy and should be forgiven his gender's inborn foibles, plus I didn't doubt he'd used plenty of knots in mountaineering, but I'd tied alpine butterflies scores of times in sailing, so I wasn't about to give in. When he declared, "That's just not how it's done," I replied, "Who says, Big Guy?"

"I say," he pronounced, in Godspeak. "I have spoken."

"Don't make me puken," I smirked, to his feigned indignation, as I tightened the knot my way. (Truth is, the damn thing would probably be considered legit his way too, as I acknowledged that night.)

We can relish a dose of convention, though, and we welcomed an opportunity for one when Uncle Yeshe offered to arrange a Tibetan wedding for us during our first visit to Gnam Yuljongs as a married couple, a year ago October. It was an honor to be pampered and treated like a Tibetan bride for twenty-four hours. Kurukulla worked hard helping Sonam with the feast preparations and told me it helped make up for her not having been able to participate in her two sisters' weddings (to two brothers—a not infrequent practice hereabouts) in a village far away. I was presented with a necklace of colorful beads and a white silk shawl and Den received a fox fur hat that he wore for the rest of the ceremony. After a feast at which Uncle Yeshe recited a traditional wedding speech in Tibetan—much of which I could understand only through the deep feeling in his voice—everyone in the village joined us for hours of dancing and singing by a bonfire in the pasture.

At one point, when I was dancing with Renzin and Lasya, I saw Sonam looking at me and I could tell she was wondering when Den and I will get around to sleeping together for Nature's intended purpose. (I would differ a bit with her on that view of human sex—there's a reason we call it lovemaking vs. baby making—but never mind. We could agree that reproduction is on the official Sex Purposes List.) Den and I talked about having a child again that night in our tent. Raising a child together in a genuine paradise has its appeal, but a child brought up in New Hale might not fare much better in civilization-coping skills than one raised by wolves. Without exposure to the wider world, the kid would miss most of her or his infinite possibilities (and incidentally be unable to understand our work). It'd be rough all around to be bottled up in the cave with a crying infant during the monsoon, and if there were any kind of injury or illness that we couldn't handle ourselves, we'd condemn ourselves to a lifelong punishment of regret. Why do I get keep getting myself into these binds? In my pre-Den life I traveled so much I couldn't even have a dog, and I adore dogs. Our life is exotic and challenging and we're carrying out the mission we've set for ourselves, but the idea of having a child here is absurd and a meticulous rhythm method must remain a fixture of our lives. But, as Den says, we're young yet.

As to the mission: the progress I described when I was logging regularly that first year has continued apace. Our rate of success triggering eviola rejection is about five out of six. We've become finely attuned to each other's inspirations and cues and we're learning a bit more of each other's specialties—that is, Den has managed a few marginally successful projections and I've gotten some incipient radar going, but we don't dabble that way often, because every visitation requires peak performance. We can't take chances when a big game is on the line, and our game is always on the line and very big for somebody. Sometimes we've tried to aim our visitations at potential recruits who might join our ranks, but we couldn't tell if we'd gotten anywhere, and without clear evidence we were succeeding, we couldn't justify diverting energy from our primary objective.

Three visitations and one family matter bear mentioning at this time. Last October, an eviola incident struck home for me literally and figuratively. We'd come upon a piece of male sub-human scum in his forties whose interior world was crawling with psychopathology. We watched as he entered the bedroom window of a girl about twelve in the middle of a fun slumber party and kidnapped her with a knife at her throat before her pale, terrified friends. He threw her in his car and drove her to a field where he raped her in a ditch. Nothing we did raised a blip in his consciousness. When he began to smother her, I became hysterical and injected images into his soulspace of myself stabbing his head and body with his own knife, making vile mincemeat of that abomination of pseudo-human plasma. If anything, his suffocation of the girl became even more fierce. When I saw the life pass out of her eyes, I screamed. Den yanked me away with all his psychic strength.

I returned to New Hale a wrung-out wreck. As an undeputized public safety officer, I'd not merely stepped over the line of objectivity, I'd leapt far over it and crash-landed. The Dalai Lama would not be pinning a medal on me for heroic conquering of my anger and hatred any time soon. I took it so personally in part because the crime took place not far from my former home in California. On the killer's drive from the girl's house, I recognized the area as Petaluma, a town where I'd once done a guest speaker appearance as a videographer at a local grade school. For all I knew, the monster's victim was one of the kids I'd let shoot some footage on the playground. Then there was the girl's age, undone by evil at the same time of life when my mother was murdered while trying to shield me from gunfire.

I was inconsolable for almost a week recovering from that murder. For the next few months, crimes involving prey like that girl were absent from the range of crises Den found for us, to the point that I suspected that he was consciously or subconsciously avoiding subjecting me to them. I didn't call him on it—after all, there were scores of life-or-death situations we were attending to all along—but I began to feel guilty that the lives of vulnerable girls might have been sacrificed in a sense, denied our help on account of Den's fear of triggering a nervous breakdown in me.

So by February I was primed for a jab from my conscience and I got one. We visited Gnam Yuljongs at Losar, Tibet's New Year festival, and were enjoying a traditional mutton feast when I saw Lasya smiling at me idolatrously, and I suddenly grew ashamed of the weakness I'd manifested after the kidnapping, for it was indirectly preventing me from providing other children like Lasya what protection I could. I told Den that I wanted him to make certain he wasn't excluding such situations in his scanning for targets. He didn't admit to having done so, but the following week we found ourselves in a similar situation in the Mediterranean and a couple more incidents since then followed suit in Africa and Appalachia. It was rough going, but the kidnappers' plans were successfully defused through projections of guilt, threats of imprisonment among short-eye haters, and prospects of public humiliation.

The second incident to alter the lay of the land occurred a couple of months ago. Our subject was a white man in his mid-twenties whom we found walking around a US federal office building in a medium-size city, probably in the Midwest, judging from the architecture and flat horizon.

The plethora of memories in his soulspace reflecting time spent on the front lines in the Gulf War indicated that he was an ex-soldier.

Unlike most of our subjects, this guy was not heated by passions of power or perversion. The totems in his soulspace displayed an odd mixture of patriotism and hatred of the US government. One clue to this guy's animus was an endless loop of a firefight scene that kept turning up in different parts of his mind. This had nothing to do with Iraq; rather it looked a lot like a photo I'd seen in a newspaper down in Zhangmu last year of a battle between a law enforcement squad and a sect holed up in a huge ranch house in Texas. Our subject's version of the incident was littered with images of burning bodies, which I'd not seen in the published photos. Children were among the victims.

I could only guess at how that played into the plot this guy was weaving as he studied the ten-story office building. A lot of children were being ferried into the building by parents, presumably because of an on-site day care center. As an eviola virus neared him, he sneered, envisioning a montage of schematics and chemicals culminating in a tremendous explosion destroying the building and everyone in it.

Den called my attention to one of the guy's combat memories in which he'd performed well and was enjoying the accolades of his comrades in arms. He was suggesting that I put American military hero material into play as a bulwark against the subject's planned terrorism. I concocted a scenario of several of those war buddies surrounding him in the downtown street, urging him in macho brotherhood vernacular to let it go, acknowledging his conviction that the government was pocked with shitheads, but insisting that blowing up scores of children and their parents would only stir up pro-government loyalty in the general public.

The strategy seemed to work. In his soulspace vision, our subject, however disgruntled, agreed with his pals and he backed off, his violent imagery subsiding as he walked back to his car and drove off. "Cool," part of me wanted to say to myself, "dodged that bomb." But deep down, I didn't buy it. This guy's meticulous planning was different from the acutely crazy passions of most of our subjects. I was disturbed by the thought that any seeds of horror that had been dissolved would revive and germinate in his deep hatred. We returned to New Hale in low spirits that night.

Well, having reached this spring in my account, I must relate the story of Uncle Yeshe. A month ago Den and I were sleeping outside at New Hale for the first time since last fall. In the middle of the night I dreamt that Den and I were engaged in a visitation to someone with a wild cacophony of sounds in his soulspace, yet there was no hint of eviola. He was chasing demons in his soulspace walls and seeing them also through his window, dodging around as if searching for something. Periodically, a sleeping figure and people huddled in near-dark candlelight would appear in the window, too. Imagine my shock, when, amidst that visual confusion, I caught a glimpse of my drawing of Uncle Yeshe as a sleeping Buddha—followed by a clear view of the sleeping figure, revealed as Uncle Yeshe himself. And he wasn't asleep—he was in a coma, breathing with great difficulty. Our subject held a candle near his face and lifted his right eyelid, and there was no reaction.

The dream was so vivid and upsetting that I woke up gasping, and discovered Den sitting up, staring at the setting moon. I knew why, without asking. I said, "Uncle Yeshe?"

He nodded. "They must have a shaman working on him—we've got to get down there."

I was out of the sleeping bag before he finished his sentence. "First light must be less than an hour off," I said. "I'll fix some tea and toast. Will you pack?"

As it happened, we'd been planning to return to civilization later that week anyway, for a long-planned visit with Jyoti and her parents in Zhangmu. When Jyoti turned thirteen in December, she told her parents that all she wanted for her birthday was a chance to visit me in Tibet. Through several letter exchanges, we'd agreed to meet them in Zhangmu for a couple of days in April. I knew that the crisis at hand could throw a bag of wrenches into the works, but we could only take one step at a time, and the first ten thousand of them led straight to Gnam Yuljongs.

We made our way downhill with a quick pace and nervous hearts. When we approached the village at mid-morning, Lasya and Renzin noticed us, but instead of running to us as usual, they ran into Yeshe's house. A moment later they came out with Sonam, all of them looking relieved to see us.

When Sonam reached us, she said, "You know," as unsurprised as if she'd expected we'd heard the news on television. As we hugged her, she told us, "The healer is resting in my house. He told us he'd found the angry demon and persuaded him to unleash Father and now he is awake."

We entered Yeshe's house and found Kurukulla and a few other neighbors sitting at his bedside. They made way for us to approach him and we saw his haggard face light up. I was so happy to see him smile, I teared up. The whole way downhill I'd been afraid we'd find him dead.

Yeshe had suffered an episode of congestive heart failure, a condition I was only too familiar with from my father's battle with heart disease. I was buoyed by the recollection that my dad had recovered completely from his first battle with it. He managed to escape its clutches for almost three more years before the grim reaper returned, meaning business.

Yeshe was drained but able to speak in little spurts. He told Den, "I wasn't worried about you over winter. I'm sure you are as strong as Yeti."

"Of course," Den replied. "I'm your nephew, and you're strong enough to scare off a heart sickness demon!" Yeshe smiled and settled into some much-needed rest. We stayed beside him for a while, noshing on some tsampa and butter tea Sonam brought us, and quietly exchanged news with her. Throughout it, Den or I would hold Uncle Yeshe's frail, cool, hand.

That was April 9th. We were scheduled to meet Jyoti and her parents in the lobby of the Cloud Peak Friendship hotel in Zhangmu at noon on the 12th. I'd been tossing around plans to get word to them that we'd have to reschedule our reunion—news I knew would devastate Jyoti, not to mention the cost her parents had incurred to get the three of them from Bombay to Zhangmu—but as everyone relaxed about Uncle Yeshe's incipient recovery, we decided that if he remained stable, I could go on to Zhangmu by myself in a couple of days. Not only would I save Jyoti (and myself) from a major disappointment, I could pick up some much-needed medicinals the healer wanted the family to have on hand for Uncle Yeshe in the event of a relapse.

Before leaving on the morning of the 12th, I gently hugged Yeshe as he slept and whispered that I loved him, and that I'd be away for a bit but would see him again in a couple of days. Den walked me to the top of the pass for my first solo hike down to the road to Zhangmu.

I made good time, caught the bus to town, and arrived early. I'd barely had time to greet Lin-Chee and sit down in his hotel lobby, when in walked Jyoti and her parents, also an hour early. I almost didn't recognize Jyoti, who had shot up seven inches in height with maturity to match. She ran up to me but halted suddenly, uncertain as to whether it was all right to hug me. Her concerns melted when I embraced her. I felt a rush of protective big sisterly feelings—with maternal overtones that were no doubt expected by those looking on, since, at thirty, my having a thirteen-year-old child would be common in this part of the world.

Jyoti's parents, Rishi and Manjula, were justly proud of having pulled off this expedition, given the difficulty non-Nepalese foreigners face trying to enter "China" from that part of Nepal. However, Rishi is a successful Indian businessman, and I got the distinct impression that to get his family across the Friendship Bridge for a day and a half, his friendship handshake with the sentry had been lubricated with Rupee Brand palm grease.

After lunch at a Nepalese eatery, Jyoti and I went for a long walk while her parents indulged in a shopping spree. For a few hours, we sampled the civilization casserole that Tibet, China, and Nepal have cooked up near the Bhotekoshi River. As we walked up a path beyond the edge of town, I learned that Jyoti's early fascination with my work in nature cinematography had spurred on an insatiable curiosity about natural science, biology in particular. She loved hearing about sea slugs and how various marine organisms were contributing so much to medical research. I got the feeling that if I'd offered to fly her that moment to the Caribbean or the Red Sea for a research dive, she'd have fired off a loving goodbye telegram to her folks and leapt onto the plane.

When it came to technology, Jyoti's life has become a lot more far-ranging than mine. She reported seeing Japanese businessmen in the airport who spoke on telephones they carried around in valises. And there are computers in her school that are networked with computers in governments and museums and even stores scattered around the world, so a student can hop hither and yon and see whatever these non-material bulletin boards want you to see.

When we regrouped for dinner, Jyoti was all a-jabber about the adventures of wildlife filmmaking. Pride and premonitory sadness mixed it up in her parents' faces, since it was becoming obvious that someday, not that far off, their little girl would be spending a lot of time far from Bombay. Already she was campaigning to be allowed to visit Den and me in our mountain home—a notion I quickly scotched as too risky for a young person's safety (and, though I left it unmentioned, a violation of our agreement to keep our hideaways hidden). But I did suggest that someday she could visit us in Gnam Yuljongs and get a feel for the warm life in a cool mountain village.

Dinner lasted well into the evening, after which we retired to our rooms. After nearly three years of life in conditions ranging from somewhat to knockout primitive, the luxuries of hot running water and a cushy mattress in a $35 a night hotel felt like a stay at the Grand Hyatt Maui. But I had no desire to stay another day. To an inhabitant of New Hale and the Andromeda Range, the noise and pollution and material razzmatazz of Zhangmu left plenty to be desired.

We'd expected to spend much of the next day together, but I awoke before dawn with a terrible anxiety, fearing that Uncle Yeshe had taken a severe turn for the worse. I had to return to Gnam Yuljongs without delay. I knocked on the door of my friends' room and explained why I had to beg off of our plans. They dressed with the speed of firefighters to join me for a quick continental breakfast before I bid them adieu and raced off in a ride up the road I was able to arrange through Lin-Chee.

I re-entered the village in mid-afternoon, having hoped against hope all the way over the pass that I wouldn't be too late, but that hope died while I was still a half-mile off. I could see people hugging each other in the street. Den got word I was coming and walked deliberately up the trail, only fleetingly permitting me visual contact with his red eyes. Uncle Yeshe was no more.

When Den reached me, I cried piteously on his shoulder—quietly, though, since sobbing near the newly deceased is considered injurious to the soul in transition. I felt so bad for not having been with Uncle Yeshe when his life deserted him. Den got it without my saying anything. His first comment was, "He suffered a reversal at midnight and slipped into a coma. He had no idea who was with him." I appreciated his reassurance but didn't buy it. When my father was in a coma during his first heart failure, I talked to him for hours even though his doctors had told me he wouldn't hear me—but I knew that, at some level, he did. A year later, out of the clear blue, my dad told me, "I don't think about that incident in the hospital often, but when I do, I'm convinced that you had a lot to do with my surviving that night." So it's been a source of deep regret these last several weeks that Uncle Yeshe did not hear my voice during his final dreams. We're in Tibet, where no one buys my dad's doctor's story, where they've believed for thousands of years that the soul of the recently deceased continues to hear us and must hear us and be coached as it begins its journey across the passage between lives known as the bardo.

We stayed on in the village for the funeral, as did the shaman. Someone who knew the prayers was with Uncle Yeshe at all times, so that he would hear comforting guidance as we prepared to bear him up to the ridge overlooking the village, while being carried and placed on the pyre, and while his physical remnants were transformed by flames to smoke rising to the clear blue sky. He heard, along with all of us and any animals within a mile of us, blasts on four long Tibetan horns that must have been borrowed from the orchestra that trumpeted Creation at the beginning of time.

Throughout the ceremony, my fragmentary comprehension of the prayers would be supplemented by brief translations, which I much appreciated. Seeing the gray-haired head of someone you love in flames could be an awfully traumatic sight, but for the shock-softening, comforting imagery of light and blissful deities he was advised were welcoming him. There was no horror or wailing grief surrounding this phase in the life of Uncle Yeshe's soul. He had been taught about the time between death and life throughout the long period between his birth and his death and all were confident that he felt secure as he embarked on his latest journey.

The prayer imagery was not all rose-petal pretty, not by a long shot. Mantras were chanted to ward off wrathful deities and to keep evil at bay throughout the world. Gnam Yuljongsians take a long-familiar, global approach to evil, much different from the individual telepathic struggles Den and I engage in, but they share our yearning for humanity to overcome the evil bane of its existence. Taking part made me feel more centered in the tradition of the land I've finally made my own, eighteen years after I first set eyes on its thrilling, mountainous skyline.

We stayed one more day after Uncle Yeshe's departure and said our good-byes for the summer the following morning. Sonam's family accompanied us to the edge of the village and watched us begin our ascent to New Hale, our private earthly heaven.

Den and I hardly spoke on the way back. I'd been obliged to entertain some rather somber thoughts along the way, such as, if Den and I continue to make these mountains our home for the rest of our lives, who would care for the body and soul of the one of us to die last? Which led to other morbid ponderings such as the thought of one of us having to cope in utter isolation with the death of the one who died first. I recognized that such thoughts must come to everyone at some point, perhaps first as an unpleasant surprise in the full vigor of adulthood when suffering the loss of a parent, then more frequently as years pile up. Of course, like ambulance drivers, Den and I have had to deal with death hundreds of times in the course of our work, and we've developed a shield of professionalism around our emotions to get through the nights. No such protection was possible or desirable when it came to losing Uncle Yeshe, and so we grieved in silence, with the echoes of Tibetan Buddhist prayers offering a bit of comfort.

With this journal nearly full, I regret having to add the third grim report alluded to earlier, because it comes down heavily on the opposing side of the case we make to ourselves that human evolution is on the right course. After our arrival in the Andromeda Range last week, Den and I went to work as usual one night, expecting to find this or that impassioned vengeance seeker or sociopath on the brink of a psychotic break, only to discover that nearly three years' experience in the field reckoning with evil had left us ill-prepared for what we were about to witness.

I'm not going to subject you to the grisly details, but rather will simply state that a slaughter is going on in Central Africa right now on a scale that is unimaginable. Some tribal thing—I have no idea what's behind the insanity between these rival tribes that I can't even tell apart, but whatever it is, it's triggered an unimaginable killing spree. Not for these aggressors the precision clockworks of Birkenau or the business dividends of slaves harvested for labor camps—these guys brook no distractions from their mass murdering frenzy with machetes and guns. We've visited half a dozen of them over the last week and everywhere we go we've seen scores or hundreds of men, women, and children being hacked or shot to death. In one instance our efforts at dissuasion had some impact, when our subject retreated from a hut in which a grandmother and grandchild were huddling in terror, but the tidal wave of murder being perpetrated by his fellow maniacs limited the merciful extension of those two lives to forty seconds. Having soaked the ground of one enclave in blood, they would jump in their jeeps and hit the next one, killing everyone they saw. Their only breaks came when they found they'd been beaten to the punch at a village that had already been snuffed out by some other cadre.

"Never again," my father's people had said about genocide, but in the present African mass murder, genocide has again engulfed a region in evil. I turned on the shortwave last night, hoping in vain for news of some imminent intervention. News wires are reporting stories of rampant butchery in Rwanda, thousands of murders every day perpetrated by Hutus on Tutsis, who incidentally had gone on Hutu-killing rampages of their own previously. If the UN or anyone else is thinking about stepping in to halt the killing, no sign of it has emerged yet.

Despite that disheartening development, Den and I remain committed to our course, because we *know* that every time our work saves a life, our energies have been well invested. Anyone who escapes evil due to a prospective killer having changed his mind values his or her life as much we value ours, and were we to be similarly spared, our gratitude for whatever had saved our lives would be incalculable.

Today Den and I walked off our frustration—well, his frustration, my despair—about the Rwandan atrocities by taking a hike to a peak I found around a bend in the range off to the west. It serves as a local surrogate for the Spire when we're away from New Hale. We took off our shirts under the high spring sun. Den sat with his back against a rock and I sat with my back against his chest. As we watched the clouds play shadows-on-the-valley, our shining, warmed skin and our nerves within murmured languid thanks for our indulging them with a sunbath in our al fresco spa. After a spell, we allowed mortality to sink back into our consciousness.

"So," I began.

"So?"

"Any misgivings about what we've gotten ourselves into?"

"Hell, no." Den arced his neck around to where he could look at me askance. "Are you going wobbly on me?"

"Big picture, Den. Didn't you think that by now there might be some propitious cycle starting up, some hint that maybe things were improving out there? I've got a sneaking suspicion those butchers in Rwanda will be issued get-out-of-jail-free cards by some truth and reconciliation commission like the one they set up in Chile for the disappearance squads, some panel that will let the killers go right back into the neighborhoods of their victims' families in exchange for a 'Mea culpa.' Nobody offered a truth and reconciliation pat on the head to Jeffrey Dahmer and he was a piss-ant perp compared to the mass murderers in Bosnia and Rwanda who might get cushy commission wrist slaps."

"But if it's all you can get, public acknowledgment of evil is better than nothing. It's a temporary preventative measure, like emergency food aid in a famine—it's no substitute for a healthy food system but it can get you through the night." Taking in my glum expression, Den added, "Look, Calieze—nature paces itself and so must we."

"But maybe we're overreaching. Many a downfall has sprouted from grand expectations."

"As well as all successes. This is keep-on-keeping-on time, Calieze. We can't quit just 'cause we're not being served pie in the sky."

Wistfully, I flashed on the peaceful face carved out of the mountain in Ellora's Cave 10, and sighed, "Sometimes I wish I could trade in a truckload of our visitation anguish for a smidgeon of the Buddha's cosmic bliss."

"That'd be peachy, Calieze, but I don't think we're gonna get there as long as we've been called to do this first."

"Called? Do you think we've been recruited for this job?"

"Let's just say that Buddha bliss would feel hollow to people like us if it came from abandonment of the world for the sake of private nirvana. The beauty of Creation demands that we do what we can to enable everyone to enjoy it."

"Point taken. It's hard to see how people blessed with a strong, healthy love like ours could feel enlightened while leaving the suffering to fend for themselves."

"Sitting still and inaction are not the American way."

"They're not very Jewish either."

"Or Jesusish, for that matter."

I agreed and reminded him that he hadn't answered my question about being recruited.

"I'd hate to think of anyone scouting Earthlings getting a look at what's doing down in Rwanda."

"That would create a bad impression."

"Bad impression? It would raise a five-alarm galactic emergency to contain a lethal epidemic and prevent the eviola virus from leaping to other worlds before the anipoxi develop space travel and endanger the galaxy's spiritual gene pool." I figured he had one more engine backfire of pessimistic speculation on the way and summoned sufficient patience to let him get through it. "We'd be lucky if they didn't run a hose from Venus's tailpipe to suffocate us with CO_2, assuming we don't get the job done for them."

"Your pep talk just slid off the rails, Coach."

"Sorry. Please ignore me when I go off like that."

"I do. Your answer?"

"As to whether I think justice and peace scouts are somewhere out there looking for recruits? Do you?"

"I don't know. Sometimes I wonder when we're up in places like this or the Spire."

"I think my father was trying to recruit me to find a way to help stop evil without killing others."

"Check."

"Check, thanks to you."

"Thanks to you, Den—I might have quit if it weren't for your shoring-up."

"That was the search-and-rescue mindset. If you find four dead and one still alive, you can't let regret over the deaths diminish the horsepower of your rescue of that one survivor by an iota. We must keep at it and remember that this Rwandan massacre shit will end, as will the Chinese government's killings of Tibetans. They will pass from the Earth like the murders perpetrated by the Khmer Rouge—"

"—and the Nazis—"

"—all of them. In the meantime, armed with the power to stop some of it and the perfect setting and freedom to use it, we've got our marching orders."

I felt a bit abashed. What a morale-busting injury evolution would suffer if people fighting evil were to up and quit! I've got to punch up my game by an order of magnitude, to the point that despair dare not show it's shriveled and shriveling face around me. As co-writer and actor, I'm putting myself back in the show.

Good timing for that, with this book almost full. This record has served an important purpose, one even more interesting than a film on bar-headed geese. Setting down these words has helped me stay centered in the voyage of a lifetime. I thank God for our many blessings and hope we can hang onto them in whatever unknowable winds shall blow through the future.

[4-2]

early A.M., 9/12/2001
New Hale
CZM

Viewed for the first time from seven years above, the journey down our past reminds me of a crazy quilt my Sonoma landlady bestowed on me long ago to keep me warm in my caboose. It's like an experiential patchwork knitting a radiologist's reports on supernatural CAT scans together with memos from Scotland Yard, spiritual combat debriefings, and a young couple's travel diary. Penned by bushy-tailed novices, it throws off memory sparks of a past as distant as the first year of medical school might seem to veteran brain surgeons.

It took some high-powered idealism for a couple of bright-eyed young adults raised in the West to cut the cultural apron strings and commit to a risky mission in a foreign, mystical, almost unpeopled mountain land with no one else to rely on as guide or protector. But guess what: we made it. Now, way into our thirties, our eyes are brighter than ever, illuminated by visions that left subtle crows' feet nearby. Den and I keep forging ahead, engines thrumming, through adventures so numerous and wild as to make the *Odyssey* look like the police blotter in a one-intersection town on a slow day. We know what we're doing now and have become sufficiently toughened to make it through whatever comes our way, no matter how extreme. Even last night's incident on the Spire.

But first, some notes on background. Den and I are stronger than ever, individually and together. We are thwarting eviola ingestion at a rate scarcely imaginable in the early days, probably eight or nine hundred times a year during the nine or so months we are together. (We've even managed connecting to each other when we're apart, though successful visitations that way are too infrequent.) The resurrecting number Den ran on me during the early days of Rwanda proved lasting. Now when we lose, I'm up off the mat as fast as he is, in hours or minutes, rather than weeks. Physically, I could hold my own with the best of the rowers I used to crew with in San Francisco Bay. My husband and I are wound tightly together in every way except genetically, and even that remains a possibility.

That particular fantasy was spotlit during a long, harrowing night two years ago last spring, when our own lives were on the line in a snow cave we had to engineer in a few blizzard-swept minutes about a mile from the Andromeda Range. Den had met me en route from my place back to New Hale. I hadn't expected him—I thought he'd be away on one of the short camping trips he sometimes takes while we're apart. My plan had been to surprise him by being home at New Hale when he returned, but he met me in the late afternoon a half-hour into my trek.

He'd been to hoping catch me before I left to alert me to an extreme avalanche risk, neither of us aware that a spring snowstorm would soon pose a threat of its own unlike any we'd faced in the previous seven-plus years. The blizzard came on as suddenly as a dam break. As we dug furiously in a thickening white-out, Den insisted that we keep carving till we could fit in the fishing rod he'd brought to snare snow trout from the creek below Andromeda Cave. Throughout the snowfall the rest of that day and night, he employed the pole to maintain a vent so that we didn't become encased in ice frozen from our own moisture.

I can see how many might surrender in such an ordeal, for the fear of being buried alive can wield quite the mental strength-sapping. Den and I prevailed by focusing on our future.

After we'd managed to sate our pent-up hunger for each other with a few creative workarounds, I murmured, "Den, it's getting harder to ignore a certain feeling tapping on my door every once in a while."

"Yeah? What's that?"

"I'm driving an empty womb around and I'd kinda like to pull up to the TD station and 'say fill 'er up, please.'" His pain-tinged smile left no doubt I'd struck a chord. "I've begun thinking of my body as an instrument designed over billions of years of evolution to join the team creating the next generation of sentient beings. Sometimes I just want to blow up the rules of rhythm and get it on as Nature intended. Blessed with all I could want in body and love, I feel like I've set a thick glass case around a Stradivarius to prevent anyone from playing it."

"Excuse me, ma'am. I've played that instrument a thousand times. No musician has known greater joy."

Several ripostes occurred to me but none was necessary. Den knew what I meant and it saddened him as it did me. We'd run through the gamut of child-rearing scenarios set here, there, and everywhere and had yet to find a satisfactory one among them. Looking up into the pitch darkness while Den twirled the pole through our vent, I commented, "Feels kinda selfish, enjoying myself up here and depriving some soul looking for a new home in our arms."

"Uh, 'selfish' is not a term that comes to mind when I think about what you're engaged in here." I kept quiet. "However, I do grant that the world should not be denied a child with your genes."

"Yours too!"

"Yeah, ours especially. To raise such a child would be joy abounding. But, look, darlin', we've plenty of time to figure this out."

"I'm almost thirty-eight."

"So? That still leaves us years to decide. In the meantime, we're getting in parenting practice with Jyoti."

True that. Jyoti had made it up from Bombay (now known as "Mumbai") to Gnam Yuljongs to visit us during each of the previous two springs and, at age seventeen, was then due for her third hegira there in what had become an annual event. She and Renzin and Lasya have become enamored of each other, the Tibetans and the Indian each enchanted by the exotic, affectionate other. In her last visit, Lasya showed off her skill making a blouse with her mother's treadle sewing machine and Renzin gave her a photo he'd taken of an orange dragonfly above a cloud. Lasya told us that her brother had lain on the ground by the bush the dragonfly was browsing through for half an hour to get the shot—a kind of dedication I well remember. Jyoti promised to frame it and hang it in her living room at home.

Jyoti's love for me is downright filial, and much reciprocated. She had long settled on me as a second mother, and I was only too proud and happy to be considered so by a girl growing up to be such an incredible young woman. Jyoti's intelligence blazes in a pearlescent crucible of love, sensitivity, and bright humor that will surely earn her the opportunity she covets to study medical science at a place like Johns Hopkins, Stanford, or Oxbridge. I adore that girl and would do anything for her.

It was natural for Den and me to think of Jyoti while encased in our emergency accommodations. It helped us stay positive as we traversed the night locked in in-flight refueling, all the while on the lookout for signs of the snowfall's end. We framed our entertainment of each other as a clever remedy for one of numerous minor hassles one must expect in return for living in a rough-hewn paradise. So we have to clear snow, tend a fire, and snuggle under the same stuff that falls on yak and geese once in a while—we live and breathe majestic beauty, practice an extraordinary, mostly gratifying art, and haven't idled an engine in a traffic jam, locked a door, or received a bill in ten years.

We did not attempt a visitation to an eviola site that night—there was a bit too much anxiety knocking about for that—but we did try to contact our four parents. The experience lacked the vivid intensity of our visits to living people but it was comforting to imagine that we were feeling their love for us. It led Den to mourn the likely loss of his parents' terma. He'd neglected to stay in touch with his mother's friend Brenda, who'd accepted it for safekeeping, until it was too late. He'd received a card from the postmistress in Leadville informing him that Brenda had emigrated to an unknown location in New Mexico and hadn't been heard from in years.

Eventually, while Den was talking about his trip to Nepal during infancy, his voice became as woozy as my ears, and I drifted off to sleep, where he followed me soon enough.

We awoke some indeterminate time later to the joyous sight of a spot of deep sky blue at the upper end of our vent. With the snow's surface still powder light and uncrusted, we dug ourselves a tunnel to freedom and threw our arms around each other in wide-open space.

After getting our gear in shape for travel and grabbing a bite of jerky, washed down with fresh, mouth-melted snow, Den looked around and re-entered avalanche assessment mode. Risk factors were piling up: we were on the leeward side of a slope at the bottom of a huge bowl with a lot of loose snow lying at a forty degree angle. A grim look crossed his face and he told me we had to make a run for it. I started to question how one could "run" in deep snow when he snatched my pack and ordered me to hightail it.

"Fine, but you're not carrying my pack!"

"I know you're strong as a lovely female ox and I'm still carrying your pack—now watch your footing and run for your life!"

I heard a thundering wave of snow begin to sweep down from south to north and I ran all right, as the avalanche dusted us with the edge spray of its mountainous weight only a hundred yards behind us. I would have feared that my pack could weigh Den down, but for being able to hear him right behind me, bearing both packs like a couple of loaves of barley bread.

When the white thunder stopped rolling downhill, I stopped to catch my breath, but Den yelled at me to keep going. We kept running for another two minutes till we rounded a bend to a part of the trail that was now a half-mile from the nearest steep slope, when he finally said, "Whoa, love," and put down the packs. We walked off our breathlessness and collapsed on a snowy meadow.

"Thanks, coach," I huffed and puffed, my eyes rejoicing at the brilliant sky blue instead of the underside of ten thousand tons of entombing snowpack. "I could use a break before the earthquake and the volcano."

We were readying ourselves for the final leg of our return to New Hale when our trip unveiled one more surprise, a mystical beauty: a snow leopard performing a swift predatory dance descending across a stony slope on the other side of the draw, tracking a fox. The leopard glanced briefly our way as he pursued his prey, suddenly leaping into a glorious feline tear, up and over a ridge and out of sight. Den and I looked at each other, interpreting that vision as a reward for surviving the previous nineteen hours. That night we wondered if we'd been spared for something new and important yet to come. I know not what, but I still feel it up ahead.

Whatever it is, it had better be good to balance out something very bad and new under the sun revealed to us and the whole world last night. Prior to my imminent departure for Andromeda Cave, slated for tomorrow, Den and I had made our way up to the Spire as part of an ambitious farewell party. We decided, for the first time, to take the calculated risk of spending the night up there—the risk being lightning, given that that promontory is a natural geologic lightning rod. We figured it was worth it to experiment with visitations from that height, plus there was the kicker—the starscape, which, if it were clear, would outdo even New Hale for thin air clarity, boosting a couple thousand more stars into the visible range, plus a few million more in the Milky Way. We would be careful, gauging the skies before letting ourselves sleep and setting our inner alarm clocks to wake every couple of hours to make sure no late summer storm was sneaking up on us.

It was exciting settling in up top. We placed stones to hold down our belongings against the winds, enjoyed our al fresco supper, and set about our nightly hunt. We've been feeling plenty hardy by now, given what we've witnessed in Serbia and Rwanda and innumerable individual crimes (oh—that army vet *did* blow up that federal building a year after I'd hoped we'd dissuaded him from it). Worst of all was the slow, drawn-out manslaughter by starvation of more than a million people, mostly women, children, and the elderly, courtesy of the "military first" policy by which North Korea's "supreme leader" Kim Jong-Il and his cronies deflected famine emergency food supplies to their army—but even witnessing that couldn't stop us.

So we were beginning to think we'd seen about everything, when last night we came upon something that dropped our jaws wide open.

It began strangely when our meditation was interrupted by a horizon-wide crackling of silent lightning. At 19,000' with a 270 degree view and utterly exposed, the silent bolt gave us pause. We looked at each other, something we almost never do as we're trying to find our way to a visitation. Den shook his head the slightest bit, which I understood to mean that the lightning was too far to pose any threat, a judgment proved correct by the full minute and a half it took for the thunder to reach us that marked the lightning as being at least fifteen miles off.

We were safe from the lightning but not unaffected by it. From the moment we saw it I could feel my hair stand on end. At an elevation closer to the edge of space than most humans ever venture on foot, those bolts subtly electrified us. In the glowing darkness that followed, it seemed like the vast space beneath us had reverted to a primitive state, as the world might have been just before the start of time. The phrase "tohu v'vohu" rose up from the recesses of my memory, a phrase uttered by my father once while reading Genesis to my mother and me after dinner one Sabbath eve. He translated it as "unformed and void."

My skin prickled all over with the suspicion that we were veering into uncharted territory. After a lengthy, troubled flight, Den landed us simultaneously in the soulspaces of four different men in different locations. In ten years of visitations, we'd never visited even two soulspaces at once. These four soulspaces filled our field of view in layers that dissolved in and out of each other, each dipping and rising in prominence in waves of auditory and visual signals.

I was thinking that the Spire must confer some mighty strong mojo on nighttime meditators, when we discovered that our four subjects were linked to each other in a very f-ing sick scheme. Each of them was patrolling the aisle of a different airliner in flight, filled with terrified passengers, adults and children alike, trapped in a hijacking. Most of the passengers spoke in American English but our subjects and their teammates—all men, each communicating with a couple of fellow gangsters plus two more in the cockpits—spoke to each other in Arabic.

Oh, brother, I thought—think of the broadcast interruptions, negotiations, and the tsunami waves of fear that must be sweeping over the USA right now. The hijackers were telling their captives they'd be landing soon and to pipe down, but people were crying and shuddering about dead bodies—one or two in each cabin compartment, crew members who'd had their throats slashed by the hijackers' to make the point that the passengers had best stay in their seats.

I was so absorbed in grasping the scenes visible in the subjects' soulspace windows that it was several minutes before I got a handle on their pathological plot. These guys had already treated themselves to large servings of eviola—their pustule covered inner faces betrayed that as much as the dead bodies crumpled against the bulkheads—but more tempting, steaming second helpings were hovering right near them and their worst gorging was yet to come. They were going to crash the planes, their passengers, and themselves into buildings filled with thousands of people. Three of them had their sights set on skyscrapers at the World Trade Center in New York, a neighborhood I'd walked through hundreds of times. This was the same dark horror laid out in scrawled notes of the Osama bin Laden flunky who knocked off Meir Kahane more than a decade ago and later repeated in the diaries of a couple of murderous Colorado high school dweebs who shot up a bunch of their classmates, a teacher, and themselves—it was finally coming to pass. The fourth gang was targeting the *Pentagon*. This paltry gang of killers were so enamored with mass murdering Americans, they were willing to die for it.

I reeled, unable to focus on my job. What could I do? These crazies had already gone so far, they were not going to turn back. But I was compelled to try, so I focused on one of the subjects envisioning the Trade Center towers. That plane carried several small children. I reached into his soulspace chamber and seized on an image the subject harbored of Mohammed. Somehow this bloodthirsty nutcase was convinced that he was committing his crime in the service of Islam. He even imagined Mohammed welcoming him into some kind of sultry paradise with scores of beautiful virgins awaiting him. But I'd known Muslims in Israel and elsewhere and I knew that Mohammed comes off in much of the Koran as a stern moralist and protector, so I projected an image of Mohammed standing between the subject and the crying kids on the plane, as if to protect the children, threatening eternal retribution if the hijackers went through with the crash.

It gave the man pause. Confused, he sat down in one of the empty passenger seats. I could see his manic partners conversing through the open cockpit door. In his soulspace chamber wall, he fought with my projection and tried to wrench Mohammed back into his previous guise. Becoming more and more agitated, he got up and grabbed one of the other hijacker's arms but when he saw his partner's wild eyes, he stopped and leaned over to look out the window.

Sure enough they were heading right toward lower Manhattan. These maniacs weren't going to land in Cuba, Arabia, or anywhere else but hell, and as that dawned on the passengers, they began screaming at the top of their lungs. A few men got out of their seats and charged the hijackers in the aisle, but at five hundred miles an hour they had no time to avert the calamity even if they'd known how to fly passenger jets. One of the towers loomed up in our view at incredible speed and *BAM!*—our subject, everyone else on the plane and doubtless hundreds in the building were killed instantly. The last thing we saw in his soulspace window was the inside of a vast, fiery explosion.

Stunned, Den and I found ourselves miles above the city looking down on a smoky fireball near the tip of the island. The other three subjects were still alive, carrying on with their business, but, terror-struck and absolutely helpless, we catapulted ourselves out of the nightmare and retreated eastward, seeking the Asian night.

We returned to the Spire short of breath and discovered that the lightning storm was heading our way at all deliberate speed. I did notice the odd sight of a pair of stars moving around in a momentary parting of the clouds at the zenith, but there was no time for stargazing. We packed up and headed down off the promontory, pronto, in a mostly conversationless two-hour descent in pitch darkness broken only by lightning and our solar-powered flashlights.

We got back to New Hale a few hours ago, too wired to sleep, despite the exertions of the hike. We talked about how the world had suddenly pivoted into a new dark period of history. It wasn't the number of deaths involved—no matter how many people perished in the four plane crashes, it couldn't compare to the death tolls we'd seen in North Korea and Rwanda, let alone the predations of the Third Reich. It was that so many evilsick perverts hungered to kill so badly on such a grand scale—not for treasure or tribal, nor for political dominance, for no hijacking thugs, no matter how insane, could think they'd be able to conquer the United States—but for a hatred so intense they were willing to kill themselves to satiate it.

The 21st century has been attacked by a new, Nazi-class form of eviola-fed hatred. How tragic for Islam, one of the great religions, to be scarred by the vermin emerging from that cesspool. How many years—or generations—will it take for the vast, sane Muslim majority to condemn and extinguish this wildfire and assure the world, as Germany has, that such crimes will never again take place in their name? How many people, Muslim and non-Muslim, will die because of a tiny minority joining the ranks of the disgraced abusers of God's various names, the pathetic freaks who've trampled through history with twisted justifications for the fiery sacrifice of babies, the Crusades, Aryan purification, and ethnic cleansing? Any fools still bleating that all religious paths are equally worthy of respect will be ridiculed by history as surely as the abusers of religion themselves will be shamed.

That's what was buzzing my brain a little while ago when Den suggested that I dig out this old notebook to record what had transpired. I'm glad I did so, though I'm sorry to see this journal end on such a troubling note. However, I've known for years that we're in this for the long haul and that evil on a global scale is not going to fade away just because Den and I manage to turn some people away from it most nights. Humans have been sucking in eviola for thousands of years and with six billion people out there, there'll likely be hosts aplenty for a long time to come. Both despite and because of the manifold blessings Den and I share, we're going to have to subject ourselves to tense and painful ordeals night after night for a long time to come.

The last thing Den said before he dozed off was, "Hey, your star eyes." He was looking up at the smudged painting in the center of our ceiling. There is some similarity between what remains of that old painting and the odd star-like lights I'd pointed out to Den in the wake of the lightning we noticed from the Spire. It's strange how two adjacent, similar lights in the dark, like the stars in Scorpio's tail, can suggest eyes. Thinking about them retriggered the weird sensation I've had from time to time that we're being watched. Perhaps that's an effect of being isolated for so long at such high elevation. It's hard to be engaged in a life like ours without feeling that something mysterious is afoot.

Whatever that may be, I conclude this account of My Trip To Tibet certain that the path I've taken in life was the right one for me. Had that girl with my name at the Art Institute twenty years ago received a post card from the future assuring her that if she would trust her instincts, she would find a great husband and a thrilling exciting job in an exotic and mysterious and unpredictable place, of course she'd have taken that deal. All I yearn for now is a mite more assurance that our having set forth on this expedition will help the world someday celebrate a century of spirit-brightening liberation from its worst curse.

Thanks for being here for me, Old Log. When the bar-headed geese come by this fall, I'll tell them you said hello.

[4-3]

<u>April 28, '04 – N.H.</u>

I've always been glad I got this log going long ago. It served as a record of Calieze's and my early life together and enabled us to lay down discoveries, theories, and techniques at the foundation of our work. Considering its purpose largely fulfilled, I've seen no reason to add anything to it for more than a decade. It's almost full anyway.

However, this morning, the lady of the house urged me to resurrect this archive and use its final few pages to report on a recent conversation I took part in down in Zhangmu. It was just some random bar chatter, but I've got to admit it bore some relevance to the very nascent science of soulology, so here it is.

The day before yesterday Calieze and I journeyed to town to escort Jyoti back to urban civilization after her annual spring visit to Gnam Yuljongs. This was her first trip to Tibet on her own, accomplished with aplomb (and considerable cost to her parents' nerves), flying into Kathmandu and hiring a car and driver to take her to the border where we met her. She's twenty-two now, and undoubtedly the only blossoming female genetics student in all of India who spends her spring vacations in a remote Tibetan village far off the grid.

Jyoti's rampant curiosity extends to all corners of the world, which unfortunately includes New Hale and thus obliges us to keep deflecting her requests that we allow her to visit us here. Instead, we stay with her in the village for about five days each April, where she joins in the spring potato, chili, and barley planting and assists Lasya and Renzin in the hunt for medicinal caterpillar fungus. The five of us go hiking together in various directions other than the one that leads here. The rest of the time Jyoti celebrates life with the locals and relishes her growing status as a beloved honorary Gnam Yuljongsian.

Jyoti still regards Calieze as a mentor, and not just because of Calieze's past as a field biology filmmaking pro. Jyoti has a strong spiritual bent that's not uncommon among Indian scientists and she seems sufficiently open-minded to be receptive to the reality of telepathy and the notions that the soul and evil can be studied as phenomena of nature. Accordingly, while Calieze has not been explicit with Jyoti about our visitations, she's not kept them entirely secret either and Jyoti's interest has been piqued.

Now a grown woman with big career plans, Jyoti has been contemplating getting involved with a young agronomist she met in Mumbai. Their proto-romance has begun to founder on account of her imminent move to Bangalore where she's scored a fellowship with a biotech firm, to be followed by a graduate program in the UK next fall.

That delicate drama compelled her to seek some private girl-talk with Calieze while we were in Zhangmu, which left me with some time on my hands on a hot day in the high tropics. The town was clogged with the clatter of trade and tourism on the rise so I sought some good old hang time at the quaint lounge in the Cloud Peak Friendship Hotel.

I sidled into a seat at the bar, anticipating a rare opportunity to quaff a cold one while giving free rein to my thoughts amidst the jocular hubbub, then being generated principally by a couple of white men seated nearby. From the sound of them, they were Irish and American, one each.

"Halliburton's out to maximize profit, like everyone else, Reed," declared the Irishman, clad in a warehouse rack sport jacket. "Just like every chai chugger in India asking for twice the price they're willing to sell for."

"You got that right, O'Connor," replied the pink-faced American, emphasizing his point with a wave of his sunglasses. "When Indian street marketers saw my wife coming, they creamed, and it wasn't because of her body." He glanced at the bartender. "Sorry, Prakash."

The Indian bartender tsk-tsked as he wiped down shot glasses. "No need for vulgarity, now, is there? Our street marketers are just trying to make a living, like yourselves." Turning to me, he asked, "And how may I brighten your day, kind sir?"

"Light beer, please. Whatever's on tap."

The Irishman slapped the counter in delight. "Didja catch that mellifluous twang, Reed? Another Yankee for your side!"

"Funny, he doesn't look Yankish." Reed lifted his mug in my direction. "Welcome to the Orient, friend."

"Ah, but that accent's a dead giveaway," countered his fellow barfly as he offered me his hand across the corner of the bar. "Martin O'Connor, Dublin born and bred. Duane Reed is a tourist, the sort of Western chap my firm hopes to hook with travel packages too good to refuse. Reed's from your neck of the woods—Anaheim, California, the happiest place on Earth. Prakash here at the wheel hails from Delhi, India, where he'd be right now had he not made a bride of the lovely daughter of the Nepalese mogul who owns this hotel. How about yourself?"

"I'm from Colorado."

"Coloradans dispense monikers to their wee ones, do they not?"

"People call me TD."

"All right then, TD from Colorado it is. That's where Denver situates itself, if I'm not mistaken. Isn't that near Anaheim, Reed?"

"Not by a long shot."

"Well, it's in America, so I wager that TD can weigh in on my Halliburton theory."

"Have at it, O'Connor. Flaunt your anti-American vitriol."

"Clean, cold logic, Reed—logic is impervious to crude sentiment and irrationality.

"Now TD, I was simply speculating that Halliburton, a company that *happens* to be American, might have an R&D team looking into packaging the meat of dead American soldiers to use as hamburger filler for the food they serve the troops on the bases they're supplying in Iraq."

Reed snorted in disgust. "We expect snide prejudice from jealous micks and frogs, O'Connor, but that's downright repulsive."

"Aye, we're jealous, I admit. There's nary a man, woman, or child in all of Ireland who doesn't awake to the sun's rays inflaming the clouds nestling in our deep green valleys and glistening off the snow-white blossoms of shamrock-clad hills without cursing and praying, 'Sweet Jesus, deliver me to Anaheim!' But hold your fire, Reed. Let him hear me out.

"TD, 'twas your own literary luminary, Ernest Hemingway, who pointed out that soldiers' sacrifices in an unnecessary war are like the stockyards at Chicago if nothing's done with the meat but burying it. So it's only natural that an enterprising firm like Halliburton might be looking to monetize a resource that would otherwise go to waste. All they'd need do is stuff the pockets of the morticians with dollars and the coffins with dummies and, bingo, another eco-recycling business is born. Or better yet, share the wealth with their friends at Blackwater Torture Amalgamated. They could team up to replace Iraqi morticians with American contractors to procure Iraqi man meat and increase their supply forty-fold! Cost overruns, no problem—just peel off a few chunks from the pallets of taxpayer cash the US sends Iraqways. Clever, don't you figure?"

This grating diatribe merited no response from me, but I couldn't dismiss it either. Things were going on I didn't know about and he could see the ignorance in my face.

"Whoopsy! Mr. Reed, your compatriot's let slip a clue that he's been hiding under a log recently. Skipping the nightly news, it seems. Maybe one of the last people walking the Earth without a bone in his nose still unaware of the torture festival your country's military police have held in that palace of Baghdad prisons"—he called it something like "Abu Greb" and gleefully turned back to me. "Aye, it's only too true, laddie. Your Baghdad Boys band have begun the buggering beguine, begorrah. Electroshocks, whips, German Shepherds, all varieties of torture too vile for those of delicate constitutions, such as, perhaps, your very self."

True, I hadn't heard of Abu Greb or the accusations he was sliming the American military with. But whatever it was, O'Connor's reference to it stilled my inclination to punch him out for his remark about my supposedly delicate constitution. I really wanted to quit the scene, but there was a mole scurrying about beneath the surface that needed watching. With O'Connor eagerly awaiting the results of having baited another American, I demurred. His story smacked of hogwash and I decided to call him on it. "Clever and/or repulsive, I don't get the joke, O'Connor. Halliburton is a luggage manufacturer."

"Hah! There's a laugh and a half! It appears you really have been holed up in a cave for the past year!" Had to let that slide. "Luggage was Halliburton's discarded fingernail. Its giant, bloated torso is an enormous oilfield services operation that got giddy at the thought of a war in a country with one of the three largest oilfields known to man. And your man Dick Cheney was the head of Halliburton before he took on the additional duties of de facto President of the United States!"

"Dick Cheney's not my man," I informed him. "I haven't been near the US in thirteen years."

"You'd best stay away another thirteen, lad. The way things are going in the land of the free, if you don't wave the stars and stripes frantically enough, you might find your bum swept into a soccer stadium on lockdown as a perk of the Patriot Act."

"Typical Europaranoia," griped Duane Reed. "Conspiracies, fascism, and nefarious powers in the shadows. And you wonder why Americans gag at the mention of Europe."

"It's in all the newspapers, Reed. Cheney's the grand vizier with the devil standin' in him who fed Bush the kind of road apples he fed Congress and the press about shady links between Al-Qaeda and Iraq. Oh, and for dessert, heaping portions of whiskey cake 'n bull about Iraq's so-called reconstituted nuclear weapons program that the UN weapons inspectors had found no evidence of." O'Connor trained his sights on me. "Now why do you think Cheney and his minions went to all that trouble, mate?"

"Something tells me I'm about to be enlightened."

"He was on assignment, Mr. D! Scooping up installments on his eight-figure golden parachute emblazoned with the Halliburton logo. Now you or Duane or Prakash might pray that your employer is crazy enough to offer you thirty million dollars when you quit to go to your next job, but it would have been crazy for Halliburton *not* to slip a sum like that to a rainmaker who could shower them with an eleven-figure bundle of government contracts without the inconvenience of having to submit a bid. Mighty fine return on investment, that! The bloke was worth every penny. And think of the trees and American taxpayer funds spared by dispensing with the paperwork required for a bidding process! If I were American, I'd thank your administration for that from the heart of my bottom."

Reed groused, "I'm beginning to tire of this socialist yap, O'Connor."

"Och, I've touched a patriotic nerve, it seems."

"This war got started in self-defense. You can be smug, 'cause Ireland doesn't have Muslim crazies trying to destroy her. But I'll bet Prakash understands. After 9-11 there was a Muslim suicide attack right in the Indian Parliament."

"True," nodded Prakash. "There is much fear among Hindus about such like happening again. And it probably will, because there's been too little outcry against it from our Muslim brothers. They fear the fanatics in their midst who've heard Osama bin Laden echoing the Sword of Islam's boast to his enemies, "I have come to you with an army of men that love death as you love life."

"Well, we in the States had our own good reasons to be concerned," Reed declared. "The CIA had picked up chatter that Saddam Hussein was preparing to nuke us. We had to stop him."

"Don't you just love Americans, Prakash? Never a more trusting lot has tread upon God's green earth. They can be knee-deep in bullshit and convince themselves they've found a pond of fresh chocolate pudding they'd not previously observed."

"We Indians find much to admire in American optimism," commented Prakash. "Without Shiva the Destroyer hovering overhead for thousands of years, Americans see sunny skies and a bright future everywhere they look."

"More than that, Prakash: Americans do have Darth Cheney hovering overhead and they're *still* optimistic." He turned back to Reed. "Duane, however, you're not so much optimistic as willfully blind. Mr. Bush primed your nation in his State of the Union speech with the specter of Saddam getting uranium from Niger even though the CIA had made him delete that from an earlier speech since the evidence had been faked. He claimed that British intelligence had *learned* it— not "suspected" or "was investigating," but *learned*, as in facts, like two times two is four. That's Big Lie marketing, Reed, right out of Hitler's playbook. This whole war of yours was cooked up as a public relations ploy in the War Fomenters Cabal just for consumers like you. They put Colin Poodle into a dog and pony show at the UN and ignored protesters all around the world."

"We had many protests against the Iraq war in this country," chirped Prakash. "Ten thousand people showed up in Calcutta alone."

"Tens of *millions* showed up worldwide—it was the biggest pre-war anti-war protest in human history. But the great white Cheney shark trolls the waters offshore Congress, scaring the people's representatives into sticking up their trembling thumbs, their constituents be damned. Next thing the military from generals to privates are buzzed, recruiters cast nets in the ghettos, purchase orders are couriered to private contractors, and Gentlemen, start your tank engines! After that, the machine runs on bumper sticker fuel demanding support for the troops that the Pentagon is shoveling into a combat maw without the courtesy of body or vehicle armor. American war machine standard operating procedure, all of it."

O'Connor's suggestion of war fomenting sharks swimming through the jet stream in Air Force Two deflected my attention from his ongoing oration. It kicked up a recollection of an old Hawaiian myth Calieze had once told me about the shark-man, a fin-backed human-like creature who walked on land and warned people about the terrors of the deep, only to devour them himself. It brought to mind the finely-coutured anipoxi at the cognac-scented Wannsee gathering at which nazis with manicured hands devised the "final solution" in 1942, all the mannerly deciders who inflict no physical discomfort on anyone directly, yet set in motion mass slaughter far bloodier than any Texas chainsaw massacre.

The bar was doing a poor job of providing the moment's peace and quiet I'd hoped for when I'd bellied up to it. Equally displeased for his own reasons, Reed snarled, "You've got a lotta nerve knocking our military, O'Connor. It was our guys and the Brits and even the Russians who took down Hitler, while Ireland sat on the sidelines. How proud are you of that?"

"Not particularly, Reed, but we can be proud that, as we sit here, our babies fresh out of school aren't soaking an oilfield desert with their blood to boost Halliburton's quarterlies." O'Connor paused to survey the audience he'd succeeded in depressing. "It's crazy, boys. You don't know crazy, do you, Prakash. India's kept its nose clean of real war for a long time."

"Oh, India is quite good at crazy, Mr. O'Connor. We have people who eat burning human flesh in religious ardor."

"I grant you, I've never seen the good reverend Father Gallagher gobble charred corpse after a eulogy at St. Mary's. Score a crazy goal for India. But better those who feed at funeral pyres than warmongers who make other people die to sate their lust for wealth and power. Profiteering warmongers have no more regard for the lives of others than serial killers, Osama bin Laden, the janjaweed who beat mothers in Darfur with their own babies, or the militiaman in—"

I shall skip the details of O'Connor's grand finale. It was a story making the rounds about atrocities perpetrated by some soldiers in a stadium in West Africa upon civilian prisoners who'd been rounded up in a scourge of supposed enemies of the state. It included an act of murderous sexual savagery upon a young woman that's too horrific to repeat. I won't even name the country, out of respect for its millions of inhabitants who must endure the ghastly wound of knowing that such evil was perpetrated in the service of the government bearing their country's name.

O'Connor's report made my gorge rise in sync with the troubling mole that suddenly thrust its snout above my mind's surface. It triggered a dark flashback to Calieze's and my visitation to the presidential palace in Belgrade, ten years ago, when another voracious power-lusting head of state unleashed his human pit bulls to perpetrate horrors on the people of Vukovar far away. That knocked my thoughts into Nixon prolonging the Viet Nam war to boost his election and re-election prospects, and the depredations of Genghis Khan, Stalin, Pol Pot, Mao, and Shitler. Images of all the ethnic cleansers and fomenters and chieftains of wars for greed and power splayed about before me, none of them prosecutable under their country's own laws, basking in chauffeured limos while garden variety serial killers and the press engorge each other in their sleazy, symbiotic frenzy.

The twinned nauseators—sharkmen and African stadium killers—catapulted me out of my seat. Barely one inch into my beer, I dropped a few 5-yuan pictures of Mao on the counter, muttered, "Have a pleasant evening, fellas," and made my exit.

I walked the streets at the edge of town for while, trying to lose the shade of pessimism that had clung to my back at the bar. I resisted succumbing to a sense of futility of saving individual lives while the sharkmen continue to have millions slain and reminded myself that if a single life saved were mine or Calieze's or that of anyone else I've loved, it would mean the world to me.

By the time I'd circled back to the hotel and found Calieze, Jyoti, and Jyoti's driver waiting for me, I cheered up enough to bid Jyoti good-bye, but as we made our way back to Gnam, I thought, wow—getting humanity to a plateau where we can detoxify the planet's spiritual atmosphere is going to be a heavier lift than even I realized. We're gonna have to put more effort into finding potential allies and any active ones already out there, because there ain't no getting around the need for a spiritual troop buildup to redirect evil's trajectory toward extinction.

I'm convinced we'll succeed, my confidence no doubt fueled by having alongside me for real the woman who was but a fleeting dream when I started this log. My gratitude for that great fortune, like our view from the world's rooftop, is boundless.

[4-4]

8/22/04

Darling Den,

I'd so hoped to find you home. Jyoti is in terrible jeopardy and I'm going to India to find her. I awoke last night from a visitation nightmare—the most vivid ever—to a psychopath kidnapping her in the parking lot of the building where she was working a night shift. He's a vile rapist and he's planning to imprison her in his jungle hovel. I tried everything and got nowhere.

Watching this from far away is intolerable. I must go now, my waiting another day or two until you get back could cost her her life. Every hour counts, especially with this break in the weather. *Please* try not to worry about me. I'll be careful. I'm taking some money and two of the diamonds so I can grease the wheels at the borders and move around as needed. I'll leave news with Lin-Chee in Zhangmu and you can get word to me through Rishi and Manjula in Bombay (see Jyoti's last letter for their contact info).

Holding this record of our early days in my hands makes me cherish our good fortune all the more, for I love you far more now even than I did then. But I love Jyoti too and I must try and save her (and us) from a calamity.

I know you'll want to join me but having both of us running around India trying to find each other could create hopeless chaos. You've got my heart as always and the rest of me will rejoin you as soon as I find Jyoti, hopefully within a week. Huge love,

C

[4-5]

8/23   Damn! Missed you by a single day. If you're reading this note by yourself, you've managed to get back safe and sound—thank God for that, in advance—but there's no way I can sit here leaving you to tackle this situation without backup, Calieze. I'm leaving this afternoon to find you. Now that you're back, please, stay put. Coming back to no Calieze would rupture my universe.

"I love you" doesn't cut it but it's all I've got for now.   — Den

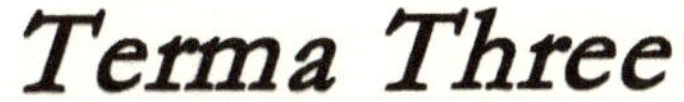

Terma Three

[5]

<u>Aug. 30, '04 – Kumily, India</u>

For a long time now, I've thought of the logs Calieze and I wrote years ago as the products of youthful metamorphosis, like cocoons left behind by free, adventuring ceanothus silk moths repurposed by Pomo Indian shamans for rattles in their healing rituals. Now it turns out our two-terma archive was but a prologue to a report of a life-changing encounter with raging evil that blasted a high-voltage shock into our lives eight days ago.

I had been bivouacking in a valley a day's hike over a pass northwest of New Hale. Calieze was away at Andromeda, a summertime first that had been in the offing since she came back to New Hale this spring declaring that she wanted to try being on her own for a while during the monsoon. I had what I thought were a few more weeks to myself before fetching her, so off I went on a three-day jaunt to one of my favorite watersheds.

On the second night, I awoke with a creepy feeling that something was wrong. I tried toughing it out, assailing myself for becoming a worry wart, but throughout the day my apprehension intensified, and by nightfall I was determined to decamp at first light. When I reached our cave entrance and found Calieze's old notebook lying open on our stone table, I knew something deadly serious was afoot. Within fifteen minutes of reading her message on the inside back cover, I was heading downhill towards civilization with three diamonds from southern Africa tucked into my waterproof sack.

I spent the night in Gnam Yuljongs because my chances of catching a ride to the border in the middle of the night were nil. The family had clearly been shaken by Calieze's demeanor the day before. They're so used to her joy light that her tense report of a dream about Jyoti being in peril was doubly upsetting. Calieze had told them that if her fears weren't assuaged by phone calls she intended to place to Jyoti's family from Zhangmu, she'd make her way to Mumbai and figure out what to do from there.

I slept in Uncle Yeshe's old house, which had been taken over by Renzin, now a wiry twenty-four. I thought about my first nights there long ago, when Calieze haunted my sleep as a beautiful phantom whose role in my life was still but a thousandth of what it would become a half year later and an infinitesimal hint of what she means to me now.

The next morning, I bid hasty farewells to the family and left the valley. Once I reached Zhangmu, with no interest in trying to finesse either Chinese or Nepalese border officials, I hiked several miles along the Bhotekoshi till I found a crossing just eighty yards wide. The river was high, but I figured I'd had plenty of experience traversing that distance evading three-hundred pounders hell-bent on bringing me down, so I could muscle my way swimming around a few stock-still river boulders. The maneuver spared me the two-day climb over the mountain pass I'd used to enter Tibet in 1991. From there I hitched a ride with a rice trucker across Nepal's narrow north-south passage to the Indian border, where, hidden under a pile of canvas tarps, I slipped past the late night, glazed-eyed surveil of an Indian border guard.

By the time I reached Darjeeling on the 25th, I'd been disappointed by a spate of Hindi voice-mail announcements at Jyoti's parents' number—a dismally thin lifeline that made me wish irrationally that Calieze and I had outfitted ourselves with cellular phones, like half the people in Zhangmu. I found a jeweler in town and metamorphosed a stone from my diamond stash into enough cash to pick up an old jeep from a local tour guide, leaving me plenty to spare for the road, which I hit straightaway.

On the 26th, running low on gas and sleep, I rolled into Varanasi, a/k/a Benares, on the banks of the Ganges. Somehow the uplifting spirituality of the holiest city in Asia, if not the world, eluded me at first, as I saw kids stuffing burning paper between the toes of a stick-thin man too weak to stand up and women bearing dead-looking or sleeping infants begging Westerners to pay six dollars for a small bottle of milk to the shopkeeper running them like a pimp—stains of the old India that the new one, resurgent in the glory of its high-tech boom, cannot wash away.

But old India has its own glory that cannot be washed away either. As I neared the river, passing some of the countless temples to which Varanasi is home, I was briefly surrounded by a procession of chanting men bearing a corpse adorned in silks and jewels down to the burning ghats at the waterfront, where sadhus bathed nearby and prayed over holy books on the steps of temples that counted their ages in centuries.

However, spiritual transcendence was neither goal nor option for a worrying dervish obsessed with the bodily well being of the two people he loves most here in the Mayasphere. Needing a place to clear my head, to empower myself for the search that lay ahead, I sought comfort at Mother Ganga's breast on the steps of a faded edifice built by a 17th century raj overlooking the river. It was several hundred yards from the nearest burning ghat, so I couldn't see the wrapped corpses being bathed in the river and set upon their pyres. I wasn't in the mood to think about death just then; I was busy enough convincing myself that the floating body-sized debris floating down-river were idols cast adrift during the previous night's religious ceremony. Drawing on my meditation training with Coach Yeshe, I tried to reduce the fresh hot visions of Indian death and misery to planets too distant to draw me into their gravitational fields; but unmooring myself from my immediate surroundings only exposed me to soul-shredding scenarios of what might be happening at that very moment to Jyoti and Calieze.

Thus rattled, I re-opened the newspaper I'd picked up near the urn market where I'd parked my car. In my earlier quick scan of it, I'd been disappointed to find nothing on the story that I naively expected to be plastered on the front page. But closer examination revealed a three-sentence squib of interest near the bottom of page 16. Detectives were looking into a report of possible foul play in the disappearance of the 22-year-old daughter of Bank of India employee Rishi Patil, who'd last been seen on the night of August 21ˢᵗ, leaving work at a biotech center in Bangalore where she was pursuing a fellowship in genetic engineering.

So Calieze's nightmare vision was accurate and somebody was paying attention. I had to start making calls to the police, the press, and the biotech industry in Bangalore, and if necessary, drive down to the southern part of the country and make inquiries in person, hoping to succeed with a mix of standard gumshoe work and whatever telepathic leads I might be able to muster in the Indian lowlands.

I bid good-bye to the Ganges and wound my way back into the welter of urban distractions downtown to look for a phone booth to use as home base for my detective work. I planted myself in one inside a currency exchange office, armed with a pile of coins. I took a deep breath and thought how, for almost all of the last thirteen years, Calieze and I have lived together alone, collaborated on a mission no one else is aware of and which few would believe, and grown our love for each other to a height few could comprehend. If a vicious criminal got the jump on her and took her life, he'd effectively be taking mine as well, unless you include living in unmitigated pain in your definition of life.

I grabbed the phone and asked the operator to get me the Bangalore police. Big help—a police detective in Bangalore started asking me a bunch of questions to get a fix on my coordinates, reeking with suspicion that I might be angling for a ransom payment. Either way, it was offensive and I hung up on him. Of course it didn't help, the way I dodged his questions as to how and when I knew Jyoti Patil was in trouble or what my connection was to another woman (accomplice?!) who might be with her, whom I wouldn't name out of fear that my interrogator might sic his dogs on my visa-less wife.

I restrategized and started dialing down a yellow pages list of Bangalore hotels asking if a Rishi and Manjula Patil were registered there. After an empty-handed hour of that, I moved on to biotech companies, hoping to find someone who worked with Jyoti and perhaps had heard her speak of Calieze and me. I spent a second hour on that track in that sweltering booth before I succumbed to the futility of accomplishing anything while seated a thousand miles from the crime scene. Ferreting out a signal of Jyoti's distress while immersed in the distractions of an Indian metropolis would be like trying to pick up one radio station while signals from thousands of louder ones crowded atop it. It was time to hang it up and resort to measures more familiar to me.

I hit the road and headed south, toward Bangalore, planning to find a location better suited to visitations by nightfall. Within an hour I'd left nerve-battering urban India far behind in search of whatever simulacrum of New Hale I could conjure from the countryside.

That night I pulled off the road in Maihar along Panna National Park and sat myself on the hood of the jeep for half an hour, looking into the darkness. I was trying to operate my onboard mental radar at a far lower elevation than I'm accustomed to while still a bit jumbly from being tossed about by the crashing waves of Varanasi chaos, but I did sense this much: Jyoti and Calieze were both still far to the south of me and nowhere near each other. Beyond that one paltry finding, nothing. I cleared a stretch of ground with my feet, threw my sleeping bag down, and had almost conked out when a casual scratch of my earlobe yielded a slimy thing on my finger, which I examined with my flashlight—a leech! I scrambled up and started pulling the little bastards off my pants leg, shirt, even my hair. I retreated to huddle in the back seat of the jeep, where time calmed me and eventually handed me off to my demanding creditor, sleep.

Come morning, I sank into a twelve hour drive on narrow, often twisting and/or cattle-clogged roads. Ugly fears churned beneath the jeep rumble, which I attempted to keep in check with auditory pit stops on the Indian radio band. I was invited to imagine the sultry gazes of sari-draped mademoiselles trilling Bollywood ballads from films where handsome turbaned dreamboats inflamed their hearts from afar—ill-fitting reminders of the absence of my own lover. As night shadow coated the forest with darkness, I remembered Calieze's phrase "tohu v'vohu," a line from the Bible that described the world just before the dawn of Creation, that seemed apt for my present limbo. If Calieze were to lose her life to Jyoti's captor and the very phenomenon she had worked so hard to protect others from, my whole life would become unformed and void. Returning to New Hale or Gnam Yuljongs or the *Iyerpadi* or Estes Park, hooking up with the old poker game, looking up Bridget or Linda (now probably the mothers of teenagers) marrying another woman, starting a new career, carting the remaining husk of my soul off to some new land—all of it inconceivable, absurd.

I pulled off the road near the town of Dichpally in the Ghandi Hills, yearning for a spell of peace to cleanse my mind of morbidity and engine noise. I wanted to settle into the darkness of jungle-draped mountains redolent of orchids, sandalwood, and dwarf coconut trees, and glean one ray of cheer by detecting some signal of Calieze, safe and sound. I mind-surfed the spiritual waves for hours, till exhaustion drifted me away, certain only of what I'd concluded the night before: Calieze and Jyoti were alive and apart somewhere in Southern Tohu V'vohu, far from the heaving technometropolis of Bangalore.

I awoke the day before yesterday with a road-miles hangover and got off to a late start. After sweating through another long drive in India's beastly August, I sought a night's refuge in a flimsy hotel at the edge of Chikballapur, about an hour north of Bangalore. I needed a place to clean up and grab at least a little half-decent sleep before facing what could become one of the longest days of my life.

Yesterday's long drive brought me to the state of Kerala in the southernmost latitudes of India. Same time zone as home, but with some different constellations peopling the sky, different scents in the atmosphere, and different creatures hiding in the trees and on the ground. At nightfall, after scoring a carton of curry from a food stall in Anakkara, I drove deep into the vast forest of the Periyar Wildlife Reserve intent on finding a hilltop locale for more favorable meditation conditions than any I'd managed since finding Calieze's note back at New Hale a week before. My sleep of late had been jumpy with certainty that something intense was headed my way and I needed to be ready for it when it showed up.

I sat in the jeep for an hour, listening to tropical breezes rustling the leaves of the trees lower down on the verdant hillsides punctuated by the occasional howled comments of monkeys unseen and alien night birds. Suddenly a new sound slashed the aural tapestry, a pulsation of jungle air that no ears, human or otherwise, could forget: the roar of a Bengal tiger. He must have been miles away, skulking through the forest on the other side of the valley glowing in the soft light of the moon, reveling in the knowledge that every living creature in a volume of air a billion times his own size knew he was there and lived at his mercy.

I stashed my sleeping bag against the passenger door and put my feet up on the seat, staring into the darkness which the tiger's threat had unsettled and braced myself for the vision thundering my way. Overhead bats darted silently between giant palm fronds silhouetted against the last portion of the Milky Way not already obscured by sullen clouds. Barely audible inner ululations clamored to be recognized, pressuring me to recognize that I can't face down inchoate fear without the courage to look it in the eye.

The tiger's brain-trembling warning had made my spine shiver in a way that puzzled me. I share Blake's admiration for tigers and I wasn't in danger. Rather, its announcement had resonated with something else lurking just beneath the surface of my sea of consciousness. I peered there with my inner eyes for a few minutes until there emerged a mindless blade, the sign of another powerful predator on the hunt—a man-eating shark. No—a *sharkman.*

The chilling, Guinness-fueled rant of the Irishman in the Zhangmu bar jammed my eyelids open, forcing me to recognize the spiritual phenotype linking the war-ginning, world-trashing sharkmen with Dahmer, Manson, and all serial killers, the whole lot of exulting anipoxi including Jyoti's kidnapper, who at that very moment was relishing whatever he was doing or had done to my surrogate daughter and possibly to my wife. It was tantamount to standing naked above one's foxhole in the high pitch of war, but I couldn't stop myself. My mind became a cauldron for a hot bubbling broth of fear and anger. I realized more than ever how much eviola afflicts everyone, not just those killed on its account. A bad viral epidemic, like the Spanish flu that felled people around the world at eight times the rate of the Great War it overlapped in 1918, injects a stream of fear into the bloodstream of all who survive its passing. But that epidemic evaporated in a year, while eviola lives on, century after century, tearing at the edges of the spiritual tissue of those not killed with pity for the victims and fear for themselves and their loved ones. And the longer we tolerate eviola, the longer it has to metastasize, aided by technology that gets perverted (trains and ovens) or devised (suitcase and car bombs) to aid its spread.

Visions of the rise of the anipoxi exploded like mortar fire inside my skull. I saw eviola poisoning the planet's atmosphere, each new copy of the virus further potentiating the next one by rendering more of the unthinkable thinkable. The anipoxi began to perceive the respect for life instinct as a threat to their rapacious lust for dominance. A vicious cycle of viciousness began to stir, sweeping humanity into a non-tribal world war in which both sides welcome volunteers and coerce recruits regardless of race, creed, or nationality, caring only about their predilections for or against evil, a world of look-alike mortal foes, slathered in paranoia and suspicion. Sharkmen using cutouts to enlist Manchurian solopsycho candidates to have their way with realized and potential Ghandis, Kennedys, Kings, Silkwoods, Lennons. Some of them at that very moment planning to round up their usual suspects for capital woodshedding, stadium-style, and, if necessary, dropping the big one on any metrocluster of alarmed humans they deem dangerous to their way of life and death while they secrete themselves on vast estates in hardened domes and underground skybox-lush bunkers to wait out the fallout. Mulling over cannibalizing their own when things really get tough. Revolted by the post-menopausal groupies wrapped in tattered hundred-K chinchilla coats with talcum-tipped warts pocking their faces, gabbling deranged of their readiness to raise more election campaign funds for an alpha sharkman pol before whom they shiver in titillation at the scowl chiseled into his head like a serrated wedge cut into a petrified block of German cheese.

Disturbance, the invisible assailant from my long-ago first monsoon at New Hale, slipped in under the walls of my mental tent and shot up the place with macabre apparitions. Illuminated by jagged lightning, giant wrathful deities leered down with bloodshot eyes between needle spike eyelashes while scooping up human entrails with bloody chapatis, pulling wrist and nose cartilage from between smelly fangs that protruded down to the level of their many elbows, impaling the skulls of their human prey, gobbling away while overlooking plains of gasping, grass-thin, woeing Munchesque sufferers. Ape-shaped hollows in the mountains watched with eyeballs excited by lightning stabs, poking out of cliff walls before slipping back in like noodles sucked into invisible stone mouths stinking of flesh-rot. Demons fondled the self-bunkered anipoxi, adored them as they devised schemes to reproduce without inbreeding their line to extinction by capturing female humans from the poison zone for raped reproduction purposes, women who would rather set their bodies ablaze than allow their wombs to be used to perpetuate the anipoxi line.

At rape, the juggernightmare boomed open to the real and present danger that had flung me from the heights of the Himalaya to the edge of the sub-continent's tropical jungle. Stuffed somewhere in the bowels of that humid forest hid the agent of Jyoti's suffering.

As I fought off images of what was happening to her and the possibility of injury or worse to Calieze, the cruelest demon of all appeared and gleefully flung me into a visitation in the soulspace of Jyoti's kidnapper, scorching me with my worst fear. An Indian man, thirty or forty years old with greasy hair hanging down past his shoulder blades, wearing a filthy dhoti, stared at Jyoti splayed out on a dirty mattress on the dirt floor of his lantern-lit hut, her spirit severely wounded, her beauty dirtied and emaciated. Her feet and hands had been tied with elephant chains to four of the hut's metal anchor poles. Her eyes were half-open and glazed. A plastic raincoat cast atop her evidently naked body rose less than an inch with her depressed, staggered breath.

A grotesque fantasy began to play in the kidnapper's soulspace walls. The kidnapper imagined himself frightening Jyoti by displaying his cock with pathetically exaggerated dimensions. In an eyeblink, a cluster of maggoty eviola viruses materialized before him; he inhaled them into his mouth and nostrils, ripped off Jyoti's covering and his own, and plunged his raping member into her, grunting in psychotic ecstasy, forcing from her body agonized gasps.

Nothing Calieze and I had experienced in all the thousands of visitations to eviola suckers prepared me for the waves of revulsion I felt toward this puny, vile monster. I wanted to bind him in his own elephant chains, enucleate his eyes and cram his severed body parts into the emptied eye sockets. I craved the power to restore him from his resulting death to life so that I could kill him again, swinging his head into giant thorn bushes hoping he could see blobs of his brain meat dripping onto the ground, then bringing him back to life once more to stuff his nostrils and mouth with shavings of his eyelids, toenails, and lips, harvested carefully to keep him conscious throughout the proceedings.

As I felt a trace of humiliation arise within me for having slid into such repellent floodwaters, a cool zephyr blew down over my face from a hole in the clouds above. The horrors froze, amazed as I at the sudden shift in the temperament of the sky. Disturbance's legions pixelated and shrank, their power fading in the celestial glow of a radiant Blue Tara, the goddess described in Bon and Dzoghen termas as she who strengthens the afflicted by melting away anger and fear of enemies. Suspended in a mandala etched in golden-white flames above dark-grumbling clouds, this gently powerful, sensual angel swept her six arms in benediction pacifying the wrathful demons, stilling their viral replications and guiding them to evanescence in the thunderhead rim glimmering in her light. As I thanked her for her fortifying, lightning-flickered grace, a smile radiated through all my cells before I consciously realized that her features were metamorphosing to those of Calieze. I lifted my face to receive her telepathic caress. Wherever she was, Calieze had found me in a dire state and was calling me back to work on the most critical challenge of our lives. Understanding but brooking no nonsense, she laid it out: I had to resuscitate my wits—i.e. conquer my anger and hatred—and join with her to effect Jyoti's rescue, now.

Easier said than done, I exclaimed to Tara-Calieze. That volcano erupted out of nowhere. I had no idea if it were a true visitation or how to set about achieving one that we could share now as we had so many in the past. I'd never exercised that power below an alpine timberline or in a crowd of three much less near sea level in a country teeming with more than a billion.

No matter. You have a hilltop and relative solitude in a lightning storm; now concentrate and find her, before it's too late.

She faded into the blackened sky and I was alone, chastened into clarity by ass-kicks from electrons tearing along neural highways in my brain. Yes, I'd let my mind slip out of control, even though I well knew the consequences of distractions during a search and rescue operation. It is hard enough to live with a failed rescue of a stranger, let alone the soul crushing I'd have to endure, were I to sacrifice a slim opportunity to rescue someone I loved by wasting time with senseless fantasies of revenge. My rescuing prowess itself needed rescue, and fortunately it had materialized. Calieze had reached me and shaken me free of my self-crippling rage. We had the mission of a lifetime on our hands and no time to spare.

Like a busted dam releasing a flood of arsenic-laced mining spoils, my load of vengeance had spilled away. I knew what I must do. I listened to the sodden breathing of the jungle, the purple-tailed giant squirrels turning in their tree nests, neighbors to the moths, hornbills and plaintive laughingthrush, and scanned for the tormentor of the young Indian girl we'd watched grow up, who had trusted us as mentors, mother-aunt and father-uncle, infusers of confidence.

And then it came—a discordant signal of the twisted soul that was subjecting Jyoti's loveliness to his savagery. His grimy machinations emanated from a point on the jungle floor miles further south. I floated up from my post and slid through the night sky in that direction, gripping my foreboding in a vice of resolve. Nothing would stop me from finding that anipox and coming to my grown child's rescue.

A tremor of fear over what I would find was rippling through my body when, out of the dark nowhere, Calieze emerged by my side, her soul no longer embedded in the guise of a Vajrayana goddess, but as herself, my still safe and strong co-pilot in one more visitation that recast all those in the past as training exercises for this night's mission. We flew in silent, tenuous confidence that the skills we'd forged through years of fiery visitations would give us a fighting chance to save our surrogate child.

In time, our flight slowed and a gray cloud emerged from the darkness; we'd reached the border of a soulspace with a repulsive odor. Calieze took up her position high on the side opposite from me and we trained our sights on the figure within.

The Indian man I'd envisioned earlier stood before us, lending my nightmare heart-stopping credence. He was walking toward what appeared to be the shrouded body of a woman, but when he reached down to remove the coverlet, we saw instead a stack of elephant tusks, four to five feet in length, lying on the floor in the corner of a crude structure. He picked one up by its blood-encrusted wide end and turned to carry it out a doorway covered by a torn-open burlap bag.

Through his window we saw him carry the tusk out the door to a dilapidated pickup truck parked at the edge of a path of crushed undergrowth that served as a makeshift road in his jungle hideaway. He stuffed the tusk in the back beneath some sugar cane and a tarp and turned back to his dwelling, a tin shack hidden by thick forest on all sides. I held my breath as he re-entered it, waiting for his first glance in the direction he'd not looked before, and when it came, my heart lurched in my chest. There lay Jyoti, exactly as I'd seen her during the rape, in a state worse than death. The poacher of women and elephants stuck a jackfruit in her mouth. Listlessly, she spat it out. In the wall to the left of his window, we saw what had to be either a memory or a fantasy of himself sticking a flower behind the ear of the body of a young woman who looked a lot like Jyoti that had been dined upon by vultures. *Focus!*

Calieze and I settled in to work over this perp. We kept at it for two full hours, bringing to bear every technique we could remember from all our years performing rescues, trying to come up with something that would steer the kidnapper away from temptations of rape and murder toward some notion of freeing her, letting her weak body loose in the jungle or dropping her by a roadside somewhere, anything that might lead to preserving a core from which the flesh of the life she was entitled to might be regenerated. We took great care not to inflame the psycho in such a way that he'd carry out his murder fantasy. Utilizing fragments of raw ore from his memory bank, we concocted streams of guilt and inspiration and fear of retribution from wrathful deities, supernatural summonings, and endless combinations thereof and dozens more approaches we'd never thought of before in a desperate attempt to bolster his atrophied RLI.

Throughout this spell, the criminal completed loading the ivory he'd harvested from elephants whose bodies were no doubt decomposing in the surrounding forest, cooked himself a snake, and retired to his cot for a nap.

Then, out of nowhere, a strange and wonderful thing happened. Two more souls appeared in the upper walls of the subject's soulspace walls, first an elderly woman who looked Nepalese, followed by a man about my age who may have been native to South America. Calieze cast me an amazed glance; the newcomers must have found the scene of our crisis by the same means and for the same reasons we had found thousands of others before. We looked at them and each other as we absorbed the astonishing proof that we were not alone, neither in our night of need nor in what could be the signs of an incipient worldwide campaign to dissuade weak souls from succumbing to evil. A wave of gratitude swept from us to our reinforcements as we welcomed the balm of their reassuring aid. The arrival of these allies sparked an idea in Calieze. "Den!" she whispered. "Let's leave the visitation to our helpers while we try to find Jyoti in person. Do you have any idea how far away you are from her?"

"My sense is that she's within thirty to sixty miles of me, to the south of Anakkara."

"In Periyar?"

"I think so."

"Then they're probably to the east of me, about the same distance away. You've got to get behind the wheel and use whatever radar you've got working—"

"—while *driving?*"

"Yes, while driving, and while driving as well I'll try to stay hooked to you so I can meet you there."

"We can't drive with our eyes closed."

"No, so we must work a visitation with our eyes open and on the road. If we get nowhere, after a couple of hours, we can each find another hilltop and reconnect the way we're doing now."

Time to push the skills envelope. We tendered our helpers a word of thanks and took our leave.

I opened my eyes back in my jeep, struck by the contrast between the quiet of the jungle night and the violent vibes in the kidnapper's hut, which I could still feel clinging to me like singeing tar. I got out of the car, stretched, splashed some water on my face and looked up at the clouds that still popped with flashes of lightning.

Back in the car, eyes open, I sought a distress beacon. In a couple of minutes, my sense of direction locked in on a signal emanating from a spot in the jungle south by southeast. I waited for a sense of Calieze accompanying me, and when it came, washing my mind with relief, I fired up the engine and got on the road, double-tracking what I was taking in from the sensors in my retinas and elsewhere in my brain as the clouds began to deliver on their threat of rain. Navigating became all the harder as I had to keep my eyes peeled for road hazards amidst flashes of lightning alternating with images of Jyoti's tormentor's soulspace, but the pressure sharpened my vision and reflexes as never before. I gauged at top speed the maximum rate with which I could safely get my four-wheel drive vehicle around or through each pothole and bend in the road, only too aware that my allowance for accidents was zero.

After half an hour, I swung off the pavement onto a soggy, forest road that was so bumpy with strewn rocks that I had to slow down to preserve what was left of the jeep's suspension. I felt Calieze's presence intensifying and hoped it was due to her wending her way toward me.

A dim lantern light flared in the criminal's soulspace window; he had awakened. Surrounding the window were images of gendarmes creeping towards him through the forest. I wondered if the projections of enforcers arose from the work of the newcomer eviola hunters who'd joined us in our visitation, from Calieze, or from the subject's inherent paranoia.

I saw the kidnapper go to his doorway and peer out into the dark downpour. Far in the distance he saw a bouncing light, which could only mean that a vehicle of some kind had entered his sector of the forest. I hoped it was my car, which would confirm that I was within a mile of him and Jyoti. My stomach and mind curled in parallel, realizing that I was seeing myself, or my car, approach the rapist through his own eyes. As I maneuvered around the muddy road ruts, a dim light appeared in the distance through my windshield, moving around in sync with the lantern light I could see the criminal carrying through his soulspace window—I had him on both planes now. Had I a high-powered rifle I could have stopped the car and taken him out right then. I braced my vertebrae for repeated hammer blows from the bumpy road as I tore toward my target, while soldiers and police in his soulspace walls converged on him through the jungle.

He began to panic. As he looked towards his truck thinking to escape, *another* pair of headlights appeared in his visual field and the number of his imagined pursuers—now commandos bearing rifles—doubled.

A set of headlights appeared in my rear view mirrors, about a half mile behind me, bouncing in sync with those visible in the rapist's view. My spirits leapt at the likelihood that they belonged to Calieze. She appeared in the perp's soulspace and called to me that she could see me and that the squadrons pursuing the frightened kidnapper in his soulspace were projections from her and our new allies.

Hope and fear soared together in the lightning-cracked forest as I raced over what I was now sure was the path to the hideout. I was still two minutes away when the rapist turned his eyes on Jyoti and begin yelling at her. He shoved his feet into some boots by the doorway and yanked the raincoat he'd thrown over her, cursing all the while. As he fended off imaginary gunfire aimed at him from the soldiers haunting him, he ran out his door, then turned back, bellowing at the naked, wide-eyed girl. He grabbed a flaying knife from a hook by his door way and stalked towards Jyoti. As I heard Calieze scream, "No! No!" the monster plunged the knife into Jyoti's chest.

I yelled in sync with Calieze and gunned my engine, tearing off my right fender on a tree stump and hurtling the jeep towards a yellow light up ahead that had to be the killer's flashlight as he exited his hideout. Through his soulspace window I could see his view of the tangled jungle thickets sweeping by him as he made his way by flashlight and intermittent lightning. As I kept my eyes peeled for a shack buried in the darkness, my inner sight revealed the rapist's fumbling view as he scrambled through the soaking wet branches for a couple hundred yards. Suddenly he let out a hideous scream that I could hear over the noise of the jeep and when the lightning flashed again, Calieze and I shared with him the final sight of his life, his own blood spattering the regal face of a Bengal tiger.

Fifteen seconds later my headlight beams bounced off a truck by a wall of corrugated metal and I slammed on the brakes. As the clatter of Calieze's car approached, I leapt out, leaving the headlamps on for her, pulled my flashlight from my jacket pocket, and entered the shack.

Jyoti lay on the cot, breathing but in shock, with an eight-inch knife protruding from her chest above her left breast. "Jyoti, it's Terma Den," I told her as I began untying the chains. "Calieze is almost here. We're going to take you to safety." Her eyes caught mine for a moment, widened, and shut. She must have thought I was a hallucination at death.

I covered her with my jacket and lifted her from the cot in both arms, taking care not to jostle the knife, as Calieze's car came to a halt outside the shack. We met at the doorway. As Calieze took in the sight, her first breathless words were, "She's alive?!"

I nodded. Calieze touched my head with one hand and stroked Jyoti's face with the other. "Darling," she said to Jyoti, "it's Calieze. Den and I are going to take you home. "

Jyoti's eyes opened, and her eyes widened in a mixture of joy and fear. "Oh, no!" she cried. "He killed you too?"

"We're very much alive, and so are you." Jyoti's eyes darted around in fear. "And that man will never hurt you again. You're safe now. Den and I are going to take you to a hospital to get you fixed up." Calieze turned to me. "I passed one in Kumily, about eight miles from here."

We stepped out into the rain and surveyed the penny-stamp parking lot. "Your car looks more comfortable."

"Forget it," she answered. "Half the chassis bottom's loose from hits it took on this road."

"Never mind, we'll make it in the jeep."

"I'll drive so you can monitor her."

"Exactly." Calieze helped settle Jyoti's upper body on my lap in the jeep's back seat. We stole a half-second kiss, aborted by a chilling sound that rose over the dwindling rain—the chuff of a satisfied tiger.

Calieze got behind the wheel, backed the car through the narrow slot remaining between the other two vehicles and the trees till she could maneuver a turnaround, and plowed on back through the dense jungle. While checking Jyoti's vitals, I noted each turn in my memory for the real police.

We made it to the E.R. in Kumily in twenty minutes, at 2 AM this morning. The hospital staff, several of whom had heard of the kidnapping the previous week, whipped into action. We stayed with the doctors as they anesthetized Jyoti and removed the knife. When they set to cleaning and suturing the wound, they asked us to retire to the waiting room. They assured us Jyoti would live, and heal.

As Calieze rested her head on my shoulder, I thanked God for the zillionth time for letting me have her in my life and for permitting her to remain as strong and energetic (and as gorgeous) as she had been at twenty-seven. The gray strands I noticed arcing behind her ears for the first time are a sign of how long my love for her has been growing. (Later, washing my face in the bathroom, I noticed with a rueful smile that I'd sprouted more gray than she.)

Police from Kumily came by. Leery of bringing too much information about our non-documented selves into the picture, we stuck to the essentials and then pleaded exhaustion, suggesting that we'd fill in any details with detectives in Bangalore who'd been assigned Jyoti's case.

Around 4:30, a nurse came and told us "Your friend has awakened in the recovery room. She said she'd been rescued by angels. I told her that her angels are human and would like to see her."

We visited Jyoti for a few minutes to give her a kiss and set her on the long road to recovery from multiple physical, psychological, and spiritual wounds. She came up with her parents' cell phone number, which we called from the nurse's station, awakening them in a hotel room in Bangalore. Manjula and Rishi, wrecks delirious with relief, wrapped their minds around the news of their child's survival, injury, and rescue. When they asked Calieze how we'd found their daughter, she responded that it was a long story and assured them that we'd not leave Jyoti's side till she was home with them in Bombay. They were transferred to Jyoti long enough to soothe her and themselves and rang off to find a flight down here. Calieze then accompanied Jyoti to a four-bed ward on the surgery floor. Apart from one interval when the nurses allowed me to bring Calieze some breakfast from the cafeteria, she's been alone with Jyoti and the medical staff ever since.

It was on that errand that I scored this unused ledger from the cafeteria's manager—hence the faint blue and red column lines and chapati flour peeking through the report I've drawn up over these last several hours.

I'll need to leave for the airport to pick up Rishi and Manjula soon. Calieze and I will spend a few days assisting their family, but beyond that, our future is indeterminate. Some silent and invisible force has been at work transmuting it, either in parallel with or arising from the exponential surge in our telepathic powers, without which we could never have found or saved Jyoti. We need to get back behind the Himalayan fortress walls that will shut us off from India and the rest of civilization. A call awaits us, invisible and immense.

[6]

Sept. 6, '04
Namchi, Sikkim
CZM

I used to play the piano, and then I stopped. And the longer I went without playing, the harder it became to go near a piano again, to face what it would take to get the level of my performance up to where I felt it should have been.

So it is holding this log in my lap for only the second time in more than ten years. Life has preoccupied me enough to preclude recording even a scattershot account of Den's and my explorations. Instead, a mile-high stack of blanks shall remain unfilled in, but the essentials of the most recent two weeks must be noted nonetheless.

When I jettisoned the solitude of the Andromeda range a couple of weeks ago, bearing a couple of diamonds and a yoke of fear, I knew Den wouldn't stay put and await my return, sparing me the worry as to his whereabouts. But I had to leave—no future existed for me that did not include doing everything in my power to come to the aid of a young woman who is, in a way, my own and only child.

I spent the first night in Gnam Yuljongs, but had little time to socialize with the family. I was out of there before sunup and made it all the way to Kathmandu that day, thanks to a Nepalese trucker Lin-Chee hooked me up with in Zhangmu and a border guard who, for a "deposit," was willing to overlook my passport being supposedly shuttled between the American embassy and Nepalese authorities in Kathmandu. A similar strategy was applied with ease on the Indian border the following afternoon, when I crossed over in a chauffer-driven Lexus with an Indian businessman and his wife, whom I'd met outside a fancy Kathmandu restaurant. Sometimes a small dose of corruption can be just what the doctor ordered.

I entered India on the 24th, a day ahead of Den, and transmuted one of the diamonds into a Tata sedan I bought off a glass shop owner. It was old and creaky, but it ran. I headed towards Bombay, rarely interrupting my drive except to try and reach Jyoti's parents on the phone. Due to a wave of terrorist paranoia, Indian hoteliers usually check the passports of foreigners, so each night I had to finagle alternative accommodations, once at a small dairy farm and once courtesy of the proprietor of a curio shop.

By mid-afternoon on the 26th I made it to the Patils' apartment building overlooking Chaupati Beach in southern Mumbai. The doorman informed me that the Patils were away, but he allowed me to hang out in front of the building to speak with exiting and returning tenants to glean information. They all knew that Manjula's and Rishi's daughter had disappeared in Bangalore and that foul play was suspected, but nobody knew how to reach them. A kind upper floor resident, an art history professor named Devika I'd have loved to jaw with under other circumstances, took me in and let me work her phone until nightfall. My calls proved fruitless, but later, on Devika's balcony, less than fifty yards from the apartment where Jyoti had been raised, I picked up a sense of Jyoti's location in the southeast, not Bangalore, but further away, in a remote forest.

I thanked Devika profusely and took off in my clunker without delay. The farther I got from that cluster of twelve million people, the more focused I became. By the time I reached Kerala I was certain that I was getting close. At dusk on the 29th, I made my way into a lush forest and found a pullout on a hillock that offered a view of my surroundings in the brief moments lightning struck the night sky.

It was there that I latched onto the twinned nightmares of Jyoti's captor attacking her and the tempest of rage in which Den was engulfed. Apart from seeing my mother's murdered body, witnessing that monster attack Jyoti was the single most traumatic experience of my life. I needed Den, but he needed serious help before he'd be in condition to help anyone else. I had to reach out to him and project an image that could lift his sights above the vortex of his hellish revenge fantasies so we could get on with the search and rescue work for which we'd descended to the subcontinent. I found a key deep in the layers of memories he'd absorbed over years of poring over deity images: a Blue Tara. Thank Goddess, it worked; I could not have handled this crisis my own.

Den came around quickly and we set to work on the most exhaustive visitation labor of our career, hoping in vain to reshape the thoughts of Jyoti's anipox captor to get him to release her alive. The astonishing discovery of two new rescuers, as welcome as strangers showing up to help battle a fire in a remote cabin, gave us leave to find Jyoti in the physical world. We sped off from our separate points of departure, struggling to maintain our connections to each other and to our target over twisting jungle roads. I clung to Den's psychic wake the way I slipstreamed behind a log truck for ten miles in Humboldt County late one night when my car was running on fumes, banking on another driver to keep me going.

Den's report spares me having to detail the shock waves we endured passing through terror to joy as we found Jyoti alive after fearing that she'd been killed a minute before. As Den held her in the back of the jeep speeding toward Kumily, I felt reverberations of the trauma I underwent clinging to my wounded mother in the East Village and I prayed that this time my loved one would recover.

In Kumily I stayed by Jyoti's bedside day and night, coaxing the remains of her dreams for her future back out of the dark hole where they'd lain crushed for more than eight days. Jyoti knew something of our life's work and relating how we'd found her helped her reorient herself. A more bare-boned suggestion of what took place had to suffice for her parents. The police detectives who came down from Bangalore were told that we were nature-lovers with a penchant for nocturnal birding on a nighttime outing who happened to hear Jyoti cry out. True enough for government work.

In the midst of that long, slow-motion swirl in the hospital, Den handled the logistics of getting us to Mumbai on a small charter jet, accompanied by the trauma surgery resident overseeing Jyoti's recovery.

The trip cost the Patils a pretty rupee, but they knew how much Jyoti depended on me and there was no way Den or I would be allowed on a commercial aircraft without proper documentation. Upon leaving the hospital, Den and I lightened the loads of Jyoti's two nurse's aides by giving them the keys to our vehicles and instructions on how to find mine. By the time the plane lifted off the tarmac, our hearts were filled with hope that Jyoti's eventual recovery from her physical and psychological wounds was assured.

Jyoti and I became closer than ever as we talked for hours, working through the nightmare of her kidnapping by a guy who'd done a brief stint as a substitute security guard on the campus of the genetic engineering firm where she'd been serving her fellowship. He grabbed her from the back seat of her own car at 11 o'clock on the night of the 21st and ordered her to drive to the outskirts of town with his knife pressed between her ribs. We treated the wound of that story with happier stories of her life since her visit to Gnam Yuljongs the previous spring, spiced with sprigs of excitement about her plans to study in the UK next year and the visit she would pay us at Gnam Yuljongs at the end of the school year.

My five days at Jyoti's side meant the world to me, but they couldn't extinguish the growing sense I shared with Den that we didn't belong in that megalopolis or any place like it. For one, living as a hermit couple for so long in so vast a wilderness, I'd lost much of my once abundant capacity to engage with a buzzing, modern society. I could carry on carefree interaction with people in an urban environment only so long before I'd find myself looking on and asking, *what am I doing here?*

More important, a powerful force was tugging us back to New Hale. While Jyoti was napping comfortably during our second afternoon in Mumbai, Den and I were sitting at the Patils' living room window, looking down on the zany Brownian motion of exhaust-spewing cars, trucks, and buses seven stories below, and we found ourselves discussing exit strategies, the decision to leave soon being a foregone conclusion. Our brainstorming came to an abrupt end when Rishi and Manjula overheard us. Eager to do whatever they could for us, they gave us the use of one of their cars, insisted on paying for our gas, and arranged for us to stay at the home of friends of theirs in Sikkim, a recent addition to India appended to its northeast border with Tibet. It would take us a little over two days to reach Sikkim, which is a long way east of Mustang and Nepal, but reducing our international border crossings to one rugged hike would simplify things a lot. The car would be returned to Bombay a month later when their friends' son came down for job interviews.

We bid Jyoti and her parents adieu the day before yesterday and began our drive clear across India, alone with each other and our reflections on the tumultuous previous two weeks. We welcomed the spiritual salve of India's checkerboard of lush forest and roasting plains dotted with small towns, but it was not enough to make us want to return there any time soon. Living so isolated in a great wilderness for so long had woven a skein of alienation between us and the day-to-day street life of the rest of humanity. I felt much affection for the people we saw, whether children walking through traffic on their way to school, peasant women guiding long-horned cattle down the country road, or the men hanging out on the front stoops of trade stalls selling cell phones, lumber, produce, tea, and candy, but it was the kind of affection I could feel for deer or swans, wishing them all the best but without the common ground for conversation that came naturally to me before New Hale. How close could you feel to people with whom you could not mention your spiritual foundation, the defining moments of your life, or even your home or occupation?

But compassion—of that I had mountains. I hoped that all of them, the comfortable few and the vast majority for whom conditions were harsh, would eke out their shares of joy in life and escape the torturous pain that could be visited upon them suddenly by people infected with evil. They all seemed so vulnerable. After a lengthy silence, I mumbled aloud, "I don't know how to work this. I just wish they could be *safe*." My voice cracked as I felt myself slip into the chasm with Jyoti the night of her kidnapping. I grew dizzy with the terror she must have felt, the painful and humiliating crushing of all her bright dreams of love, family, and a career of discovery, and before I knew it, I was crying, for the first time since we saw the Petaluma girl taken from her bedroom and brutalized ten years ago.

I turned away to hide my tears from Den—a dumb instinctive move since he'd probably know if I were crying three light years away, let alone three feet. Not surprisingly, he'd been brooding about the toll anipoxi exact so relentlessly from the innocent. Seeing me cry would throw him, but I couldn't stop myself. Two weeks of tears built up behind the dam had broken through.

He stroked my cheek. "That was a tough one." I squeezed his hand to let him know I appreciated his solace. Out of the corner of my eye I saw the swallow in his throat and the steel building up in his jaw as his protector instinct took the helm. I knew he would not rest until he figured out how the curse of evil that had made such an unholy mess of the world could be exterminated. No matter how far beyond our capabilities it might be to pull it off, he had to at least conceive of a strategy that could work, over time. I felt likewise.

After I stopped tearing and a spell of silence, Den said, "I know how you feel—the theft of safety and happiness and all. In an odd way, it fits with a strange nightmare I had last night."

"I was wondering if you were having a nightmare."

"Sleepless ruminations, actually—same difference."

He fell silent again, so I nudged him. "And?"

"I dreamt I'd slipped back in time to when humans like us and Neanderthals co-existed. There were conflicts and a dawning recognition that one of the two species was going to triumph and the other would die out. It was heavy. Lose that contest and instead of a locker room sulk, you face extinction while the other side owns the world.

"Once I woke up, it didn't take long to see where that had come from. Few people have awakened to what's at stake between us and the anipoxi. Again there's an interspecies war going on that most people can ignore in their day-to-day lives, but this time it's trickier because the two species look alike and it's more treacherous because technology has helped rev up evil's kill rate to one more fatality every forty-five seconds. If we don't do something to stop it, what do you think will happen?"

A rhetorical question. I awaited his answer.

"Humans can't keep tolerating this devastation, Calieze. We might as well invite flesh-eating bacteria rotting our feet to work their way up. The longer we wait, the stronger the anipoxi can get, so that if they ever do feel threatened, they might cook up the mother of all pre-emptive wars, with the sharkmen giving marching orders to their military forces and using dog whistles to whip up all the solopsychos, haters, gangsters, and tribal crazies they can lure out of their rat holes. World War III will show up at last, vomited up from the belly of the beast with invisible enemy lines no one conceived of during the Cold War."

"They'd still lose," I interjected. "The Nazis did."

"Yes, maybe someday new allies will bust in on the final stronghold of the last surviving sharkman and haul him off. Maybe they'll dump him in a public cage plastered with photos of him caught with blood and guts dangling from his mouth over his messily dissected half-eaten family—"

"—Aack!"

"—living by dint of a victim-consuming habit he'd acquired from Liverlips Lecter that he turned against his own people when his food supplies dwindled to nothing. Visitors will gawk aghast through three-feet thick transparent walls at the last vestige of anipoxi with his broken Himmler spectacles dangling from one ear, as he growls and hurls his feces in their direction."

"Gross, Den." He was driving and I debated suggesting that we switch the subject until he was less wrought up.

"But sitting idly by and hoping for the best isn't much of a battle plan against an enemy with its paws on nukes and radiation-proof bunkers—"

"—bunkers again? Come on, Den. Lighten up."

"Hey, you can't prevent a disaster you won't let yourself envision. Play it out. From their hidden redoubt, the anipoxi carry out raids hunting for humans and destroying Michelangelos and holy places the way the Taliban blew up the great Buddha statues and the Chinese Communists destroyed Tibetan monasteries." I thought of Aurangzeb declaring music and dance dead, but I was not about to bring that up. "And anyone they suspect of being human they'll ship off to one of their Abu Ghraib franchises."

"Are you done? Because this Evilgeddon talk is sapping my strength like kryptonite. How about we focus on ending evil before that can happen?"

He cleared his throat. "Fine." He became silent for a minute. The road had become a spillway for thoughts we'd had about the context of our work for a long time. "Whatcha got?"

I took a slow swig of bottled water and stared out the window, trying to push my mind onto prospects of undermining the ancient cult of sharkmen, but I was hungry and tired. We'd reached the hill country around Darjeeling, where dragonflies and blossoming tea plantations invited our eyes to the dance. I told Den I'd take him up on his invitation after we took a break from this subject and the road.

We stopped for dinner in a tiny restaurant run by a kindly Sikh man who let us spend the night on a rain-sheltered spot on his back porch. Come morning, we took a walk through a low maze of tea bushes across the way, where an elderly tea master told us that the plants had just been removed in the adjoining field to make way for the new planting that takes place once a century. I thought of the planters putting in the new crop knowing that some day the plants would be tended by the grandchildren of people not yet born. It helped clear my head before we hit the road again for our final drive, so I was ready for his challenge.

"So?" Den began. "Your prescription for whacking evil?"

"Viruses, Den—eviola, variola, any infectious agent—eradicating them requires quarantining the infected and building up immunity in everyone else. We've got to isolate the anipoxi and boost respect for life around the planet, pole to pole. Respect for life has got to trump every possible competing claim from crazies and all the nationalist, racist, sexist, or religious zealots who are breaking the world by rationalizing murder. It's got to be taught by parents to their kids, teachers to their students, pastors to their flocks, and vice versa, if necessary. Once that gets rolling, evil will begin to drop and keep on dropping. Viruses, like any other pathogen or enemy, will die without sustenance."

"'Isolate' sounds a little cushy for anipoxi," Den retorted, still festering over what had happened to Jyoti. "Murderers have got to face ultimate punishment."

"Terminal punishment, I'd call it. Not capital."

"I know—I didn't think dangling ourselves down in the killers' abyss was your style."

"Or yours, despite your rage at Jyoti's captor and our unavoidable satisfaction at his immediate death. But for us to get behind capital punishment would be pure hypocrisy. Better, 'terminal,' meaning permanent, solitary, perkless confinement. Survival basics so minimal that terminally punished killers might give up the ghost on their own and other criminals, even rapists and torturers, will think twice on the brink of murder."

"Rapists and torturers have to be hit incredibly hard."

"I agree, Den, believe me. But I've known several women who've been raped and the ones who weren't murdered got a shot at recovery and seventy more years of life. The difference in punishment may be what saves most rape victims' lives. Rapists and torturers must face terrible consequences, but there's got to be some distinction so they can't think they're better off murdering their victims. It's the killers, most of them, who must expect to be condemned to a hell on Earth."

"What do you mean, 'most of them'? Don't you think lax judges and parole officers have done enough damage?"

"They've done massive damage, but we still can't automatically throw a one-size-fits-all sentence at every person who kills someone. Shooting a rapist who's about to thrust a knife into your daughter's chest isn't a crime anywhere I know of, and shouldn't be. In some cases even someone who commits an evil killing might be eventually earn a measure of forgiveness and redemption."

"Redemption? As in, 'Sorry I lied us into war. Waiter—more caviar over here!'"

"I'm not talking about mass murderers and serial killers."

"As in 'Gee, I'm awful sorry I iced my ex. Can I go now?'"

"No, Den—as in 'I was kidnapped at age nine by an African militia, drugged up, and told my family and I would be tortured to death if I didn't shoot the people I'd been told were our enemy, *and* I've spent ten years atoning for it, five of them in prison and another five trying to make it up to the families I hurt.' I'm just allowing some limited leeway for the rare human with a weak RLI who follows up a bad mistake with extraordinary long-term rehabilitation. My father used to quote Micah to me about God wanting us to love mercy <u>and</u> do justice. We can't let either one destroy the other."

"That's a slippery slope, Babe. Next thing you know, someone like that former cop who assassinated your mayor in San Francisco pleads temporary insanity for eating too many Twinkies and gets out in five years."

"Five with conjugal visits with his wife. That time the justice system was almost as twisted as the killer."

"'The alcohol and Twinkie debbil *made* me do it,'" Den whined. "'The bad genes debbil *made* me do it. Daddy's hitting me *made* me do it. My mania *made* me do it, or maybe it was my pills for mania.'" He dropped the impersonations. "Juries and parole boards who buy that poisoned baloney are unwitting death squads freeing thousands of killers every year. It's cruel and unusual punishment of the survivors, the victims' families, and all the innocent people put at risk. They might as well let a bunch of ebola victims into the schools to spew infected bloody vomit in the kids' faces."

"Thank you for that image. My brain cleaners will be working overtime on that one. Trust me, I get your point, which I've agreed with all along."

Den took a big breath and whistled. "Well, what odds of success do you give this grand plan for evil eradication? The world's full of status quo addicts who will say evil is here to stay just because it's been around forever."

"Someday they'll have to eat crow. Humanity tolerates evil out of habit the way Bangladeshis in cholera zones keep drinking water with shit in it. They'll resist change but once they get over it they'll be glad they did."

"'Someday' seems a long way off."

"Hard to say. The end of apartheid and the USSR seemed a long way off a couple of years before they occurred. And even if taking down evil is a very long way off, we can't get there unless we take the first steps, like those tea planters. I saw a temple at Ellora that took two hundred years to carve. Big picture thinking, Den. A work crew has got to set to work carving out a global mindset change."

Den stared at the road a moment without quite seeing it, shaking his head at the brief dustup between his doubts and his innate optimism. Then he came to and craned his neck to the left to catch the retiring sun on the horizon. "I wish I knew if the Andromedans had sent us a bottle containing the secret to downing evil—if they even made it long enough to have figured it out."

"Only the Preoccupied Gardener knows," I replied. And there was no more talk of evil, then or since.

We made it to Namchi a few hours ago and met up with the Patils' friends in their hillside bungalow above a pepper and cardamom orchard. After dinner, we retired to the little room our hosts' son Norbu had vacated for us. We've relished the luxuries of a hot-water home for the fourth time this week and this decade, but we're yearning for the exalted solitude of New Hale. As we sat for a while in the dark, gazing out the window at the silhouette the Himalayan ridge cut out of the northern starscape, Den broke the silence. "I'm not sure how, but I think we're headed for some big changes up there."

"So it's not just me. I've been identifying with the guys on Apollo 11 a few days before they strapped themselves into their space capsule."

"I'm identifying with the first lung-breathing amphibians, with just enough consciousness to know we're part of a quantum jump in evolution, the details of which are too vast to imagine." It was dark, but I think he knew I was nodding in agreement.

In the quiet that followed, I drifted off to sleep for an hour. I awakened from a dream that I was a mountain shaped like a lotus and Den was a mountain shaped like a snow leopard and when his mountain climbed atop me, I could see moonlight streaming through a mandala nebula reflected in his leopard eyes. I let Den sleep while I wrote these pages by candlelight, but in the morning, after Norbu drops us off at the end of a road four miles south of the border where we can thread our way on foot over a pass that will land us back in Tibet, I'll tell him that dream.

[7-1]

September 14, 2004 - Nightfall
New Hale, Tibet
CZM

Maintaining my equilibrium while sliding up and down heaving seas, I must record one more entry with some ambivalence about delving into thoughts that could be perceived as crazy. I prefer to view them as exulting in adventure.

Den and I fled the babel and lather of India last week for the peaceful quiet of New Hale only to become electrified here by energetic skies, as lightning from the south began sweeping into Tibet towards our hazardous perch on the Spire twenty hours ago.

We hiked up there yesterday evening determined to try something new, even though we knew—all right, *because* we knew—that the lightning season was still on. We had witnessed how, despite our shredding fear for Jyoti's safety, our power grew beneath the jungle storm lightning the night of Jyoti's near-murder, even in those low hills. We *had* to test our momentum in a lightning-laced sky at our peak elevation.

As soon as lightning appeared in the southern sky, we found we could reach many subjects at once—first several, then a dozen, two dozen, and before long, as the lightning drew within ten miles, we established ourselves in at least a hundred soulspaces simultaneously, multiplexing signals in different locations around the world in a flood tide of crises in which those we resolved slipped away to be replaced by new ones. It was like thinking a hundred thoughts at once, all with perfect clarity, in calm intensity, easing paths for our subjects to dismiss the eviola virus by boosting the frail output of their RLI lights.

It went on for hours, during which it seemed there was no one succumbing to eviola lust anywhere. When lightning struck within three miles, I wanted to stay on, but my SAR partner wouldn't have me risking my life and insisted we leave. I protested; I climbed into his lap to embrace him and a thrill shot through us when the next lightning strike hit nearby. Looking up to the sky's zenith, we beheld a storm cloud opening like an iris, revealing seven pairs of brilliant, stellar diadems gathered in a circle, looking for all the world like eyes peering down at us. These were not stars—they glowed and steered around the rim of the hole in the clouds, gliding through color temperature changes as they stared. They injected my mind with a sense that we had been targeted for some vitally important communication by beings with strange, commanding faces—I imagined a deep crimson one shaped like a wide diamond, another, anemone-like with an eye at the tip of each tentacle— who would sweep us up and transport us to another world with alternating lateral bands of ocean and land.

Another lightning strike just a mile from the Spire jolted us back to the realization that our lives could be in imminent danger. We fled, abstaining from glances at the sky, our eyes on the declining mountain terrain, gingerly descending in the storming dark all the way back to New Hale.

We got back around 2 AM and collected our thoughts. Den had experienced the same vision as I but was more cautious in drawing conclusions. As for our hours-long visitation cascade, he noted that, with studies having pegged the death toll from murder and war at some two thousand victims a day for decades, our having blocked several hundred such kills in four hours suggested the possibility that during that time, few people—*if any*—had perished from evil anywhere on Earth.

If so, even had it been the first such spell of that duration in centuries, it would have escaped notice. Had a homicide detective in

Detroit chatting with a colleague in Chicago observed that both their domains had had a quiet afternoon, it would have been considered a meaningless, minor coincidence. Yet it might well have been a microscopic snapshot of a long-term embryonic process beginning to unfold around the world, an early spark in an erratic series that could ultimately catalyze a recomposition of the planet's spiritual atmosphere. Even if much more blood is shed along the way as anipoxi isolation and anti-evil culture take hold, the time may come that several days will pass without a single death from murder or war occurring anywhere, a time when homicide rates in El Salvador, Congo, and Iraq will have dropped by half or three quarters within a few years of each other, when the coroners of Juarez and Mogadishu and New Orleans, finding themselves with a lot of free time on their hands, will turn to each other and connect the dots until it becomes common knowledge that humanity has pushed itself into a propitious cycle in which instinctual respect for life is becoming immanent throughout the world.

Absent proof for or against that thesis, we revisited the watchful stars. Like the Japanese soldiers cut off from the rest of the world in Iwo Jima caves during a different kind of battle, we could only speculate what was going on, and we had to, for our nature abhors a vacuum of understanding. We began to sort through the gathering assortment of clues.

Three years ago, during our first lightning-spurred multiple visitation (to the aircraft hijackers in the States), we had witnessed a lesser but similar celestial display. Why ascribe to these phenomena the consciousness of advanced beings who would take interest in our actions? To begin with, acknowledging the existence of highly intelligent extraterrestrial life requires no great leap of faith. The Drake Equation, positing the likelihood of thousands, perhaps millions, of other civilizations co-existing with us in our galaxy has been around for more than forty years. With so large a sample, how many might have blossomed far beyond our provincial notions of intelligence? With our solar system being younger than tens of billions of others in the Milky Way, how many might have burgeoned forth eons before humans appeared on Earth, with ample time to develop telepathic and/or physical interstellar exploration?

I asked Den, if there have been such advanced species before we came along, how likely is it that none of them had ever had to reckon with evil? "Surely somebody's seen this movie before."

"Maybe trillions of somebodies over millions of years," he acknowledged. "Perhaps many whose civilizations had paid the ultimate price for failing to contain evil that produced kill rates worse than Earth's."

"For all we know, humanity is a specimen on an eight thousand mile-wide petri ball being examined in a study of conflicting species given free rein with extinction and survival at stake."

"The data from those trials would make interesting reading."

We agreed to put the discussion on hold in favor of catching up on sleep, but sleep played hard to get, leaving us to toss and turn with several long hours to go before first light would slide into our cave entrance. I lit a candle, thinking I'd log what had transpired since yesterday evening, and readied myself for the task by staring at the ceiling.

As the hushing contours of the Tibetan highland pillowed the woodwind chorus sweeping through the nearby forest, an internal thunderclap reverberated in my mind, as I noticed something that had nagged at my subconscious for thirteen years: the exposed fragment of the soot and moss-covered painting on our ceiling near my more recent artistic offering featuring Den and me as avian astronauts. I recognized in it an image of what Den and I had seen at the zenith at midnight atop the Spire. Whoever had inhabited this cave in the 1800s might well have been as stunned as we by the same celestial phenomenon.

I made up my mind on the spot: on the chance that our predecessor has painted his own visual terma of the revelation he'd witnessed, I would do whatever it took to restore it to its original glory. With the makeshift tools at hand, I'd take on the task with the same passion as an art restorer coaxing the beleaguered beauty of a Rembrandt canvas recovering from three hundred years in a mildewed attic.

I let Den sleep until dawn before I heated up some water and rummaged around for an old toothbrush, some sourdough bread (a useful supplement to a brush for sensitive areas), and a crumpled old box of TSP I'd once dragged up here from Zhangmu. I would compensate for the crude composition of my DIY restoration kit with extreme care. When Den got up and took a look at what I was doing, he got the picture, but said only, "Hm."

He set about chopping firewood for the charcoal pit, out of habit rather than from any clear plan for what else we might do today or the rest of our lives. The time called for a sheet of calm contemplation to be laid over our intemperate mix of anxiety and excitement.

I worked on the painting for hours, even though it was clear almost from the beginning that my suspicions about the artist's inspiration were being confirmed. I'd gone into mental labor, birthing an idea with careful breaths. When I'd laid the original bare, seven stellar eye pairs looked down at me. I called Den over to lie next to me and stare back at them.

Neither of us spoke for ten minutes. Imagine then how I was taken aback when he finally said, "You told Jyoti how to find this place."

He'd leapt forward to the possibility that we might be on the verge of leaving New Hale forever and backward to guessing what Jyoti and I had talked about during our long hours alone. "Not exactly," I began. "But more or less. I've been meaning to tell you." He nodded his request for me to continue. "She was begging me again to invite her to our home. She went on about how she felt disconnected from us, having no idea what kind of world we inhabited. Her curiosity had been fired up almost beyond control. So I took pity on her and made a deal that I'd describe it and give her some idea of where we live as long as she never came up here uninvited…unless…"

"Unless?"

"Unless she hadn't heard from us for two years." Now my eyes had a number of reasons to dart away from Den, who tapped his fingers on my side. "I've been reluctant to tell you because I was afraid you'd think it morbid of me to envision a scenario in which we might not be around." He picked up this journal, probably imagining someone other than the two of us doing likewise someday.

"Look, Den, she might as well know. And Renzin and Lasya too— you saw how those two were when we passed through the village the other day. They're getting older and they're feeling left out of the Magic Wonderland they imagine us living in. They have an idea where it is already. And face it, with these curious young cats, our days here have been numbered for years. We're destined to move on and it won't be to any city—the ordeal in India made that crystal clear. I've been figuring we might move to Andromeda Cave, or maybe find some new place altogether, much farther away. And now—this."

"And by 'this' you're referring to the possibility that some beings from afar just paid us a recruiting call. Pretty much what you mused at Andromeda ten years ago, after Rwanda."

"Frankly, yes. Maybe they concluded that we've qualified for something and our number's up."

"So we're hot prospects being called up to the majors, now, is that it?"

"Well?"

"Needed somewhere else so badly that our services on the planet that's been home sweet home for forty-one years can be dispensed with?"

"There are others on Earth doing what we've been doing—we've known that since the night of the jungle. And we must have seen a score of them last night. Maybe the watchers feel the time's come to put us on their team elsewhere."

"And they'd like to swing by and pick us up on of one of the world's most prominent lightning rods."

"Den, our abilities seem to intensify exponentially the closer we've let ourselves get to lightning, so for that reason alone I'd think you'd want to go back up to the Spire tonight, and see what happens."

"While conducting another slew of visitations?"

"Maybe. Or maybe it's time to replace our receivers with a broadcast transmitter and seed the noosphere as much as we can with encouragement about eradicating evil, as we talked about while driving across India. But in any case, hanging tough and not running away as the lightning approaches."

"I gotta admit, if you're gonna be pulled up by a trillion volt Bon sky cord, a spot atop a spire in the Himalayas would be just the place for it. But *you've* got to admit—"

"—I do. I admit we could get struck by lightning and end up as a couple of dead dopes."

"Well, not necessarily *dead* dopes. People survive lightning strikes every day. A buddy of mine in the Park Service got struck and survived twice. Being of pretty tough mettle, you and I might well survive being lit up that way, but there's a risk, all right. We could be performing our own sky burial up there."

"Simultaneous attainment of the rainbow body with interlocked bones doesn't tempt you."

"It'd be hot—thirty thousand degrees hot."

"Yikes."

"I don't know, baby. I sure treasure our life."

"So do I, Den. But we might be on the brink of treasuring our life in a wholly new chapter."

"And form."

"Perhaps."

"It'd be hard to beat the bodily abodes we've been enjoying the last thirteen years. I don't regard them as old lizard skins at shed time."

"Neither do I."

He arched an eyebrow in my direction. "Not to mention the bodily abode for the interlaced DNA whom you and I have fantasized about."

"Whew," I swallowed. "Now you're touching me below the belt. I still dream of giving life and upbringing to a child who's equally you and me. But if we're being called to service by cosmic deities, it's got to involve some other kind of birth far away. And, on the other hand, if we get up to the Spire tonight and find we think better of risking that kind of birth, we can turn right around and return and get on with the traditional kind whenever we want." I kissed Den and stood up. "Think on it. I'm going to take a walk and then come back and put together some soup. By sunset we should make up our minds." I poked my head out of the cave entrance. "The sky looks moody-perfect, Den."

I left to get some water down at the creek and spend one more hour by myself to check my center. I've had my moments but I've never been crazy and I wouldn't condone it now. I sat on my favorite boulder with a view through the trees straight to the Spire some seven miles west and almost a mile further into the sky it has scraped in majestic silence for hundreds of millennia. I listened to my inner voice. Hearing it clear and vibrant and calm, I headed back home, up the hill.

I found Den above the cave, watching the sun settle on the horizon. He embraced me and we kissed. The decision had been made.

When we returned to our entryway, Den saw me aim for the pantry nook and stopped me. "I'll fix us a snack. Perhaps you should take advantage of the chance to log a few notes about all this."

I realized I'd better seize the opportunity. In the next few days, perhaps tonight, we shall leave New Hale and these three terma behind.

Having logged a third of my life on this planet in one of its highest and most magnificent dwellings, I look back with great affection for the naïve lass who arrived here not quite twenty-eight years old. How trusting and innocently she trudged up here, utterly clueless as to the riveting life that awaited her; but her sneaking suspicion that her journey might lead her to the love of a lifetime was bull's-eye accurate. I now believe that Earth's sky is not the limit.

I thank my parents, and you too, Sonam and Lasya and Renzin and beautiful Jyoti and Uncle Yeshe for all the love and wisdom with which you've blessed us. Know that we love you, wherever we are, and may you and anyone else who reads these pages keep the faith that the world can cure its own disorders and become fully healthy, and must.

As for you, my bar-headed friends, I thank you for inspiring me to venture to the top of the world and for your flights of grace and peace, seeing unaided further into space than any Earth creatures before or since you first appeared in the Himalayan skies. I can trace evolution's arrow from inanimate matter and eukaryotes right through you en route to the rise of human beings and our present aggregate of foibles, greatness, and love in countless forms. With that momentum, the world might yet achieve universal respect for life and yield an Ellora Buddha's successor with eyes open in delight that liberation from the confines of the non-worldly is cause for a smile sweeter still.

And, hey, Dad: why is this century different from all other centuries? Because in all other centuries we either ignored evil when it victimized others or grappled with it through dim-sighted containment schemes; in this century we shall begin eradicating it forever throughout the world.

God, my heart is racing—in exhilaration, not fear. I'll need sure footing on the wet uphill trail ahead, so I'll do some deep breathing while Den signs off. Then we'll get on the move.

[7-2]

<u>Same time, same place</u>

Wellsir—ma'am, whoever—my wife's confidence in the wisdom of this visit to the Spire is hovering a good twenty-five points above mine, which is holding steady at about sixty-five percent—not very high for an SAR guy feeling utterly responsible for his woman's life. We're taking a bet Calieze would never have made if not for me and the engulfing embrace with which I greeted her when she came to New Hale. But great instincts lace through her gifted brain, backbone, and heart, so with my curiosity at phenomenal record levels, I've locked in with her. If her recruitment hunch is correct, it will be an offer no SAR guy could refuse.

Besides—Denver, Leadville, New Hale, Wherever We're Headed Now—every ten or fifteen years I've found myself some place a thousand times more removed than the last and my explorations a thousand times more wild, beautiful, and fascinating, so why stop now?

If my parents are watching this, I hope they'll trust my judgment, appearances notwithstanding. In taking this risk, I'm not throwing away the gift they bestowed on me; I may be fulfilling it. Balancing risk on a scale with somebody's survival is the foundation of SAR strategy. When the survival of an entire species of intelligent life is at stake, we need to up our quota of risk. There may be plenty of intelligent species out there up against a natural selection test who could use some extra time for their RLI and social justice systems to grow strong enough to prevent extinction by soulpox. They might appreciate some help, much as I'm indebted to every soldier who landed at Normandy knowing that they were risking everything to be a millionth part of an effort necessary to save scores of millions. Without them, the two kids who became Calieze's parents would never have made it through the war and the central light of my life would never have been lit.

Perhaps my father had an inkling of this in mind when he wrote me that postscript in Tibetan. What other destiny could better titrate Tibetan wisdom and American wild colt spirit? Those stellar recruiters may be freeing us to recognize the myopia in the old saw, "Either we're alone or we're not, but in either case the thought is staggering." We've had nothing to do with whether we're alone or not; but alone or not, we intelligent beings, by our own free will, may either end evil or let it end us—either way, that's more staggering by far. And if the Intelligence League acquits itself respectably, who knows? Maybe the Prime Mover and Shaker will promote us to partners in Creation. Nothing beats collaboration with someone you love.

Calieze has begun pacing around outside, waiting for me under the crackling sky. We're on our way.

EPILOGUE

The passage above was the final entry in the logs penned by Terma Den Sherab and Cali Zigana Moss.

The three notebooks were found in a remote cave northwest of Zhangmu, Tibet in the spring of 2007 by the young woman then named Jyoti Patil in the company of Renzin Quring and his sister Lasya, three individuals named in the texts. Ms. Patil now goes by her married name which she does not want divulged. Like myself, she seeks no personal attention in connection with the publication of this work.

Ms. Patil had spent the better part of three years wrestling with a growing concern over the welfare of Calieze and Terma Den, from whom she had heard nothing since they left her in Mumbai in August of 2004. By the time her birthday and the annual invitation to visit had twice passed without contact from Calieze, Jyoti wrote Lasya to broach the subject of an expedition to find New Hale. Working with Lasya, who had since married and moved to Zhangmu, and Renzin, she formulated a plan to visit Gnam Yuljongs the following spring to make a foray into the mountains west of their village in the hope of reuniting with their solitary friends, or, failing that, recovering the written logs Calieze had mentioned to her.

By the middle of the fourth day of their search, with discouragement overlaying anxiety about the nearing onset of the monsoon, Jyoti observed through her binoculars a pair of symmetrical mounds some five hundred meters away. Within minutes, the trio had come upon the charcoal pits, the former home of Calieze and T. Den, and the waterproof sack containing their written logs. A glance at the ending filled her with a twinging mixture of sorrow and hope.

Renzin suggested that they take the books with them and perhaps return them later in the year after they'd been photocopied, but the two women were loath to remove such precious and personal artifacts from the place they had been left. It was decided they would photograph the entire manuscript, two pages at a time, which they proceeded to do over the next hour and a half. Within a few months, a copy of the manuscript was in my hands.

Despite the limitations of the authors' knowledge of biology, their use of virology and speciation models and their analysis of ongoing human evolution nonetheless demand some respect. Their thesis cannot fairly be dismissed in favor of the orthodox view of evolution as having culminated with the emergence of *homo sapiens* two hundred thousand years ago. Scholars and researchers as diverse as Harlow Shapley, Eric Chaisson, Teilhard de Chardin, and Darwin himself all called for the inclusion of broad developments in human behavior as necessary to a full understanding of evolution as an ongoing process.

However, taking on the phenomenon of "evil"— a vaguely defined category of human behavior normally relegated by science to the boondocks of mysticism and religion—constitutes a daring and controversial expansion of the study of evolution, hardly typical fare for someone settled comfortably in his white tower habitat. Yet I believe that we ignore the Sherab-Moss summons at our peril. Our action or inaction with respect to the eradication of evil and the strengthening of what they term the "respect for life instinct" might well have a central role in the destiny of our species. It is an ambitious project, to be sure: even ridding the world of public slave markets, which took generations, is small beer compared with eradicating evil altogether. But given the authors' common sense analysis, the range of prognoses they present, and their proposals to achieve that goal, it would have been hypocritical of me as an evolutionist not to lend a helping hand. Hence I committed myself to take Jyoti and her document under my wing.

I began by engaging in ancillary research to better inform myself about various social and historical themes dealt with in the journals. Joe Bageant's *The CIA's Secret War in Tibet*, Eileen Kernaghan's *The Nameless Religion*, and Vajranatha's *Ancient Tibetan Bonpo Shamanism* were particularly helpful in that regard. And, in light of the concept of an ultimate creative partnership with the Creator touched upon by Mr. Sherab in his final entry, I undertook a study of Alfred North Whitehead's work on that theme in his development of process theology.

The more time I spent with the Sherab-Moss story, the more I became convinced that it was incumbent upon me to perform some professional due diligence by examining the original documents myself *in situ*. (I admit that, my confidence in Jyoti's veracity being quite sufficient, a taste for adventure—within reason, of course—had something to do with it.) Jyoti was reluctant to disclose the location of the text and the cave to anyone, but, appreciating my respect for the material and the seriousness of my offer to facilitate its publication, she relented. With all the time consumed in procuring visas and leaves of absence, it was 2010 before I was finally able to set my eyes on the original log books in their remote Himalayan abode, exactly where Jyoti had left them almost three years before.

Having spent so much time in my mind with Terma Den and Calieze, it was moving to discover their fire circle with a couple of ceramic teacups resting to the side and weathered sleeping bags, blankets, utensils, gardening tools, drawing materials, books, and a heavy duty backpack nearby. Imagining the incredible experiences they had lived through in that very location reminded me of my past visits to Runnymede and the Acropolis. It was eerie, as if the souls of the former residents had left behind a resin redolent of the daring and passionate life they'd carried on there before moving on. I was stirred by the sight of the promontory that surely must have been the place they referred to as the Spire. I quelled a fantasy of attempting a climb there. Aside from such a venture being foolhardy for someone with my minimal acquaintance with mountains, any remnants associated with the former denizens of New Hale that might have come to rest upon that peak, where winds must routinely whip past at fierce speeds, would have disappeared long ago.

Throughout my investigation of the authors' accounts, everything that was confirmable therein checked out to the last detail, down to the description of the landscape and the paintings by Calieze and the cave's former tenant. With Jyoti's blessing, we photographed the paintings, but refrained from doing likewise with the local environment so as to preserve the secrecy of New Hale's location.

Terma Den's family in Gnam Yuljongs proved marvelous hosts to us in the two days we spent en route to and from New Hale. Their recollections of their cousin and his wife were vivid and heartfelt; it still pained them to have had no word from them in six years.

For providing us their colorful alert alongside a dazzling and plausible alternative vision for the future, I am grateful to Mr. Sherab and Ms. Moss, wherever they may be. I wish them and the rest of our species good fortune.

One final note: About a month after our return to England, I received a letter from Jyoti in which she made a confession of sorts. I shall close with an excerpt from that letter, and leave any commentary to the reader.

> *I've wrestled with the question of whether to relate the following to you, out of fear that you'd think me dotty. In the end, because of your generous help, I've decided to let you know what impelled me to seek you out years ago and to let you think of me what you will.*

> *One night about six years ago, while home on holiday in Mumbai, I'd been out with friends and not gotten to bed until nearly midnight. I felt sufficiently wiped out to sleep twelve hours, but at some point scarcely an hour later, while dreaming, I felt a powerful surge coming on, as if God were about to smash open the singularity and ignite the universe into being. I thought I heard an ear-splitting crack like lightning splitting open our roof and the sky itself. I flung myself upright in bed, my eyes suddenly open but not recognizing my whereabouts for close to a minute. My hair felt like it was standing erect on my head, and I was gasping for breath, trying to comprehend what had happened, indeed what was still happening—and in the seconds that followed, a beautiful image of Calieze's face filled my mind, overflowing with love and reassurance and good blessings reaching down to the depths of my soul. Terma Den was there too, looking fondly at both of us. With my eyes wide open I watched that transcendently blissful specter, almost blinding to my mind's eye, glimmer and fade away, leaving me bereft but comforted and immensely intrigued by a profound*

sense that Calieze wanted me to know how much she valued our friendship and that she was counting on me for something that, regrettably, I could not discern. I stayed up for hours, wondering what might have triggered such a galvanizing connection to my beloved friend.

As time went on over the next few years, that thunderstriking awakening slipped my mind. But in 2007, after returning from Tibet and devouring my copy of Calieze's and Terma Den's journals, that middle-of-the-night shock flash-flooded my memory. I dug up my diary to find the account of that vision and discovered that the incident had occurred during the first hour of 15 September, 2004.

Perhaps this will aid your understanding as to why, by getting their journals out to the world, you have put my heart at ease.

With fond gratitude,

Jyoti Patil

C. G. Sloan

<u>Acknowledgments</u>

I am deeply grateful to Lucille Lang Day, Patricia Dedrick, Craig Lambert, Ancil Nance, Lawrence Rosenwald, David Rottman, Deborah Schneider, Mark Terry, Ben Teton, and Jennifer Scott Teton for their comments on the material; also to Michael Ray Allison for co-designing the book's cover and Justin Mikkelsen and Aidan Terry for their assistance with it; to Esukhia in India for excellence in translation, assisted in the US by Lobsang Ghadong, Paul Hackett, and Kamala Chhetri; to Sage, Ben, and Zoe for their colorful and loving gifts too numerous for words; and to my wife Jennifer for her all-encompassing elevation of my life.

Praise for *Upsurge*

"An artful blend of well crafted science fiction, revealing social criticism, and a thoroughly engaging love story, John Teton's *Upsurge* will strike an immediate chord with anyone who has experienced outrage at the persistence of hunger in the midst of potential abundance…At once a sci-fi fantasy and a thoroughly engrossing love story of family relationships, this book…raises fundamental questions about the fate of humanity and entertains at the same time. Bravo!"

Janet Poppendieck, Professor of Sociology, Hunter College, City College of New York
Author, SWEET CHARITY? EMERGENCY FOOD AND THE END OF ENTITLEMENT

"*UPSURGE* is a great, evocative, thought-provoking book…an engaging and personal drama that takes us on a voyage of inner discovery of moral and scientific transformation"

Tyler Volk, Associate Professor of Biology, New York University
Author, GAIA'S BODY: TOWARD A PHYSIOLOGY OF EARTH and METAPATTERNS

"*UPSURGE*, like its predecessor, *APPEARING LIVE AT THE FINAL TEST*, proves again that literary realism can hold its own when interwoven with fantasy elements, even those as wild and original as those in these books. Teton's characters and their emotional complexities are so firmly established early on that by the time readers are transported to his dizzying alternate realities, we're hooked for the duration."

Debo Kotun, Producer, Pacifica Radio Network, Author, ABIKU

"A rare treat...John Teton brings to life a family in crisis—a father on the verge of an earth-shattering scientific discovery, a mother approaching childbirth, and a teenage daughter who runs away when she becomes overwhelmed with despair about poverty and hunger—a theme that runs throughout the book. *Upsurge* brings real family dynamics and real politics together in great science fiction."

Eric R. A. N. Smith, Professor of Political Science and Environmental Studies
University of California, Santa Barbara
Author, ENERGY, THE ENVIRONMENT, AND PUBLIC OPINION

Praise for *Appearing Live at The Final Test*

"fantastic...defies typecasting...grounding in everyday human fears and troubles, along with mind-blowing scenes which venture into questions about creation and the role of human beings in it."

Santa Barbara News-Press

"*APPEARING LIVE AT THE FINAL TEST* is a genre-breaking story unlike any other. Its scenes range from a scarily realistic depiction of an urban nuclear event to mind-stretching intergalactic travel--all related in the author's savvy, wise-cracking, original, and sometimes hilariously hyperbolic voice."

Craig A. Lambert; Deputy Editor, Harvard Magazine

"*APPEARING LIVE AT THE FINAL TEST* is an extremely well-written novel--a pleasure to read, a wild ride of depression at some points, exhilaration at others. John Teton has raised some serious concerns regarding the fate of civilizations, and our consciousness is raised with this thought-provoking work."

Eric Chaisson, Professor of Astronomy and Physics, Tufts University
Director, Wright Center for Science Education, Author, COSMIC EVOLUTION

About the Author

John Teton was born in Chicago and earned degrees from Harvard and the San Francisco Art Institute. He directed the films *Thunder Head Clearing* and *B'raesheet* and produced the cosmology film program *Visions at T Minus Zero*. In addition to *Elevation*, his fiction includes *Appearing Live at The Final Test* and *Upsurge*. He directs the campaign for the International Food Security Treaty (IFST), which arose from notes for *Upsurge*. On behalf of the IFST, he has made many public appearances at universities and written numerous articles including *The Armless Hand*, published in the Yale Journal of International Affairs. He and his wife, Jennifer, are the parents of three and live in Oregon.

www.ingramcontent.com/pod-product-compliance
Lightning Source LLC
Chambersburg PA
CBHW050616110726
47899CB00001B/135